LATENT PROWESS

ORDER OF SCION
BOOK 1

TOBY NEIGHBORS

MYTHIC
adventure
PUBLISHING

To George Lucas, for opening the door and inviting us to dream of adventures long ago and far, far away.

In the celestial spaces above the Earth's atmosphere; in which spaces, where there is no air to resist their motions, all bodies will move with the greatest freedom; and the Planets and Comets will constantly pursue their revolutions in orbits ... by the mere laws of gravity.

SIR ISSAC NEWTON

In 'General Scholium' from *The Mathematical Principles of Natural Philosophy* (1729), Vol. 2, Book 3, 388

CHAPTER 1

EVERYONE HAS BAD DAYS, but Mitch Murphy hit the trifecta. It started out like any normal day. He woke up at six in the morning, his alarm clock blaring.

"Shut it off," his wife growled, poking him in the side.

He was already starting to reach over to hit the alarm clock but knocked over his glass of water in the process, and his nightstand drawer was open.

"Dang it!" He snapped.

The accident forced him fully awake. He grabbed a towel and began soaking up the water. His wife groaned angrily, even though he was trying to be quiet. A few minutes later, after cleaning up the spill, Mitch went to start some coffee. His job was in the business district, which required a ninety-minute train ride to reach. He normally prepared one cup of coffee in the morning to give him the jolt he needed to shake off sleep. Only that day there was no coffee in the empty container. It was a shocking disappointment.

By that point, it crossed his mind to just get back into bed. And as nice as that might have been in the moment, he had bills to pay. Not to mention that his wife would be furious if he skipped work.

She didn't like surprises and claimed that she needed peace and solitude in the mornings. He quietly stepped into the tiny bathroom and shut the door before turning on the light. Once he got the shower running, he had to wait for the water to warm. He tapped the mail icon on the bathroom mirror and several urgent messages appeared. He was behind on his mortgage and several credit cards. It had cost all of their savings to buy the little apartment. Three tiny rooms on the backside of a semi-respectable building cost nearly half his salary each month. They could just get by, but then the Homeowners Association doubled their monthly fees, and there was a significant property tax increase that left Mitch scrambling to pay the bills. Every day he got notifications that left a burning sensation in the pit of his stomach. They would need to sell the apartment and move, but his wife wouldn't like that. And the market was down, which meant they would be lucky to get out from under the place.

When he finally got out the door, he was on the edge of despair. The only good thing that happened that morning was finding a seat on the train that wasn't next to a homeless person. The commuter trains that brought workers from the suburbs into the city proper had become a haven for transient people down on their luck. The police ignored them, and the riders as they were known, could be dangerous. Mitch breathed a sigh of relief and sank into the hard plastic seat he found unoccupied and clutched his satchel close to his chest.

Every day the people on the commuter trains were subjected to advertisements on display screens. The audio was hard to hear over the rumble of the train cars and the hubbub of voices, but there were no windows to look out of and no one wanted to stare at the other passengers. So, they watched the advertisements and tried not to garner the attention of the transient riders.

Mitch was sitting beside two older men who knew each other. He couldn't help but hear their conversation. It was the usual back and forth until the advertisement for the new Latent Tech. The video was a montage of young, fit people, and doctors in lab coats.

"Now, that's crazy," one of the men beside Mitch said.

"Gotta be off your rocker to sign up for that," the other said.

Mitch was familiar with the advertisement. People called it the Escape Plan, but it was actually for a company that had developed bio-enhancement techniques. Latent Tech was the research and development arm of the Colonial Marine Corps. And they were desperate for people to join their mission to help protect New Terra. For half a century, humans had been trying to gain a foothold on the new planet. Space travel had been limited to the solar system. The very best engineers still couldn't design a ship that could survive interstellar travel, or engines that could even approach the speed of light. But explorers had found a wormhole, some people called it a portal through dimensional space. It was essentially a door to another star system. New Terra was a planet with a thin atmosphere that barely supported life. Most of its water was frozen, and much of the land in the warmer climates was still barren. That didn't keep humanity from jumping at the chance to colonize the world, but there were a host of obstacles, from wildlife that hunted humans, to other intelligent races who had shown up in the system shortly after humans did. New Terra was a battleground.

There had been a lot of fanfare about Latent Tech, with claims of amazing technological breakthroughs in human physiology enhancement, but like most government programs, there were just as many conspiracy theories. It didn't help that the therapies they offered were only for people willing to join the Colonial Marine Corps. And those individuals were shipped out on one-way trips to New Terra.

"You'd have to be a fool to fall for that load of crap," the man sitting next to Mitch said.

"It's a death sentence," the other man added. "I know a guy in government. They say the supper serum has a fifty percent failure rate."

"Failure?" the first man asked.

"The lucky ones never wake up," his companion said. "Those that do aren't always better."

"Why would anyone risk that? You'd have to be pretty pathetic to sign on with Latent Tech."

Mitch didn't disagree. He was ten years out of university, still paying off his student loans. Married, with a mortgage and a job in finance. Things weren't good, but people ran into speed bumps in life. Despite his terrible morning, he still felt like things would turn around.

When the commuter train finally reached his stop, Mitch disembarked into a crowd of people. They were all moving in one direction, into the city, toward the towering buildings where millions worked ten hours a day and couldn't afford to live in the ritzy condos on the edges of the business district. Mitch entered the drab building where Sterling Investment Corporation had its Western Offices. Ten years in, Mitch was still an assistant buyer. It was an entry-level job, but everyone paid their dues. His peers had moved up or moved on to better jobs, but Mitch felt loyal to the company that had taken him on right out of college. And the job market was very competitive; his window for finding something better had closed. Employers would want to know why he hadn't been promoted in ten years. He had no good reason to tell them. He was a good worker, but he wasn't aggressive or very confident for that matter. Sure he had hopes and dreams, but things hadn't broken in his favor, and he had sunk to the murky middle where he learned to keep his head down and not attract attention.

His workspace was a narrow desk with a computer in a cubicle that was identical to fifty-nine other cubicles on the thirteenth floor. He dropped into his chair and woke up his computer to log in for the day. He was on salary, but still required to log into the system and account for every hour. Only when he put in his password, the computer informed him that it was no longer valid.

"Are you kidding me?" he snapped, typing in the password again, and a third type after that.

"Problem?" Lois Burman, the frumpy woman who occupied the cubicle next to his asked.

"I can't log into the system?" Mitch complained.

The only response was silence. Mitch stood up and looked over the cubicle wall. Lois was frowning.

"What is it?" he asked.

"Nothing," she lied.

"What?"

"I just heard a rumor, that's all."

"What about?"

"Downsizing," she said softly, looking down at her desk, refusing to meet Mitch's gaze.

He dropped back down into his seat, his heart suddenly beating at twice the normal pace. He felt tired and scared. The hair on the back of his neck stood out, and his hands were suddenly ice cold.

"Murphy!" a gruff voice called. "I need to see you in my office."

It was impossible to ignore the looks from the other assistant buyers and market analysts as he walked down the aisle between the rows of cubicles toward the manager's office. The gruff voice belonged to Stuart Bellamy, who was in his late fifties with only a ring of gray hair left on his head, and a bulging stomach that strained the buttons on his shirt. He was never in a good mood, and always complaining about something. A trip to his office was bad and Mitch felt a strange numbness as he entered the glass walls of the tiny space. Stuart Bellamy's desk was slightly larger than the others, but not by much. He wasn't in a cubicle, but the glass-walled office was barely large enough for the overweight manager to squeeze around his desk.

"Close the door," Stuart ordered.

Mitch pulled the glass door closed and looked at his superior. The man's face had no compassion.

"Orders just came down from the twentieth floor," Stuart said, his voice a grumbling monotone with no real emotion. "They're trimming the fat, so to speak. You'll have an official letter of termination in your inbox by now. The severance package is pretty generous. It's been nice working with you."

"I'm being laid off?" Mitch asked.

"No, you're being fired," Stuart said. "The company won't be bringing you back on."

"But I..." Mitch started to argue, which was unusual for him. But he realized he had nothing to say.

"You've got two weeks of pay in that severance package. A full month of medical covered," the manager said. "That's plenty of time to find a new job. You'll need to gather your things and leave the building, Murphy. Is that going to be an issue? Do I need to get security involved, because if I do, I'll have to put a report in your personnel file, and that will follow you into every interview you take."

"No," Mitch said.

"Good," Stuart said, standing up. "Good luck, Murphy. Send Jennings in here, would you?"

"She's pregnant," Mitch said.

"Hey, I don't make policy. I just carry out the orders they send down."

Mitch opened the glass door and looked out at the dozens of his former co-workers. No one was looking at him. They were suddenly all very, very busy with important work that couldn't wait. Mitch shuffled out of the office and down the row of cubicles. He slowed at Kimberly Jennings's cubicle. She was three months pregnant, and not yet showing. There were rumors that she was faking the pregnancy. It was idle water cooler talk, and Mitch had never joined in, but he saw the framed ultrasound photo on her narrow desk.

"Bellamy wants to see you, Kim," Mitch said.

She was crying before she even got to her feet. Mitch felt hollow inside. The storm clouds that had been hanging over his head for days were brewing. His life had been shattered.

"You okay?" Lois asked as he picked up his satchel and jacket from his cubicle.

"Terminated," he said.

"So the rumors are true. I'm sorry Mitch."

"Ten years," he said. "I've been here ten years."

"You'll land on your feet."

That thought made him almost laugh out loud. He had worked feverishly to get through college, and he had done so with middling grades. Still, he had a degree and nearly two hundred thousand dollars in debt. Everyone told him that it was okay, that he would get on his feet soon. But he had never quite managed to achieve any real stability. His job at Sterling Investment had seemed amazing at first, but he soon found the work to be incredibly boring.

His marriage had been a bright spot. Megan Aubry was two years behind him at the university, and pretty. She wanted nice things, and he had gone into more debt to get them, always believing that soon he would get on his feet. Somehow, he never managed to get ahead. Ten years into his career and he was still living paycheck to paycheck, with mounting debts he had no way to pay off. She would be furious that he had lost his job, he realized. They had agreed that she would stop working and concentrate on getting pregnant. The idea of having a child terrified Mitch, but he wanted to make Megan happy, so he agreed. She had seemed more like the girl he had known in college for a while, but had not been happy for long, and no matter what he did for her, it was never enough. For some reason he couldn't quite explain, he loved her, at least he thought he did. And that was what mattered, he told himself, not quite believing it.

Normally, the commuter train ride seemed to take forever, but lost in his thoughts Mitch reached his stop in what seemed like record time. He considered stopping for coffee and pastries but decided against it as he shuffled toward his building. They were going to have to make changes, that was all. Megan would need to go back to work, and they would have to sell their apartment. Which also meant they would have to wait to get pregnant, but he couldn't help it. The real difficulty was going to be finding a job that paid anywhere close to what he had been making at Sterling. He had a college degree and a solid work history, but no real achievements to speak of. Still, Mitch tried to think that maybe he could find an occupation that he actually enjoyed. He had worked himself up into believing that maybe losing his job was a good thing. Perhaps, he thought, it was the catalyst he needed to finally do something different and get ahead in life. His student loans could be deferred for a while, and they would probably have to move out of the city, but he was starting to think shaking things up was exactly what they needed. But what he found at home dashed all that to pieces.

CHAPTER 2

HE OPENED the door and stepped into the tiny living room. Music was playing from the bedroom, but that wasn't unusual. Megan liked music and listened to it while she showered. He could also hear the water running. Mitch dropped his satchel, which had his generic reading device, and his sack lunch. He laid his jacket on a chair and walked to the bedroom. There was no door between the small bedroom and the only bathroom. Megan wasn't fastidious about keeping the apartment clean, but she didn't like him leaving his clothes on the floor. And at first, Mitch thought that what he saw was his own clothing. He had an impulse to pick it all up and stow it in the dirty hamper, but then he realized he didn't wear the name-brand jogging pants or the expensive sneakers.

He was dumbfounded, standing at the foot of his bed, looking at the trail of clothing that led to the bathroom. There was a loud ringing in his ears, and he could somehow hear his heart beating at the same time. Laughter broke through his befuddlement.

There was someone in the apartment.

At first, Mitch desperately wanted to believe an intruder had broken in, but he was too smart to accept it. He walked slowly toward the bathroom. The shower was tucked behind a wall, the semi-clear door completely fogged over from the steam, but Mitch didn't need to see what was happening. He could hear the voices and other things. Pain broke through the fog in his mind. His wife was cheating on him. She was laughing in a way he had never heard, or at least, hadn't heard in years. That made him feel like someone had stabbed him through the chest with a sharp object.

The water stopped and shook Mitch out of his daze. He suddenly realized that he didn't want to see who his wife was cheating on him with. Nor did he want to face her anger at being caught. He stumbled out of the bedroom and through the living room. He managed to pick up his satchel, but not his jacket. Megan called out as he opened the front door.

"Is someone there?" her voice reached him just before he closed the door and hurried away.

An hour later he was in a bar. He didn't remember getting there, or even realize where he was. There was a drink in front of him. Whiskey from the looks of it, with ice melting into the brown liquid. Mitch wasn't a heavy drinker, but he needed something to ease the pain. He was lost, not that he couldn't find a way back to his apartment, but it no longer felt like home. The future was bleak. He had no job, very little prospects, a mountain of debt, and a marriage he couldn't face.

"You okay, pal," the bartender asked.

"My wife's cheating," Mitch confessed. He didn't know the man, and the bartender didn't know him. Most places had replaced humans with android servers, but for some reason, people still liked human bartenders. Perhaps it was because most people drank to avoid their problems and there was something about a stranger willing to listen that people enjoyed. Mitch didn't enjoy revealing his failings, but he couldn't hold them back any longer.

"That's horrible," the bartender said as he dried a glass with a clean, white towel. "You just find out?"

"Yeah," Mitch said, swirling the ice in his whiskey, but not drinking it.

"Someone you know?"

Mitch shook his head.

"Been going on long?"

"I didn't stick around to get the details," Mitch said. "I just ran away."

"Nothing wrong with that," the bartender said. "It's better than killing the guy, and I'm guessing you'd have wanted to do that if you stayed."

Mitch looked at his drink and wondered what he had become. He had been in his share of fights growing up. He played ball in school and was athletic, but somewhere along the way he had lost all of that. His instincts were gone, beaten down with fear of upsetting his wife, and the pressure of his mounting debts. That wasn't the way life was supposed to turn out. He had plans but he couldn't remember what they were exactly. His friends had all drifted away. All he ever wanted to do anymore was eat and sleep. When he got home from work on most days, he watched television and tried to avoid the fight with Megan that never seemed to end. On the weekends, he could hardly get out of bed. He told himself it was a phase, just a minor case of depression brought on by the debts he was laboring under. But as he stared at the ice melting into the whiskey, he realized that he had lost himself. Worse still, he had to admit that he and Megan would be better off if he was dead.

"How much do I owe you?" Mitch asked the bartender.

"This one's on me, pal. You deserve it."

"Thanks," Mitch said.

He took a drink. It was foul and burned his throat, but the heat that spread through him felt nice. Still, he didn't want to get drunk. He pushed the glass across the bar, stood up, and nodded to the bartender who returned the gesture. Leaving the bar, he knew he had to do something. He stopped at a bench long enough to eat the sandwich in his satchel. There was plenty of traffic on the street, people walking, hover cars humming by city aircraft gliding above him. Everywhere he looked there was life, but he felt dead inside. It wasn't until he was halfway through his sandwich that he noticed the Colonial Marine Corps recruiting office across the street. It was colorful, with the same advertisement he had seen on the train that morning playing soundlessly on one of the window displays.

Through the traffic, he read the colorful slogans on the recruiting office windows:

Ready for a new life?

Wish you could do the things you did when you were younger?

Are you looking for exhilaration and excitement?

Join the CMC and discover a galaxy of adventure.

Mitch didn't make a conscious decision. There was no reasoning, or rational in his mind. But he remembered what the two strangers on the train had said about the program. People died from taking the super serum that was advertised as being a way to bring out a person's strength and vitality. And Mitch wanted to die. He had been contemplating the many ways he might do the deed. What he didn't want was to be considered a coward. He was tired of being invisible and settling. He wanted to do something bold, something that would show people that he had taken control of his life. Suddenly, he was on his feet, his sandwich forgotten on the bench, as he strode purposefully through the traffic and pushed open the door to the recruiting office.

There was a man in military uniform sitting at a desk. He looked up at Mitch and smiled.

"Welcome to CMC recruiting. Can I help you, sir?"

"Yes," Mitch said. "What do I have to do to join?"

"That's the right attitude," the recruiter said. "We'll have to do a few tests and see if you're compatible."

"Compatible with what?"

"The Latent Enhancement Protocols," the recruiter said. "It's not for everyone."

"And if I am compatible?"

"Then we've got a lot to talk about Mr..."

"Murphy. I'm Mitch Murphy."

"It's nice to meet you. I'm Sergeant Lopez. Come with me and we'll get started."

Mitch followed the recruiter into a small room with a bench against one wall and a medical scanner against the other.

"Strip down, get inside, and the system will start all by itself," Lopez said.

"What is it, exactly?" Mitch asked.

"It's a scanner. One pass to make sure you don't have any unexpected disease, then another to see if you're compatible."

"How long does it take?"

"Not long. Once it's done, the door will open. You can get dressed and come on out. I'll be looking over your results."

"Okay," Mitch said, realizing the sergeant was younger than he was.

The hopeless feeling was back. And Sergeant Lopez didn't seem too optimistic either. In fact, he didn't seem to be very good at recruiting. So far, he hadn't done anything to make Mitch feel wanted. But that wasn't surprising. Mitch shut the door and pulled off his shirt. He was pale and on the cusp of chubby. Ten years of sitting at a desk was not a recipe for physical fitness. Megan had insisted that they get a gym membership, but by the time Mitch got home from work he was too exhausted to exercise. He felt a surge of emotions that nearly wrecked him. Looking at himself in the mirror he felt worthless, and instead of fury at Megan's betrayal, he wondered how she had stayed with him so long.

The scanner door was open, and he stepped inside. It sensed his presence. The door closed and a series of instructions flashed on the display. He stood still while the scanner ran up and down the chamber. It was a lot like the tanning booths at Megan's gym. Most doctors used handheld scanners, and the automated medical booths seemed clunky in comparison. The first scan took ninety seconds, the second was longer. But the entire process lasted less than five minutes.

By the time he got his clothes back on, Mitch was ready to find out the bad news. He was in the middle of the worst day of his life, and if the Sergeant told him he had a terrible disease, it wouldn't have surprised him. But the smile on Lopez's face when he opened the door was unexpected.

"Mr. Murphy, the results of your scan were excellent," Lopez said.

"They were?" he asked, feeling nervous.

"That's right. Come with me and we can discuss your options."

CHAPTER 3

THEY DIDN'T RETURN to the reception room where he had walked in off the street. Instead, Sergeant Lopez took Mitch into a room with reclining theater seats and a massive video display screen.

"Have a seat," Lopez said. "It's a little quicker if you watch the recruiting video. Then I'll answer your questions."

"Okay," Mitch said.

He sat down in the plush, faux leather seat which automatically reclined. The video display screen lit up and Mitch saw the Latent Tech logo rotating slowly as Sergeant Lopez sat in the other recliner.

Suddenly, a man in a lab coat appeared on the screen. "Hello, I'm Doctor Theodore Packerman, head of the Latent Enhancement program. Several years ago, the CMC enlisted us to produce a series of protocols meant to enhance the latent skills and abilities of the average person. Building on the work of Lewis Musthaven and breakthroughs in DNA research, we have created a formula, part serum-based injections, part environmental optimization, that can bring out the latent abilities inside a person. What does that mean? Let me show you."

The video changed from the man in the lab coat to an animated child, but the voice of Theodore Packerman continued speaking.

"This is Teddy. He was born with a wide spectrum of natural talents, but like most people, many of those talents went unrecognized."

In front of the child, a road appeared, and then it split into several more, and each of those roads split into even more.

"Life is a series of choices," the voice of Doctor Packerman continued. "Some lead to wonderful opportunities, but they are also limited in scope. Some natural skills and talents fail to be recognized or encouraged to grow and develop."

The animation of the boy began to change. He grew taller, passing through the teenage years and into adulthood.

"In most cases, the needs of life such as working and family, continue to limit a person's opportunity to hone and develop their talents and abilities. Those innate, but unused talents are considered to be latent. Teddy could have been an outstanding football player, but his mother didn't like the idea of him playing contact sports and his father was too busy to encourage his son's athletic abilities. Instead, Teddy's enjoyment of computer games led him to focus on mental disciplines that eventually coalesced into a job as a computer programmer for a major corporation. But buried deep inside of Teddy is the ability to gain strength and develop agility."

The animation of adult Teddy looked a lot like Mitch. He was pudgy, with poor posture, thinning hair, and a look of defeat. But then the image of Teddy walked into a room where several men in lab coats were waiting. They sat Teddy down and began a series of injections.

"The Latent Enhancement Protocols will not just reactivate Teddy's dormant natural abilities, but they will give his body the chance to recover from a lifetime of poor choices," the voice of

Doctor Packerman continued, while the animated Teddy laid down in a strange-looking cylindric chamber. It looked a lot like the medical scanner that Mitch had been in, only it was vertical instead of horizontal. The lid closed and a clock appeared with hands that spun much faster than normal. When the lid opened, Teddy sat up and then jumped out of the machine. He was taller, his hair thick and wavy. His chest was broad, his shoulders wide, his arms bulging with muscles while his waist was thin. And instead of the look of depression he had before, Teddy was smiling and bright-eyed.

"The LE protocols aren't magic, and not every individual has the same latent abilities, but if you're watching this video, it means that you have scored high enough in the DNA scanning procedure to be a top-tier candidate for the LE program."

The video animation dissolved and Doctor Packerman reappeared on screen. "This is your chance," he said, "to discover all that you could have been and make a difference. LE participants will undergo a series of procedures at our private facilities and then proceed via starship to New Terra. As you can imagine, accessing the full range of a person's latent abilities would make them far superior to the average person here on earth, and laws were passed long ago that forbids the use of DNA enhancement. But on New Terra, there are no such laws. You'll be entering a world full of opportunity, with a chance to make history. You can say goodbye to the troubles and disappointments in your life, and yes to a whole new you. The best part is that it's absolutely free to you. In fact, your recruiter will walk you through the many benefits we offer to LE candidates. Once your affairs are settled, you'll be taken to our laboratory on Space Station Epsilon in orbit around Venus where you'll be taken through the protocols to bring out the very best latent skills and abilities you never knew that you possessed. I encourage you to take part in this exciting program and discover all that you can become."

The video ended, and Mitch's chair returned to the normal

sitting position. He looked over at Sergeant Lopez who smiled invitingly, as if he had just offered Mitch a billion dollars.

"What did you think?" he asked.

"I think it sounds too good to be true," Mitch said. "What's the catch?"

"No catch," the sergeant replied. "In exchange for the LE protocols, you must agree to a standard CMC enlistment. But with your background, you'll probably qualify for officer training shortly after you complete the basic training program on New Terra."

"Military service?" Mitch asked. He wasn't opposed to the idea or even the danger he knew that was inherent to joining the Colonial Marines, but he didn't like the idea of being locked into a career for several years.

"Trust me," Lopez said, "if the protocols take, you'll want to do something physically challenging. They don't call it super serum for nothing, if you know what I mean."

"What do you mean *if* they take? I've heard that some people die."

"The protocols can be intense," Lopez said. "No pain, no gain, my friend. But the results are spectacular."

"What other benefits are there?"

"We want you to leave Earth with no debts. We'll pay them off for you, up to half a million dollars, with the remainder held in escrow for you."

"Debts?" Mitch asked. "I have a mortgage."

"You're married," Lopez said. "I ran your financials already. We'll pay off the credit cards, and get your mortgage caught up. After that, you can decide how much to leave your wife, if anything at all."

"When would I leave?" Mitch asked.

"I can have you on a shuttle to Epsilon Station tomorrow," Lopez said. "Unless you want more time. The payments to your creditors go out when you report here for enlistment."

"Tomorrow works," Mitch said. "Where do I sign?"

"Follow me, Mr. Murphy. We'll do the paperwork and have you on your way."

He signed no less than forty electronic disclosures. And didn't bother reading any of them. It was as if someone had given him a get-out-of-jail-free card. Yes, he had lost his job. Yes, his wife was cheating on him. But in one fail swoop, the CMC was removing him from those painful realities and giving him a new shot at life. Mitch didn't care if the LE protocols failed. He could die knowing that he wasn't a burden to Megan.

It was late afternoon when he got home, but much earlier than he normally arrived. There was no evidence in the apartment of the man Megan was cheating on him with. And Mitch really didn't want to know who it was. All he cared about was saying his good-byes. He sent his parents an email. Perhaps they would miss him, and regret his decision, but Mitch hadn't been close with them since marrying Megan. They hadn't approved of her and weren't supportive of him moving to the city. Over the years, their relation-ship had become perfunctory, just a card on his birthday, an email at Christmas.

It was almost dark when Megan arrived home. By that point, Mitch had already packed his bags. He wouldn't need much once he reached Epsilon Station, but he didn't want to leave Megan burdened with his belongings. He had a change of clothes and a few keepsakes in his satchel. Everything else had already been taken to goodwill. When Megan got home the disappointment on her face was obvious, but Mitch didn't care. He hopped up and gave her a hug. She was stiff and eager to pull away.

"Let's go to dinner," he said.

"What?"

"Dinner," Mitch said. "I'm hungry."

He had already checked his bank account. The severance pay had gone through the banking system. It wasn't much, but it was more than enough to keep Megan going for a while. Mitch had decided to use some of the half-a-million bonus to pay their mortgage for six months. That would be enough time for Megan to get it sold. The money in their joint checking from his severance package would be enough to buy food and pay the utilities for a few months. After that, she was on her own, but he decided that it was more than enough considering Megan's behavior.

"What are you doing home, Mitch?" Megan asked.

"I have good news. Let's go celebrate."

"What?" she asked suspiciously.

Maybe she was being paranoid, or maybe she was suspicious because she felt guilty about her illicit behavior. Mitch knew she wouldn't be happy about him leaving her, and he didn't want to endure an ugly fight, hence the idea of going out for dinner. She had never liked making a scene in public, and he had every intention of using that weakness to his advantage.

"I'll tell you over drinks at La Trattoria," he said. "I've already called ahead. Let's go."

"I don't know, Mitch, I've had a long day," she said.

He was prepared for her to resist and wasn't above simply emailing her the news that he had left the planet. But he wanted to see her face when he told her he was leaving.

"I understand," he replied. "But you can't deny that going out with me would be better than cooking something here. The fridge is nearly empty anyway. Come on, let's go. We don't have to stay out late."

"Fine," she relented. "Just let me get a shower first."

"Can't," Mitch said, knowing that if she saw the tiny space in their shared closet where his clothes had been she would know something was wrong. "I called ahead, remember? They're already expecting us. Let's just go."

She wasn't happy but didn't resist when he took her hand and led her toward the door of their apartment. He locked it for the last time but didn't bother looking at the small abode before leaving. There were so few good memories in the home, which had been a financial weight around his neck from the moment they had bought it. Instead, he walked away feeling light, as if that weight of being behind on his payments was finally gone. For the first time in a really, really long time, he felt a spring in his step.

"What's your news?" Megan asked as they rode the elevator down to the lobby of their building.

"It's a surprise," he said.

"I don't like surprises," she snapped. "You know that."

"It's good news, I promise," he assured her.

La Trattoria was only a few blocks away. They walked. She didn't cling to him the way some couples did. And they didn't talk about anything important along the way. He did ask what she had been up to. She gave him a list of things, half of which weren't true. He knew she hadn't gone shopping that morning since he had been at home and seen exactly what she was up to.

At the restaurant they ordered drinks. She had a glass of white wine, he had a rum and soda. Normally, he hated buying cocktails at restaurants. The drinks were ridiculously overpriced, but he made no comment and even ordered an appetizer of roasted Brussel sprout chips with a fancy sauce drizzle. For dinner, he was having lobster risotto with beef tenderloin medallions and a side of steamed vegetables.

"Seriously?" Megan asked when he tapped the order into the tabletop touchscreen ordering system.

"Yes," he said. "I'm hungry."

"That's one of the priciest things on the menu," she whispered. "I thought we were behind on the bills."

"We were," he said. "But we're not anymore. Get whatever you want."

She ordered a salad, probably just to be obstinate. Mitch didn't care. With every passing moment, he felt better, lighter, freer, and happier. Not that he wouldn't miss Megan or grieve that she had cheated on him. There was pain coming, but he was focused only on the freedom of the moment. For the first time that he could remember, he had found a way out from under the crushing pressure of life. And the relief was so great he was almost giddy.

"What is going on?" she asked quietly.

Megan didn't want to be overheard. She worked hard to maintain the illusion that she had her life all together. But Mitch knew better. He saw her without makeup and knew she sometimes wore a tight-fitting body suit under her clothes to help hold in her stomach. He also knew that the marriage she had pushed so hard for in college was just another false front, a façade to hide her infidelity.

"I got a promotion," he said simply.

"What? You got a promotion at work?"

"Sort of," he said. "They let me go."

Megan stiffened, her face turning slightly red. "You got... fired?" she demanded.

"Yep," Mitch said. "It was terrifying at first. But then I came home."

Her eyes narrowed, and the red flush intensified on her face. She leaned toward him.

"Not here," she said.

"I have nothing to say, Megan," he told her. "But I did have a revelation."

"I won't discuss it."

"Good, just listen," he told her as a short droid delivered their appetizer.

Mitch snatched one of the chips from the bowl. It was drizzled with a sweet glaze, while the crunchy Brussels sprout leaves were covered with salt. He popped it into his mouth and enjoyed the delicious contrast of flavors.

"I don't know what you think you know," Megan said, "but you need to rein yourself in."

"I was there," Mitch said. "I saw it all. But that's not what we're celebrating."

"You're losing it."

"Actually, I'm in control for once," he assured her. "Things are going to get better for both of us."

"No," she said in a furious whisper. "You don't get to decide that for the both of us."

"It's already done. I joined the CMC today. I'm leaving tomorrow."

"You're leaving?" she said, louder than she meant to. Her voice was strained, and she leaned forward, her hands gripping the sides of the table. "You're leaving me? Why? What do you think I did?"

"I think you're cheating on me," he told her. "I saw you in our shower with him, Megan. But I'm not mad at you. I know I'm not the man I was in college. Life has beaten me down and I quit being the man you needed a long time ago. For that, I'm very, very sorry."

"So, you're just running away? You can't do that, Mitch. We have obligations."

"Which I have taken care of. Tomorrow at nine a.m. the mortgage will be caught up, and the credit card bills will be paid off."

"What?"

"Part of the incentive program," Mitch explained. "I'm also making sure the mortgage is paid for the next six months. There's money in our account for you too. Enough to get by for the next couple of months. That's plenty of time to get the apartment on the market and maybe get yourself a job. I've already signed a release, so the house is all yours. Whatever you want to do, you can do it."

"I don't understand what you're telling me. You joined the CMC? That's Colonial Marines, right?"

"That's right."

"You're really leaving the planet?"

"Tomorrow."

"And they paid you, Mitch. They paid you."

"I'm going into the Latent Tech's enhancement program. You've seen the commercials."

Her eyes got big and she shook her head. "No. No that's not okay, Mitch. You know what they do to people. Are you crazy?"

"I don't really have anything left to lose," he said. "You don't love me anymore, Megan. I don't have a job, and I don't have prospects. We're behind the eight ball here. Even if I could get another job, we can't keep the house. Either way, you've got to find a job. At least we didn't have children."

"No, I don't want you to leave, Mitch," she argued quietly. "I know things have been off, but we can come back from this."

"I don't want to," he said. "This is it. The final meal. Let's go out on a high note."

She sat back and there were tears in her eyes. The serving droid returned with their food. She didn't touch the salad, but Mitch ate his dinner with gusto.

"This is delicious. You want a bite?" he asked.

She shook her head. "I can't believe you're leaving me."

"I'm not leaving you alone," he said.

"That hurts," she responded.

"I know it, and I'm sorry. But we both know this is the best thing."

"I don't know anything of the kind."

"You're going to be fine. I've seen to that. As soon as I arrive at the recruiting station tomorrow it's all official. It'll be the same as if I died. Our marriage will be dissolved and you can move on with your life. No more sneaking around. No more fighting. Find someone who makes you happy, Megan. That's all I ever wanted for you."

He pulled his wedding band from his finger. It wasn't worth much, but the gold had some value. He slid it across the tabletop toward Megan. She looked at it for a moment, not moving. Suddenly, he pushed back from the table. Her demeanor changed without warning.

"I hate you," she snapped.

"What?"

"I hate you for doing this to me."

"Okay," Mitch said, not sure how else to respond.

"I wasted ten good years of my life on you. I dropped out of college so we could get married."

"That was your idea," he told her. "I promised you I would wait."

"And we both know that you wouldn't have," she snapped. "Now, I have to find a job and some way to support myself. That's the coward's way out of a relationship, Mitch."

"I thought it was the chivalrous thing to do," he replied, feeling a rising sense of anger. "I'm not holding anything against you."

"You made every decision without me. Then you brought me here so I couldn't fight for my marriage."

It was Mitch's turn to lean close and speak softly. "You had another man in our home, Megan. I think you quit fighting for our marriage the moment you agreed to cheat on me."

"Bastard," she snarled.

In an uncharacteristic move, she stood up so fast her chair toppled over, and everyone looked at her. She threw her napkin onto her untouched food and stormed away. Mitch was shocked, but he noticed that she had taken the ring. Soon, the other diners returned to eating their meals as if nothing had ever happened. And Mitch finished his meal, although he didn't taste it. When he finished, he paid the tab and left the restaurant. Megan was gone, and he didn't try to find her. It was clear what she thought of him. And while he felt like he had done right by her, despite her infidelity, he still felt guilty. Worst of all, he knew he would never see her again. The life he had lived for thirty-three years was over. There was no looking back. It was time to train his eyes on what lay ahead, whether for good or for ill.

CHAPTER 4

MITCH SPENT the night on the town, mainly walking the streets. He wanted to see people and remember Earth. What lay ahead for him was a mystery, and there were things he would miss about his home planet. The time passed remarkably quickly. He found himself at a park when the sun came up. He sat on a bench, weary but satisfied, taking in the beauty of the gold and crimson sky. After that, he had breakfast at a busy diner, then walked back to the recruiting station where his adventure had begun.

"Right on time, Mr. Murphy," Sergeant Lopez said. "I take it your affairs are in order."

"Yes, I'm ready."

"Good. Your new life begins today."

They took a hover car to the airport, and from there, Lopez gave Mitch instructions. A shuttle flew him up into orbit, then a military transport flew him to Epsilon Station. Mitch slept on the flight. He wasn't exactly rested by the time he arrived, but he wasn't exhausted either. He expected a rough and loud drill sergeant to welcome him to his military service. Instead, he was checked into what appeared to be a hospital room. All the medical equipment made Mitch nervous, even though he told himself he had nothing to lose.

An orderly gave him a hospital gown and told him to change clothes. Then a full battery of tests began. He was poked and prodded, scanned, and examined by doctors as well as by medical droids. Eventually, a woman around his age came into the room.

"My name is Doctor Emily Thessle," she said shaking his hand. "I'll be overseeing the LE protocols."

"Okay," Mitch said, feeling self-conscious.

"Don't worry," she urged him. "I'm here to answer your questions and make sure you're fully at ease."

"That's kind of hard at this point," Mitch said.

"You're having second thoughts?"

"No," he told her. "It's just... well... there are a lot of rumors about people dying from this."

"Some do," she said, her honesty shocking him. "Overall, the morbidity rate is around fifty percent."

"That's not encouraging," he blurted out.

She raised a hand to show that she wasn't finished. "But that's overall. You're a top-tier candidate, which means latency markers were abundant in your DNA. The statistics cover mid and low-tier candidates too."

"You do this on low-tier candidates?" Mitch asked. "Why?"

"Because they want it," Doctor Thessle explained. "Most are military. They've seen the results and want to go through the protocol. The statistical success rate for top-tier individuals like you is around ninety percent."

"Well," he said, breathing a sigh of relief, "that's better."

"I'm glad that you're concerned. It shows you have the desire to live. Believe it or not, not everyone who comes into the program feels that way. Some actually hope they don't survive. And a person's mental state plays a big role in the outcome of the protocol."

Mitch felt a wave of embarrassment. He looked down, hoping

that the doctor wouldn't notice. He had felt pretty hopeless when he stepped into the recruiting office. And he thought that dying wouldn't be bad. His life had been a disappointment, and the pressure he was under was enough to make him despair. But after being accepted into the LE program, and knowing that he was finally getting ahead, the thought that he would be better off dead had disappeared. In its place was a strong desire to live, and to make the most of his new opportunity.

"Let me tell you what to expect," she continued. "In the morning, we'll be giving you a series of injections. It won't be pleasant, but it's not horrible either. The serum begins to work immediately by opening the pathways in your nervous system. It's a necessary evil."

"Evil?" Mitch asked.

"Because you'll be sensitive after that. It's a little hard to explain but think of it like stepping outside in a snowstorm while you're all bundled up. It's cold, but you have protection from the elements, right? Now imagine doing the same thing completely naked. You would feel the cold all over, the frozen ground beneath your feet, the snow turning to water as it hit your body, the wind, everything. That's what this is like, a new awareness of your body that you've never experienced before. It can take some time to adjust, so you'll stay here for phase one until you're ready to continue.

"Phase two," she said with a smile, "is a refresh of your circulatory system. The serum in that phase will strengthen and enlarge your arteries. It will begin to increase your blood supply, and the blood's ability to carry oxygen to every part of your body. We call it a refresh because most patients feel younger and have an exponential increase in their energy levels. In phase two, you'll want to do things, and we'll move you to a different part of the station where you'll have the freedom to be active."

"That's sounds good," Mitch said.

Doctor Emily Thessle smiled. "It's an exciting part of all this," she told him.

"Have you done it?"

"No," she admitted. "I'm not a top-tier candidate. My job is to help you go through the protocols. It's a bit like seeing people reborn. At least that's the way many people describe the process. Phase three will enhance your skeletal system and includes growth hormones so that you reach your physical potential. It includes bone density and muscular growth. Most people sleep a lot during phase three, which will take place on board the transport ship taking you to New Terra. From there, you will take a variety of oral boosters to help you complete the enhancement process."

"You won't be with me?"

"No, I don't leave Epsilon Station, but the CMC is experienced in helping recruits through the process. You won't be alone."

"How long does it all take?" he asked.

"That depends on the person, but on average, three weeks. We try not to rush our patients, but the body responds quickly. Any more questions?"

"No, I think I'm ready," he told her.

"Good. Get some sleep. We'll begin in the morning."

The room wasn't uncomfortable. There was an entertainment unit and for a while, Mitch flipped through the available options but was too nervous to land on anything. He slept fitfully, and when morning finally came, he was standing by the video window, which showed a feed from the station's external cameras. Venus was a swirling pink orb below them, and the sun was a huge ball of fire. He was surprised at how much familiar things could change from a different point of view. Another camera with telephoto lenses showed Earth. It was surrounded by space stations and large ships that were built to traverse the solar system. There was a ring of satellites around Earth too, many with large solar sails to catch the light that powered their onboard computers and positional thrusters.

For a while, Mitch felt out of place. Earth was no longer his home, but Epsilon Station was foreign too. He felt awkward, his body restless from nerves. Doctor Thessle hadn't been very encouraging about the procedure he was to undergo. She had explained what it did, but not how it would be performed. Eventually, a woman in a nurse's uniform came in. She had a disposable cup and a bottle of water.

"Good morning," she said in a cheerful voice. "How are you feeling today?"

"Nervous," Mitch admitted.

"Don't worry," she said. "You'll be fine. And this will help."

She handed Mitch the disposable cup. Inside was a small pill. He looked up at the nurse, who was smiling. She was younger than he was, and very pretty. Nursing jobs on earth were done by droids, but the staff at Epsilon Station wanted to put their patients at ease. The nurse did a good job of that.

"What is it?"

"Diazepam," she explained. "It will relax you."

Normally, Mitch was hesitant about drugs. He wasn't worried about healthy habits or anything like that, but he had a small fear of addiction. But he told himself he was in the care of trained professionals. And if they thought the Diazepam would help, then who was he to argue? He took the pill from the disposable cup and swallowed it with a gulp of water.

"What's the schedule?" he asked.

The nurse flashed a smile that seemed to say he had asked a great question. It gave Mitch a little thrill. Normally, he did his best not to notice other women. He was a married man after all. But there was a small part of him that wanted to keep the nurse smiling.

"In about an hour, they'll take you to the procedure room. It's right down the hall," she said, her voice smooth and reassuring. "It doesn't take long, then you'll be right back here for the rest of the day."

"Sounds easy enough," he said.

"It is," she replied. "I'm Heidi, by the way. I'm your nurse."

"Mitch," he said, extending a hand. "Mitch Murphy."

She shook his hand and he could see the white strip where his wedding band had once been. His mind wrestled with guilt at feeling something for another woman, but he had ended things with Megan, both personally and legally. He wasn't really divorced, and not dead either, although there wasn't much difference officially.

"It's nice to meet you, Mitch. Do you need anything?"

"Breakfast?" he asked.

"Not before the procedure. Once you're back here we'll get an IV started and make sure you get all the vitamins and minerals you need until you feel like eating."

"Is it that bad?" Mitch asked.

Heidi gave him a non-comital shrug. "Everyone responds differently," she explained. "I've seen patients back on their feet the next day, and others that need more time to adjust."

"Adjust to what?" he asked, hoping she wouldn't say pain.

"That's a little hard to explain," she said but leaned a little closer in a friendly, reassuring way. "Don't worry, though. It's not a bad thing, just different. And I'll be here. If you need anything at all, just ask me."

Mitch felt a flush of heat through his body. It wasn't just that Heidi was pretty, Mitch thought, but she was nice too. Megan had never been very patient or understanding when Mitch got sick. She wasn't mean, but she didn't mask her annoyance and frustration either.

There were a couple of comfortable sitting chairs in the room. Mitch sat down in one while Heidi picked up the remote control for the entertainment system.

"Do you like music, Mitch?"

"Sure," he said.

"Normally, I don't recommend easy listening, but a lot of people say it goes well with the Diazepam."

Music began to flow from the sound system. It wasn't loud or upbeat, and maybe it was the medication, but it almost seemed soothing to his ears. Heidi made his bed and straightened a few things, but Mitch didn't move. He felt like he was sinking into the chair, and every worry and concern fled his mind. By the time a pair of med techs showed up to take him to the first procedure, Mitch was so high on the medication that he didn't care. In fact, he didn't even have an original thought. He was just being, not really thinking or doing anything. His body had no feeling, not even a numb sensation. He was completely relaxed but had no trouble standing up when they hoisted him to his feet. They set him in a chair on wheels and rolled him to the procedure room. It had the sterile feel of an operating theater, with big lights and some type of large robotic arm that was mounted in the ceiling.

Some small part of him knew he should be afraid, but it was easy to dismiss with the Diazepam coursing through his veins. The medical techs moved him to a padded table with strange holes in it. He didn't resist, and hardly noted as they strapped him down.

"Is that necessary?" he asked when one tech fed a thick, leather belt over his chest and began to tighten it down.

"Actually, it is," the man said.

"You got a problem with needles?" the other med tech asked.

Mitch had to think about that. The technician looped a narrow strap across his forehead. "No," Mitch finally replied.

"That's good," the med tech responded. "These straps are just to keep you from moving, guy. I promise it's not as bad as it looks."

"What?" Mitch asked as they strapped down his arms and legs.

He was completely immobilized when the two med techs left the room.

"Hello?" he asked, his voice sounding strange to his own ears.

A voice responded through hidden speakers in the procedure room. "Mitch, this is Doctor Thessle. Just relax, okay? You can close your eyes if you want."

Mitch had a tremor of fear, but it was quickly squashed by the

Diazepam. They could have gutted him alive at that moment and he wouldn't have cared. Above him, the robotic arm began to unfold. There were dozens of thin hoses connected to the arm, and as it rotated toward him, he saw needles. Not just individual hypodermics, but clusters of them. At some point, the med techs had taken off his hospital gown and Mitch didn't even remember it. He tried to raise his head as the robotic arm moved toward his legs, but the straps held fast.

"What? What's it doing?" Mitch asked, his voice sounding strange in his ears.

"This is phase one, Mitch," Doctor Thessle's voice explained. "We're going to inject your major muscle groups with a patented blend of pharmaceutical agents that will invigorate your nervous system. Just lay still, the procedure won't take long."

The first cluster of needles pierced his left thigh. Pain registered in Mitch's mind, but not so much that he couldn't stay nestled in the warm embrace of the Diazepam. The medicine pumped into his body was cold, the fluid stinging its way through his muscles and into his bloodstream. Two cluster injections went into each thigh, and the robotic arm rotated around to the underside of the table Mitch was strapped to. Another injection was given in each calf muscle.

The procedure continued from below. Two injections in his gluteus maximus, and then several on either side of his spine. The injections became increasingly more painful. He could feel hot rivulets of blood running down his thighs. The robotic arm rotated again, injecting each shoulder, and then piercing his chest. The stinging medication didn't seem to be absorbing right. It certainly wasn't fading, but rather the sting intensified into a burning sensation that covered his entire body. The robotic arm injected into the sides of his neck, and the final stabbing treatment was applied to the base of his skull. When the procedure ended, Mitch felt like he had lost a knife fight and been thrown into a fiery furnace.

"We're done, Mitch," Doctor Thessle's voice assured him. "The medical technicians will be in soon. We're just going to run a few scans first."

Mitch didn't answer. He was focused on breathing through the pain. It was all he could do. The medication Heidi had given him either wore off or was swamped by the agony in his body. He felt as if he'd had a thousand holes punched in his body. He could feel hot blood on his skin and sweat that made the injection sites sting even worse. Inside, there was a fire that coursed through every vein and inflamed every muscle fiber. A scanning ring passed back and forth over him, but Mitch hardly noticed it.

When the med tech's came in, they were grinning, as if the procedure was a joke. They unfastened the straps. When Mitch could look up, he saw the injection sites on his chest and legs. Blood had welled up and in places, it ran down his body. The techs were prepared. They had clean gauze that soaked up the blood and sweat. They ran the pads over his body, then helped him sit up. His head was spinning, and his stomach pinched into a hard knot.

"You did good, pal," one of the med techs said.

"Most people pass out cold," the other said.

"It's burning," Mitch managed to mumble.

"That's your nervous system," the first tech said. "It won't last long."

They wrapped a flimsy, hospital gown around his body, and put him back on the wheelchair. He was slumped over in pain as they pushed him back to his room. The gown was soaked in sweat and stained with more blood when they stood him up. His muscles were trembling, and he felt dizzy. He wasn't sure if he was going to faint or throw up first. But the medical technicians were fast and efficient. They stripped off the soiled gown and tucked him into the hospital bed.

Heidi came in as soon as he was covered up and began activating the bed's monitors. His pulse rate, blood oxygen, respiration, blood pressure, and even his brain waves were recorded. She didn't speak, and neither did Mitch. He closed his eyes and struggled not to moan from the pain. The burning wouldn't stop and there was no way he could lay that would alleviate the pain even for a moment. The injection sites were sore to the touch. Just lying in the bed was torture.

Eventually, Doctor Thessle came into the room. She stood beside Heidi, both medical professionals more interested in the readouts than in his agony. Mitch lay curled on his side, facing away from them, but he heard what they said.

"Remarkable," Doctor Thessle remarked.

"He's adapting fast," Heidi replied.

"It's amazing. Some people just respond to the therapy very, very well."

Mitch didn't think he was responding well, he was miserable, but the doctor and nurse didn't seem to care about that. Time lost all meaning to Mitch. He lay with his eyes closed, focused on his breathing until the pain became so intense, he had to roll over. If he could have killed himself in that moment, he would gladly have done it. But there was no escape from the pain—just the never-ending fire eating through his body. And Mitch was forced to consider that maybe he had died and gone to hell.

CHAPTER 5

AT SOME POINT, Heidi managed to get an IV into his arm. Mitch didn't remember much about it, or the fact that she strapped his arm to the side rails of his medical bed to keep him from pulling the needle free as he thrashed around. There was some type of painkiller in the drip, and as the fire in his body subsided, he fell into a deep sleep.

Waking up was surprising. Not that he thought he was dying, but even before he opened his eyes or moved a muscle, all sorts of information was flooding his brain. He could feel everything, from the compressed foam mattress on the bed to the stiff sheet that covered his naked body. He could feel the hair on his chest moving with each breath he took. The curve of his spine on the hospital bed felt just right, but the skin on his jaw was prickly and needed a shave. Chapped lips and little spots of dried blood around the injection sites were sensitive and a little bit painful. He could hear someone moving in the room, he even smelled her perfume. Never in his entire life had he felt so alive, and he was barely awake.

When he opened his eyes, he found Heidi nearby making notes

on a digital, touchscreen tablet. The stylus she used to input data tapped lightly on the surface of the device. He could even hear her slow, steady breathing. When he moved, he felt his skin rubbing across the bed sheets. His bladder was full, and his stomach was empty.

"You're awake," Heidi said. "How do you feel?"

"Strange," Mitch said, noticing a difference in how his voice sounded to him.

"Can I get you anything?"

"Clothes," Mitch said. "I need to use the bathroom."

She turned to a small closet built into the wall that Mitch hadn't even known was there. It sprang open when she pushed what looked like just another wall panel in slightly. Several hospital gowns were hanging inside. She handed him one.

"I'm thirsty too," Mitch said.

"I'll get you some juice," she said. "But don't get out of bed before I come back. You might not be as steady on your feet as you think you are."

He waited until she was gone to pull on the gown. The injection sites on his chest and thighs looked exactly like what they felt like. Dozens of tiny stab wounds in tight formations. The skin around them was red and hot. Some of the holes had bled enough that little rivulets had dried on his skin. They were starting to itch, which he guessed meant they were healing. He sat on the edge of the bed and let his feet dangle toward the floor. A moment later Heidi returned. His first procedure had been torture, and yet there was something about seeing the young nurse that made him not care about that at all.

"Apple juice," she said, holding a little cup with a tiny straw. "Sip it slowly."

He nodded. She held the cup and he took a sip. The sweet liquid was cold and surprisingly delicious. He felt it run over his tongue and down his dry throat. His body had been hydrated by the IV fluids, which were demanding to be released from his bladder, but his mouth and throat felt bone dry. His eyes opened wide and he had to stop himself from gulping the juice down.

"Where has apple juice been all my life?" he asked.

Heidi smiled, and Mitch was shocked by how beautiful she was. He felt a yearning for her that was strong. The temptation to reach out and touch her was powerful.

"It's good, huh?" she asked.

"Delicious," he said, taking another sip.

"You can have the rest but take it slow. I've got breakfast on the way."

"You're an angel," Mitch said.

"You're feeling better," Heidi said with another smile.

"I am," he admitted. And not just to her, but to himself too.

It wasn't just his awareness of the heightened physical sensations either. His depression and sadness were gone. The normal sense of fatigue he usually felt after waking up wasn't there. He felt more refreshed than he ever had in his entire life, but with none of the usual drowsiness that followed sleep. Most of all, there was a budding sense of hope inside him. He felt like anything was possible, all he had to do was make it happen and he could achieve anything he wanted. Even though he didn't have any plans or dreams, he felt good about the future.

She took his arm as he stood up, but he didn't need help. He wasn't unsteady at all, even though he could feel some residual soreness in his legs and back from the injections. Still, he didn't complain about Heidi helping him. He liked that she was holding his arm as he walked to the bathroom.

"What's next?" he asked.

"Breakfast, then a complete physical," Heidi said.

"You sound surprised," he said as he went into the bathroom alone.

"You're responding quickly," she said in a voice loud enough to be heard in the small bathroom. "That's a very positive sign."

"Yeah, I feel great," he replied as he washed his hands.

"Doctor Thessle will be coming by soon. She'll want to examine you herself."

He came out of the bathroom and moved toward one of the sitting chairs.

"You should really get back into bed."

"I don't feel sick," he said. "In fact, I'm full of energy. Where's that breakfast."

He sat down while she went to get the food, but he was soon up and pacing. He could feel the muscles in his legs and core flexing. It was a novel sensation. Not that Mitch hadn't been athletic in his teenage years, but he had never had such a conscious awareness of his body before. And the idea of sitting around doing nothing was not appealing in the least.

Heidi returned with a tray of food. There were scrambled eggs, bacon-flavored protein wafers, toast, a bowl of oatmeal flavored with dehydrated fruit, and a tall glass of orange-flavored drink. He devoured the meal. Every bite filled his mind with a flood of information about what he was tasting and he could even feel his body absorbing the nutrients.

As he drank the last of the orange drink, Doctor Thessle walked in. She looked surprised to see him sitting in a chair instead of lounging on the hospital bed.

"Good morning," she said.

"Excellent morning," Mitch replied. "I feel fantastic."

"Tell me about it?" Doctor Thessle said, nodding at Heidi who began recording everything on her tablet.

"Well," Mitch said, a little surprised by the question, "I can feel my body, the muscles, the joints, even the blood pumping through my veins. And I've got energy, loads of it. Nothing hurts except some residual pain around the injection sites. They're still a little inflamed but everything else is good. It's better than good, it's great."

"That's excellent, Mitch. Can you get on the bed and let me run a few scans?"

"Sure," he replied.

They spent an hour doing tests, from the automated body scans to hands-on examinations. Doctor Thessle even pulled out a rubber hammer to check his reflexes and Mitch had only seen that sort of thing in old movies.

"I think it's safe to proceed to phase two," the doctor said. "I'll get it scheduled for first thing tomorrow."

"So, what are we going to do today?" Mitch asked.

"Rest."

"What? No way. I feel too good to just lay around. I need to do something. It's been... well, I don't ever remember feeling this good. I don't want to waste it."

"Mitch," Doctor Thessle said. "This is just the first step in your new life. You're going to feel better and better. It's okay if you just let your body adapt and heal from the first procedure."

"I'm not sure I can just lay around here," Mitch insisted. "Please, let me do something."

"We could move him down to his new room," Heidi suggested.

Mitch looked up hopefully.

"Fine, but I want full scans at noon and this evening," Doctor Thessle said. "Mitch, if at any point you get tired, or feel sick in any way, you have to tell us immediately."

"I will," Mitch said.

"Alright. You can move rooms, but I want you to get a full night's sleep, is that clear?"

"Yes doctor," Mitch said.

She reached out and touched his shoulder. "I'm happy for you, Mitch. Your reaction to the serum is very promising indeed."

"Thank you," he said.

An hour later, Mitch was following Heidi through the corridors of the space station. They passed administrative offices and took an elevator down to the lower level. When they stepped off the elevator, Mitch was delighted to find a wide open area. There was a walking/jogging track around the outside and all sorts of exercise equipment in the center. The lower level had only a few patient rooms, and they were all empty.

"Can I play?" Mitch asked.

"No," Heidi said. "If you overdo things, you could have a setback."

"Can I at least walk the track?"

"As long as you promise to go slow and not get too worked up."

"If you knew how I felt you wouldn't hold me back," Mitch said.

Heidi flashed a smile that made him feel weak in the knees. She was much younger than he was, and he knew she wasn't flirting with him. But he couldn't deny the attraction. A voice in the back of his mind told him to simply take her. He felt strong, almost ferociously so, more than enough to overpower Heidi and do whatever he wanted. But the thought of that was also abhorrent to him. He wasn't a rapist and had never even stolen anything in his life. It had never even crossed his mind to force himself onto a person, and yet that thought seemed to play at the edges of his mind with Heidi. She was young, beautiful, and readily available. He was strong, full of energy, and ready to test himself. But he forced the abominable thoughts down. He wouldn't give in to his base urges, not even if he had the strength and energy to carry them out. Mitch was in control of himself, and he was determined to be a gentleman, as well as a good patient.

Lunch was a grilled chicken patty. He didn't know how much was real meat and how much was protein filler. It was either grown in a vat, or pressed into shape, but tasted good. The chef at Epsilon Station was excellent, and the meat well seasoned. Along with the chicken were mashed potatoes and a variety of steamed veggies in a creamy sauce. Mitch ate his lunch alone, and after getting a medical scan, spent the afternoon walking the track. He wanted to run, but he had promised not to. That evening, he watched two movies on the station's excellent entertainment library. His new room was slightly bigger. The bed was still a hospital-grade device, but the sitting chairs were more comfortable, and the bathroom was slightly larger. There was even a small desk.

He ate an early dinner and got another medical scan. Eventually, he went to bed and fell asleep with no trouble. The next morning, he woke up feeling good again. He had slept six solid hours but felt completely refreshed.

"No breakfast this morning?" he asked when Heidi arrived.

She shook her head. "No, not until after the procedure."

Mitch nodded. He didn't need a sedative before being taken to a small room near his own. There was no examine table, or hospital bed, just a large recliner and an entertainment unit in front of it. A med tech was there with a machine that had several clear hoses. Doctor Thessle was there too, waiting and watching as Heidi started an IV in one arm, and the medical technician started one in the other arm.

"Mitch, today we're going modify your circulatory system," Doctor Thessle said. "This is a simple bypass machine. Your blood will come out of one arm and go through our patented infuser where it will be mixed with the serum that will enhance the ability of your blood to carry oxygen, produce antibodies, and repair your systems. It takes about eight hours to completely pass your blood through the system three times. You might feel cold, and fatigue is a normal symptom of this process. Don't worry about it, the machines are doing all the work."

"I just sit here?"

"Yes," Doctor Thessle said. "Think of it as a physical supercharge. This phase of the LE Protocol will not only enhance your blood, it will clean and strengthen your arteries, preparing you for truly remarkable physical transformation."

"Alright," Mitch said.

The idea of sitting around all day wasn't appealing to him, but he didn't argue. There were monitors built into the recliner, and Heidi brought him a blanket. Mitch binged a show about spies infiltrating and sabotaging an oppressive, galactic regime. And he did feel weak as the day progressed. When it finally ended, he was happy to get up and stretch his legs, but he was nauseous and dizzy. Heidi helped him to his room and he skipped dinner, opting for a nap instead. When he woke up a few hours later, he was hungry and very thirsty. Food and a fruit-flavored drink with electrolytes and amino acids were supplied, first by Heidi, then by a male medical technician. He could feel that something inside him was changing. When he went back to sleep that night, he could hear his heart beating slow and strong in his ears.

The next morning, he was completely changed.

CHAPTER 6

"HE'S in the top ten percent of patients we've seen," Doctor Emily Thessle said. She was speaking to a room that was half administrators, half military officers. They were assembled around a table watching edited and annotated footage of the procedures that had been done to Mitch Murphy. "His recovery time is exceptional."

"He's already completed phase one and two?" one of the administrators asked.

"That's correct," Doctor Thessle said. "My guess is that by tomorrow he'll be ready to start testing himself. We'll get a baseline on all the regular physical exercises. If all goes well, we'll be ready for phase three in a couple of days."

"That's excellent," a four-star general said, leaning forward. "What do we know about him?"

"Mitch Murphy, thirty-three years old," another officer said, reading from the tablet on the table in front of her. "Born in the Boise/Salt Lake megatropolis. He attended Boise State University and earned a BA in Business. Went to work for Sterling Investment Corp in the Bay Area but did not progress in that career. Was terminated... wow, just a few days ago."

"What did he spend his signing bonus on?" the general asked.

"Looks like he paid debts," another officer replied. "Seventy thousand in credit card bills, and a little over a hundred grand to pay off his student loans. The rest went to catching up his mortgage, he was a month behind, and paying the next six months' worth of payments. He also owed forty thousand to the HOA."

"Family?" the general asked.

"Parents are retired," an administrator supplied that answer. "They still live in the BSL megatropolis."

"He was married," a military officer commented. "But he used the program to end it."

"Married to who?" the general asked.

"Megan Murphy, formerly Megan Aubrey, also of BSL," the officer continued. "Unemployed. Went to Boise State but didn't finish. My notes say she's already got someone living in the apartment with her."

"Not a roommate?" the general asked.

"Doesn't appear that way, sir. There were indications of a preexisting relationship."

"So, you're saying she cheated on him," the general said. "Surprise, surprise. A broken marriage, dead-end career, and now he's with us. Doesn't sound very promising."

"His latency markers are very high," another administrator said. "He's a top-tier candidate for the program."

"And making remarkable progress," Doctor Thessle said. "Whatever his past may be, he's not dwelling on it. I think he's ready for a new life, General. Eager isn't too strong of a word."

"He isn't milking the situation," a female administrator said. "I've seen plenty of candidates who thought of this process as a free vacation."

"Recommendations?" the general growled.

"He's got the education for officer training," one person said. "What's his personality?"

"Friendly," Doctor Thessle said. "Self-control is high. He hasn't made a pass at Heidi Strong yet. That's saying something considering the increase in testosterone. We've had other patients who performed as well as Murphy, but none who didn't step out of line along the way."

"Is he gay?"

"No, sir. No indication of that," an officer said.

"He's friendly with Heidi, but has maintained decorum," Doctor Thessle said. "I believe he could be the best candidate we've ever had."

"Or he could be non-aggressive," the general argued. "We don't need a super soldier who doesn't like to fight."

"He'll be ready to test himself tomorrow," Doctor Thessle said. "The next day at the latest. Abu Kahn will test his aggression via grappling and hand-to-hand combat. You'll have all that information before he's put on board your ship."

"Very well," the general said. "And there's nothing negative in your testing? No flaws?'

"No one is perfect," Doctor Thessle said. "Murphy has a deficiency in his nutritional habits, and my guess is he'll bulk up, so speed may not be as high as you are hoping for, but everything else is at the top of the chart."

"Eyesight?" the general asked.

"Normal for a man his age. The circulatory enhancement will correct whatever deficiency might be forming," an administrator explained.

"Very good. Let's give the recruiter a commendation. We need more of our people targeting people with high debt and low career advancement. Doctor Thessle, I want to know his limits. Don't hold back."

"Yes, General," she said. It was what was expected of her, but not what she wanted. Mitch Murphy wasn't a racehorse. Pushing him too hard, too fast would only slow down his progression. Of course, the general didn't care about that. He wanted a weapon, and she was creating one. In a few days, Mitch would be sent to a dangerous world and expected to fight. It might be honorable, but it seemed like such a waste to Doctor Emily Thessle. And she knew once he set foot on the CMC ship, she would never see Mitch Murphy again.

The meeting broke up and she went back to her office. The latest scans by Murphy's medical bed showed that his blood volume was already increasing. It was impossible to know his red, white, and T-cell counts without drawing a sample, but she could guess that his body was reacting as well as any she had personally worked with.

"You need anything else today?" Heidi stepped into the office and asked.

"No," Doctor Thessle said. "Get a nap. He'll be raring to go in a few hours."

"He's a machine," Heidi said.

"But you are not, my dear. You need your sleep."

"On it," Heidi said.

Doctor Thessle stood up, stretched, and realized she needed some sleep too. But she had a report to finish and tests to schedule. She brewed herself a cup of coffee and then settled back in for a few more hours of work until Murphy woke up. She was tired, but also excited to see how he performed. He had come to her broken and completely unimpressive. And yet physically, his body had responded better than she had dared to hope. Even with the high latency markers, she hadn't expected him to adapt so quickly. And his mental attitude was equally impressive. The sudden surge of energy and physical prowess hadn't caused him to act out. Many top-tier candidates had simply lost their minds. She had patients who attacked their female nurses, or who nearly killed the trainers who helped test their physical limits. Some had to be restrained, and others were locked away. She guessed that some were even terminated. It was within the administration's purview to have a patient put down. It was sad, but necessary, both for the safety of the faculty, and it also gave them an opportunity to do testing on the subject's body and brain. They had learned so much over the past few years, but there was still so much to discover. Fortunately, it didn't appear that Mitch Murphy would need to be terminated. He was going to make an excellent soldier, at least as far as Doctor Thessle could tell. His superiors would be the real judge of that.

She sipped her coffee and made the arrangements for the tests that would soon take place. Once that was done, and she had administrative approval, they would move into phase three. It was, by far, the most dramatic part of the protocol. She wouldn't get to see it in person, but she would get reports. And that would be enough for her. By then, she would be on to a new patient.

†††

General Stanley Mercer was the newly assigned head of Special Operations for the Colonial Marine Corps stationed on humanity's sole planet outside of the Sol System. He was one of the few people who knew the full story of how the wormhole was found. Another officer was in charge of protecting the passageway and defending the solar system from any non-human vessel that might pass through. It was a threat that was becoming all too real.

New Terra was a unique world, what the egghead scientists called a *Cold Swamp* ecosystem. Most of the planet's water was frozen, but there were areas where liquid water stood in fetid pools among lush vegetation. There were no oceans on New Terra, which left a lot of terrain, but it wasn't all habitable by humans. There were vast deserts, with no water available at all. There were rocky canyons, and deep crevices, tundra, and swamps. In general, it was a cold planet, but one rich in natural resources. When humans had first discovered the wormhole, and the habitable planet in the system beyond it, there was hope that they might also discover other intelligent beings. There was plenty of animal life on New Terra, but nothing with the capacity for true intelligence. But soon after the first colonies were established, humans discovered they were truly not alone in the galaxy.

General Mercer had made his stars fighting the raiders, slavers, and predatory races that seemed to show up in the Terra system or on the planet itself. Humanity was in a constant struggle to maintain a presence on the planet and ensure the safety of the colonists. But their settlements and electronic gear, such as satellites and early detection systems were constantly being disrupted if not outright destroyed. Latent Technologies' Super Serum as the LE Protocols were commonly called, had seemed like a game changer. It produced a team of special operators who could thrive in New Terra's harsh environment longer than regular Marines. And when it came to fighting, they were absolutely ferocious, but the results were spotty at best. Some recruits only excelled in a single area of latent prowess. Others went crazy or died in the process. He had been fully briefed on the LE Protocols, and none of it sounded like anything he wanted to endure. The results could be fantastic, but they could also be disastrous. Better to let the raw recruits take those chances, while the invaluable senior officers, which was how General Mercer saw himself, called the shots from the safety of a command ship.

He was on Epsilon Station for the first time as his battle cruiser prepared to make the trip to the wormhole. With the latest engine technology, they could reach a speed that approached one-quarter of light speed. It still would take his cruiser two weeks to reach the wormhole. While the top speed was high, it took a ship days to reach that speed, and sometimes even longer to slow back down. The wormhole was between the orbits of Neptune and Pluto. At top speed, they could cover the distance in just under one standard days' time, or twenty-four hours. But it would take the cruiser five days to reach that speed, and another six to slow back down. Once in the Terra system, it would take them ten days to reach New Terra.

General Mercer was eager to get going but having a top-tier

candidate for the Super Special Operations (SSO) program was worth waiting for. He gathered his staff in the Cruiser's wardroom. The ship itself was crewed by Space Force personnel and the ship had a naval feel to it. But as a battlecruiser, it had a full fighter squadron and a battalion of Colonial Marines. General Mercer had his own wardroom, and his personal quarters included an office, and sitting room, as well as the usual sleeping berth and bathroom. The wardroom had a long table, several beverage dispensers, and all the fine china for the senior staff under Mercer's command. They used the room for meals, but also for staff meetings.

"What's the latest word from NT?" Mercer asked.

"We just got word that a Grumbler ship touched down in the southern hemisphere," Lieutenant Colonel Jerome Banks reported. "The Graylings are in the system but have not landed to our knowledge. We have Jesters raiding Colonies four and seven. They're taking the Rare World Minerals."

"Easier to steal them than to mine them yourself," Captain Frank Marcs claimed.

"Indeed," General Mercer said. "What do we know about the Grumblers, Captain Swift?"

Elaine Swift was a xenobiologist and the resident expert on the ETIs (Extra-Terrestrial Intelligence). She looked severe with her long hair tied up in a tight bun.

"We know they're forty feet tall and hard to kill," she said.

"Tell us something we don't know," Captain Marcs said.

"The ones we've encountered before didn't seem to be directly aggressive. They breathe carbon dioxide and have very efficient atmospheric generators."

"Which is why we've had to hit them before," Banks said. "Those gennies will make the atmosphere unbreathable if we don't take them down quickly."

"Any other threats?" the general asked.

"We'll know more when we get there," Captain Swift said.

"The new operator the eggheads are prepping has a fast

recovery time. I want to put him straight into officer training, as long as he's sufficiently aggressive."

"I thought they were all hyper-aggressive," Captain Lindsey Priss, the logistics officer said.

"Some are," Captain Marcs said. "I've seen 'em go nuts. They can be hard to control."

"The doctor is convinced her new guy is the real deal. Brains and self-discipline, but we'll have to see for sure. Marcs will do the physical training, I want Swift on leadership. Make sure he's ready to lead a team on the ground."

The officers all made notes on their tablets, either typing with modified hand motions or using a stylus.

The general leaned back in his seat and spread his hands on the table. "Two more days, and we dust off. We'll be ground side in four weeks' time. I want to hit the aliens hard and fast. No excuses. Lieutenant Tosh will coordinate with the rifle platoons for support. SSO teams will be the point of the spear. Let's make sure everything is ready."

CHAPTER 7

AFTER HIS BLOOD TRANSFER SESSION, Mitch was surprisingly tired. He felt sick, even though he hadn't eaten since the night before. All he wanted to do was sleep, and the medical staff encouraged him to do just that. He slept all through the evening and night, a full fourteen hours. But when he woke up the next morning, he practically jumped out of bed. After his first session of the Latent Enhancement Protocol, Mitch could feel everything. His nervous system functioned like it hadn't in years, maybe never. He reminded himself of a child with bountiful energy.

But after the second session, Mitch woke up feeling like he could do anything, as in run through walls kind of powerful. And he wanted to be moving, to be active. He immediately dropped to the floor and started doing push-ups. As a teenager, he could do twenty push-ups no problem, but over the last few years, he had gotten weaker and heavier at the same time. Just a few push-ups were difficult. But the first day after his blood transfusion Mitch did twenty pushups as easily as one might stroll through a shopping mall. He kept going, thirty, forty push-ups and he wasn't even breathing hard. When he stopped it wasn't from fatigue, it was from boredom. His enhanced blood was so efficient at carrying oxygen to his muscles that he felt invincible.

When Heidi came in a few minutes later Mitch had already showered and shaved. He was pacing in the room, anxious to see what the day held.

"Good morning," she said. "I brought breakfast."

"Great!" Mitch said. "I'm starving."

"Eat up. You're going to need it."

She sat the tray down on the desk and Mitch dove in. He ate fast. The food tasted good to him, not just the flavors on his tongue, but the way they fueled his body. He could sense the nutrients filling him with energy.

"What am I doing today?" Mitch asked Heidi, who was making notes on her tablet while he ate.

"Everything," she told him.

Mitch couldn't help but smile, and she wasn't lying either. As soon as he finished eating someone knocked at his door.

"Come in!" Mitch said.

Heidi smiled as a short, swarthy-looking man entered. The stranger gave Heidi a hug and Mitch was suddenly filled with an intense jealousy. He felt himself on the verge of rage and had to look away from the pair. He took a deep breath to calm down, but the feeling was still there, lurking in the shadows of his mind. He felt a connection with Heidi that he knew on a logical level didn't make sense. It was a simple crush. She was young and attractive, as well as friendly and encouraging, but he hadn't even flirted with her. And she certainly hadn't made a pass at him. He knew he had no claim to her, but he still felt anger at seeing another man be so familiar with her. Part of Mitch wanted to rip the newcomer's head right off.

"Mitch," Heidi said. "This is Abu Khan. He'll be putting you through some training today."

"It's a pleasure to meet you," Abu said, extending his hand and offering Mitch a smile.

It took all of Mitch's willpower not to react in jealousy. Instead, he stood up and shook the stranger's hand.

"Are you ready to begin?" Abu asked.

"Yes," was all Mitch could manage to say at that moment.

"Then we shall," Abu said. "Come with me."

They spent half an hour warming up. They did basic exercises and stretching. Mitch's fury slowly subsided, and by the time Abu let him run on the track, he was anxious to get moving. As a teen, he had run to train for the sports that he played, but he never ran for pleasure. But after his second procedure in the LE Protocol, he ran with abandon. It was partly because running allowed him to fully engage his body. The energy buzzing in his brain needed a release and running allowed him to let it out. But there was something completely different about running when the activity didn't wind him at all. His enhanced blood was so proficient at carrying oxygen to his body that after five miles, Mitch still wasn't out of breath. His body felt like a well-oiled machine, his arms and legs pumping in rhythm, his breathing controlled, yet fueling his body with all it needed to perform at its peak.

After his five-mile run, Abu took Mitch to the resistance machines. Epsilon Station was positioned in orbit around Venus so that it took advantage of the planet's strong gravity field, but it still didn't make sense to have free weights in space. The resistance machines instead used cables and weighted planks to create resistance. Mitch was stronger than he remembered, but he didn't have super strength. He lifted his maximum weights on a variety of machines, with Abu taking notes on each one.

"Why are we doing all this?" Mitch asked.

His body was fully engaged, and the exercise was releasing endorphins into his brain chemistry that made him feel good. But his mind was just as active. He wanted to know what Abu Kahn was doing as he made his notes.

"We're forming a baseline," Khan said. "The next phase of the LE Protocol will make you bigger, and stronger. We need to know how much of an increase you get."

"Makes sense," Mitch said.

Abu offered Mitch a break once they had gotten his max on every resistance machine, but he didn't feel like he needed it. Lifting his maximum made his muscles tired, but never for long. A few moments rest was all he needed to recharge.

After lifting weights, they moved to the grappling mats. Abu Khan was an expert in hand-to-hand combat and had trained in a variety of martial arts. Mitch knew nothing, but they were soon rolling on the ground, flipping and twisting as Mitch tried to catch Khan in submission hold or pin him to the floor. Khan wasn't as strong or as fast as Mitch, but he had years of experience. Every time Mitch came close to catching Abu, the smaller man squirmed free. Dozens of times Khan caught Mitch in a submission hold, causing him to tap for Khan to release him. It was frustrating, but fun at the same time. And Mitch realized he no longer wanted to kill Abu Khan.

At lunch, Mitch ate a full meal, while Abu gave Doctor Thessle a report. They didn't hide anything from him and talked freely in his presence.

"Aggression?" Doctor Thessle asked after hearing the list of maximum weight Mitch had lifted.

"High, but he's got more control than any of the others," Abu said. "And he's learning fast too."

"Excellent," the doctor said.

They ran a full scan on him, checking all his vitals. Mitch had worked out hard all morning, a full five hours of constant, hard exercise. There were times when he felt his strength waning, but it only took a few moments of rest before his energy returned. After lunch, he was raring to go again. Abu took the time to teach him some of the basic hand-to-hand combat drills that he would be put through in his military training, then Mitch ran again. In fact, he ran ten full miles on the track. It was, he found, a great way to bleed off the excess emotions he sometimes felt, like his desire for Heidi, his jealousy of Abu Khan, and even the anxiety he sometimes felt about the LE Protocol. When his body fell into the rhythm of his run, his mind cleared, and he found that he could think.

After training all day, Mitch took a long shower. Dinner was brought to his room, but Heidi and Abu stayed. They talked and laughed. It was the most normal thing Mitch had done since leaving Earth. It was clear that Heidi and Abu were friends, but nothing more. And she was friendly with both men, but not flirty. Still, she didn't have to flirt to make Mitch long for there to be something more than friendship between them. But by that point, his emotions were in check. He felt the same desires, only not as strong as before. And he felt more in control of himself.

"You'll be leaving soon," Heidi said. "It's too bad."

"You'll miss me?" Mitch asked.

"Sure," she said.

"It can get boring up here," Abu said. "We do the same thing, day after day."

"Only the subjects change," Heidi said.

"When I leave, you'll have someone else to look after," Mitch said, feeling an all too familiar stab of jealousy.

"After a short break," Heidi said. "Only most of the patents that go through the protocol aren't as fast to recover as you are, Mitch. They take a lot more time and work."

"It's not the same for everyone?" he asked.

She shook her head. "No, everyone has different latent abilities, and they all respond differently to the protocols. We're still learning. There's a lot to the science."

"How long have you done this?"

"A few years now," Heidi said.

"I've been here two years," Abu spoke up. "Before that, I was training professional fighters on Mars."

"The cage fights?" Mitch asked.

Abu nodded. It was a fast-growing sport. Mars had a much smaller population than Earth. Many of the people living there worked dangerous jobs in the red mines. Cage fighting was very popular among the citizens on Mars, and the top-ranked fighters earned the right to compete on Earth.

"Yes," Abu said. "I enjoyed it, but then Doctor Thessle poached me."

"Five years here and you can go anywhere," Heidi said. "Earth, Titan, Hollywood Station..."

"I'll go to New Terra," Abu said. "I want to see a new world."

"What have you heard about it?" Mitch asked.

"Same as everyone else," Abu replied, but Mitch sensed he was hiding something.

"Come on, you're part of the CMC. You have to know more about it."

"What's to know that isn't public knowledge," Heidi said. "They report it on the news every night. Another colony raid, another alien species entering the system."

"They make it sound like a rough place," Mitch said.

"It is," Abu replied.

"So why would you want to go there?"

"I'm a fighter, Mitch. But sport fighting is like play-acting. I'm not saying it isn't dangerous, but I don't want to fight for money. I want to fight for a cause, for freedom, to protect the weak. I want my training and my skill to mean something more than a number in a bank account."

"What about you?" Mitch asked Heidi. "Do you want to go to New Terra too?"

She nodded. "I feel like I can help."

"So why not just go? Why spend years here first?"

"If I'm honest, I guess I'm hoping they'll perfect the protocol and make it available to everyone," Heidi said. "Seeing what people can do with it is amazing. I can't help but want that same opportunity."

"But you didn't want to sign up with the CMC?"

"I'm not a fighter Mitch," she said. "I'm a nurse. I want to help heal."

"Doesn't the CMC need nurses?"

"They need boots on the ground," she said. "Working here is better for me."

"What about you, Mitch?" Abu asked. "Why did you sign up?"

He thought about his answer before replying. "It was time for a change."

"So, get a pet, or change jobs," Heidi said. "You don't have to leave Earth forever and go to war just to shake things up."

Mitch shrugged. "I was at a point where I didn't have a lot of options. Maybe I could have found something else, but no one was in a hurry to hire me. I had fallen into a pattern of mediocrity, and I needed to do something to break out of that cycle."

"That takes wisdom and courage," Abu said.

"Well, you're certainly not the man who I met just a few days ago," Heidi said. "You give me hope that what we are doing can be more than just a super soldier program."

"What's wrong with humanity the way it's always been?" Abu asked her.

"Nothing," Heidi explained. "But we're not alone in the universe. And if we're going to compete with other races from other worlds, we need to be the best we can possibly be. I mean, just look at humanity. We have a pretty short lifespan, just eighty-odd years if we're lucky. The LE Protocol could be the key to unlocking longer life and higher thinking. You're not just a physical phenom, Mitch, your mind will expand too, if you exercise it along with the rest of your body."

"You're saying you think everyone should go through the protocols?" Abu asked.

"Once it's perfected and safe," Heidi said. "Yes."

Mitch didn't disagree, although he liked feeling special. Still, he wouldn't deny someone their opportunity to excel in life. Not

Heidi, or Abu, or even his ex-wife Megan and her mystery lover. Mitch had been filled with jealousy that morning when Abu Khan gave Heidi a friendly hug. But he hoped that was just a glitch, maybe his brain chemistry needed time to level out. Whatever it was, he no longer felt it, even though part of him still wished that Heidi felt more than just friendship for him.

"What about children?" Mitch asked. They had finished their dinner and were sitting around in comfortable chairs. The big display screen had a beautiful video feed of Venus swirling with color below the station. Mitch wasn't tired, but he felt calm and peaceful after a long day of training and physical check-ups. His mind was fully engaged in the conversation while his body was content to be at rest.

"Children?" Abu asked.

"You mean can people enhanced by the serum have kids?" Heidi asked.

"Yes," Mitch replied.

Heidi looked at Abu and shrugged. "Who knows? I don't think many live long enough to procreate."

"It would be interesting to see how their children were physically," Abu said. "Can an enhanced man get a normal woman pregnant? Would their child have only half of the enhanced skills?"

"I'm not sure even an enhanced couple would have enhanced children," Heidi said. "The capacity is there in most people, but it has to be unlocked. Enhancement doesn't change your DNA."

"So how does it work?" Mitch asked.

"It's more like a computer upgrade. It's the same software but on a faster, more powerful mainframe."

"Fascinating to think about," Abu said.

"You should see what it feels like," Mitch told him.

"What does it feel like?" Heidi asked.

Mitch thought for a moment. "Everything is clearer," he said. "It's like going from a dark, shadowy room, to having someone turn on the lights."

"So, it's all mental?" Abu asked.

"No," Mitch replied. "Physically I feel better. In fact, I can feel things I never felt before. But the old aches and pains are gone. The mental fog has cleared, and nothing is a struggle. When I breathe in, I can feel the oxygen flooding my blood supply. And I feel more capable of doing things. Did you guys ever roller skate?"

"I did," Heidi said.

"Not me. That's a good way to get injured," Abu replied.

"When I was a kid, we used to roller skate. They're heavy, the skates," Mitch explained. "You don't notice while you're doing it, but when you finish and you take them off—"

"You feel light," Heidi said with a nod. "Like you're walking on springs."

"That's what this is like," Mitch said. "It's like someone took the skates off my entire body. I feel like nothing I want to do is a burden."

"Sounds wonderful," Heidi said.

"Yes it does," Abu agreed.

Mitch thought he was the luckiest man alive at that moment. Little did he know he would feel exactly the opposite in just a few short hours.

CHAPTER 8

"PHASE THREE IS INTENSE," Doctor Thessle said. "So far, you've excelled, Mr. Murphy. There's no reason to think you won't continue to exceed our expectations."

He was sitting on another padded table with holes in it. Above him was another robotic arm. The first phase of the LE protocols had been incredibly painful. But he'd had a powerful sedative before that procedure and no one had offered him anything when he had gotten up or been called into the room where the next phase would be carried out.

"We're going to inject the patented formula into your large bone centers," Doctor Thessle said. "Right into the marrow of your femurs, femoral heads, acetabulum, and scapula."

Mitch was confused and looked over at Heidi.

"Your thigh bones, hips, and shoulder blades," she explained.

"The serum will, in time, strengthen your bones, enabling you to grow stronger, and less susceptible to injury," Doctor Thessle continued. "But the recovery process is much longer than the other phases. We'll also be injecting a combination of the LE serum with growth hormones into your large muscle groups. The procedure takes a few hours, and I'm afraid it's painful."

"No sedatives though?" Mitch asked.

Heidi looked away and had a pained expression on her pretty face. It seemed unnatural and Mitch would have done anything to make it go away.

"I'm afraid not," the doctor said. "Sedatives and narcotics would only interfere with the process. The results, however, will be well worth the pain."

Mitch thought that was easy to say by the person not going through the painful procedure, but the results of the first two phases of the LE Protocols had resulted in excellent benefits. He didn't want to endure a painful procedure, but he knew he had no choice in the matter.

"Let's get it over with then," he said.

"Excellent," Doctor Thessle said. "Let's begin."

"I'll be here when it's over, Mitch," Heidi said. "Good luck."

"Thanks," he replied, not quite sure why he needed luck.

The two females left, while a pair of medical technicians entered.

"You'll need to strip down," one said.

"All the way?" Mitch asked, already guessing the answer."

"That's correct," the technician said.

Mitch complied, glad that Doctor Thessle and Heidi weren't in the room, but also certain they were watching via the mounted cameras on the ceiling. Once he was out of his clothes, he laid down on the padded table. Just like during phase one, he was strapped down. Then the med techs retreated from his sight, but he could hear them in the room. Doctor Thessle's voice could be heard over hidden speakers.

"Let's begin."

The robotic arm whirred as it swiveled down into the position of his right thigh. With his head strapped down he couldn't see the thick needle or the tiny drill bit inside it. But he felt the needle punch through his skin and stab through his quadriceps muscle. His entire body was still sensitive to every sensation, good or bad. Pain shot through his leg and it took all his strength not to cry out in pain.

"Try not to tense up, Mitch." It was Heidi's voice that came to him over the speaker. "Do your best to stay relaxed."

It may have been good advice, but it was easier said than done. When the drill began to bore through his thigh bone, Mitch groaned in agony. By the time the medicine was pumped into the bone marrow, he was sweating, and his breathing had increased. In the control room, they were monitoring all his vital signs.

"His heart rate is at one ten and holding," a med tech announced.

"Respiration is elevated, but well within acceptable levels," another said.

"He's strong," Doctor Thessle said.

"That doesn't mean he isn't in pain," Heidi pointed out.

"It's what he applied for," Doctor Thessle said. "Unpleasant, but necessary. We've been through this many times, Ms. Strong."

"That doesn't make it any easier to watch."

"Your presence here is essential, but you do not have to monitor the patient," Doctor Thessle said. "I'll tell you what to say when it's needed."

But Heidi didn't look away. Nurses saw patients come and go all the time. Her work on Epsilon station was no different. And it wasn't lost on her that she had been recruited for her looks as much as her education and skills. Heidi believed in the LE Protocol, and she knew that her presence often set her patients at ease, especially her male patients.

The robot arm finished its work on Mitch's right thigh and moved over to his right hip. Mitch noticed blood oozing from his leg just before the drill went to work on his hip. The pain was exquisite, but strangely enough, at that moment, he found that he could isolate it. He felt the electrical impulses flashing through his nervous system, relaying the terrible pain to his brain. Somehow, he managed to dim his mental receptors. As the pain raged in the procedure room, his mind focused on a warm, sunny place. He imagined himself on an island, basking in the sunlight, while the waves lapped at his feet.

The robotic arm finished injecting the medicine into the ball joint of his hip, moved over a few inches, and injected more into the wide socket. The pain of the tiny drill boring into his bone was the worst, but the medicine felt out of place too, and the burning sensation that had tormented him after his first procedure returned, only it was worse than before. It was bone deep. Mitch had to move his consciousness away from his body and focus on the details of his imaginary seaside escape. He felt the sun on his face, the ocean breeze playing across his skin, and the sand swirling around his toes as the tide ebbed and flowed.

In the observation room, the technicians were amazed.

"His heart rate is actually coming down," one tech said.

"Respiration, and blood pressure too," the other pointed out.

"Did he pass out from the pain?" Doctor Thessle asked.

"No," Heidi said. "Look at his brain waves. He's conscious."

"Remarkable," the doctor observed. "I've never seen anything like it. We've had stronger candidates. Some faster, a few with more stamina, but I've never seen anyone deal with the pain so adroitly."

"You're doing great, Mitch. We're halfway there," Heidi said over the intercom as the robotic arm finished injecting the medicine into his shoulder blade.

Mitch heard Heidi's voice. In his fantasy, he turned and saw her walking down the beach. She was beautiful in nursing scrubs, but in his mind, he imagined her in a swimsuit with a silky robe-like cover. It was a modest fantasy, and he envisioned palm trees swaying over the beach. He had never been to a tropical island, but it was a pleasant diversion from the awful pain that wracked his body. He could still sense the agony but did his best to ignore it, and somehow the effort was working.

It took a full hour to complete the bone injections, and then the technicians from the observation booth had the robotic arm swap out the big needle and drill for the cluster of hypodermics. They injected the LE serum into the same muscles as before but added more to each side of his stomach and the muscles in his shoulders and biceps too. By the time the procedure was complete three hours later, Mitch was so weak he couldn't sit up on his own. The med techs came in, moved him to a gurney, covered his body with a sheet, and rolled him back to his room. Heidi was waiting there. She oversaw the transfer to the bed. Mitch couldn't keep his mind shut off from the pain any longer. It was different than the acute agony of the injections, but more overwhelming to his mind. If he could have reasoned he would have seen that with his entire body reacting to the serum, there were simply too many signals reaching his brain to isolate them all. He lay on the bed trembling as Doctor Thessle came in to check on her patient.

"How's he feeling?"

"He's conscious," Heidi said.

Doctor Thessle stepped to the bedside. The rails were up on the bed, the wireless sensors monitoring his vital signs.

"Mr. Murphy, can you describe your pain on a scale of ten, with zero being no pain, and ten being—"

"Ten..." Mitch said through clenched teeth, "thousand!"

"You're a highly sensitive person to the protocol," Doctor Thessle said. "It's why you've shown such marked improvement. The pain will fade, and you'll feel sleepy. Don't fight the sleep. It's your body's way of healing. Stay with him, Ms. Strong. I want regular updates until they take him onto the ship."

"Yes, ma'am," Heidi said.

The technicians left, and so did Doctor Thessle. Heidi pulled a chair right next to his bed. She took his hand and held it tight.

"You'll get through this Mitch," she said. "It won't take much longer. The pain will recede."

"Glad... you're... here," he said, looking at her with feverish eyes.

"Me too," she said.

He didn't know if she really meant it, or how she felt for him, but he enjoyed holding her hand. And the pain didn't continue unabated for long. Half an hour after reaching his room, the pain began to ease. Or maybe he was just so exhausted that he passed out. Either way, he fell into a deep, sleep. He was completely unaware that Heidi removed the sheet, cleaned the sweat and blood from his body, and dressed him in lightweight scrubs.

He slept through the rest of the day, and all through the night. Heidi stayed, recording his vitals. It wasn't necessary, the bed was keeping a record, and it was synced to the space station which was recording updates every few minutes. But Heidi was a medical professional, and her report was essential for the LE program. Early the next morning, a pair of Marines showed up. Heidi stepped aside while they unplugged the medical bed and unlocked the wheels to move it to their ship.

"What's happening?" Mitch asked in a groggy voice.

He was barely awake. His body felt as if it had been run over by a giant boulder, but through the haze of pain and fatigue, he knew something was going on.

"Mitch," Heidi said. "These Marines are taking you to their ship. You'll finish your recovery there."

"Won't see you again," he said softly.

"You can write me," she said, tucking a plastic card with her personal contact information printed on it. "Maybe our paths will cross again."

"Thank you," Mitch said, his voice barely more than a whisper.

"Take care of yourself," Heidi said.

"We're moving," one of the Marines said.

They wheeled the bed from the room, and Mitch drifted away. He was in a sleep fugue for several days. Eventually, he woke up and found himself in a tiny berth in the ship's sick bay.

"How are you feeling, recruit?" a doctor in a military uniform asked.

"Tired," Mitch said.

It was an understatement. He had gone from feeling more energized than he could ever remember, to being weak and helpless.

"You need to eat. We've been giving you nutrition via the IV, but your body is in a state of rapid growth," the doctor said.

"I could eat," Mitch said.

"That's good," the doctor replied. "I'll have something sent to you."

Mitch dozed until a private appeared with a tray of food. Mitch devoured it. The moment he smelled the food he felt like he hadn't eaten in a week.

"Can I get more?" he asked the private.

"I guess," the Marine responded.

From that day forward, Mitch spent an entire week eating and sleeping. He was always hungry. And his rest was often disturbed by aching pains in his legs, arms, and back. The fifth day after waking up, Mitch felt like he had the energy to get out of bed. But he was groggy, his body sluggish and clumsy. It was nearly two weeks from the procedure before Mitch realized what had happened to him. When he finally looked into a mirror, he didn't recognize the person looking back.

CHAPTER 9

"WE'RE PREPARING to pass through the portal now," a naval officer said.

General Mercer was a guest on the ship's bridge. His post, in a conflict situation, would be in the Command Information Center or CIC. From there, he could direct his Marines into the fighting. But the *Wellington* wasn't his permanent post. He was a guest on the ship, with his command staff and a single new recruit. Once they passed into the Terra System, he would transfer to a group post, while a regular fire battalion would embark on the *Wellington* for the return trip to the Sol System.

"Very good," the ship's commander said. "Steady as she goes. Full impulse power please."

"Aye, Con, full impulse power," the aviation officer said.

Flying an interstellar ship was a bit like playing a computer game. It was a simple matter of pressing the right buttons at the right time. General Mercer knew his naval compatriots had skills that he didn't understand. The military battleships had fought several engagements in space around New Terra. But the humans had yet to win a decisive battle in space. The other vessels were more advanced, which essentially meant faster and more agile. But they had their place, the general knew.

"Passing the event horizon now, sir," the navigational officer announced.

General Mercer didn't feel anything as the ship moved from one system to another in the blink of an eye. He didn't know how the wormhole worked, but he understood the concept. It was a passage through time and space. Without it, humanity wouldn't have left their own solar system yet. The technology to increase speeds to a level fast enough to travel between star systems was still out of reach. And even if they could venture out of the Sol System, the dangers of space debris wrecking their ship were much too high. The eggheads, as General Mercer thought of the researchers and engineers who worked to come up with ways to make the rest of the universe more accessible, understood what was needed, such as a Faster Than Light engine system and expandable laser shielding. It wouldn't do them any good to go faster if they couldn't protect their vessels from the small bits of matter that floated in the great voids between the systems.

"Give me a plot," the ship commander barked.

"We have enemy ships in system," someone on the bridge shouted. "Designating Echo one, Echo two, Echo three..."

"We have a clear run to the planet, sir," the navigation officer said, as a hologram of the Terra System sprang to life.

General Mercer could see the plot clearly. The sun, planets, and moons were shown, as well as their position and several other Space Force ships. There were also red holograms of alien ships. They weren't as clear and distinct as the Space Force vessels. Little designation markers appeared by the ships as the fire control officer barked them out.

"... Echo nine. I think that's all sir. Two other ships appear to be leaving the system. They're outside the scope of the plot."

"Very good, Henderson," the ship commander announced. "Give me firing solutions on Echo three, four, and seven. Spin up stealth torpedoes in the bow launchers and open the bomb bay doors."

"Aye, Con, spinning up stealth torpedoes," the gunner said. "Opening outer bomb bay doors. Pressurizing the launch area. We'll be weapons hot in four minutes, sir."

"Copy that, four minutes," the captain said. "Nav, what's our route into orbit?"

"We'll reach the space dock here sir," the navigation officer said, pointing to a tiny looking dot on the hologram near the planet. From there we can slingshot around Luna Blue, or swing around the planet to get our speed right."

"Very well, make it so," the commander ordered.

It was all by the book. The navy pukes had their routine down. There were enemy ships in the area, mostly Graylings, which were rarely hostile. It was widely believed the Graylings were observers only, although whether they were gathering intelligence, or just watching the humans for sport was still undetermined. The Grumbler ship was a massive vessel and probably had massive armaments. It might be a tempting target but was a little like a mouse challenging an elephant.

"Trouble, Commander?" Mercer asked.

"Negative, General. We have an unobstructed path to the space dock in orbit. You'll have no trouble getting your people down to the surface."

"Outstanding," Mercer said. "ETA?"

"Navigation?" the ship commander barked.

"Six days, eighteen hours, and forty-four minutes, sir."

"Call it a week," the ship commander told General Mercer. "That work for you?"

"It will have to," Mercer said. "We'll be ready. Permission to leave the Bridge?"

"Permission granted," the commander said, turning his attention back to the plot.

The ship commander was actually lower than General Mercer

in rank, but the Marines operated on the battle cruisers under the orders of the ship commander. It was a complex affair, but a space-ship was in many ways a country unto itself, with the commander acting as a dictator over everything that went on inside the vessel. Mercer might not like having to ask permission, but he respected the chain of command, so he did it.

Leaving the Bridge, he began the winding route to his own section of the ship eventually reaching the Ward Room where he spent most of his time. Captain Frank Marcs was there, sipping a cup of coffee and watching as their new super serum recruit got dressed in the sick bay via a ship video feed.

"He ready?" the general asked.

"Looks like it. The doc cleared him."

"He's a big one."

"Looks that way, sir."

"Well, show him who's in charge. I want to know what he's capable of. You've got five days."

"Roger that, General. Five days."

"That's three hours in the morning and two in the evening," General Mercer explained. "Captain Swift will be taking him through an abbreviated officer's command school."

"You really think that's necessary?" Marcs asked.

"Regular Marines can't keep up," the general said. "We both studied the reports. In the field, discipline breaks down. They're getting their orders, but with no one to enforce them, the inmates start running the asylum. And you saw what happened to Lieu-tenant Griggs. They broke him to pieces when he tried to stop them."

"That was outrageous, sir," Marcs pointed out.

"It was a learning experience. Lieutenant Griggs did the right thing and will be remembered in the history books for it."

"That's a small comfort, sir."

"What more can I tell you? Those animals were put down. They were highly aggressive to begin with. These super serum recruits are dangerous. Controlling them requires walking a razor's edge. We've got one now capable of being in charge. Let him take the risks of commanding a squad of enhanced Marines. You just need to ensure that he will follow orders, and you've got five days to do it."

"That isn't much time," Marcs said, dumping the remainder of his coffee down a small sink.

"It's all we've got. We'll be in the Orbital Docking Station in a week and have boots on the ground the day after. Recruit Murphy will have to hit the ground running. And it's up to you to make sure he doesn't fall flat on his face."

Captain Frank Marcs saluted sharply, then hurried from the room. He's used to a lot of uncomfortable situations. Just being on a battleship was difficult. It was claustrophobic, too small a space, and too many people. There were bad smells, narrow corridors, and a constant barrage of noise. But that was life in the CMC. Frank Marcs had served for seventeen years. He was on the cusp of making senior rank and had the combat experience to rise to the very top, but he liked where he was. He liked mingling with the special operators, or Spec Ops as it was often referred to. They were the best of the best in the war business, and he was in charge of combat operations. In his mind, it didn't get any better than that.

He met recruit Mitch Murphy just as he was stepping out of the sick bay. He was wearing an extra, extra, extra-large sweat suit that looked too small on him. Frank Marcs had to crane his head back to see Murphy's face.

"You Murphy?" Marcs asked as if he didn't already know. And it wasn't just because he had been watching the new recruit on the video surveillance system. There was only one Marine over seven feet tall on the *Wellington*.

"Yes sir, Mitch Murphy."

"Recruit will do for now. Come with me, Murphy. Let's see what you're made of."

CHAPTER 10

MITCH WAS speechless as he got dressed. The ship spun through space like a bullet, creating a weak, false gravity, but that wasn't what made him feel so strong. When he had gotten out of bed, his arms and legs felt too long. When he looked into the mirror, it was a shock. He had the same face, but his body was too big and muscular. Not like a bodybuilder, but his arms, legs, shoulders, and chest were thick with muscle. And he was taller too. The ship was built for men and women of regular height, with ceilings as low as seven feet in some places. The sick bay had an eight-foot ceiling and his head nearly touched. He had grown nearly an inch every day since his last procedure.

When Captain Frank Marcs showed up at the sick bay, Mitch had just finished getting dressed. He was wearing sweats, but they seemed too small. And he had felt clumsy getting them on. Especially the shoes. Tying their tiny laces with his thick fingers was a challenge, but he'd managed it. The captain led Mitch through the narrow confines of the ship. At times he had to duck under conduits, heating ducts, and doorways. When he saw the naval crew, they stared at him in surprise. It was a surreal experience.

And as he walked, he discovered that his body, though strange to him, fell into a rhythm where everything worked together. And he was anxious to find out more about himself and what his new muscular body was capable of.

They ended up in a training area around the ship's two massive engines. A track of sorts had been set up that circled the big, loud machines, and in between there was exercise equipment. It was fancy and looked clean, but it was well-used. There were members of the ship's crew there exercising when Mitch and Captain Marcs arrived.

"Get warmed up with a run," the captain ordered. "Move!"

Mitch was all too happy to comply. He felt like a wild stallion that was set free. He started with a jog, nothing strenuous, just feeling his long legs striding. Before the final phase of the LE Protocol, he had felt full of energy, his blood pumping oxygen to his muscles so that running and strenuous activity didn't strain him the way they always had before. And even though he was bigger, with larger muscles, he had also gained more blood volume and greater lung capacity. Running was easy, his arms and legs churned in perfect synchronization. Despite his big feet and long legs, he didn't pound around the running track, which was really just a metal deck painted red. His feet rolled from heel to toe so smoothly it was almost graceful. He felt his muscles heating up, calves, quads, abs, and back. He felt strong and full of energy, so much so that running wasn't a chore, but a joy. There was a lot to think about, but as he ran, his jog growing into a fast run that stretched his long legs, his mind settled into a peaceful bliss. Perhaps his old life had fallen into shambles, and there had been terrible pain in the LE Protocols, but it was all behind him. Perhaps he was on a military battleship, traveling to a distant system, to fight alien enemies, but that was fine as long as he could keep running. The release of his pent-up energy, along with his fears and frustrations, was almost joyous.

"That's enough!" Captain Marcs barked.

The track was roughly a kilometer around the two big engines. Mitch hadn't bothered counting his laps or even noticed that he was flying past the other runners like they were toddlers on a playground. He didn't hear Captain Frank Marcs give an order that cleared everyone else out of the training area. It was normally open to everyone on the ship but was designated as a Marine training area, which gave Marcs the authority to send everyone else out. The officer was waiting in the exercise space between the two engines.

"That's good enough," the captain growled.

Mitch couldn't tell if the officer was actually angry or not. His voice was gruff, but there was a twinkle of excitement in his eyes.

"Let's start with resistance exercises," he ordered. "Bench press."

The training area wasn't large. There was just one resistance machine with several exercise stations built into all four sides. The bench press was an upright chest press. Gravity was weak on the ship, which might have accounted for the ease of Mitch's run, but the resistance machine used thick elastic bands to simulate lifting heavy weights. The max on the chest press was three hundred pounds. On Epsilon Station, Mitch had maxed out at one hundred eighty pounds. But on the *Wellington,* he set the machine to its maximum resistance and easily pushed out fifteen reps. He could feel his chest muscles flexing, and his triceps bulging from the exercise, but it didn't feel overwhelming or tiring. In fact, it was just the opposite. It felt good to utilize his muscles. And he quickly moved on to the next exercise, and once more did the maximum resistance.

"Don't get cocky, recruit," Captain Marcs snapped. "Everyone in the LE Program sees a big improvement in strength."

Mitch didn't talk back. He was thrilled at his new abilities, but still felt a little intimidated by the stern officer. And there were no other recruits to commiserate with. Being the low man on the totem pole felt lonely. On Epsilon, he had Heidi there to buoy him up during the hard times. On the *Wellington,* he was all alone.

After working through every exercise on the resistance machine, Marcs had him climb a thick rope that was attached to the ceiling some thirty feet up. There were no safety lines, and no mats to dampen a fall. Mitch felt a little intimidated looking up, but he could make out several names scratched into the paint around the cleat that held the room to the ceiling of the training room.

He took the rope in both hands and started to pull himself up. It had never been an area he felt confident in. Before the LE Protocols, he could barely do one pull-up. But like every other area of his body, his back and shoulders were much stronger than before. He went up the rope easily enough, the thick nylon weave seemed small to his big hands. When he reached the top, he could see several names scratched into the paint, and even found a spot where he planned to leave his own mark. But that would have to wait. He climbed back down and did pushups, sit-ups, and squats. He broke a sweat keeping up with the captain's fast pace, and after the exercises was sent on a ten-kilometer run which the captain timed. Pushing himself, Mitch fairly flew around the track. When it was over, Captain Marcs turned Mitch over to a naval enlisted man who took him to the Marine berths. He showered in a room built for a dozen people, but he was the only enlisted man on the ship.

When he was cleaned up and shaved, he found more sweats to wear, and his bunk was one of many in a long room with a low ceiling. He took the bunk closest to the door and felt completely isolated in the empty room. After what seemed like a long time, he was shown to the chow hall. It was a big room with lots of tables. The chairs were little round stools that were bolted to the floor. His food came from a dispensary built into the wall. It wasn't good, but he was too hungry to care. There were ship's crew eating in the room. They all stared at him, but none spoke or invited him to eat with them. He settled at an empty table and ate two full meals from the dispensary machine, all the while wondering what he had gotten himself into.

CHAPTER 11

"OFF THE CHARTS," Captain Frank Marcs said.

General Mercer's command staff had reassembled in their Ward Room to hear the progress report from Captain Marcs.

"Aren't they all?" Lieutenant Johnny Tosh asked. He was the General's new executive assistant, and like many Marines, had a natural prejudice against the super soldiers as the LE candidates were often called.

"No," Captain Elaine Swift explained. "Most only thrive in one or two areas, and even then, their enhancement is rarely significantly higher than the average Marine."

"This one is significantly higher," Captain Marcs said. "Hell, we practically couldn't find clothes big enough for him."

"I can't wait to see him in theatre," Lieutenant Colonel Jerome Banks said, rubbing his dark hands together. "He's aggressive, right?"

"Not like most," Marcs corrected his superior. "Nothing I said or did rattled him at all. He's a cool customer."

"That is unusual," Captain Swift said, and it was obvious that she was anxious to meet their new recruit.

"I'm having some new clothing made up for him," Captain Lindsey Priss said. "I just need to get his measurements. We'll need to adjust the armor and probably his field pack too."

"What does off the charts mean, exactly?" General Mercer asked.

"He's strong," Marcs explained. "Maxed out the resistance exercises. I hammered him with all the regular exercises. He hardly broke a sweat. Ran the ten-kilometer test as fast as anyone I've heard of, and looked to me like he could have run another. He wasn't even breathing hard, and that was after I pushed him to do the final five laps at a full sprint. The system clocked him at almost fifty kilometers per hour at the end."

"Fifty?" General Mercer said. "That's what, thirty miles per hour? Is that really possible?"

"Professional athletes can reach twenty-three, twenty-four miles per hour in small bursts," Lieutenant Tosh said.

"Our boy kept it up for five kilometers," Marcs said.

"He's not a boy," Captain Swift pointed out. He's thirty-three years old."

"And a failure at everything's he put his hand to," Jerome Banks said. "I'm not sure giving him command of anything is a good idea."

"Elaine will sort that out," General Mercer said. "Tell me more about his demeanor."

"Like I said, he's a cool customer," Captain Marcs said. "Very even-keeled, doesn't get bothered by much."

"But you could tell he's aggressive?" The general questioned.

"He followed orders, absorbed my criticism without even blinking, and when it came to the exercises, he was a beast. He threw down three hundred pounds on the chest press like he was in a fight. Not straining, just eager. I don't know how he'll respond to a fight, but I think he's good."

"Find his limits," the general instructed. "I want to know exactly what he's capable of."

The meeting wrapped up and Captain Elaine Swift went

immediately to meet with Mitch. She sent an order for him to meet her in the simulator used by the Marines to simulate battlefields and practice coordinated responses to danger. She didn't need to simulate a fight, but she could use the program to take Mitch through the officer training videos.

When she arrived, she found him waiting. He was inspecting one of the virtual reality harnesses and the omnidirectional treadmill. When she entered, he didn't exactly come to attention, but he stood up straight and looked at her. He was tall, over seven feet, and well-proportioned. Elaine didn't know how much the LE Protocol affected the participant's physique, but there wasn't much fat on him. He had a narrow waist, broad chest and shoulders, and thick legs. His hair was too long for a Marine, and his eyes were expectant. There was none of the usual disdain that many of the super soldiers clearly felt around their superiors. Elaine was a biologist by training and an expert on alien forms of intelligent life. She also knew a lot about the psychology of the Marines who had been given the Latent Tech serum. Increased levels of testosterone often resulted in aggressive behavior, and that combined with their enhanced abilities gave the LE participants a belief that they were better than regular people. So, a normal officer giving an LE super soldiers orders sometimes made them bristle. But all she saw on Mitch Murphy's face was hope and excitement.

"I'm Captain Swift," she said, extending her hand. I'll be doing your military protocol and officer training."

"Officer?" Mitch asked.

It was Elaine's turn to smile. "If you qualify," she said, "you'll be the first Enhanced Marine Corp officer. You have a B.S. in business, is that correct?"

"Yes, ma'am."

"So, let's start at the beginning. Right now, you're a recruit. Our goal is to take you through an expedited boot camp here on the ship, and hopefully have you hit the ground running once we arrive on New Terra."

"When will that be?" Mitch asked. "I'm allowed to ask questions, right?"

"That's right. Let's sit down," she said, then raised her voice to give the ship's computer an order. "Simulator, give us a table and two chairs."

In the center of the simulation room a plain, four-legged table rose up from the floor. There was a straight-back chair on either side. Elaine sat down and Mitch did too, only he was clearly too large to be comfortable on the little chair.

"We'll reach orbit in six days," Elaine said. "Unless the situation on the ground changes before that, we'll take a shuttle straight down. In one week, you'll be an officer in the CMC. You'll have to wait a few months for your commission, but the field promotion will go into effect immediately."

"Wow," Mitch said.

"You shouldn't be surprised," she told him.

"I am," Mitch said. "Things happen fast here."

"The moment we passed through the wormhole, we essentially entered hostile territory. There isn't time for decisions based on committee. A good officer carries out his orders to the best of his ability, which often includes making decisions quickly. Would you consider yourself a decisive person, Recruit Murphy?"

"I don't think I've been in a position to be decisive in a long time," he admitted.

"And why is that?"

Mitch shrugged. "I was married right before I graduated from business school and went right to work for a big firm."

"Where?"

"San Francisco," he said. "Sterling Investment Corporation."

"What was your job?"

"I was an assistant buyer. It was very competitive."

"And were you, competitive?"

"No," he admitted. "I fell into some bad habits. Everyone around me was very loud, very opinionated. Our politics didn't exactly line up and I'm not the type that will stab a person in the back to get ahead."

"And you became invisible," she said with a knowing smile.

"Essentially, yes," he told her. "At work and at home. I thought if I did my job and kept my mouth shut, everything would work out."

"Did it?"

"No."

"So you joined the program."

"And here I am," he said with a small grin.

"How do you feel about that decision?"

"So far... outstanding," Mitch replied enthusiastically. "Don't get me wrong, the process was extremely unpleasant, but the results are undeniable."

"What effect has it had on your cognitive abilities?" Captain Elaine Swift asked.

"I honestly don't know. It's all new and I'm still figuring everything out. But there are some changes."

"Like what?"

"My physical senses have grown. I can feel every part of my body, and not just when something hurts. I can feel the blood supply, the muscle movements, the joints, the function of my organs, everything. And I feel stronger. No more aches and pains. It's like I turned back the clock."

"And you think that maybe your cognitive function has increased the same as your physical body has grown?"

"I don't know for sure, but that makes sense. I'd love to find out."

"You're about to go through a course that most officers take six weeks to complete," she said. "I'm going to be showing you videos that are sped up. And you'll be taking strategy and tactical tests using the simulator. How does that sound to you?"

"I'm ready," Mitch replied. "I want to know what I've gotten myself into."

"Good, let's start with the basics. When you meet a superior officer, you will salute. Stand up."

He did as instructed. She looked down at his feet.

"Heels together. Okay, head up, eyes straight ahead. Bring your arm up, hand stiff at your brow, and wait for a response. Once you get it, bring your hand down sharply."

"Like this?" Mitch asked.

"Yes, that's perfect. There will be a short video that goes over all this, and you'll have time to practice it on your own. But perfecting the basics will help you have confidence when you are with the other members of your squad. Which brings us to the next thing you need to know. You are not going to be part of the standard Colonial Marines. The LE program has changed you, and despite the fact that we are on the same team, we have learned that standard rifle platoon Marines feel that you are not the same. They don't mind fighting behind you, but they may not fully accept you. And being an officer will further isolate you. Don't let that get you down. Fortify your mind to understand your role and know that you are not alone. You are in the largest, most talented fraternity in the galaxy. Friendships will come. Are you following me?"

"It's new information," Mitch said. "I knew I was changing careers, but now you're telling me I'm in management. That will take a moment to wrap my mind around."

"It seems to me your emotional intelligence is right where it should be."

"Thank you," Mitch said.

"All the LE candidates are part of what is called Super Special Operations, or SSO. General Stanley Mercer has just been placed in charge of the SSO. We are based on New Terra, and divided into small, five-man teams. Most are led by regular Marine officers, but your team will be unique. You will be paired with experienced Marines whose enhanced skills and talents match up to create a balanced, Spec Op unit. SSO squads are given the most dangerous assignments, and often lead the charge in battle."

"Sounds dangerous," Mitch said.

"Fortunately, the LE program seems to give the participants strong and speedy healing abilities. That doesn't mean they can't die, just that many manage to avoid it. We've seen your kind do some amazing things."

"My kind?" Mitch said with a grin. "Not very politically correct, is it?"

"It's reality," she said. "You can do things that regular humans can't. And you'll be asked to do things that seem impossible. As an officer, your job will be to carry out your orders to the best of your abilities... which are substantial."

She loaded him down with materials. Normally, he would have been discouraged, but he was full of energy and stuck on a ship with nothing to do. There were binders full of reading material, and videos he needed to watch on everything from military protocol, history, and regulations, to strategy and tactics of small squads, platoons, and special operation units. It would have been a daunting task, but for some reason, he didn't mind. He was anxious to learn about his new career, essentially his new life.

After two hours with Captain Swift, Mitch was sent off to lunch. Elaine went to her tiny office on board the *Wellington* to contemplate what she had learned. Mitch Murphy was still a big question mark. He was certainly intelligent enough, but he had endured a decade of failure. And Captain Elaine Swift didn't know if that would make him a good officer, or bad.

CHAPTER 12

MITCH WASN'T BOTHERED by hunger, but he found that when he thought of eating, he was always hungry. After lunch, he dove into the materials. After reading for nearly two hours straight, he was called back to the training area. Captain Marcs pushed him hard, but nothing that he asked of Mitch was too difficult. Running, climbing, push-ups, and sit-ups all managed to work up a sweat, but they didn't tire or exhaust Mitch. In fact, he enjoyed the challenge. Everything he was ordered to do came easy to him.

"Now, we'll do some hand-to-hand combat training moves," Captain Marcs said. The man was frowning, and Mitch thought he was impossible to please. "Obviously, you're too big to square off with regular humans, so you'll be working with a weighed grappling bag."

Mitch was starting to grow sensitive to the term *regular humans*. He was still a human after all, just maybe not regular. But that didn't make him a freak or an outsider. He had signed up for the CMC with the hope that he would find a place where he belonged. But on the *Wellington*, no one seemed to think he did.

Captain Marcs opened a locker. Inside was a big punching bag that was shaped like a person.

"Pull this out," he ordered. The bag was heavy, at least three hundred pounds, even in the light gravity of the ship.

They spent over an hour learning judo hip throws and jujitsu incapacitation holds. Mitch learned quickly. Afterward, Captain Marcs forced him to run ten kilometers on the track. He would never have been able to do such extended physical training sessions before the LE Protocols. There were times in his old life when walking down the street winded him. And stairs always made him sweat. It was a little embarrassing, but he spent most of his days sitting at a desk, staring at a computer screen making buy and sell orders that were handed down to him from the traders in the Sterling Financial Corporation.

"Tomorrow, we'll start weapons training," Captain Marcs told him. "Keep it up, Murphy, and you'll make a decent Marine. Hit the showers."

It was as close to a compliment as he got. After cleaning up, he had another session with Captain Swift. Mitch enjoyed talking with her but felt a little like he was being tested. Not over the material, which he was absorbing quickly, and found easy to retain. But rather, he was being tested as a person. She asked a lot of questions about his old life, and he found that he wished he could just lock it away and not think about it. He still felt pain when he remembered Megan's infidelity or thought about the fact that she and her lover were probably enjoying themselves in the home he had paid for. Not that Mitch was concerned about money. He had gladly spent the signing bonus paying off his debts, and leaving Megan with a safety net, but in many ways that only made her infidelity more painful.

When they talked about his grades in college or his job with Sterling Financial, he found it to be just as painful. He had gone into college in an almost carefree fashion. School wasn't simple, but it had never been difficult or required much from him. At the university, he had been forced to try a little harder, but he didn't have the drive to excel. And it seemed to Mitch that he was being judged for his past behavior. It made him angry to think of the promotions that he had missed out on in his job, and he was a little ashamed that he had never stood up for himself. He had fallen into bad habits, and while he understood that he couldn't allow himself to do that as an officer when he would be responsible for the lives of other Marines, it still bothered him to feel judged. In the past, he didn't have the same kind of motivation. And while he wasn't proud of his mediocre record, he didn't feel like it defined him. In fact, since the LE procedure, he didn't even feel like the same person.

After two hours with Captain Swift, he ate dinner and then retired to the empty barracks berth. It would have been a difficult place to study in had the room been occupied by anyone else. But he was all alone, able to spread the materials out. He had been issued a table to take notes on and watch the assigned videos. And while he knew he should be exhausted, he didn't feel tired. His body seemed to have two modes, either he was working hard, or he was at rest. And his mind was like a dry sponge that soaked up everything. He flew through the material. Even reading was easier. He merely had to scan the page and the information seemed to flow into his brain. It all made sense, even the things that had seemingly no basis in logic.

The next day, he worked out hard in the morning, then shifted into the simulation room where he got his hands on actual weapons. Captain Marcs gave a full lecture on the weaponry. His hands weren't too big to work regular guns and rifles, but with his size, he was a perfect candidate for the .50 caliber machine gun. Over the centuries, firearms had changed, but one thing remained the same. They still fired real bullets. Laser weapons and various projectiles had been developed and tested. But plasma weapons and laser guns lacked the stopping power of a physical bullet. Soft lead was still preferred in combat, although with a depleted uranium tip for penetration. The 50 Cal was a belt-fed machine gun that was normally fired from a supported position. In other words, most people needed to set the weapon on its bipod legs because it was heavy and hard to control, but the gun seemed small and light to Mitch.

"We've increased the weight for simulation," Captain Marcs said. He was still gruff, but his enthusiasm for the weapons he was lecturing on showed. "It should be about the same weight as a live weapon in real gravity. This one has tactile simulators which will make it buck and rock when you shoot it in a VR training session."

"I'll get to shoot it?"

"By the time we reach New Terra, you'll be an expert."

He was also issued a Dessert Eagle .45 caliber pistol. The firearm was big, but so was Mitch. Captain Marcs put a heavy backpack on him and wrapped a thick belt around his waist with two ammo canisters of the belt-fed ammunition for the machine gun. They went through simulations that were basically a digital shooting range. The machine gun was not easy to control, but it did have a standard rifle stock which Mitch could press against his shoulder and as long as he fired in short bursts, allowed him to hold the weapon steady enough to hit what he was aiming at.

"You'll practice every single day," Captain Marcs said. "PT and marksmanship are absolutely essential for every Marine."

"Yes, sir," Mitch replied.

"That weapon is your life, recruit. You have to know every single part of it. You have to clean and maintain it because your life depends on it working. The last thing you want is to get into a fight and have your gun malfunction."

He showed Mitch how to take the weapon apart and put it back together. It wasn't a functioning rifle, so there was no need to clean the various parts. That lesson would come later, just as the pack he was wearing, which weighed nearly eighty pounds, was just filled with space holders. He wouldn't get the real gear assigned to a Marine until they touched down on New Terra.

And so the days passed in a rush. Mitch was just beginning to adjust to his routine when they reached orbit. Mitch had done all his physical training with his weapons and gear pack in place. He could climb the rope to the ceiling, which he did over and over again, with the weighted pack and his rifle slung over his shoulders. He could run ten kilometers in combat boots, with all his weapons and gear, and still never lost his breath.

It was a fascinating time in his life. Not only was he learning so much about being a Marine — and learning that he loved it — but he was also learning so much about himself. His lung capacity and enhanced blood were very efficient at feeding his big body the oxygen and nutrients it needed to perform at its peak. It was a bit like having purchased an expensive sports car that one carefully maintains. Mitch didn't have to baby his body either. He was functioning well on just five hours of sleep a night and waking up feeling refreshed and energized. And the extra time in his day allowed him to read all the training materials and watch all the videos that Captain Swift had assigned to him. What was truly amazing to Mitch was his mental recall. If asked a question from the materials he had studied, it was like he could see the page, or the vid screen in his mind. His physical traits weren't all that were enhanced during the LE Protocols.

Captain Swift took him through command exercises in the simulator room. Most were small unit exercises, giving commands, setting positions, identifying ambush sites, and planning fields of fire for maximum impact. He learned to call in air support using standard military radio protocol. And occasionally he was tasked with leading different kinds of units in the simulations such as mechanized battle tank divisions, or mixed infantry, armored, and airborne Marines working in concert. It was challenging and exciting. Mitch loved the strategy of command, and there was a thrill to being in control. But he knew that soon enough he would be ordering real people into dangerous situations. The weight of that responsibility wasn't something his enhanced body or mind could make any easier. It was, in fact, heavier than any weight or physical test he took.

On the last night aboard the *Wellington*, Mitch returned to the training area. He had been issued a K-Bar combat knife along with the uniform, fatigues, boots, and gear that had been modified to fit his body. The week of hard exercise had trimmed away the softer edges and left him with a lean body that any athlete would have died for. He put the knife in his teeth like a pirate and climbed the rope to the roof of the training area. The engines were thrumming on either side of him, and there were members of the ship's crew working out below him. Most of them stared but never spoke. A few had over the last week and were friendly enough, but Mitch had yet to make any friends. He got to the top of the rope and then used the knife to carve his name into the paint. It only took a minute, and his muscles weren't burning or trembling from the effort of holding himself up. Satisfied, he returned the blade to his teeth and slid back down to the floor. His boot camp was over, they would leave the *Wellington* the next day, and Mitch felt satisfied that everything had gone well. He couldn't say what the future held other than danger, and he felt ready to face it, come what may.

CHAPTER 13

"SHUTTLE IS TWO HOURS OUT SIR," Lieutenant Tosh announced. "The *Wellington* should make the orbital station in about forty minutes."

"Go and see that everything is packed, Johnny."

"Yes sir," the lieutenant said, snapping to attention and saluting before turning on his heel and hurrying away.

General Mercer was on his way to the CIC. He felt anxious and impatient. It had been that way before every deployment. The wheels always seemed to turn slowly. He was ready to assume command and make a difference in the fighting, even though that wasn't a given. One wrong decision could ruin his entire career. But the SSO division was where the action was. It was the one command that would really make a difference, not just to his career, or even to the Marine Corps, but to the history of mankind. His name would go into the books that recorded what the humans did on New Terra, and how they overcame the alien threats. He tried not to think about the fact that probably every general tasked with the SSO division felt the same way. So far, they had won battles and pushed back the various aliens invading the new planet, but none had done so in a decisive fashion. The aliens were still coming, and it was up to General Mercer to clean them out. Not that he would do it alone, or actually do any of the fighting himself. He was a commander, not a grunt on the battlefield. But it would be his strategy and tactics that made the difference. And he planned to hit the aliens with shock and awe as he drove them out of the system.

"General," the ship's commanding officer said as he entered the CIC, "looks like you've got your work cut out for you."

"Tell me," he said.

"Graylings in the system, of course," the naval officer said. "They've had a constant presence almost as long as we've been here. There's a Kistor ship inbound for the planet. We may be able to dissuade them, but they typically drop pods from orbit. No one knows how far out they can send their spawn. And there's a flotilla of Porg ships. Right now, they're just gathering information, but who can say what they might do."

General Mercer grunted at the news. In the six days it had taken to pass from the wormhole to the planet, the system had grown much more hostile. He didn't like the Porgs. They were small, aquatic aliens that no one knew much about. Humanity had not cracked their language or made any sort of diplomatic inroads with them.

"On the ground," the ship's commander continued, "you've got a colony of Grumblers, and several bands of Lomtuc raiders. But you already knew about them. Since we've entered the system, we've spotted a Lymie pod cluster and several Brascus ships make planetfall."

"Sounds like a party," General Mercer said. "It's time to introduce the guests of honor."

"Your new super soldier seems promising," the commander pointed out.

General Stanley Mercer grunted again. He knew it was one thing to see a super serum Marine up close, and even to see one working out. But to see them in combat was something completely different. They were monsters, designed for killing. And Mercer was in charge of them. He was going to turn New Terra into a slaughterhouse for any species other than humans."

"He is," Mercer replied. "He'll be the first commissioned officer of their kind."

The ship commander shook his head. "I don't envy you, General. I'll be taking the Second Battalion back to the Sol System. You'll be short-handed until the next transport arrives."

"What's the ETA on that?"

"Ten days... maybe more, but never less. No one is in a hurry on their way in."

"We'll just have to make do," General Mercer said.

He wasn't in charge of the regular Marine platoons. The CMC kept two full battalions on New Terra, and there were enough SSO super soldiers to make up two platoons. He wasn't exactly sure what the state of those Marines were. Some would almost certainly be dealing with wounds and injuries. Others would already be deployed on various missions down range. He would have to get his boots on the ground and receive a full assessment before he could begin sweeping up the unsavory ETs.

"I suppose you will," the commander said. "We're coming into port now. Your party has priority to the shuttle bay."

"Thank you, Commander Templeton. It's been a pleasure."

"The pleasure's all mine, General Mercer. Good luck and God be with you."

There were no salutes. Officially, Mercer outranked the ship's commander, and while Marine and Naval forces had always worked hand in hand, there was no real camaraderie between the groups. General Mercer left the CIC and met his staff officers in the Ward Room. They were all waiting, their gear packed and ready.

"Where's our boy?" the general asked.

"Meeting us at the airlock, sir," Captain Marcs said.

"Very well, what's the word Lieutenant?"

"We've got everything," Tosh said. "We're ready to disembark, sir."

"Outstanding. Time to get off this tub. Let's move out."

Mercer led the way through the narrow corridors of the ship. They found Mitch waiting at the amidships airlock. He was in his new uniform, which had no rank at the moment, no name tag or insignia. Not that he needed it. He was taller than the senior officers and had a hard-sided gun case as well as his standard issue rucksack. The logistics crew on the *Wellington* had outfitted Mitch with everything he needed. Eventually, there would be more forms to fill out and sign, but that would have to wait.

A chime sounded and the airlock opened once the ship was securely attached to the orbital docking station. It was a long space station in high orbit, with docking arms that extended outward. It was a gravity-free space, and they used small magnets in their boots to hold them to the floor. Mitch had to bend low and duck through the airlock. It was a novel sensation moving in zero gravity. He felt like he was going to float right out of his combat boots, but they held him fast. It was a bit like walking on a very sticky floor.

From the docking arm, they entered the main concourse which was wide with kiosks down the center between rows of plastic waiting chairs. The ceiling was thirty feet high and transparent. Looking up, they could see a dazzling display of stars. General Mercer led the procession through the space station, which was full of Marines from the Second Infantry Battalion waiting for their ride back to civilization. They came to attention as the senior officers passed, most throwing up salutes. Then their attention swiveled to Mitch, and they stared at him. It was something he realized he would have to get used to. He was a full head taller than Captain Marcs, who was six feet, three inches tall himself. And he was wider through the shoulders than most people. This uniform was tailored to a snug fit. He had on dark blue slacks and a tan, short-sleeved button-up shirt with the CMC logo over his right breast pocket. His combat boots were size seventeen, and his biceps bulged in the short sleeves. He could feel the eyes of the other Marines, but no one spoke, and General Mercer never stopped walking.

They reached a docking arm on the opposite side of the station from where the *Wellington* was berthed. A short corridor led to a comfortable shuttle with reclining seats. Mitch sat in the rear, while the general and his staff sat near the front. There were plenty of empty seats, but the officers were the only people going down to the planet. They buckled in and sent word via the deck sergeant that they were ready to go.

The flight down was rough but didn't last long. And when the ship landed at the Alpha Colony CMC space field, they got their first real taste of New Terra.

"Smells like a farm," General Mercer said.

"They use animal refuse as fertilizer," Lieutenant Tosh said. "About half of the produce consumed on Earth comes from New Terra these days."

Mitch Murphy was astounded. The world seemed so wide open and completely different from Earth. He had been on space stations and spaceships for so long, that he had forgotten what it was like to be out in the open. New Terra had a brilliant, blue sky. In the city where Mitch had spent most of his adult life, a sickly, yellow smog layer covered the sky. And what greenery there was had to be carefully cultivated in tiny little parks and recreation spaces. He had grown up in the Boise Salt Lake Megatropolis which had more trees and open fields than San Francisco, but it was nothing compared to New Terra. The skies above the BSL Megatropolis were always filled with climate control gases that made it look dirty gray. But there was nothing but deep green and brilliant blue around him on New Terra. Even the dirt under the grass seemed dark and rich. There were several buildings nearby, and beyond them were crop fields. The neat rows stood straight and swayed in the breeze.

The air was thick with humidity. Alpha Colony was built on high ground, but most of the world was swampy. They were near the equator and it was still chilly in the middle of the afternoon. A major in dark green fatigues hurried up to the group. He came to attention and saluted the general.

"General Mercer? I'm Major Wong, part of General Polk's command staff. If you will come with me, there's an engagement underway. Your SSOs are fighting a group of Lomtucs about two hundred klicks west of here near Foxtrot Colony."

"Lead the way, Major," General Mercer replied.

Mitch followed along. No one had told him any differently yet, and until they did, he would stay with the senior officers he had come in with. They went directly to the command center, a concrete dome, that was built to withstand bombardment. They passed through what had to be four feet of reinforced concrete in the outer shell of the dome. Inside, they went down a series of stairs and straight into the command center. Large screens on the walls showed a combination of aerial drone feeds and body cam footage in real time. The generals met and shook hands, while the rest of Mercer's staff spread out in the back of the room. There were drone controllers lined up in a row on a lower level of the room, which was built like a theater. They had big monitors and wore what looked like VR headsets. They sat with their backs to the big screens that the other officers were facing. There were several communications specialists, and officers controlling the radar at Foxtrot and monitoring the colony's defensive measures.

"Pay attention, Murphy," Captain Marcs snapped. "You can learn a lot."

Major Elaine Swift stepped up beside Mitch and whispered, "This is real combat. Not a simulation."

The combination of aerial feeds and body camera footage was fascinating to observe. His mind quickly formed a mental composite of the area and the fighting taking place. The Lomtucs were strange looking aliens. They had two legs and well-muscled bodies that were almost human. But that's where the similarities ended. The Lomtucs had four arms, two on each side, and instead of a neck and head, two antennae rose up from their shoulders. The CMC researchers had learned a lot about the aliens, mainly from after-action autopsies. They had humps on their backs where their brain was located. The antennae performed a variety of functions that included hearing and a kind of smell that was more like taste. They also had a form of biological sonar that served as their sight and made them excellent marksmen. They fought with small arms and rifles, all shooting long, narrow rounds that looked almost like construction nails.

There were nearly forty of the aliens in two vehicles that had been brought down with shoulder-mounted rockets. Mitch knew the Lomtucs had excellent armor on their vehicles and military craft. There were scorch marks near the engines of the alien aircraft, and the armored fuselage was dented. The rockets had done enough damage to force a landing, but not enough to kill the occupants, who had come spilling out armed to the teeth.

"Two SSO squads," Swift said softly. "Romeo and Tango. They've got natural COs. Both squads are behind cover."

The ground around Foxtrot colony was pure swamp. There were wide areas of standing water, and lots of bushes sticking up. The ground wasn't flat, but undulating, which gave the Marines plenty of cover to work from.

"They have snipers in place," Swift whispered. "The heavy gunners are moving closer."

"Why don't the Lomtucs retreat?" Mitch asked.

"They either don't realize what they're up against or believe they can still win the fight," she said. "They aren't the most intelligent race we've encountered. Most learn from their mistakes. These are about it."

"Eight against forty?" Mitch asked.

"Wait and see," she told him.

A strange wailing sound came over the speakers in the

command center as the Lomtucs charged. They were savage beings, but unorganized and undisciplined. Most carried pistols in each of their four hands. The sound of the soft, popping reports from their pistols could be heard too. Then a human voice, laced with static spoke.

"Tango squad in position," a male voice said.

"Romeo is ready," a female voice added.

General Polk was a tall, skinny man with gray stubble around the crown of his head. He leaned toward a microphone built into one of the communication consoles.

"Engage, engage, engage," he ordered.

"You heard him!" someone shouted over their radio. "Give 'em hell!"

The human weapons sounded loud and lethal. They were spread out in an arching line that curved toward the aliens. They hit the Lomtucs with overlapping fields of fire. The battle only lasted a few seconds. The aliens wore some sort of light armor, but it wasn't capable of stopping the bullets fired at them. Forty aliens died in a savage slaughter that both saddened and excited Mitch Murphy.

"Fast," he said.

"Fast and clean," Major Swift said. "No casualties on our side. The colony is safe."

"What would they have done if we hadn't stopped them?"

"They're raiders. They steal anything that isn't bolted down, including people and children."

"They deserve what they got," Captain Marcs said. "Dirty, bug-eyed, bastards."

Mitch watched as a few of the Super Special Operators walked to the aliens and checked for any survivors. They were bleeding a black liquid that looked more like motor oil than blood. The Marines poked a few with their weapons, but none appeared to have lived through the well-executed volley. Their antennae lay limp on the ground, some were even flopped back under their bodies.

"Looks like a total victory," a plain looking lieutenant said. He wore a smug expression even though he hadn't been involved in the fighting.

"Any casualties on our part?" General Polk asked.

"Negative, a few flesh wounds, but nothing serious."

Mitch saw one of the operators with several pins sticking out of his shoulder. He looked miserable as a female Marine pulled a pair of standard needle-nosed pliers from her belt and started tugging the pins free.

"That doesn't look pleasant," Mitch said.

"Don't worry," Major Swift said. "That Marine will be fine in a few days. He won't even have scars from those wounds."

"Sorry for the unorthodox welcome," General Polk told General Mercer, speaking loud enough for everyone to hear him.

"I can't imagine a better one," Mercer said. "We're all anxious to get started."

"That's good. There's several groups of various aliens we're doing our best to keep tabs on. But New Terra is a big world, and there's lots of places to hide. Let my people show you to your new quarters, and we'll meet in say, an hour, to hand over command of the SSO."

"Works for us," General Mercer said. "I look forward to working with you."

They shook hands, and a lieutenant led the way out of the command bunker. Officer housing was in a dormitory nearby. The lieutenant walked quickly through the ground floor, which had a lot of tiny rooms. The senior staff would have larger quarters on the upper floor, but he was assigned a tiny room on the ground level.

General Mercer stopped long enough to make an announcement. "Recruit Murphy, step forward," he said. "I'm giving you a field promotion to second lieutenant, effective immediately."

He handed Mitch a pair of pins with a single gold bar on it.

Mitch recognized them. It was junior officer rank insignia, and he was surprised at how happy he was to receive the commission.

"Thank you, sir," Mitch said, taking the pins and shaking the general's hand.

"Make us proud, Murphy. We'll be watching."

Mitch saluted, the general returned the salute, and then he joined the rest of the senior staffers on an elevator. Mitch walked into his quarters. It was austere, just a narrow bed, and desk. He did have a closet with hangers waiting, and there were drawers along the bottom of his bunk. There was one bathroom with shower stalls and multiple sinks. None of it was built for people Mitch's size. His bed, just like his bunk on the *Wellington* was too short, and barely wide enough when he laid on his back. But Mitch was still too excited about the many changes to complain.

On the top floor of the four-story building, General Mercer's quarters were much larger. He even had multiple rooms, with a sitting room outside the bedroom, and his own private bathroom. His sitting room had a built-in mini-fridge and microwave that looked like storage compartments under a built-in bookshelf. There was already a crystal wine decanter and three whiskey bottles waiting to be filled with whatever spirits the general preferred. An ice machine sat on one shelf beside a row of tumblers. The sitting room had two leather sofas with big brass studs on the arms. There was also a wide-backed, reclining chair that matched the sofas and full entertainment system.

His bedroom had a double-sized bed, two closets, and a built-in desk by the windows that looked out over the city. Alpha Colony had been the first and was still the largest of the New Terra colonies by far. Built on the equator, there was another colony town every fifty miles in either direction east and west. There were resource camps in various places, but the colonies were where most people lived and worked. Twelve had been established before the first of the alien invasion forces landed on New Terra. Two had been lost. Three were still vulnerable, but the CMC had made the planet much more secure.

General Mercer was happy with his new domain but still looked forward to returning to the Sol System as a conquering hero. Eventually, he would leave the service and step into politics, but that would be after a career that reached the highest level. He was only one promotion away, and then he would reach the top of his field, which would open up new realms of power. And really, what else was life about than to conquer one's enemies and relishing personal achievement? His aide de camp, Lieutenant Tosh was busy bringing in the general's personal items and getting everything settled. Soon, he would go to work. The regular Marines could fortify the colonies. He would take his super soldiers into the field to seek out the enemy and destroy them. Along the way, they could take as much advanced tech as they could get their hands on to turn over to the Marine Corps' R&D department. And like a captain of a prize ship, he would take the lion's share of credit and reward.

CHAPTER 14

MITCH ONLY HAD time to linger in his new quarters long enough to unpack his rucksack before Major Swift arrived.

"Come with me," she ordered.

He did as he was told without question. He still had a lot of things to get used to, but following orders seemed natural enough. They left the officer's building and went out to a row of buildings. They were low and plain looking, none were very large, but all had insignias, with names or mascots painted above the unusually tall and wide doors.

"These are the barracks for the SSO squads," she said. "You'll be put in charge of Leo Squad, code name Lions."

Mitch could see the barracks with *Lions* painted above the door. On the door was a picture of a lion's head with a thick mane, its jaws open wide in a savage roar that revealed the massive teeth. It looked fierce, and Mitch was simultaneously excited and nervous.

"You'll be their new CO," Major Swift continued. "They don't need to know much about your past or your training. I wouldn't tell them how recently you went through the LE Protocols. Let your work speak for you. Today you meet and begin training. This evening you'll receive a schedule of simulations and exercises. It's no different than what we did on the *Wellington*."

"Except with real people," Mitch said.

"They're Marines," she reassured him. "You'll have to prove yourself, but they will follow orders. A word of advice?"

"Please," Mitch said.

"Take your time. Get to know your squad mates. Look for their strengths and weaknesses, not just physically, but in relation to the job. It will help you to know what your people can do and who you can trust to get things done. That's what being a leader is all about. Your job is to bring out the best in them, so that the team performs at the highest possible level, no matter the task."

"Good advice," he said. "Thank you."

"If you need anything, Lieutenant," she said, tapping the single gold bar that he had pinned to the collar of his uniform shirt. "You can reach out to me. I'll message you later today so you'll have my contact info."

"I don't have a tablet or phone or anything," Mitch said.

"You will soon," she told him. "It will all be delivered to your quarters, Lieutenant. You're an officer in the Colonial Marines Corps. That's something to be proud of."

She led him to the door with the lion's head and pushed it open. The barracks building was simple. The first room was a recreation space, with a loose assemblage of furniture around a poker table, and another set near an entertainment console. There was a folding table with guns in various stages of assembly near one wall, with a gun rack attached. In the back of the barracks were the sleeping quarters. Each member of the squad had what amounted to a cubical. Standing shelves were flanked by full-size metal lockers to make one wall. The back of the next person's shelves and lockers made another, with the oversized bunks in between. Each sleeping area was closed off with a curtain. Between the bunks and the recreation space were the shared bathrooms, some to the right, others to the left. Mitch would soon learn that while most Marines had no modesty, the bathrooms were segregated.

There were five people in the recreation space. Two men, one tall, thin, black man, and one hugely muscled white man, were playing video games. A woman with brown skin and tattoos was at the gun table cleaning a long rifle of some sort. At the other table was a man and woman. The man was carefully sharpening a dangerous-looking curved knife, with a ring at the pommel. The blade made a steady rasping sound across the whetstone. The woman at the table was playing solitaire. She had raven-colored hair and dark eyes. She called out the order to come to attention.

"Officer on deck!" she shouted.

The five Marines all dropped what they were doing and popped up onto their feet. Mitch felt self-conscious, but with Major Elaine Swift beside him, he felt the response was aimed toward her, not him.

"At ease, Lion Squad," Swift said. "Meet your new CO. This is Lieutenant Mitch Murphy."

"He's an officer?" the muscleman asked.

"That's right. He's the first officer to have the LE Protocols, and you're lucky to have him. The eyes of the entire Corps will be on Leo Squad. You've got the day to get to know one another. Range time is reserved at fifteen hundred hours. Show him what you're made of and get ready for a busy schedule."

"Sure beats the hell out of sitting around all the time," the man with the knife said.

Major Swift turned toward Mitch and nodded. "They're all yours, Lieutenant. Good luck."

"Thank you, Major," he said.

She left and Mitch turned back toward his people. They had moved closer and were standing together as they looked at him. Mitch was only a little shorter than the tall, black man.

"Let's start with names," he said, giving his first order.

It felt a little strange to be put in charge, but good too. He had spent years just blending in, trying not to get called out for doing anything wrong. But that was his old life. He had taken charge of himself, and his future. The LE Protocols had not only changed his physique, they had also changed the way he thought about himself.

"I'm Lee Jenkins," the black man said. "They call me Flash."

"Good to meet you, Corporal Jenkins," Mitch said, memorizing the name.

"He's crap at video games," the big muscleman said. "I'm *Lance Corporal* Cameron Gustave. They call me Jingo."

"Slow as a seven-year itch, too," Flash commented.

"Nice to meet you," Mitch said.

"Corporal Casey Brown, sir. They call me Ninja."

"I'm Marauder," the woman with dark eyes who had been playing solitaire said. "Sergeant Mara James. And this is Sergeant Estelle Flemming, code name Hawk."

"Thank you, Sergeant James. It's a pleasure to meet all of you."

"They put you through the protocols, huh?" Flash asked. "They order you or was it voluntary."

"I volunteered," Mitch said.

"What's your, specialty, sir?" Ninja asked.

"Specialty?"

"We all got one, sir," Ninja said. "Mine is stealth, Flash is speed, Jingo is strength. What's your specialty?"

Before Mitch could reply, the woman who called herself Marauder spoke up. "He's got it all, Ninja, can't you see that? They wouldn't make a normal grunt an officer. They waited until they found someone with the total package."

"Honestly, I'm just a few weeks out from the procedure," Mitch admitted. He planned to take Major Swift's advice, but he still had a lot to learn about himself. It seemed right to be honest about that. "I haven't had the opportunity to really test myself."

"We can help with that," Jingo said with a wide grin.

"Good," Mitch said. "I look forward to learning from all of you."

It was lunchtime on the base, and while Mitch had access to the officer's dining room, he chose to eat with his squad. The SSO had their own training areas and their own chow hall. The only thing they shared with the two platoons of regular Marines stationed at Alpha Base was the gun range. They ate a hardy meal together, the portions were large to fit the typical SSO appetite. Mitch was pleased with how accepting the squad was. He got some looks from the other Marines in the chow hall, mostly because he was wearing a uniform instead of fatigues and had his second-lieu-tenant gold bar pinned to his collar. There were no other SSO offi-cers, he was the first. And most of the looks he saw were either surprise or admiration.

After lunch, they went to a large building filled with training equipment. Jingo wasn't the only super soldier whose primary skill was strength. There were dozens of hulking Marines that would have made a champion bodybuilder look puny.

"Home away from home," Jingo said, leading Mitch to a specially built wide bench press station. "What's your max?"

"Three hundred was all they had on the ship," Mitch confessed.

Jingo snorted. "Flash can bench three. You gotta do better than that if you're going to be the head Honcho around here."

"Honcho, I like it," Flash said.

"Yeah, it suits you, LT," Ninja said.

The two female sergeants were hanging back. And some of the other Marines were taking notice that Mitch was an officer. They stopped their own workouts to see what he could do. Mitch took off his short-sleeved button-up shirt and hung it on a rack of heavy plates, while Jingo loaded the bar with weights.

"We'll start with three fifteen," he said, sliding three forty-five-pound plates onto each side of the forty-five-pound bar.

Mitch laid back on the bench. He felt self-conscious, but also excited to finally get to really test himself. There was no doubt in his mind that the Marines in his squad would push him to his limits. He put his hands up on the bar, pushed it up, and then lowered the bar toward his chest in a smooth, controlled fashion. He pushed it back up easily enough. The weight was substantial, but he had worked out on the chest press machine on board the *Wellington* for a full week at three hundred pounds. He was used to the weight and did six reps before setting the bar down.

"He's warm now," Jingo declared.

"Let's go!" Flash shouted.

Ninja and Flash placed another forty-five-pound weight onto each end of the bar. Jingo stood in the spotter's position just above Mitch's head.

"Four oh five, Lieutenant. You ready?" Jingo asked.

"Yes," Mitch replied.

The weight was enough to make the barbell bend a little, and Mitch felt the strain in his chest and triceps, but he lowered and raised the bar.

"Nice," Jingo said.

"He did that easy!" Flash declared.

"Keep going," Ninja urged.

They pulled all the forty-five-pound plates off the bar and put on the big hundred-pound weights, two on each side, bringing the total to four hundred, forty-five pounds. Mitch pressed it and nodded for more. By that time every person in the gym was watching. Most were cheering him on. Mitch noticed that Hawk rarely spoke, even when they had lunch. And Mara seemed to be holding back, reserving judgment of him.

They added a twenty and a five-pound plate to each side of the bar. Mitch pressed four hundred and ninety-five pounds, straining for the first time. The twenty-fives were replaced with a forty-five on each side, bringing the total to five hundred and thirty-five pounds. He lifted it from the rack. Mitch felt his entire body tense, his muscles quivering. Bringing the weight down wasn't easy. It felt like it was going to crush him. But he brought it to his chest, let it touch lightly then started pushing. It took all his strength, every muscle straining, but the bar slowly moved upward. Jingo stood ready to help, as did Flash and Ninja on either side. But Mitch got a full extension, then lowered the barbell back onto the supports with a clash. To his surprise, the other Marines began to clap and cheer. Mitch sat up on the bench. He was sweating and breathing a little faster than normal.

"That was impressive, LT," Jingo said.

"Five hundred ain't no joke," Ninja said. "He ain't wearing any assists either."

Mara mixed up a recovery drink in a shaker cup and handed it to Mitch as they moved on to other exercises. He squatted nearly half a ton and curled three hundred and twenty pounds. His squad was gaining respect for him with every lift he did. He would have liked to keep going, but after the three essential lifts it was time to get their weapons and head for the range.

Mitch strolled back to the officer's building to retrieve his weapons. During the flight through space, Mitch had read up on the .50 caliber machine gun. It was called an M50AX on the manual, but MAX by the Marines who used it. In the regular platoons, the strongest person carried the MAX and was called the Machine Gunner. There were also two assistant gunners in each platoon to help carry the cans of belt-fed ammunition and set the large weapon up on support legs that were attached to the front end of the barrel shroud. Mitch was expected to do all of that on his own. But the bulky rifle wasn't too heavy or awkward for him. He had consistently built his skills over the week of simulator training on the *Wellington*.

He also had a laser-guided rocket launcher. It was a short, wide-barreled gun, too big to be a pistol, but much shorter than a rifle. It had a laser built into the top of the barrel that guided the rockets, although they could be synced to another device if need be. His Desert Eagle automatic pistol went into a holster with a flap cover that strapped to his upper thigh. Mitch carried all three weapons to the gun range where he met back up with his squad. They were all carrying weapons. Cameron Gustave (Jingo), Lee Jenkins (Flash), and Casey Brown (Ninja) all carried the standard weapon for SSO, the GAR, or Garrison Assault Rifle. It was a long-barreled tactical gun that fired standard .232 rounds, although theirs were explosive-filled hollow shock bullets in full metal jackets. Estelle Flemming (Hawk) was their sniper and carried a Long Range Railgun with a special telescoping laser sighting device that linked to a monocle on her helmet. Mara James (Marauder) carried an automatic shotgun with a big, barrel clip that held fifty rounds. The shotgun shells could, of course, be filled with just about any munition available, from buckshot pellets to armor-piercing explosives, and even large bore slugs that would knock down anything short of a full-size Grumbler. It has less range than the GAR, but the auto shotgun was perfect for laying down a blanket of fire that allowed the other members of the squad to close in on the enemy, or make a hasty retreat.

Everyone took a turn on the range so that Mitch could see what they were capable of. They were all excellent marksmen with both rifles and sidearms. For Mitch, it was the first time he had fired live rounds from the MAX. It was a little like holding a wild animal. Every shot made the weapon buck in his hands like it was trying to escape his hold. When he fired multiple rounds, as the fully automatic weapon was designed to do, the movement grew. Fortunately, it was also predictable, and it only took Mitch a few minutes to get the feel of the big, bulky rifle.

The MAX was made for shooting a lot of rounds in a short time. But that was all the weapon was designed for. The GAR that Jingo, Flash, and Ninja carried had built-in bayonets that could spring forward, turning the rugged assault rifle into a short spear that was deadly in close quarters.

Hawk's weapon was completely different. It didn't fire using explosive gel or gas. Instead, it hurled objects along a zero friction rail, that allowed for maximum distance. The bullets were longer than a man's middle finger, with tiny little fins on the back. Each one was carefully engineered to provide the maximum distance with reliable accuracy. Hawk had no trouble hitting bullseyes the size of a plum at five kilometers down range. The Long Range Rail Gun or LRRG was her primary weapon, but she also carried a compact tactical submachine gun. Mara's automatic shotgun was an impressive weapon, chugging out maximum damage so fast that it was hard to keep track of.

Then it was Mitch's turn. He had already warmed up with the big .50 caliber machine gun, which hung from its sling over his right shoulder. But shooting with an audience was different.

"Let's see it LT," Ninja said.

"Chiefs got the big gun," Jingo added.

"But can he use it," Mara wondered.

Mitch flipped off the safety with his thumb and fired a quick burst. The target was shaped like a man and set up a hundred feet from the firing line. The bullets ripped across the chest portion of the target.

"Not bad," Hawk said quietly.

"Can't miss at this distance," Mara said. "Take it back fifty, sixty meters. Let's see how he does with that."

Normally, a fifty-caliber machine gun was a mounted weapon with mechanical advantages to make firing it easier. The MAX was designed for Marines who had undergone the LE Protocol. At seven and a half feet tall, Mitch was big and strong enough to handle the otherwise bulky weapon. The belt-fed ammo came straight from a box that was attached to his belt at the hip. He didn't need the strap to hold the rifle up, but it did give him a means to better control his rifle. It wasn't the type of weapon one held to their shoulder and aimed down the top of. He fired from the hip, letting the tracer, one every five rounds, guide his shooting. It was, he had learned, a very intuitive style of shooting. Hawk was a sharpshooter taking careful aim to hit the smallest of targets at maximum range. Mitch, on the other hand, was there to lay down the maximum amount of ammo into a target.

"Sixty meters," Flash said. "Coming right up."

He punched in the distance on the target controls. The paper target hung from a wire and had tiny little weights attached to the bottom to hold it steady. With the new distance punched into the system controls, the target flew backward. Sixty meters was nearly two hundred feet, which was four times as far away as Mitch had been practicing. He knew that .50 caliber weapons had been used as sniper rifles for a long time. The MAX was powerful and accurate. When the target settled into position, he took a breath, released it, and fired a five-round burst. The first two shots were wide, but the other three stitched across the target.

"That's a kill," Ninja said.

"Nice shooting," Hawk replied.

"What about the pistol?" Mara asked.

Mitch set the safety on the MAX, then let it hang from the carry strap as he drew his pistol. He held it in two hands, just the way he had learned from the video lessons, and from the simulator training. After adjusting his feet, he let his focus on the target go and instead saw the front sight of his pistol clearly. The rear V-shaped notch was slightly blurry, the target just a blob in the distance, but the front sight was clear, and he held it in the center of the target, both eyes open, and fired six shots. The big Desert Eagle was a powerful handgun loaded with gas-powered hollow points that would knock down a man in full combat armor. The target was already compromised by the powerful .50 caliber rounds, but when Mitch fired six quick shots with the semi-automatic pistol, it hit the target in the center upper portion of the figure's chest. It wasn't necessarily a tight grouping, but they were all on point.

"Boo-ya!" Jingo declared.

"The LT can shoot," Flash agreed.

"Sure, if he has time to stop and aim," Mara said with grudging respect, "and no one is shooting back."

They spent two full hours working with their weapons. Everyone knew, either from personal experience or in Mitch's case, from his training, that keeping their weapons primed and their skills polished was essential in combat. Mitch practiced everything, loading and reloading, clearing jams from the belt-fed ammo, practicing a variety of shots at a variety of distances. And there was camaraderie in the practice. Everyone had a word of advice for Mitch, which he listened to and applied.

"Focus on your breathing," Hawk recommended.

"I can show you some good exercises to increase your grip strength," Jingo told him. "Holding that beast steady can wear you down."

"Anticipate the movement," Flash urged. "We're shooting stationary here, but in the field, you have to always be moving. And you'll be shooting at moving targets."

"Switch to a body harness," Ninja said. "A gun that heavy shouldn't be on a single strap."

"Keep your weight balanced on both feet," Mara said, he couldn't tell if it was a friendly word of advice or a chastisement. "You're putting all your weight on your back foot when you fire that behemoth."

When their time at the range ended, they went back to the barracks and cleaned their weapons. Mitch broke down the big MAX and took his time oiling each component as he listened to the easy conversation between the members of his squad. They were friends, and friendly to him, everyone except for Mara, who seemed not to trust him. Mitch knew the others were probably offering him a greater form of trust simply because he was like them. Every other SSO squad had a regular Marine CO. And Mitch could understand how difficult it might be to take orders from someone who couldn't match him physically and mentally. In his years as a businessman working for Sterling Finance Corp, he saw plenty of people get promoted who weren't good at their jobs. In the business world, the old saying *it's not what you know, but who you know that counts,* was absolutely true. Some people got promoted because of the school they attended, or because they were good at buttering up their superiors. And some got the nod because they did things for their boss off the clock. Mitch knew one person who got ahead by taking his boss out on the town when a superior was going through a divorce. It was how the game was played. Mitch had naively thought the business world was merit based, but that was wrong, and he had suffered the indignity of being passed over for promotion time and time again because of it.

Mitch ended his day with a run. Like most people who had gone through the LE Protocol, he was drawn to physical training. It just felt good to push himself, especially since he was constantly discovering new things about himself. His squad was going for a trail run and Mitch went with them. They started outside the barracks, then quickly moved off base. As the sun went down, the temperature dropped steadily. A trail wound down the hill the city was built on. The sound of animals and insects humming and chirping in the twilight was loud. The trail circled the big hill, slowly angling back up. When they finished Mitch felt good, his body warm, his joints and muscles loose. He wasn't even tired and thought he could have made the long circuit again, but his squad was going to chow. Mitch would have liked to have joined them, but he needed to check his room for the rest of his gear that Major Swift had promised him. And he was ready for a hot shower too.

When he reached his quarters in the officer's building, he was pleased to find several items waiting for him on his desk. One was a large computer tablet encased in a hard, military style protective sleeve. There was a card lying on the dark screen with instructions for setting up his account.

Beside the table was a wrist cuff with a flexible, touchscreen control interface, and a tiny holographic projector built in. There was also a Paper-thin reading device, a charging unit, and a small banking fob. The latter had instructions for getting into his MFA or Marine Finance Accounts. He powered up the tablet, quickly found the banking icon, and opened his account. His first pay was the standard recruit rate, just two hundred credits per day. He had officially been in the CMC for one month, for a total of six thousand credits, minus the two thousand, four hundred credits for taxes, which wasn't bad considering the fact that he had no bills. His housing, clothing, equipment, and meals were all provided by the CMC. And since his promotion to Second Lieutenant, his pay had gone up to five hundred credits per day, nearly equal to what he was earning at the Sterling Financial Corporation. It was a pleasant surprise that he hadn't really considered before joining the Colonial Marines.

The Paper-thin reader had several technical manuals already loaded onto it, including the instructions for his holographic data cuff or HDC. It was his link to the military communications and information systems when he was in the field. He put it on and activated the device. With a slide of his finger across the touchscreen controls, a holographic image appeared just above his wrist. The icons on the HDC were touch-activated, but the interface was via the hologram. He opened the navigation app, which displayed his current position on a holographic map of the base and surrounding town. A squeezing gesture with the fingers of his opposite hand on the holograph zoomed the image out. The reverse gesture zoomed in. Another icon brought up the messages on the planetary network. He had a recorded video from Major Swift waiting and pointed at it to activate the message. Her face appeared above his wrist. Major Swift had short hair on the sides and back, barely more than stubble. The hair on the crown of her head was longer and braided tight. Her skin was smooth, her lips full, and her eyes large. Mitch couldn't help but admire how well the holograph captured her likeness, even though he could technically see through it to the top of his desk.

"Good evening, Lieutenant Murphy. I trust that you are finding everything in order there in your quarters. If you get this message in time, please join me in the Officer's dining hall at nineteen hundred hours. I'd love to hear how your first day as an officer went."

The message ended, and her face remained hovering above his wrist. Mitch made a simple swiping away gesture and the hologram of Major Swift disappeared. In its place was a circle of icons, many of which he didn't recognize right away. In the center was a time readout that showed he had only thirty minutes to get cleaned up if he was going to meet the major for dinner. He powered down the data cuff, took it off, then grabbed his clothes and toiletries and headed down the hall for a shower.

As the hot water in the privacy stall, which was too small for him, cascaded over his strangely large body, Mitch considered how much his life had changed. When he joined the CMC, his only thought was getting out of the crushing debt and broken marriage that were making him miserable. He hadn't known if he would live or die, and honestly, he hadn't cared. Then the LE Protocol had been both torturous and exhilarating. He had been so pleasantly surprised by the results that he had been completely mesmerized by the moment, with almost no thought of his future. Likewise, on the *Wellington*, he had been so overwhelmed by the prospect of being an officer in the CMC that he hadn't had much time to reflect. But in those few moments, while he washed off the sweat and gun oil residue from his skin, he realized how much he was enjoying his new life. He was in a good place, with good people, making friends, and excelling at the things he put his hand to. His future seemed bright, and he couldn't help but feel excited about where he was and what he was doing. The old Mitch, physically stunted, and stuck with no prospects in life, was gone. And he had absolutely no regrets.

CHAPTER 15

THE POD CRACKLED open and a hiss of nutrient-rich gas escaped. It was thin, the rich nourishment having been consumed by the thing inside. The pod was barely thicker than a soap bubble and broke apart like glass. Inside, something was stirring.

"Arise, there is work to be done," a huge, four-legged alien called out in a chitter-chatter language that humans had yet to decipher.

The creature inside the pod came out. It wasn't young, as one might expect. The pod wasn't an egg, however much it might appear to be one, but rather an organic hibernation device that the aliens known as Lymies used on their long, interstellar voyages through space. The pod was protection, and nourishment, rejuvenating the aliens. The one inside the delicate membrane was known as Skar, but he was just one of several hundred of the large, insectile aliens who had been dropped on New Terra by a seed ship.

They had four, hairy, multi-jointed legs that ended in pointed feet that stabbed into the strange new ground Skar found himself on. The ground was soft and wet, the air rich with a mixture of gases, some beneficial, others not, but nothing was toxic. The sky above was bright blue, and nearby there were thick trees and standing pools of water.

"This is a rich world," Skar chattered.

"Succulent," another Lymie said.

They were starting to bunch up around Skar, and why not, he was the leader of their clan. They knew there was safety in numbers. New Terra wasn't the first planet they had dropped onto. And yet they instinctively knew that those first few hours as they assimilated with the world was when they were most vulnerable.

"Are we the first?" Skar asked.

"No, great one," another creature said, one of the scouts whose pod had opened early. "The seed ship has been busy."

"Is it still speaking to you?" Skar said.

"Enemies to the south," the scout said. "A new species to subjugate."

"Excellent," Skar said. "The order is given. Begin the feast."

The Lymies turned and began to devour what remained of their pods. They had thick, bulbous bodies with a wicked-looking stinger that curved down from their rear section. In front, a head pod with eight, black eyes stared up at the new world while it ate the pod with thick pincers and a long tongue that was covered with suckers. It looked remarkably like the tentacle of an octopus. The tongue extended, latching onto the pod, and tearing a piece free. It was their food and drink, the last of the rich nourishment from their home world. It would give them the strength to conquer a new one.

Skar had eight eyeballs, but his other senses were more highly attuned. He could feel the air pressure in the bristles on his body. The ground beneath his feet hummed and thrummed with the vibrations from his kin nearby and the planet's subtle movements. The alien's sense of smell was so discerning, it could make out the various animal life whose myriad scents wafted to him on the cold breeze. Most of all, Skar's entire body was like an organic antenna for psychic waves. He could hear the thoughts of his kin and those from other tribes. He even picked up the electronic frequencies of the Woo-Mans, those two-legged aliens who relied so heavily on electronic technology. As his kin finished their feast, Skar stood and absorbed what the planet was teaching him.

"We go south," Skar announced. His insectile mouth was made for chirps, clacks, and hums. The language they used was redundant since his mind was linked to the others of his clan. But he spoke anyway, his body quivering with the prospect of war. "We find the Woo-Mans and feast again."

The clan chittered and chattered their reply. They were excited. The pods were nutritious, but nothing compared to devouring warm flesh. It was what the Lymies were created to do. They were hunters, their ancestors long ago rising to become the apex predators on their world and eventually spreading to others. New Terra, as the Woo-Mans called it, would be no different. Skar learned that the earliest scouts of his kind had been killed. That was the risk they took, but they left their story resonating on the wind. It seemed to Skar's mind, like regaining a lost memory. In his mind, he saw the Woo-Man soldiers in their hardshell armor, with their projectile weapons. They had neither the strength nor the speed to close ranks with the Lymies. They had been victorious over the small bands of scouts, but the seed pods had fallen, bringing thousands of Lymie warriors to the planet. They would not be so successful again.

"Begin the metamorphous," he ordered.

The Lymies could transform their outer skin, hardening the stiff bristles into deadly spikes, and thickening their skin into hard armor. As they marched, their atrophied legs would strengthen until they could jump more than a kilometer in distance. They didn't spin webs, but the silk they did spin created a drag that allowed them to be carried by the wind to drop onto their enemies from above. Soon, the Woo-Mans would be stricken with fear of the Lymies, their ugly cities razed, their bodies consumed.

Skar had no illusions that defeating the Woo-Mans would end

the struggle to hold the contested planet. Other races were coming, some were already there. He could sense the thumping steps of the giant Grum-Lars who lurched about on two legs like the Woo-Mans. He could feel the scraping of the scaly Kiss-Tors who slithered over the ground, and the splash of the Po-Orgs in the fetid waters of the swampy world. There was a lot to be done to make New Terra a home for the Lymies, but the first step was always conquest, followed by total domination. The Lymies wouldn't slaughter all the beings that had come to New Terra. Some would be kept to breed for consumption. The Woo-Mans and the beastly Brascus were both excellent for that purpose. Soon his clan would be ready to join the fight. Skar's body vibrated with the thrill of it.

CHAPTER 16

MITCH WAS DRESSED in dark green fatigues, with his pants tucked neatly into the tops of his combat boots, and his gold bar pinned to the collar. His hair had been cut on the *Wellington* into the standard Marine style. Nothing about him seemed any different from the dozens of other officers in the dining hall, except his size. Yet, they all stared.

It was at that moment that Mitch really understood how he, and everyone who had gone through the LE program, were perceived. There was suspicion, jealousy, and resentment in many of the stares. Mitch tried to ignore it, but the volume in the dining hall had diminished significantly when he came in. And while he searched for the familiar face of Major Elaine Swift, the officers in the dining hall stared back at him with unveiled expressions.

Unlike the enlisted mess, there was no serving line in the officer's dining hall. The tables were smaller, with real chairs. Food was served by the waitstaff on real plates, not trays. When Mitch spotted Major Swift, he saw that she was seated with Captain Marcs, and Captain Priss. He went to their table, trying to ignore the stares from the other officers but it was difficult. He felt like he didn't really belong, despite his rank. And disdain was something he had experienced all too often in the business world, from bankers to his superiors at the Sterling Finance Corp, and even the clients who occasionally showed up at the office he had worked in. It wasn't a good feeling.

"You made it," Major Swift said. "Excellent."

"Thank you for the invitation," Mitch said, sitting down.

"How was your first day?" Captain Lindsey Priss asked. She wasn't as old as Captain Marcs, and had a plain, round face, with dark blue eyes.

"Good," he said, spreading the linen napkin across his leg and taking the glass of water that was poured for him by Captain Marcs.

"Tomorrow will be the real test," he declared. "I hope you're ready."

"Me too," Mitch admitted.

He was used to Captain Marcs ordering him around, which the veteran Marine usually did with a brusque manner. But his tone in the dining hall was friendly and encouraging.

"I'm madly curious about how the squad accepted you?" Major Swift said, her smoked chicken breast on broccolini with a cranberry vinaigrette, completely forgotten as she leaned forward.

"With surprise, but in a good way I think," Mitch admitted. "There was some testing, but it was all good."

"Excellent," she replied. "I've decided to make a case study. We won't know for certain until you're in the field, but I have a feeling your squad could be an elite unit. The enlisted Marines should respond to you in a way they don't with regular officers."

Mitch looked around. People were eating again and talking. He didn't have to wonder what the topic of conversation was. They were still staring at him. He felt out of place, and not just because of the reception. The table seemed too low, his chair too small, and the staff too friendly. A waiter handed him a card with three meal options. He was hungry and pointed to the beef option, with baked potato and roasted vegetables.

"Very good, sir," the waiter asked. "How would you like that cooked?"

"Medium," Mitch said.

"Give him a double portion," Major Swift ordered. "He has a very high metabolism."

"Yes, ma'am," the waiter said, before moving off.

"Thank you," Mitch said, then leaned forward and whispered, "Did I do something wrong with my uniform?"

He knew there was nothing wrong with his clothing, but he couldn't ignore what was happening. And the waiter bringing him two steaks wouldn't make him seem any more normal.

"No," Captain Marcs said. "But you are the talk of the town."

"Word broke shortly after we arrived on base," Major Swift said with a sardonic grin. "They're all jealous."

"Doesn't seem that way to me, Major," Mitch replied.

Elaine Swift sat back in her chair and looked around the room. No one paid her any attention, they were all talking about Mitch. Very few tried to hide their stares, or the look of disdain on their faces.

"Well, I have to say you're right," Major Swift said. "It seems not everyone has the same sense of genuine curiosity that I have."

"Prejudice is part of our history," Captain Marcs said.

"But we've moved past that," Captain Priss said. "Haven't we?"

Marcs shrugged his shoulders, and Major Swift raised her eyebrows. Mitch had never really thought much about it. He knew, from the videos of the intelligent species that had invaded New Terra, that he had a knee jerk reaction to their strangeness. Nothing about them seemed human, they were, in every sense of the word, alien. And he felt no qualms about hating them. Perhaps prejudice was built into the human genome, or maybe it was just a natural reaction to beings from another part of the galaxy. But Mitch had never thought that going through the LE Protocols would make him so different that people might hate him. He was still himself after all, maybe his mind was clearer, and he was certainly faster, and he was much bigger than before, but he still looked like himself.

"Maybe, they just need time," Elaine Swift said. "We'll worry about them later. Tell me everything about your day, Lieutenant. Don't leave out a single detail."

Mitch obliged, and he enjoyed his extravagant dinner. The steaks were real beef. On Earth, meat was either vat grown, or made from things one would rather not think about. On New Terra, raising animals for consumption was one of the most valued occupations. And for the residents of the colony world, getting the fresh meats and produce was certainly a perk. Mitch was given two steaks. They were grilled to perfection and seasoned well. Just half his meal, purchased on Earth, would have cost him a thousand credits, maybe even more. It was the kind of lavish meal the partners in the Sterling Finance Corporation bragged about. He was eating two at once, and when he got up from the table, he didn't feel stuffed, or sluggish. In fact, he was rested and satisfied. He felt like he could go to work at that moment with no regrets.

Returning to his room, he read all the materials that were given to him. And studied the training schedule that Captain Frank Marcs and Major Elaine Swift had worked up for the Lions. Things would kick off just before dawn 0600. His squad was due in the simulators all day, and the one after that would be live fire exercises. There was just enough time for PT and weapons maintenance each day. But by the fifth day he was scheduled to take the squad on an extended field exercise a couple of hundred miles north in the cold swamps. It would be a grueling, three-day hike, with combat exercises thrown in. After that, it was possible that his squad could face real combat. The one thing Mitch knew was that General Mercer was anxious to get the SSO busy, and like Major Swift had told him, everyone would be watching his squad.

He went to sleep at 2300 hours and woke up 0400. The day before, he had lifted five hundred pounds, and run more than ten kilometers cross country. Yet, his eyes popped open before his alarm on the data cuff went off. Sitting up on the side of his bed, he discovered that he wasn't tired at all. He didn't have to shake off the usual drowsiness, or struggle to get himself moving. In fact, he was brimming with energy and couldn't wait to start his day.

He was the only officer up at that hour and had the bathroom to himself. Ten minutes after rolling out of bed, he was on his way to the training facility. He was excited to see that his squad was already there.

"First day of school, LT," Jingo said. "You excited?"

"Can't wait," Mitch replied.

They spent half an hour warming up on the track, then a full hour in the training center. Mitch, Jingo, and Flash spent the entire time lifting weights, while Mara, Hawk, and Ninja split their time between the resistance machines and grappling sessions on the mats. They wrapped up their PT with another short run on the track. They took turns sprinting and jogging to vary their heart rate. After the workout, Mitch had just enough time to shower and change into his fatigues before hurrying out to the simulators in the combat training center or CTC. Inside, there were several rooms with different types of VR training systems. They started with recon exercises. Their job, loaded with VR equipment, was to get close to the enemy, gather as much information as they could, and escape without being seen.

Mitch was smart enough to let his squad help with the decision-making process. On the recon ops, Ninja usually had a suggestion or two. Mitch took his advice, and the others noticed, which encouraged them to share their thoughts too. They passed the recon training exercises with flying colors and were rewarded with breakfast.

When they finished eating, it was back to work in the CTC. Moving to a different room, they practiced ambush tactics. It was a lot like a video game. They were in a digital domain, but it looked real enough with the VR headsets. They were on omni-directional treadmills and moved through the simulated landscape. During the first few exercises, they had good intelligence on the enemy, and lots of options for ambush sites. Mitch didn't make decisions by committee, but when someone made a suggestion, he gave it weight. He understood from the business world that good leaders listened and set their own ego aside. Mitch felt like he could take on the world since his LE procedures, but he knew the members of his team had much more combat experience than he had. Plus, the simulations were so easy. It was more like playing a game. They gave suggestions, and he made the final call, it was that simple. Not that every ambush worked perfectly. Depending on what type of enemy the facilitators drew up, their tactics and weapons had varying degrees of success. For Mitch, it was all a learning experience. For his team, it was a chance to see what working for him was like. He didn't demand their obedience. Everything was even and calm when Mitch made the final decisions, sending people to various places and ordering them to achieve certain outcomes. Mitch learned about the terrain, and about the aliens they would eventually face downrange, as well as a lot about each member of the team.

Mara James was the unofficial leader. She had the most seniority, and the highest rank, although she and Hawk were both Sergeants. At first, she had been silent, and waited to see what sort of leader Mitch was going to be. Once she realized he didn't think he knew it all, she began making small suggestions. And once she saw that he was willing to listen, and showed her respect, she opened up even more. Mara wasn't as tall as Mitch, but over six feet. She wasn't as muscular either, her body was lean, the muscles in her arms and legs were compact but powerful. What really stood out to Mitch was how she moved. She was like a dancer, so graceful, no matter the terrain, like she was gliding wherever she went. Her walls began to come down with Mitch as the training went on. Eventually, she became his partner, helping him think through the options and their mission parameters, then calling out orders to compliment his plan.

As they trained, Mitch thought less and less of his squad as people, and more as parts of a single unit. They each had their own strengths and skills. Mara lived up to her nickname, Marauder. And when things got tense in a fight, she was savage. She could move from place to place, making good shots, pinning the enemy down without giving them a target to shoot back at. On those occasions when things devolved into hand-to-hand combat, she was a whirlwind of destruction. She could use her rifle like a club and knew how to hit and move to avoid counterstrikes. When things were tense, she tended to put herself between the danger and her commanding officer.

Of course, not all the aliens fired weapons in the way that Mitch expected. The Brascus were short, thick bodied aliens who alternated between moving on all fours and walking around upright. They had pig snouts, and big curved tusks that stuck out of their mouth. The Brascus had a variety of traditional weapons, along with guns that fired jets of acidic gel that burned whatever it touched. The Kistors and Porgs relied on laser weapons, which didn't have the kinetic power of a projectile, but they were light and easy to fire. Heat management was something the laser guns had to contend with, but for ease of use and accuracy, they couldn't be beat.

The Lymies were strange looking, spider creatures, very cunning and fast on their feet, with big, curved stingers that dropped from between the rear legs and could impale a human easily. They also had long, tentacle tongues that stuck to a person and pulled them into a set of powerful pincers that could cut a full-grown man in half. The ends of their legs were also dangerous, almost like spear points. In battle, they could lash out with their legs in any direction. The Grumblers were giant humanoids that reminded Mitch of characters from an epic fantasy movie. In the simulations, they didn't look real. They were so huge, and every part of their anatomy seemed to be exaggerated. They carried single shot weapons that looked like some of humanity's earliest firearms called blunderbusses. They had big, smooth bored barrels that flared at the end. They were usually filled with whatever would fit inside, rocks, branches, bits of metal, even ice. In the hands of the giant Grumblers, the weapons were like cannons and fired a barrage of small particles. In that way, they were like shotguns, but because they were so big and so full of ammunition, one shot could take down an entire platoon if they were massed too closely together.

They fought human elements too, from bands of bandits to well-trained militia units. It was all controlled, recorded, and scored. Mitch had no idea what his superiors thought of his approach to leading the squad, but he did what felt natural and right to him. And it wasn't until late in the afternoon that they lost an engagement. It was a successful ambush against a Marine Platoon, but they weren't an enemy unit, so they failed the exercise.

"Bad intel," Ninja said.

"They could have been militia," Hawk added.

"They looked rough," Jingo said. "Someone got their wires crossed."

"Ultimately, it's my call," Mitch said.

"And one you'll remember," Mara said. "You learn from your failures, not the victories."

"But winning is more fun," Flash said.

They dove into the next exercise and took down a Grumbler. It wasn't easy. The huge alien shrugged off Mitch's fifty caliber rounds, and Mara's combat pellets. Only the explosive charge in the GARs hollow point rounds, jacketed in depleted uranium, could penetrate the alien's thick hide. The squad had to work together to lure the creature into a kill zone, and then distract it long enough for the three Marines with Garrison weapons to cause enough damage to take the giant down.

When the day was over, Mitch was mentally, and physically

drained. They had stopped for a short lunch — cold sandwiches — but by the end of the day, he was ready for a long shower and a good meal. The week went on like that. Busy days, laughter, stress, and learning. Mitch had more than a few dinners by himself in the officers' dining hall. The wait staff didn't mind taking care of him, but the other officers avoided him for the most part. It felt a little like being a new kid in school, only he had good friendships with his squad. In some ways, he wished he was billeted with them, and could share meals with them. But he understood the need to be separate. Major Swift had emphasized that point.

"They may love you, but without some distance, you won't be able to lead them properly," she insisted. "You have to be willing to make the hard decisions. This isn't the business world, it's the military. We hold the lives of every person under our command in our hands. There will be times when you have to send those people into harm's way for the greater good. You can't do that without some distance. Perspective is vital to good leadership."

CHAPTER 17

AT THE END of the week the squad was taken by military transport to an undisclosed location with enough gear and rations for three days. The task was survival. North of the planetary equator New Terra was much colder. The terrain could be deadly with poisonous flora and sucking bogs, and there were hostile animals in the swamps as well. But as the transport flew away, leaving the six members of the Lion SSO squad all alone in the wild, Mitch felt a surge of excitement.

"Things just got real," Flash said.

"I love a good camping trip," Jingo replied.

"Dude, we don't even have s'mores," Ninja joked.

"Let's get moving," Mitch said.

"Agreed," Mara added. "I get stiff when I stand around gabbing all day."

"Why doesn't Marauder like us?" Jingo asked.

"She don't like anybody, bro," Flash replied.

Mitch led the way. He had taken Ninja's advice and put the MAX on a body harness which had to be modified to go across his wide shoulders and back. The big belt-fed machine gun had a special forward pistol grip modified for his oversized hands. It allowed him to walk and carry the gun as easily as a regular Marine carried a tactical auto rifle. On his back was eighty pounds of gear, neatly organized into a backpack. He wore armor too, with plates across his chest and stomach, shoulders and back, designed to stop high caliber rounds and laser energy. His short barreled rocket launcher with the laser guidance scope was snugged into a special holster at the small of his back, just below the backpack. From his belt hung the Desert Eagle .45 in a thigh holster with a flap cover, and slightly curved Kukri fighting knife.

What they didn't have was shelter equipment. No tarps, tents, or sleeping bags. They were going in cold, and although they had fire starters, the point wasn't to lounge around for three days. Their extraction point was sixty kilometers away. It would be slow going through the swamps. Mitch planned to skirt the standing water as much as possible, but they had to remain alert for an attack at all times. The facilitators of the training exercise had several surprises in store for the SSO squad.

"I'm hungry already," Jingo said. "Tell me someone brought snacks."

"Nah," Flash said. "We get hungry, we'll just eat you, big fella."

"He'll be too tough," Ninja said. "Can't chew him."

"And gamey," Hawk added, which got everyone laughing.

Mitch didn't mind the silly joking. It was one of the ways Marines dealt with their anxiety in a combat zone. But he didn't take part. He was the point person, and his complete focus was on finding a way through the swamps. They marched for three hours straight across the soft ground. It didn't take long for mud to cling to their boots and the mosquitos to start biting. They were all a little tired when Mitch finally called for a halt on a low, but dry hill.

"This sucks," Flash said, as he began scrapping the mud off his boots with a stick.

"Just a walk in the park," Jingo said. "I love the Corps!"

"Keep your voice down," Mara warned him.

"Sorry, Sarge," Jingo said. "I just get excited."

"Only you would be excited about a hike through the swamps," Ninja said.

Mitch didn't speak. He was cold, wet, and frustrated by their slow progress. But there was nothing to be done about it. The soft ground and standing water forced them to go slowly, and to avoid the myriad obstacles. There were thorns and bushes with toxins seeping from the leaves that would make entire body parts go numb if they touched your skin. The creatures living in the bogs made strange sounds too, and the wind was growing bitterly cold.

Hawk didn't speak either, but she pointed across a pond of scummy water. On the far side was a Razor Gator, it's triangular head barely above water, and the fin on its back sticking up behind it.

"Wow," Mitch said, thinking he was glad it was several hundred meters away from him.

"We could kill it and eat the meat," Mara suggested.

"I don't want us shooting unnecessarily," Mitch said. "The sound is bound to carry across the swamps."

"No need to shoot it," Ninja said, drawing a bowie knife that was nearly a meter long from tip to the butt cap.

Everything they had was large, or as he had heard the SSO Marines say, *super sized*. He didn't feel super at that moment. He was cold and frustrated. The great thing about the training exercises was the speed in which the enemy would appear. But the field exercise was much closer to real combat, long and boring with the threat of imminent danger to make you afraid all the time.

"You'd fight that thing with a knife?" Jingo asked.

"Sure," Ninja said.

"It might eat you, bro," Flash said.

"Not if it doesn't see me coming," Ninja replied.

"You're crazy," Jingo declared. "I ain't that hungry."

"Let's just stay focused," Mitch said. "What do we know for certain about this field exercise?"

"That the facilitators have surprises for us," Mara said.

"Exactly. My guess is they want us tired and frustrated before they strike, which means probably not until tomorrow."

"Just a long hike then?" Jingo asked.

Mitch nodded. "We get as far as we can today. Sleep when the sun goes down. And stay ready for anything."

"Copy that, LT," Ninja said.

"What if they ambush us today?" Mara asked quietly. "They might anticipate your strategy and try to lure us into an ambush."

"Yeah, makes me wish we had scouting drones," Mitch said.

They didn't have any of the gear they would normally carry into a combat zone, just the survival supplies. Mitch took a sip of the lukewarm water in his canteen. Somehow it wasn't very refreshing. He had water filters and iodine tablets to make the swamp water safe to drink but he wasn't looking forward to it. All the standing water around them was covered with a layer of thick, green algae, with wide leaf aquatic plants that looked like lily pads, and big insects buzzing over the surface. Whenever he did see the water, it wasn't clear, but dirty brown. Perhaps he would get thirsty enough to drink it, but he hoped not.

"Have you ever done a training exercise like this?" Mitch asked.

Mara shook her head. "This is a new one. I've done long distance hikes, but not field exercises so far from base."

"What about your combat drops?"

"There's usually an enemy in the vicinity," she said.

"Tomorrow we'll send Ninja ahead to scout for us," Mitch said. "I want to keep moving for now."

"You're the boss," Jingo said.

They got to their feet and checked their weapons. Mitch did a quick visual scan. The day was overcast and patches of fog hung over many of the larger ponds of standing water. Insects buzzed about, some as large as a child's fist. The big ones were easier to ward off, but the smaller ones were more invasive. They landed without notice, found the gaps in Mitch's armor, and eventually made their way to his skin.

By midday, the joking had stopped. The group had great stamina and could keep up a steady run for hours, but the cold swamp seemed to be sucking the strength from them. They were only six hours into their field exercise and their legs were covered with mud. It clung not just to their boots, but managed to get high on their fatigues, so that they were careful to keep their weapons clean.

Lunch was standard field rations. Meals Ready to Eat pouches, or MREs as they were known, were mushy bags of vat grown macro nutrients. Mitch had never eaten them before. His was supposed to be Chicken Teriyaki with rice and vegetables. But the chicken was just vat grown protein strips, the rice tasted uncooked, and the vegetables were unrecognizable. What Mitch could identify was the soy sauce. It was so salty he almost couldn't eat it, and the food made him incredibly thirsty. By the time he choked the terrible food down, he had drained most of his canteen of water.

"Looks like the LT is going to be first to drink the pond water," Flash pointed out.

"What meal did you eat?" Jingo asked.

"Chicken Teriyaki," Mitch replied.

The squad all laughed. Mitch didn't understand what was funny. They all had exactly six MREs in their backpacks. He had put in a variety of meal pouches in his kit, along with three protein bars.

"That's one of the worst," Mara said. "Stick with the pasta meals."

"Lots of carbs," Ninja said. "And the pasta is pretty close to normal."

Mitch held back a sigh. He had only one pasta meal among the remaining pouches. And his canteen was nearly empty. It was going to be a long day.

An hour later, Mitch dipped his canteen into the smelly water.

He recognized the foul, rotten egg scent of sulfur. His canteen had a filter across the top to keep foreign objects out, and another just inside the opening that was supposed to filter out impurities to make the water drinkable. He wasn't entirely convinced, but he was thirty enough to try. The squad was spread out around him as he knelt by the pool.

"You think we'll really colonize this world?" Ninja asked. "You know, drive everyone else away and turn it into something like Earth."

"It's possible," Flash said. "Be better than Mars or Titan."

"At least the air is breathable here," Jingo said. "And stuff grows in the soil."

"It just seems so wild," Ninja said. "And turning swamps into good, usable land isn't easy."

"But it's profitable," Mara said. "An acre of farmland produces a lot of high value food in the Sol System. And you've got billions of people on Mars, Titan, the space stations, all paying top dollar for whatever you can grow."

"Seems like a lonely life to me," Ninja went on. "Working the land, not seeing other people every day."

"Who knew Ninja was a social butterfly?" Jingo asked.

Mitch finished filling up his canteen and dropped in two iodine tablets, before putting the lid back on. The canteen was three quarters of the way full of pond water. It had been very murky, and the filter had turned from blue to a dark brown. Mitch shook the canteen to get mix the iodine through the water.

"Alright," he said. "I'm good."

"How's the water?" Flash asked with a grin.

"Haven't tasted it yet," Mitch said. "You want a sip?"

"Hard pass, LT," Flash said. "I'm rationing what I got."

"It all comes from the same place," Mara said. "The filters clean the water, just like the water treatment plant in Alpha."

"Maybe," Flash said. "But I don't like seeing how the sausage is made."

"Are we taking a break?" Jingo asked.

"Let's wait until we find some dry ground," Mitch said.

"There's weather coming in," Hawk said, peering through her LRRG optical scope. "Looks ominous."

They could see dark clouds far away.

"You sure it's coming this way?" Flash asked.

"Wind is blowing this way," Hawk explained. She spoke calmly, but Ninja and Jingo both chuckled.

"She's got a point," Mara said.

"Let's get to high ground and see if we can establish some type of shelter," Mitch said.

"Hang on," Hawk said, her voice so normally calm, had a note of alarm in it. "There's something else."

"Air patrol?" Mitch asked.

"Can't be," Mara said. "We would hear a vehicle already."

"Drones," Hawk said. "A squad of them. Coming this way."

"Bombers," Ninja said.

"We need cover," Flash said.

"Go," Mitch told him. "Find us something."

"On it," Flash replied.

"I'll go with him," Ninja said.

They started running. Mitch and the rest of the squad followed. Normally, Mitch liked to run, but his legs were heavy with the clinging mud. His boots, pant legs, and socks were wet. There was a feeling of oppression that grew with every passing moment as they knew the drones were getting closer. In the swamps, cover was hard to find. There were trees, but they were short and crooked. Few grew close to one another. They had to settle for clumps of bushes. The squad burrowed down into the mud and muck, cutting the branches to cover their bodies.

"If those drones have thermal imaging, we're toast," Jingo said.

"We can't stay bunched up," Mitch said. "Jingo, move in front of me, head to head. Flash, get behind Ninja and Hawk. Stretch all the way out."

"Why?" Flash asked.

"If they have thermal, we need to look like a swamp animal," Mitch said.

"Good idea," Mara said softly.

They were laying in the mud, side by side, surrounded by thorny bushes. Mitch turned and looked at her. She was looking at him. For the first time it crossed his mind that she was more than just a sergeant in his squad. It was impossible to know what she was thinking, but she was staring at him too. Maybe it was fear, or possibly just the bonding that a shared mission created, but he felt something for her that was more than just camaraderie.

"Well, this is fun," Ninja said.

"I think something just wiggled into my boot," Flash said.

"So much for no attacks today," Mitch said.

"At least we weren't caught out in the open," Mara said.

"Marauder, are you seriously thinking these bushes will give us any kind of protection?" Jingo asked.

"I think it's possible those drone operators won't even see us," she said. "There's a lot of wildlife out here, a lot of bland ground to search. They're probably sitting in a dark room in a comfortable chair, watching the vid feed while the drone cruises on auto pilot."

"Maybe I'm in the wrong division," Ninja said. "How do I get that job?"

"You have to be good with your hands," Hawk said.

"Yeah, man," Ninja added. "Speed ain't always a good thing."

It was the first hint that Mitch had that something had gone on with Flash and Hawk. It wasn't really surprising. In the movies about the Space Force, there were always love affairs between the Marines, or members of the ship's crew. Mitch guessed it had been that way since women had been allowed to join the military.

"What would you know about it?" Flash said.

"Just something I heard," Ninja replied.

"Well, don't believe everything you hear," Flash said.

"You two shut up," Mara ordered. "I think I hear the drones."

It was hard to be certain. The swamp was full of bugs, birds, and loud reptiles that croaked. But after a few more seconds, he heard what had to be a mechanical hum. It was tempting to look up, but they all knew better than that. The mud that had spattered onto them all day, and weighed their legs down, was helping them to blend in. Hidden under the shrubbery, they would look like the landscape. Mitch could only hope the way they were grouped, all six of them laying head to toe, would make their heat signature look like a big Razor Gator if they were using thermal imaging.

"Got to be bombers," Jingo said.

"How does that work?" Mitch asked, thinking they couldn't possibly be dropping real munitions.

"They aren't explosives," Mara said. "They're a type of electrical discharge device. It's a bit like sonar."

"The drones have receptors," Jingo added.

"The bombs send out an electrical wave that bounces off of us, or our armor," Mara continued. "It simulates the blast radius. We might not even know it, but it'll show up to the Marines back at HQ."

"Where they're keeping score," Jingo added.

"That's about all they're good for," Ninja said.

"That's no way to talk about your fellow Marines," Flash replied.

"You ever fought with any?" Ninja asked. There was no reply. "I did, my first tour. They didn't do much."

Mara tilted her head closer Mitch's ear and whispered. "Ninja's first squad got wiped out fighting a band of Lomtucs early in the war."

"Sounds like they're passing over," Jingo said.

The sound of the mechanical hum was starting to diminish. They continued laying on the ground for several more minutes. Eventually, Mitch gave Ninja the order. He moved slowly, and even though Mitch strained he couldn't hear the stealthy Marine.

"Sky is clear," Ninja reported.

"What about the storm?" Hawk asked.

As if in response, a crack of thunder sounded. They got to their feet, brushed off as much of the mud and muck as they could, then set out again. It took an hour to find a decent place to make camp. It was already raining by that time, but a big boulder on top of a small hill gave them some protection from the wind. Night fell fast, and the squad huddled together as the rain shower grew into a storm. Nothing about it was pleasant. Mitch was hungry but opted not to eat. His fellow squad members slept while he took the first watch. It was impossible to see anything in the darkness. Normally, they would have vision assistance built into their combat helmets with low light amplification, infrared, and thermal imaging. But the field exercise was all about surviving with as little gear as possible. Most of the weight in Mitch's backpack was ballast. He had two extra ammo boxes, with two hundred and fifty rounds each for his .50 caliber machine gun. Along with the water filters, fire making kit, and MREs, he had a pair of socks and clean underwear sealed inside a plastic bag. There was a long distance sat phone for emergencies, and a first aid kit. But nothing helpful for making shelter or seeing in the darkness. Mitch had to rely on the lightning to see anything. Every fifteen seconds, bolts of pure electrical energy ripped through the storm clouds and lit the landscape in a flash of light. There wasn't much to see. Below the hill was a narrow trail between two standing pools of water. The animals were bedded down, riding out the storm. Even the aquatic wildlife seemed quiet.

"It's my shift," Mara said quietly.

She had been sleeping beside him. No one was stretched out. They sat with their backs to the boulder, shoulder to shoulder, their heads tilted back, and their guns held ready.

"I'm not sleepy," Mitch replied.

It was true. He was used to staying up late and functioning on four or five hours of sleep. Yet, in the field, he found that just sitting still was very restful for him. Perhaps he could have slept if he tried, but there was something invigorating about being out in the storm.

The rain was cold, the temperatures just above freezing, but Mitch didn't complain. He could deal with being wet and cold. He didn't enjoy it, but it was a minor annoyance in the face of the storm.

"I'll keep you company then," she said. "Ooooh, that was..."

The rest of her response to the lightning was drowned out by the rolling thunder. Mitch waited until the sound died down, then asked.

"How long have you been a Marine?" Mitch asked.

"Twelve years," she said. "I just reenlisted for the second time."

Another bolt of lightning flashed, not as close as the first, or as long. The light was barely half a second, just long enough for Mitch to see the water drops rippling across the black surface of the ponds below the hill. They both paused, letting the thunder rumble.

"You like it then?"

"Love it," she said.

"Tell me about getting the protocol. What did you do before that?"

She chuckled. "I was a dancer."

"Really? What kind?"

"I started out in ballet, but outgrew it. As a teenager I competed in all kinds of dancing, ballroom, hip hop, interpretive, whatever I could find."

"That's impressive," he told her.

"Hey, I said I competed. I never said I won."

"Did you?"

"A few times, small competitions only. I was never going to be a star. I went to Hollywood the day I turned eighteen."

"Wow, that's exciting."

"Turns out, it's really, really frustrating. I had the moves, but not the lithe figure the casting agents wanted. I tried getting on with a musical act but didn't have the right contacts. Two years later, I was broke, living with four other girls in a one bedroom bungalow, watching my friends either get their big break, or more often flame out. Drugs were a big problem. Not for me, but I saw good friends ruin their lives. Some even overdosed, and when I started thinking that they were the lucky ones, I decided something had to change."

She paused for more thunder.

"I had to decide what my future held, it was either give in to the temptation of making decent money as an exotic dancer, or go back home and admit defeat."

"Which did you choose?" Mitch asked.

He had to wait as lightning rippled across the sky. It was so close he could feel the static electricity in the air. Or maybe what he felt was the chemistry with Mara James. She wasn't a classic beauty, and she was nothing like his ex-wife Megan. Instead, she was tall, with long legs, and wide shoulders. It was an impressive figure, muscular but not bulky, strong, but still feminine. Her face was clear, her skin light brown, what little hair she let grow on her head was curly and dark. Her eyes were brown, not that he could see them in the darkness. They both wore armored helmets, not the standard issue smart helms, but basic protection for the skulls. The helmet had a face shield that went down below their noses, so that only their mouth and chin was really exposed. Mitch kept his head pitched slightly forward so that the water dripped clear and didn't spatter all over his mouth and neck.

"That will have to remain a mystery for now," she said. "I can't believe I told you. Twelve years in and you're the first man I've told about my past."

"Well, thanks for trusting me."

"Don't let me find out it went into some report you filed."

"It won't," Mitch assured her, although he wasn't certain that Major Swift was recording everything they did and said. She could have bugs planted in their helmets he supposed.

"What about you, Lieutenant? Were you regular forces before the procedure?"

"No," Mitch admitted to her. "I was in the business world."

"Banker?"

"No."

"Real estate developer?"

"No, I was a minion in a mega financial firm," Mitch admitted.

"Wow, and you gave up the good life to come wallow in the mud with a bunch of grunts."

"Something like that," he said.

She gave him a little nudge with her elbow. It was as close to flirting as they got that night. The storm eventually ended. They passed off their watch duties and Mitch managed to sleep for a couple of hours. But they were on their feet before dawn. At first light, Lion Squad was back on the move.

CHAPTER 18

"THE DRONES DIDN'T FIND THEM," Captain Marcs said.

"Impressive, but not surprising," General Mercer said. "The members of the squad are all veterans."

They were in the CTC's bunker, sometimes called the war room. It was a round chamber, with video display walls, and a ceiling-mounted holographic projector. Mercer had all his support staff with him. Normally, he wouldn't oversee a single squad's training exercise, but he was as interested in the Lions as anyone. Putting Lieutenant Murphy into an officer's roll had been his idea, but he certainly didn't see the new Marine as an equal. Mercer was a graduate of a military boarding school, naval college, and had an advanced degree in military tactics and strategy from the Lunar War Preparatory Academy. He had more than earned his commission, while Mitch Murphy was simply a failed businessman who happened to have the right markers in his DNA to make him a candidate for the super serum Latent Tech was eager to try out on any sap willing to risk their life for a few thousand credits.

"We used thermal imaging," Captain Marcs said. "But the drone operators couldn't find them."

"They don't have any skin in the game," General Mercer said.

"Or maybe Lieutenant Murphy is that good," Major Swift said. "Don't discount what the serum has the potential to do to the human brain."

"I haven't met many geniuses in SSO," Marcs replied.

"There are latencies that can be enhanced in the human mind," Major Swift said. "You spent time with him, Captain. Tell me you didn't find him an intriguing human being and I'll back off."

Marcs shrugged. "They only made it twenty-five klicks," he pointed out.

"I'd say that had more to do with the stormy weather," General Mercer said. "They're making better time today."

"They better," Marcs said. "Seventy-five kilometers to the exfil site. And we'll be putting obstacles in their path today."

"Are the armored drones on the move?" General Mercer asked.

"We dropped them in the swamp right in the path of the Lions," Captain Frank Marcs explained. "Just twenty kilometers out."

The SSO squad didn't have bugs in their helmet that didn't come from the swampy fields they were trudging through. There was no way to see or hear what they were doing. But they had tracking data hidden in their armor. The holographic projector was beaming a three-dimensional, topographical map of the training exercise location. A blue dot represented each member of the squad. A series of red V's marked the location of the armored drones which the Lions were expected to take out with their live ammunition on their journey cross country toward the exfiltration point.

"Good. Let's get an eye in the sky," the general ordered. "I want to see this battle. I don't want to find out down the road that Sergeant James is carrying Murphy's water."

"Yes, sir!" Marcs snapped as he pressed a button on his computer tablet. "The surveillance drone is up."

"Do we have a good signal?" Mercer asked.

"Five by five, sir," Captain Lindsey Priss replied. "Picture is coming online now."

The walls lit up with pictures of the landscape below the drone. The unmanned aerial craft flew slow and steady, the signal it sent to a satellite in geo-synchronous orbit then beamed it back down to the base on Alpha Colony, where it was fed into the CTC's war room.

"Time to see what they're made of," Lieutenant Colonel Jerome Banks said.

"This better be good, Major," the general said to Elaine. "It's my reputation on the line."

"He's ready. And he's got a good team. They'll be fine."

"Fine isn't good enough," the general growled. "They better be outstanding, or heads will roll. And I'm not above busting Murphy down to a toilet scrubber on a fuel trawler if he can't hack it as an officer."

It was a stupid threat. Of course, no one who had come through the LE Protocol would ever be wasted on a menial task job. Mitch Murphy was too big to do regular duty on a spaceship anyway. And his scores coming out of Latent Tech's space station over Venus were off the charts. He was a physical phenom, one of the most well-rounded super soldiers to ever go through the program. And if Major Swift was correct, his mind could be enhanced too. General Mercer was anxious to see how the new lieutenant would perform in the field.

"Sir," Lieutenant Johnny Tosh spoke up. He was the general's administrative aid and had been tasked with monitoring the feed from the Space Force drone control center that was on another part of the base. "We may have a problem."

"What is it?" General Mercer said, not bothering to hide his frustration.

"The surveillance drone just got a radar contact," Tosh said. "They're re-tasking the drone to check it out."

"What is it?" Lieutenant Colonel Banks asked.

"Unknown," Tosh said, listening and talking at the same time. "But it's big."

"Not one of ours?" General Mercer said.

"Negative. Not us. They're getting interference... Sir, the drone pilot just lost control of the surveillance bird. No control, no information feed. It's gone."

"Was it attacked?" Captain Marcs asked.

"No sir, not destroyed. More like the signal was lost," Tosh said. "They're confused in the pilot control room."

"Tell them to get another drone in the air," General Mercer said. "I want to see what's going on."

"General, I suggest we pause the exercise," Major Swift said.

"We could have Lion Squad recon whatever it was that got picked up on radar," Captain Marcs said.

"Was it a ship?" General Mercer asked. "Some type of armored vehicle?"

Lieutenant Tosh had one hand pressed against the over-ear speaker he was wearing. He looked up at the general. "Sir, nothing is certain, but the word I'm getting said it was something on the ground. Something big."

"Moving?"

"Yes sir. South, according to the flyboys."

"In other words, it's headed for Alpha Colony," Lieutenant Colonel Banks said. "Could be another alien threat."

"We haven't marked anything coming down this close to our cities," General Mercer said.

"Doesn't mean it ain't a threat," Jerome Banks replied. "I suggest we order our SSO squads to ready status. Get some transports fueled up and ready to fly."

"Agreed," General Mercer said. "You get our people moving. We'll take point on this thing if it turns out to be alien activity. I'll notify General Polk and Admiral Wilcox. Marcs, get on that sat phone and make contact with Leo Squad. I want all the information they can get me."

"Rules of engagement, General?" Captain Marcs asked.

"Depends on what they find," the general said. "Until further notice, they're to watch and listen only. Do not attack unless they are threatened."

"Copy that," Captain Marcs said.

The game had suddenly changed. General Stanley Mercer was a firm believer in making the most of every opportunity that came his way. The radar hit might be nothing, perhaps a flock of birds they hadn't discovered on New Terra yet. Some animals had sonic frequencies. Bats, for example, and certain kinds of fish. It could be nothing, but in a world where humans only had a tentative hold, and there were enemies on every side, it was better to assume the worst. A large alien force would be a threat to the colony, perhaps all the human colonies spread along the equator. But it was also an opportunity for General Mercer to show what the SSO squads could do in close coordination. Sure, some of them would be killed in the fighting, but in the general's mind, that was a small price to pay for the glory of making history.

CHAPTER 19

THEY HAD BEEN WALKING for an hour when the satellite phone buzzed in Mitch's backpack. Walking didn't quite describe what they had to do. The ground was saturated. Mitch weighed two hundred and ninety-five pounds. Every step he took on the soft ground caused his boots to sink into the soil, which clung to him and made his feet heavy. He had never been so filthy in his entire life. Soaked to the skin, his clothes still damp and rubbing his skin raw where his body armor caused it to chaff against him. Still, he felt like he was doing something important. It might just be a training exercise, but he knew he was preparing himself for more serious missions.

"What's that?" Jingo asked.

"I think it's the satellite phone," Mitch said, turning away from Mara who unzipped a pouch on his pack and pulled out a water-proof hard case. "Let's take a rest. Someone get Ninja's attention."

Most of the squad was gathered close together, but Ninja was forging ahead, selecting the path they took through the swamps, and watching for any signs of danger. Flash jogged ahead to get Ninja's attention. The tall man was the only member of the Lion squad that didn't seem to be sinking into the mud. He was taller than Mitch, and just as broad through the shoulders, but much leaner.

Mara popped the clasps on the satellite phone case and pulled the lid back. The small device was flashing with an incoming call. Mitch picked it up and answered.

"Lieutenant Murphy," he said.

"Murphy, Captain Marcs. There's been a change in the assignment. You are to take your squad six kilometers southeast ASAP."

"Are we off course?" Mitch asked.

"No, Lieutenant. The exercise is being halted for now. A surveillance drone picked up something on radar, something big. But the fly boys lost signal. The drone is down. We need eyes on whatever it is. General Mercer is ordering Leo Squad to recon the area, find out what's there that could be interfering with our signals, and report back immediately."

"Roger that, sir. We're on the move," Mitch said, pointing southeast and waving to get the squad moving.

"I know that's rough terrain, Murphy, but get your people moving. Rules of engagement are recon only, do not engage. I repeat, do not engage with the enemy unless they fire on you. Is that clear?"

"Yes sir," Mitch said.

"Try not to be seen if you can help it. It might be some form of native life or might be hostile aliens. This is not a drill, Murphy. Listen to your people, facilitate the gathering of intelligence, and don't do anything stupid."

"Sir, may I ask a question?"

"What?"

"Is this one big something or..."

"Unknown," Captain Marcs said. "The drone wasn't close enough for video before it went down. The Space Force drone patrol is gearing up another sat bird, but they'll be half an hour at least just getting a long-range UAV up. Orbital control is trying to get eyes on the scene, but right now, your squad is the closest thing we've got. I know you've got minimal gear. Have your people dump the ballast from their packs and get moving."

"Roger that, Captain Marcs, we're on our way."

"Call me back the minute you know what's out there," he ordered.

"Yes sir."

"Very good, Lieutenant. Marcs out."

The line went dead, and Mitch tucked the phone into a pouch under his chest armor.

"What was it?" Mara asked.

Ninja and Flash were returning to the group. Mitch pulled his backpack off and started dumping the sandbags used to weigh it down and simulate normal gear.

"Dump your ballast," Mitch said. "The field exercise just got upgraded to a recon op."

"You sure this ain't just part of the test?" Jingo asked.

"That was Captain Frank Marcs on the horn. He ordered us to make our way four or five klicks southeast ASAP."

"Why?" Mara asked.

"A surveillance drone went down after getting a ping on the radar. Something was jamming the signal I guess. The satellites can't get a fix, and we're Johnny on the spot."

"Beats the hell out of field exercises," Flash said.

"What if it's just a flock of birds or a herd of cattle?" Ninja asked.

"Then we report in and wait for further instructions."

"And if it's a group of hostiles?" Mara asked, dumping ballast from her backpack.

"Then we report that too. We're not supposed to engage."

"That's good," Jingo said. "We're not really equipped to fight a real battle."

"We've got what we've got," Mitch said. "Our task is clear. Get close, see what we can see, and report back. If we can do that without being seen, so much the better."

"Sounds like a plan," Mara said.

"Flash, I want you on point," Mitch said. "Don't wait on us, but don't get seen."

"Roger that," he replied, heading out immediately.

"Alright, let's make sure we're ready if things get dicey," Mitch said.

"Our first real mission as Lions," Jingo said. "Let's show 'em what we're made of."

"Hawk, you've got the only telescopic sights," Mitch said. "We'll be relying on your eyes."

She nodded and wrapped her arm around the rifle she carried. Mara and Jingo formed up on either side of her. Ninja went ahead of them, and Mitch followed behind. It took twenty minutes. The best they could manage was a sluggish jog, but they pushed themselves. Mitch was sweating, despite the cold, wet conditions when they reached a small rise. Flash was lying on his stomach beside a clump of shrubs. Mitch gestured for Mara, Jingo, and Ninja to stay put, while he and Hawk crawled up the hill. At the top Mitch saw a wide, swampy plain that lay beyond. There were patches of fog in the distance, and through them, Mitch could see movement, but it was too far away to make anything out. Hawk looked through her scope and when she spoke, her voice was tense.

"Lymies," she whispered. "Hundreds of them."

She pressed a lever on the mounting rail and the optical scope came off her LRRG. She handed it to Mitch, who looked through it. It was difficult to hold the scope steady, and at the right distance, but he saw the Lymies. They looked like some kind of spider, only with four legs instead of eight.

"What the hell?" Mitch said.

They were moving at a steady pace, some on land, some wading through the swampy ponds. They didn't have any sort of organization to their horde, just one big group. But they didn't seem to be slowed by the terrain either. Mitch had spent more than twenty-four hours in the boggy wilderness and knew just how hard it was to maneuver through it. Even with the aliens more than two kilometers away he was certain they couldn't keep up with the spidery creatures.

"What now, LT?" Flash asked.

"Now I make the call," Mitch said, handing the scope over to Flash. "Those are Lymies? We're all agreed?"

He knew a bit about the aliens from his briefing materials which he had studied on the *Wellington*. There wasn't a lot to know about them. A few had been killed. Humans had a grasp of their anatomy, and an idea of how they fought, but no understanding of how they communicated or what they wanted on New Terra.

"Agreed," Hawk said.

"Yeah, that's them," Flash said. "Big hairy bugs, man. Nasty."

Mitch shimmied back down the hill to make his call. They still had a lot of intel to gather, but what they knew couldn't wait. The Lymies were undoubtedly a hostile force. One that had to be stopped, one way or another.

The satellite recorded the number Captain Marcs had called in on. All Mitch had to do was press a button and wait for the uplink. But instead of a solid connection like before, Mitch got a message on the display screen telling him no signal could be established.

"Problem?" Mara asked.

"The sat phone won't connect," he said.

"That's impossible," Jingo interjected. "It's supposed to work no matter where you are."

"Unless there's no satellite for it to connect to," Ninja pointed out.

"That's one possibility," Mara said. "There could be local interference."

"The drone lost signal," Mitch remembered. "You think the Lymies are jamming our frequencies?"

"Most likely," Mara said.

"Wonderful," Mitch said. "I'll have to fall back and make the call. Marauder, you take charge. We need to get closer, assess their strength, and make sure there are no more surprises."

"We'll circle in behind them," she said. "And form a communication line."

"Jingo, you're with me," Mitch said. "Make sure everyone stays alert. There's no reason to take unnecessary chances until we have orders."

"Copy that," Mara said.

Mitch and Jingo set off at a slow, lumbering jog. The satellite phone had a reception icon on the display screen. Mitch kept moving away from the enemy until he had a solid signal. Then he stopped and pressed the connect button.

"How far are we?" Mitch asked as he waited for the phone to connect.

"A thousand meters, give or take," Jingo said. "I tried counting out steps, but it's not always accurate."

Mitch nodded as the call connected.

"Captain Marcs," the stern voice said, sounding urgent through the tiny speaker. "What's the sit rep, Lieutenant Murphy."

"Sir, we've got eyes on a large group of Lymies," Mitch said. "Conditions aren't good here, sir. Lots of fog. As you know our movement is hindered by the soft ground which was only made worse by the storm."

"I don't need excuses, Lieutenant."

"Yes sir, sorry sir."

"A group of Lymies. How many are we talking about?"

"Impossible to say at this stage, sir, but more than a hundred. My gut is we're talking two or three hundred. And I'm still four kilometers out. Any closer and I lose signal, even with the satellite phone."

"Do your people still have eyes on the enemy?"

"Affirmative. They are moving closer, trying to get a better count and see if there is anything else, vehicles maybe, some type of jamming technology."

"Very good, Lieutenant. We are putting a defensive plan together. Right now, you are the only assets with eyes on the Lymies. If possible, I want you to move around behind their forces. You'll have to work out a way to get close enough for good intel but stay far enough to remain in contact. That is a mission priority, Lieutenant. We have to be able to reach you once our plan is clear. You may have to take a vital part in that action. Understood?"

"Yes sir. I'll move around behind them and stay outside their jamming signal."

"Good job, Murphy. I'm downloading info for your team. Get your data cuff on, and use the sat phone to maintain contact, but be aware, that phone only has a six-hour battery."

"Six hours, copy that," Mitch said, wondering what they would do after six hours.

He ended the call and pulled off his backpack. Down in the bottom was a hidden pouch. His data cuff had biometric security. He put it on and activated the device. It required a retinal scan, and fingerprint before allowing access to the features. Mitch tapped an icon on the cuff to connect it to the satellite phone. A moment later, the navigation app came on and projected a tiny map in the air above Mitch's arm.

"Jingo," he said, "come look at this."

The big man had been scanning the horizon for threats. He stepped closer and looked down. "That's Alpha Colony," he said, pointing at a large blue dot on the very edge of the hologram.

"And here we are," Mitch said, pointing at a tiny, yellow dot that was pulsing brighter every few seconds. He touched the dot with a finger, then moved that finger over to the blue dot. A green line appeared, and in tiny print, he saw the distance listed. "A hundred and seventy-five kilometers."

"No real terrain obstacles between us and the colony," Jingo said. "Nothing to stop that horde. You really think it's two or three hundred bugs?"

"Hard to say for certain," Mitch said. "But I'd argue that's the minimum."

"Damn, never heard of a force that big on New Terra," Jingo said.

"You think it's going to be a problem?"

"The bugs are hard to kill," he said. They have incredibly thick skin, and they can move fast. The good thing is they have to close the distance to fight you."

"No projectiles?"

"Not that I'm aware of," he said. "Doesn't mean they don't have them or haven't developed a way to counter our guns."

"There's plenty of Marines to defend the city," Mitch said.

Jingo gave him a skeptical look.

"Am I wrong?" Mitch asked.

"Never seen more than five SSO squads at Alpha at any one time," he said. "Same goes for the regular rifle platoons. There's always two battalions on New Terra. Three platoons to a company, four companies to a battalion. That's about four hundred, eighty Marines to a battalion. Rounding up, let's say a thousand regular Marines, and a hundred and fifty of us. That's less than twelve hundred Marines tasked with protecting eight colonies, supply lines, expansion efforts, ranches, scientific expeditions, the list goes on and on."

Mitch felt a shiver of fear. They needed to hit the aliens hard and ensure they didn't reach the colony.

"We're moving," Mitch said. "We'll trail the aliens. Report on what we see."

"Sounds right," Jingo said. "Once the fighting starts, we can hit them from behind. They won't be expecting that."

It took them an hour to catch up with the other members of the Lion Squad. Mitch had feared that the aliens could have supply lines stretched behind them that would see and attack his squad of SSO Marines. But the hordes of Lymies had no support.

"How many?" Mitch asked as soon as he was close enough to Mara to have a conversation.

"Can't say for certain. They aren't in columns or rows, but at least three hundred."

"HQ is preparing an assault," Mitch said. "Our job is to stay back here, and report anything that changes."

"Copy that," Mara said. "Flash is getting closer. They don't seem concerned with what's behind them."

"There's so many, I'm not surprised. Nothing could slip through the crowd, and we're probably the only ones crazy enough to circle around them."

"Yeah, speaking of crazy, they're much faster than we are. No rest for the weary, LT. We've got to hustle to keep up."

She wasn't exaggerating. The Lymies weren't marching all that fast, but they weren't hindered by the swamps, ponds, or bogs. Several times Mitch and his squad had to go out of their way to avoid standing water, or a sucking bog that would trap them in the soft, wet mud. The Lymies just lifted their bodies a little higher on their long, spider legs, and kept going. For the first time since his procedure, Mitch felt tired. Part of his fatigue was stress. They weren't just following an enemy, they were following hostile aliens. Combat was almost guaranteed. And to make matters worse, Mitch didn't have all the gear he should have. The squad had no communications equipment, no long-range radios, or even person-to-person comlinks. Not that their signals wouldn't have been jammed by the Lymies, but he would have felt better if he had his regular kit.

The biggest issue, and the first one that had to be tackled, was the battery on the satellite phone. Mitch needed it to stay in contact with HQ, but with the phone activated it had a relatively short battery life. Normally, Mitch would have spare batteries and solar charging units. There was plenty of solar energy on New Terra, but as part of the survival exercise, Mitch had been forced to leave his charger behind.

"Who's the most tech-savvy among us?" Mitch asked Mara.

"That would be Hawk. She likes to tinker."

"Have Ninja take her place," Mitch ordered. "And have her give him the scope too. I need her back here."

"Roger that," Mara replied.

The squad was spread out in a long line. Mitch couldn't even see the enemy from the back of the line. And he was a full three, maybe even four kilometers away from them. Mara sprinted ahead. It wasn't a top-speed run, just a full-out run over bad ground that made her much slower than normal, despite the effort. But she only had to run half a kilometer to catch up with Jingo, who then sprinted with Mitch's order another half kilometer to catch up with Ninja. Flash and Hawk were together, and just under a kilometer from the stragglers in the alien horde. Ninja reached them, gave Hawk Mitch's order, and took her spot. She slowed to a walk, then a stop, and after catching her breath, began walking back toward the end of the line.

Mitch had given Captain Marcs an update and gotten a rough outline of the initial battle plans. Four SSO squads were moving into position to attack the horde a full fifty kilometers out from Alpha Colony. They were paired up and split to either side of the alien mob. Drone bombers were being charged up and loaded with munitions for an aerial assault, while the rifle platoons at Alpha were manning defensive artillery and preparing to dig in between the colony and the aliens. The only issue in Mitch's mind was time. They were still over one hundred and fifty kilometers away from the kill zone. And even if the Lymies didn't stop to rest, it would still take them forty-two hours to travel the hundred-plus kilometers. Perhaps they could do that, but he wasn't sure about his squad keeping up. He had yet to really test his stamina and endurance. But he felt weighed down by the nasty conditions, the mud that stuck to his boots and pants legs, and the stress of what was happening. He couldn't help but wonder what the aliens were up to. Would they really just charge headlong toward the colony? The Lymies had been on New Terra long enough to be fully aware of what they would face going to war with the humans. And, if they were intelligent enough to traverse the galaxy, they were surely smart enough to know better than to walk straight into the massed fire of the Colonial Marines.

CHAPTER 20

THE WAR ROOM was living up to its name. It was filled with senior officers and their staff. General Polk was the ranking Marine, a four-star general with overall command of the ground forces had joined General Mercer. Admiral Darcy Wilcox of Space Force was in charge of the Terra System defenses but also had a group of drone pilots based on Alpha Colony. Wilcox was monitoring from her flagship, the *Juggernaut*. Her subordinate, Major Piper Fey, was in the War Room with the Marine generals. They were all listening as Major Elaine Swift gave a briefing on the Lymies. They all knew the basics about the aliens, but Major Swift was the expert.

"Their mouths aren't designed for speech," she was saying. "No vocal cords. The mandibles can make chittering sounds, and we've heard them humming, but no real vocalization."

"And that matters because..." Polk said.

"Because they have to communicate on a very high level," Swift argued. "It's been theorized that they have some type of telepathy, but it's also possible that those mental signals are what's jamming our radio signals."

"Brain waves," General Mercer said with a chuckle.

"Precisely. We've been measuring our own for centuries," Major Swift said.

"And we have no evidence of a technological source of the jamming?" Polk asked.

"No sir," Captain Frank Marcs said. He was there to direct the Lion Squad, while Lieutenant Jerome Banks was coordinating the SSO squads stationed at the other colonies.

"General," Space Force Major Fey spoke up. "We just lost another surveillance drone."

"Where?"

Everyone turned, a feeling of dread springing up in the assembled officers. Major Fey had a headset on and was seated at a computer console that controlled the dedicated communications line for the drone operators.

"Charlie Colony, sir. It just suddenly lost signal."

"Just like the bird south of us," General Mercer pointed out.

"How far out was it?" Polk asked.

"Nearly a hundred and eighty kilometers north of the colony," Major Fey said.

"Has to be another enemy force," General Mercer said.

"Do we have boots on the ground?" Polk asked, looking over at Lieutenant Colonel Banks. There was no need to wonder if there were regular Marine forces outside the colonies. The rifle platoons operated in and around the colonies, but never more than ten kilometers. That's what the SSO super soldiers were for, the dangerous, long-range missions.

"No sir, but I'm giving the order now," Colonel Banks said. "The Foxes have a ground skiff that can reach that area in just over an hour."

"What about orbital satellites?" Polk said angrily. "Damn it, we're blind here. And everything is taking too long."

"Satellite imagery is spotty," Major Fey replied. "Could be the storm, but there's a lot of residual activity in the atmosphere."

"If they can jam our signals," General Mercer said, "they might be hiding from the satellites too. We don't have a good explanation of their full capabilities."

"But if they're attacking two colonies, the chances are good they're attacking more," Colonel Banks said.

"How is this possible?" General Polk demanded. "We're facing armies of these aliens, and no one saw them landing ships, or traveling through the system?"

"We were aware that the Lymies dropped pods," Major Piper Fey replied. "But we didn't know what was in them. Long distance scans were inconclusive. What we knew for certain was there wasn't any technology in them."

"Seed pods," Major Swift explained. "Maybe new creatures, maybe some sort of hypostasis, it really doesn't matter. Self-contained, protective pods that sustain and nourish the occupant. It isn't unheard of. There have been theories about developing something similar to traverse the vast distances between galaxies."

"What good does it do to move people to a new planet if they don't have supplies?" Captain Marcs pointed out.

"No food, no communications, no weapons," General Mercer said. "They don't even have a way to traverse the world they landed on."

"What if they don't need any of that?" Major Swift replied. "What if they are the weapon? We know they communicate telepathically. We know some creatures can go for weeks between meals."

"They still need to traverse long distances," Colonel Banks said.

"And even our super soldiers are struggling through the swamps," Captain Marcs said. "Our people would be exhausted hiking just twenty kilometers through that kind of terrain."

"But the Lymies don't seem bothered by it," Major Swift said. "And we still don't know everything about them."

"We know they can be killed," General Mercer said. "And the sooner we start that, the better."

"Proceed with operation Extermination," General Polk said, "just as soon as the bombing drones can fly."

"Roger that," Major Fey replied.

"I guess we'll see what they're really capable of," General Mercer said. "Captain Marcs, keep your communications to the Leo Squad open. I want regular reports."

"Yes, General," Captain Frank Marcs said.

"Bomber drones are loaded and ready," Major Fey announced. "Launching now."

"How long to reach the target?" General Polk asked.

"Forty-five minutes, to an hour, depending on the winds," Major Fey replied.

"Looks like we've got twenty to thirty kilometer per hour winds moving south," Lieutenant Johnny Tosh said.

"Nose winds," General Mercer said. "That'll slow our birds down."

"At least the weather isn't keeping them grounded," Major Fey said. "Another storm like last night, and they wouldn't be flying at all."

"Hit them hard and fast," Polk commanded. "When the smoke clears, I don't want to see a single one of those creatures moving. We'll show the aliens who we really are."

"It's a good plan, General," Mercer said. "The bugs won't get past our SSO squads."

He was confident, but Major Elaine Swift wasn't so sure.

CHAPTER 21

BY THE TIME Mitch got the message from Captain Marcs, the bombers were already on the move. He sent word to the rest of the squad, which pulled back. Half an hour later, they stopped on a short hill to watch what happened when the drones arrived. The entire team was tired, but not to the same degree a regular unit would have been.

"Hell of a day," Flash said, as he stretched out on the semi-dry ground and used his backpack to support his head.

"Eat and rest, but check your weapons," Mitch said.

"There's a good chance that horde might reverse course once the bombing starts," Mara pointed out. "We could be right in their path."

"No cover out here," Jingo said. "Once they start the bombing raid, speed is the only defense."

"It looks pretty clear to the west," Ninja pointed out. "Who's ready for a foot race."

"Born ready," Flash said.

The satellite phone buzzed in his hand, and Mitch answered it. The rest of the squad fell silent.

"Yes sir," Mitch said a moment later. "We're on it."

He powered off the phone and stuck it in a loop on the front of his body armor. It was the first time in his life that he felt so frightened that his body actually trembled. His joints didn't seem to fit together right. Despite the heat he had worked up on the long hike through the swamp, he felt cold, and not from the outside in, but from the inside out.

"What's the word, LT?" Jingo said.

"The bombers are fifteen minutes out," Mitch said. "But there is concern they'll be lost due to the signal jamming."

"So?" Flash said. "They can just arm the bombs now, and if the drones go down over the aliens they'll still explode."

"They can't afford to lose the drones," Mitch said. "There are more bands of Lymies approaching the other colonies."

"Wonderful," Mara said.

"I still don't get it," Flash said. "What do they want us to do?"

"We're the distraction," Hawk said.

Mitch nodded. "We've been ordered to start an attack."

"That's crazy," Ninja said. "Just the six of us, against three hundred?"

"We're to hit and run," Mitch said. "Draw their attention, give the drones a chance to engage."

"And what if the bugs turn on us?" Flash said. "Those things could run us down in this terrain. Besides, we've got no backup."

"We've got the drones," Jingo said.

"If they work," Flash argued. "And that ain't guaranteed."

"Orders are orders," Mara said. "Killing is our business."

"And business is good," Jingo said.

Mitch felt like he might be sick to his stomach. Up until that point, the fighting had all been theoretical. He had wondered many nights how being ordered into battle might feel. He decided it was a bit like being seasick, but fortunately, his mouth was bone dry and his stomach empty.

"We'll do what we can," Mitch said. "Form a skirmish line and hit them as soon as we're in range. I want Hawk hanging back and covering us if we have to retreat."

"Go time," Jingo said.

"At least we're doing it on our terms, not theirs," Ninja added.

"Flash, you take the far end of the skirmish line," Mitch said. "If the Lymies begin to advance on us, we will fall back. Keep watch for hand signals. We don't have coms."

"Another reason we shouldn't be doing this," Flash said. "Whoever made the call to send us in with no supplies should have their—"

"Can it, Corporal," Mara growled. "Get your head right."

"Yeah, we got this," Jingo said, pulling Flash to his feet. "Time to squash some bugs."

Mitch didn't feel confident. He was afraid. Not that they weren't armed, and trained for battle, but they were still fighting what essentially looked like big spiders. Really big, and spiders were scary enough. It didn't help that there were hundreds of them. He checked his machine gun, then nodded at Mara.

"Let's move Lion Squad," she said. "On the double. Wait for the signal before you start shooting."

Mitch handed Hawk the satellite phone. "Just in case," he said.

Then they were running. It seemed completely wrong to run toward danger, but that's what they did. Normally, Mitch found running to be a good way to clear his head. That wasn't the case as he ran toward the enemy horde. He realized that the LE Protocols had changed him. He wanted to live. He wanted to keep exploring what he was capable of doing physically. He wanted to continue being with the people in his squad and seeing where the relationships went. But what he wanted wasn't important. He was a Marine, and nothing mattered more than following orders. The CMC had given him a new life, and if they opted to throw it away, he was obligated to accept that.

They didn't have the normal equipment they should have been going into battle with. His helmet's face shield didn't have a Heads

Up Display or any kind of targeting applications. It was just a protective barrier. Nor did his MAX have a scope or any kind of aiming device. It was a powerful weapon that used the tracer bullets to help the operator in bringing it to bear. He did however have his data cuff. It had been stowed in his backpack for just such an emergency. It wasn't a powerful device, but it did have a few handy features. One was a laser range finder. He used to gauge how close they were to the rear ranks of the advancing horde.

Mitch had to run fast to gain ground on the insectile aliens. Normally he could sprint for several minutes without even breathing hard. But the combination of low oxygen content in New Terra's atmosphere, combined with the boggy terrain, made the sprint much more difficult. He was breathing hard by the time he reached two hundred meters to his target. Only then did he allow himself to slow to a walk and raise his left hand. Mara was fifty meters to his left. Mitch was the anchor point in their skirmish line. Jingo was fifty meters beyond Mara, with Ninja and then Flash fifty and a hundred meters beyond him respectively. None of them stopped moving, but they slowed down, bringing their rifles to their shoulders. The Garrison Assault Rifles were powerful weapons but didn't have the range of his MAX. Not that they really needed it, two hundred meters was close enough for all of them to be in range.

Mitch's heart was pounding hard, not just from the run, but mostly from fear. He was about to draw the ire of hundreds of aliens. That thought was utterly terrifying, but he knew he had no choice. It was, he decided, time to see what he was made of. Would he stand and fight, or would he flee? Was he a warrior, or a waste of time and effort? There was only one way to find out. He dropped his arm in a chopping motion. Mara did the same thing, and on down the line. Then they opened fire.

For a second Mitch hesitated. His hands found the pistol grips of the big machine gun, and his arms brought it to bear on the aliens, but his focus was on the effectiveness of the other members of his squad. They were shooting explosive-filled rounds with depleted uranium tips. The bullets were designed to punch through plate armor, the small charges inside sent the soft metal bullet exploding into jagged pieces that would rip flesh into bloody ribbons. And that's what happened to the aliens at the rear of the horde. Blood, flesh, and body parts flew through the air. Mitch joined the fray, pulling the trigger for the first time in his life against another living creature. The MAX roared to life, the bullets chugging out in quick bursts. The tracer rounds were visible, even in broad daylight. His bullets didn't have the explosive charges inside, they were more of a standard ammunition, but they were still deadly. Legs were severed, and bloody holes ripped through the dark, hairy bodies of the Lymies. Dozens fell under the attack, and many turned to see who was attacking them. For a few seconds, Mitch felt something he had never experienced before. His fear fell away, and in its place was a sense of strength and purpose that was overwhelming. In those seconds he felt more alive than he ever had before.

And then something totally unexpected happened. The Lymies began to spin up long lines of silk. The milky white material flew upward, toward the sky, in long, shimmering lines. At first, Mitch thought it was a result of the attack, perhaps evoked by fear. But then, to his utter amazement, the Lymies were carried off the ground by the streaming lines of silk. They hung upside down, their long, articulated legs curled inward, the aliens carried away by the breeze. To his surprise, Mitch felt a sense of anger. His enemy was getting away, so he raised his weapon and continued shooting. Those that were hit, ejected blood and sometimes limbs, which dropped, but the bodies themselves were carried along by the wind that was blowing from the north, toward the south.

Somehow, through the rage that was churning inside Mitch, a thought occurred to him. He turned and sprinted back toward the hill where Hawk was waiting. She must have seen him and ran to meet him.

"The sat phone!" he shouted as they approached each other. "Have to call it in."

She pulled the phone from her armor. She had rigged the extra battery from her digital telescoping optical sight to the satellite phone. It was bulky, held in place by a bandage from her first aid kit. But she had at least doubled the battery life of the phone. She held it out to him. Mitch pressed the connect button and turned, just as the first explosion sounded. He watched as the satellite connection was made, and the communication channel opened. The drones had arrived, but just as they feared, the control signals were lost. Worse still, the Lymies seemed to hone in on the drones, detonating the bombs in mid-air. The explosions were impressive, killing a few dozen more of the spidery aliens, but mostly wasting their deadly force. The drones weren't as fortunate. They were destroyed in the explosions.

"Captain Marcs," the voice on the satellite phone said.

"Sir, the Lymies they're... they're flying sir."

"What?" the captain snapped angrily.

"The Lymies have taken flight. There are hundreds of them, sir. And they're headed due south at speed."

"Standby, Lieutenant," Captain Marcs ordered.

Mitch stood, watching in awe as the aliens flew away to the south. He felt helpless and awed by the display. And the only thing that was certain was that the battle wasn't over yet.

CHAPTER 22

THERE ARE no rules to war, but there are principles that the most successful commanders knew to adhere to, such as not splitting one's forces, or avoiding conflict on two fronts simultaneously. Another commonly quoted rule was to hope for what you think the enemy will do, but plan for what they are capable of doing. It was the type of principle meant to keep a person from getting caught unaware. But it was impossible to plan for what an enemy was capable of if you simply didn't know them well enough. Hence, another common axiom in military circles was to know your enemy.

General Mercer didn't know the Lymies. He didn't know what they wanted or what they were willing to do to get it. He didn't even know what they were physically capable of. All he knew was that several hundred were headed for Alpha Colony. Although they didn't have contact with the other groups, it was believed similar groups were marching toward the Charlie, Epsilon, Golf, Hotel, and Indigo colonies.

"They're doing what?" General Polk shouted.

"Flying sir," Captain Marcs explained. He was red-faced, his brows furrowed angrily with the satellite phone still pressed to one ear. "Evidently, they spun up some type of web that caught the wind and carried them into the air."

"That's impossible," General Polk said.

He was red-faced too, but his lips were pale, and General Mercer noticed the man's hands were trembling. It seemed obvious that the four-star general was in over his head. Caught unprepared, and his mind unwilling to deal with that fact, he was on the verge of total collapse. It was time for General Mercer to take charge.

"Do we know how fast they are moving?" Stanley Mercer asked.

"Negative," Captain Marcs replied.

Mercer looked at Major Swift. "Did you know about this?"

"No," she said. "But some arachnids are known to have a similar ability."

"Can they control it?" Mercer asked.

"I think we have to assume that they can," Swift said.

"Colonel Banks, what's the assessment from the other colonies?"

"Depending on the effectiveness of our weapons," Jerome said, "Odds are good we'll be overrun."

"No!" General Polk shouted. "We can't let that happen."

"We aren't giving up, but we need to evacuate the civilians," General Mercer said. "Lieutenant Tosh, give the order for full colony withdrawal. Major Fey, do we have any aerial assets?"

The woman shook her head. "We've lost signal from the drone bombers," she said.

"They were destroyed, sir," Captain Marcs said. "Leo team is reporting that the Lymies detonated the bombs while they were still on the drones in mid-flight."

"So they recognized the danger," General Mercer said. "Which means they are very intelligent. Colonel Banks, give the order for all SSO teams to pull back. We've got to guard the civilian evacuation."

"Wait!" General Polk said. "You can't give that order. You'll be countermanding the entire battle plan."

"The plan is finished, sir. You must see that."

"I see nothing of the kind."

"They'll fly right over the SSO squads," Mercer said. "Ground artillery will be useless while the enemy is in the air. And they can bypass the rifle platoons completely. They'll drop from the sky into the colonies. We'll be overwhelmed in no time, and the enemy will use the structures, not to mention the civilians, as cover. It will be a massacre. This is the only chance we've got."

The truth of the situation hit General Polk like a physical blow. The arrogant commander dropped into a chair, his dignity forgotten. He leaned forward, elbows on his knees, his hands in his short hair as he mumbled to himself. "How could I let this happen?"

"Major Fey, get your pilots moving. And contact naval forces, alert them we're ordering a full evacuation."

"Yes, General," Piper Fey said.

"I want transports running from the colonies to the extraction site," General Mercer continued barking orders. "SSO units will fall back to defend the colonies. Rifle platoons will rally with the civilians to form a protective detail. Rules of engagement are to shoot the aliens on sight. Give them no quarter. Get the orders out now, I want coordinated movements. Sound the general alarms and make evacuation announcements over the colony network."

The War Room transformed into a hive of activity. General Mercer was pleased to see everyone rushing to obey his orders. And it was no small victory to see General Polk still crumpled in a chair, his thinning, gray hair askew.

Major Elaine Swift sat beside Captain Marcs who was giving Leo Squad their orders.

"... haste, I repeat, return to Alpha Colony with all haste. The order to evacuate has been given. You have to reach the civilian launch pad south of Alpha Colony before the last transport leaves or you will be left behind."

"May I?" Major Swift asked.

Captain Marcs nodded. "Major Swift is waiting to speak to you. Standby."

He handed her the phone, and she held it up to her ear. The device was warm, and when she looked at Captain Marcs, she noticed a fine sheen of sweat upon his brow. She couldn't help but wonder if his reaction was fear. She knew there was danger coming, but it still felt distant to her. The order to evacuate had been given. It wasn't like they were going to fight to the last man. Maybe he was chaffing at being in the command bunker rather than down range with his SSO squads. She knew some commanders who hated being held back from the action. Captain Marcs was an interesting man, and she made a mental note to ask him about the reaction later.

It was just her nature. Elaine Swift was a naturally observant and curious person. She loved to learn. And studying life forms, be they human or alien, was her obsession. She was fascinated by what made people do the things they did. And she had a special interest in Lieutenant Mitch Murphy since he was the first LE super soldier she had gotten the chance to study up close.

"Lieutenant," she said. "This is Major Swift. How are you?"

"Fine, Major," he said, breathing hard.

"Are you running, Mitch?"

"Affirmative. We are in pursuit of the enemy, Major."

"Is there any chance of catching up to them?"

"Short of a miracle... no ma'am."

"Then don't be foolish," she ordered. "Gather your squad and make good choices. We need you here, Lieutenant. Don't let the situation rob you of your senses."

"Yes, ma'am," Mitch said. "Thank you."

"Tell me what your situation is?"

"We're still a hundred and fifty-odd kilometers from Alpha Colony," he said. "We'll be moving south with all speed."

"The evacuation is supposed to take four hours," Major Swift said. "Given the current conditions, my guess is it will be closer to twelve hours before everyone is moved off planet. The question is, will you make it back to the colony in twelve hours?"

There was a pause. No one likes to admit weakness, especially not the Marines who had gone through the LE program. They were big, strong, fast, and had incredible stamina. Still, a hundred and fifty kilometers was too long for anyone to run without stopping.

"No ma'am," Mitch replied through clenched teeth.

"Alright, keep moving, but don't wear yourself out. We don't know what you might run into between here and there. I'll commandeer a transport. Stay alert, and don't shoot me. I'm coming to get you. Swift out."

She handed over the phone, and Captain Marcs looked at her with disbelief.

"Don't you need to clear that with the General?"

"He's given his orders," she said. "We just have to carry them out."

"We?"

"Do you have responsibility over any other squads?"

"Yes, I'm in command of the SSO squads based here in Alpha; Bravo, Delta, Indigo, and Kilo, as well as Leo."

"Alright, see to the others. I'm going after Leo squad. They have no chance of making it back in time."

"You could run right into those Lymies out there," he said. "Don't be a fool."

"I'm a scientist," she said. "Lieutenant Mitch Murphy is as close to a perfect human specimen as there has ever been."

"I think your feelings are getting in the way."

"I resent your accusation, Captain. This isn't personal. It's purely, professional."

"Tell yourself whatever you need to, Major. But people don't risk their lives for lab monkeys."

Elaine Swift recoiled as if she had been slapped. Lab monkeys, really? Is that what Captain Marcs thought of the SSO Marines? Is that what everyone thought of them? It was a moment of clarity for her. She had assumed that the prejudice against the SSO squad personnel was merely envy. But apparently, they were seen as less than human by the regular forces. And her interest in them was being viewed as something other than professional curiosity. She had volunteered to join General Mercer's staff. Her position as a scientific officer wasn't necessary for his command staff, but most commanders liked having a xeno-biologist at their beck and call. But maybe she felt something for Mitch Murphy? She was a woman, after all, and he was a man. He was intelligent, and an obvious, physical specimen. Why wouldn't she feel something for him, she wondered? It was human nature after all.

Shelving her self-inspection for another time, she left the War Room and made her way out of the building. A siren was blaring from a speaker on some high building. The sound reminded her of a bad war movie, only it wasn't fiction. The colony was in serious danger. There was no denial of that. She found a hovercraft in the motor pool garage.

"I need a transport," she told the Master Sergeant who was in charge.

"Don't have one," he said. "They're all in service."

"What do you have available?"

"Just open cab hover-carts," he replied. "The ones we use for officers, mainly to taxi people back and forth to the commercial landing port."

"What's the range?" she asked.

"Four hundred klicks fully charged."

"Which ones are fully charged?"

"None of 'em," he said. "We been using these all day. We charge 'em up at night."

"I need whichever one has the most range," she said.

"That would be this one," he said. "What's your cargo."

"I'm picking up an SSO squad."

"Can't do that in this," he replied.

"Why not?" Major Swift asked.

"Look at it. She's built for just four people, Major."

"This is an emergency," Major Swift said. "We'll make it work."

"Your funeral. That much weight will take a toll on the distance she'll travel."

Elaine Swift climbed behind the controls. "Thank you, Sergeant."

He stiffened to attention, saluting while she drove away. The cart was comfortable. It was a simple, boxy design. Four seats inside an enclosed cabin, with a small storage compartment in the back. It was built on a standard repulser lift, with an electric drive engine that propelled it. She negotiated through the base, then out of the colony. When she reached the edge of town, she pressed the throttles all the way forward and took off on her rescue mission.

CHAPTER 23

SKAR WAS high enough that he could see for a long way. But the air was thin and exceptionally cold. As a soldier, he was trained to ignore the conditions, but he was also smart enough to realize the danger. With a simple squeezing motion, Skar severed the silk ribbon that held him aloft. It shot upward while he plummeted downward. It might have been frightening if he hadn't performed the maneuver on multiple occasions across dozens of planets. As he fell, he began spooling out more silk. It only took a few seconds for the ribbon to slow his descent.

By the time he was a thousand meters above the ground, he reached the critical length of webbing to stay aloft. He was still moving downward but at a slow, controlled speed. All around him, there were other Lymies in similar states of motion. The wind continued to carry them toward their destination. The winds were moving an average of twenty-five kilometers per hour, which would require nearly six hours of flight time to reach the colony. How Skar knew this was unclear. He didn't know the distance to the human settlement, or the wind speed. But he could sense a major source of electromagnetic energy ahead of him, as well as his

motion toward said energy source. The information was simply in
his mind, the way an infant is comforted by the voice of its mother
despite the inability to know who she is, or why she should care
for it.

Skar was always cognizant of the other Lymies in his group.
They had been a full three hundred strong coming out of the pods.
The humans had effective weapons against them until their outer
skeletons hardened. He felt another three hours was needed before
he was ready to go to war. It would have been better to approach on
the ground, the enemy having no knowledge of their presence. Skar
had hoped to coordinate his own attack, with the regimens taking
down the other human settlements. But in war, things rarely went
according to plan. He was used to improvising and making the most
of the opportunities presented to him. His regimen was down
almost sixty fighters. The shooters on the ground had taken out
over three dozen, and the drones in the skies had killed the rest. But
two hundred and forty was a sufficient number to attack the settlement from the air. Darkness would descend before Skar's fighters
did. And once they were in the settlement, there would be plenty
of physical dwellings to offer cover while his brothers and sisters
closed in on the enemy. Then the feasting would begin.

Drifting on the wind had other advantages too. They had all
been marching without a stop for several days. The rest would give
them a boost in energy just when it was needed most. Skar relished
the battle to come. There was nothing like dropping onto an enemy
out of the sky. It was fast and vicious, and tactically superior to
meeting them on open ground. Humans, like many other races,
were terrified of enemies who came at them from above. Skar
planned to harness the power of their fear, and let it propel him to
total victory over the human colonists. Once the world was in their
control, the Lymies could turn their attention to passing through
the portal to the next system. It was estimated that there were
billions of humans in their home system. Maybe even a trillion of
them. More than enough to feed the Lymies for years before the

humans were eradicated. And nothing could stop the Lymies. There's was a superior race, linked to a collective intelligence greater than any in the galaxy.

Skar let the wind take him. Sometimes he rose higher, and other times he descended. It was all dependent on the air temperatures. Warm air rose, and cold air fell. There was more lift over the dry land, while the colder sections settled over the wide bodies of scummy pond water. There were mists too, wide banks of fog that covered the swampy terrain. From above, he could see the wildlife. There was plenty of substance on New Terra, as the humans called it. Skar's kin would feast here and multiply their numbers. Of course, Skar wouldn't be among them. He would be sealed in a pod to rest on the long journey to the next world he was tasked with conquering. A few more hours and the real work would begin. His was an occupation of slaughter and suffering.

CHAPTER 24

"COULD BE A SCAM," Flash said.

They were jogging together in a line, the same way they ran the cross-country trail around Alpha Colony, only slower, their legs weighed down with the weight of the mud and muck clinging to them.

"Why lie?" Jingo asked.

"Motivation," Flash said. "Ain't no major gonna risk their neck for a bunch of grunts."

"We aren't just grunts," Mara said.

"Damn straight," Jingo said. "We're the best of the best."

"I think what she means is we represent a significant financial investment," Ninja added.

"The LE program ain't cheap," Jingo said.

"Besides, if she wasn't coming," Mara said, "why bother telling us anything at all? Why not just let us die out here on our own?"

It was the question that had been playing in Mitch's mind ever since he took the call with Major Swift. He knew her, but not well. He thought she was a decent person, so the promise that she was coming to their aid seemed believable. But at the same time, she was a Marine, with superiors to answer to. Mitch hadn't been a Marine very long and didn't know much about New Terra's colony administrators, but if they were actually evacuating, he didn't think they would let Major Swift run off on what would be considered a fool's errand.

Even if he could believe everything she said to him, Mitch knew there were a thousand reasons why she might never show. She could be ordered not to go. She could be killed in the process of getting out of the colony. Or she could run into a group of aliens who weren't flying on ribbons of silk that shot out of their posterior in a way Mitch had never seen or imagined before.

"It could all be part of the test," Ninja said.

"Those bugs weren't a test, bro," Flash said. "We all seen 'em with our own eyes."

"That could be a hologram," Ninja insisted. "They've got all kinds of illusions they use in psyops man. They can make you see stuff that ain't there and hear voices in your head from a thousand klicks away."

"You sound like a conspiracy theorist," Mara pointed out.

"Look around you, bro," Jingo argued. "We're running through the proof."

He was talking about the bloody body parts of the aliens that had been killed in the attack. And there were plenty of gory bits left on the ground, including quite a few of the spidery bodies. Mitch hadn't been surprised to see the Razor Gators coming out of the ponds to eat the dead Lymies. Some were pulled back to the water, others were ripped apart out in the open. Mitch had forced himself and his squad mates to rest for nearly an hour after getting the call. They sat on the wet ground, ate cold rations, and drank water that had a strange chemical taste from the iodine tablets. Still, after a long morning of recon, eventually closing with the enemy and surviving his first firefight, Mitch had needed the time to recuperate. If the warning about the colonies evacuating had been true, then they wouldn't reach them in time no matter how hard they tried. Even on level, dry ground, with a strong back wind, and plenty of rest beforehand, it was impossible to run a hundred and fifty kilometers in less than a day. But they weren't on flat, dry ground, but rather very wet, clinging bogs. They were forced to circumnavigate around large standing pools of water. After the hour of rest, they set out at a comfortable pace, but it would have taken them days to reach the settlement at that rate.

"If this isn't real, I buy you all dinner and drinks," Mitch said.

"See, the LT knows what's what," Jingo said.

"Maybe," Flash argued.

"The officers can be tricky," Ninja added.

"There's no point to any of this," Mara said. "Either they come for us, or we're screwed."

"I ain't getting my hopes up," Flash said.

They ran on for a few minutes in silence. Everyone was dealing with raw emotions. The training exercise had been bad enough, but the thought of the colonies being overrun was difficult to comprehend. But Mitch could envision it. The Lymies could fall in out of the sky. He had heard of such things happening in Earth's rainforests long ago. Poisonous spiders could drop down out of trees on tiny webs. If they fell on a person and bit them, the person would get sick, maybe die. It was a frightening prospect, but the thought of the enormous Lymies falling on a person was much worse.

Mitch had thought he knew how big they were. He had been watching them for a long time before their run between the bodies of the slain aliens. But up close he realized how wrong he had been. In death, the Lymies flopped onto their backs and their long legs curled in. They almost seemed to deflate, and yet the bodies were still bigger than Mitch was. They were big, powerful creatures, and the ends of their legs were pointed like the tip of a spear. Worst still, was the massive stinger that stuck up from the rear underbelly. In life they could drop down on a person and stab them with that curved stinger, which probably also injected some kind of toxin. It was a horrific thought.

His imaging of how one might die by the spider creatures was interrupted by a terrifying hiss. Mitch didn't have to give the order to stop. The Lion squad froze in their tracks as two huge creatures moved from behind the body of a dead Lymie.

"Razor Gators," Jingo said.

Not that anyone was in doubt of what the creatures were. They were long bodied animals, with short legs, and an arching fin on their backs. Mitch wasn't sure, but he guessed the fin was as sharp as it looked, and hence the name *razor gator*. There were no more alligators on earth. The species had gone extinct long ago, but there was video of the creatures, and their cousins the crocodile was still around in zoos. The razor gator was much the same. It had a tough, scaly hide, a long, powerful tail, and worst of all, a triangular head with dozens of pointed teeth which it revealed as the mouth opened when it hissed a warning.

"Doesn't want us getting close to its meal," Ninja said.

There was water on either side of them. Mitch looked over into the murky pools and saw movement just beneath the surface. The wildlife was in a frenzy. Going around the animals wasn't an option. Instead, he drew his Desert Eagle and fired at the Razor Gators. The pistol made a loud popping noise. The .45 caliber hollow point rounds packed punch but didn't do much damage against the razor gator's tough hide, or thick skull. The bullets just bounced off, but the animals backed up.

"Damn," Flash said, drawing out the word. "LT don't play."

"We need to keep—"

Mitch was cut off when a creature that looked like a mash up between an octopus, and lobster reared out of the water behind the razor gators. It had a dark red body with what appeared to be segmented shells along its back. It narrowed into a tail, which fanned out, but the real threat was the trio of tentacles where a lobster normally had claws. The tentacles flew forward, latched onto the razor gators and pulled them toward the water. The animals roared, water splashed, and the squad of Marines opened fire. Mara shot first, her automatic shotgun chugging in her hands and blowing chunks from the lobster creature's exoskeleton. Flash, Jingo, and Ninja opened up with their GARs. The garrison rifles fired three round bursts with every pull of the trigger. The ultra-hard depleted uranium tipped bullets punched through the scaly skin of the razor gators, and the hard, segmented shell covering the lobster monster. The beast fell back under the sudden barrage, disappearing into the murky water with a splash.

"Keep moving," Mitch shouted.

The order wasn't born out of some natural instinct to lead, but rather from fear of staying anywhere near the massive swamp creature. The members of Lion squad didn't need much prompting either. They jogged ahead, combat boots flinging up mud with every step. As they passed the pond that the lobster animal had come from, they could see the water moving in a frenzy.

"That thing ain't dead!" Flash declared.

"Nothing makes a predator into prey faster than getting wounded," Mara pointed out.

"All the little fish are getting payback while they can," Jingo said.

"Every fish is a little fish compared to that monster," Ninja added.

"I see something," Hawk declared. "Movement ahead."

"Another creature?" Mitch asked, fearing the worst.

"Looks mechanical," Hawk replied. "A hover vehicle."

"Could be our ride out of here," Mara said.

"Let's hope so," Mitch said. "Spread out just in case."

They had passed between the two ponds by that point, and the squad spread out to keep from being an easy target. It didn't take long before the dot on the horizon became a vehicle. Hawk used her optical scope to zero in on the approaching hover cart.

"One of ours," she said.

At the same time, Mitch's data cuff beeped. It didn't have real comlink features, but at close range, without interference, it could receive messages. He glanced down and saw text scroll across the device on his wrist.

"I'm approaching your squad," the text said. "Don't shoot."

"At ease, Lions," Mitch said. "That's our ride."

"Seems small," Jingo said.

"Better to be cramped than to keep running through this boggy swamp," Flash said.

They all breathed a sigh of relief as Major Swift's hover cart came into view. It was small, too small for all of them to fit inside, but they were Marines, and improvisation in hostile territory was part of their motto.

The car stopped a few meters from where Mitch stood. The sun was setting and he was grateful not to have to spend one more night in the swampy wilderness.

"You order a ride?" Major Swift said as her window opened.

"Yes, ma'am!" Mitch said. "We are grateful, Major. Load up, Lions."

Weapons were loaded into the storage compartment in the back. Mitch settled into the front passenger seat. Mara, Hawk, and Ninja squeezed into the back two seats. Jingo and Flash had to climb up onto the roof of the hover cart and lay on their stomachs. They held onto the edge of the doors, and the top of the windshield.

"Next time, order a bigger ride, LT," Flash said.

"Better hang on tight," Major Swift said. "We don't have time to stop and pick you up if you fall off."

"Wonderful," Jingo said.

Major Swift turned the hover cart around. She made a wide, slow turn, making sure that no one was shaken off the vehicle. Mitch could see that the power indicator was down to just twenty-four percent of total battery life.

"Will we make it back?" he asked.

"We're going to try," Elaine Swift said. "We'll get closer at any rate."

"Did you see the enemy, Major?" Mara asked.

"Yes," was all she said, as the officer pushed the throttle slowly forward and fed power to the repulser lift.

The cart rose up almost three meters from the ground and proceeded over land and water with ease. Not like the super soldiers, who were slowed by the soft ground and clinging mud. It was a relief to see the landscape flashing by beneath them.

"I'm assuming none of this was part of the field exercise," Mara asked.

"No," Major Swift said. "But if your squad hadn't been out here, we might have been hit completely unaware."

"Wouldn't radar have picked up the Lymies?" Ninja asked.

"It might have registered something if they took to the air," Major Swift said. "But the ground is too undulating to get a solid read on organic life. It's designed to ping off vehicles and war machines, not swarms of Lymie warriors."

"We hit them," Mara said. "They didn't seem so tough."

"Your attack was successful?" Major Swift asked.

"We succeeded in killing them," Mitch said. "Forty or fifty of them, before they took to the air."

"And they didn't retaliate?"

"No," Mitch said. "Just flew away."

"Interesting," Major Swift said.

"How's that, Major?" Mara asked.

"We've fought the Lymies before," the officer explained. "Usually in small groups of ten or twelve. They've always had very tough organic covering over their vitals, some type of exoskeletal growths. Even the GAR rounds don't penetrate it."

"The perfect armor," Ninja said.

"We've been forced to use alternative weapons and tactics," she went on. "My guess is the swarm isn't ready for battle yet. But they probably will be by the time they reach Alpha Colony."

"Any read on when that'll happen?"

"Before we're ready," Elaine said. "We're moving the colonists out to the launch area, and loading them onto shuttles as fast as possible, but people don't want to leave their lives behind. Most of the colonists are tough people, and some would rather fight than run."

"But we're not fighting?" Ninja asked.

"How many Lymies were there?" Major Swift asked.

"At least three hundred," Mara said. "They were bunched up, and in the fog, it was impossible to get an accurate count."

"That many fighters, coming by air will overwhelm the colony's defenses," Major Swift said.

"We don't have ground-to-air weapons?" Ninja asked.

"We do, but they're designed to hone in on high, heat-producing engines, not organics."

"Bullets will do the trick," Mitch said. "Won't they?"

"Maybe," Elaine consented. "It's possible you forced their hand and maybe they aren't ready to go to battle. But if they are, bullets won't work. And shooting straight up is dangerous."

"You think they'll just descend on the colony?" Mitch asked.

"It's a sound strategy. My guess is they'll attack after dark. We won't have all the colonists out by then. The stubborn ones won't leave, and we won't have time to go door to door. The rifle platoons are set to guard the civilians waiting for transport at the launch port. We've got more coming in from the other colonies too."

"They can't make orbit from their own cities?" Ninja asked.

"They can, but there are only so many shuttles. When people are afraid, they get anxious and do stupid things."

"Some will be left behind," Mitch said, realizing the danger, "while they're trying to get to Alpha Colony."

"We'll do all we can, but we can't protect everyone."

"We need aerial support," Mara said. "Gunships to attack the Lymies in the air."

"Correct," Major Swift agreed. "Only, there aren't any."

"No gunships?" Mitch asked.

"The fighters in the ships protecting the system can't fly in atmosphere," she explained. "The colonies were supplied with drones for aerial support."

"And they can't fly because the Lymies jam the signals," Mitch said. "The perfect storm."

The hover car fell silent for a while as everyone contemplated the situation. Thousands of aliens were advancing on the human colonies. The best the CMC could do was slow them down. People were going to die, both Marines and civilians. Mitch wanted to do something, but there was nothing he could do. They were stuck in the little vehicle, still eighty kilometers from Alpha Colony. They all watched the power supply on the hover cart dwindle down toward zero. It was down to just fourteen percent, and dropping fast.

CHAPTER 25

THE HOVER CART was still thirty-eight kilometers from Alpha Colony when it lost power. It slowed, losing altitude, but Major Swift had been smart enough to drop them down to half a meter from the ground when the vehicle dropped to three percent power. They hit with a thump and slid several meters before coming to a complete stop.

Flash's face appeared in front of the windshield. "Bathroom break?"

"Very funny," Mitch said. "We're hiking in from here."

They climbed out of the hover cart and retrieved their weapons. Jingo spoke up, "We got a decent look at the bad guys."

"Did you get a count?" Major Swift asked.

"More than two hundred," Flash replied. "Some were pretty high up, others, looked to be descending."

"How far back?" Mitch asked, as he slung the MAX support harness over his head.

"Twenty-five or thirty klicks," Jingo answered. "As best as I could tell."

"That was our assessment too," Major Swift said. "We're just under forty to the Colony."

"Once we get moving, we'll stay ahead of them," Mitch said.

"I'm in decent shape," the major said. "But I can't run twenty-four miles."

"Run while you can," Mitch suggested. "When you get tired, Jingo will carry you."

"Got any weapons, Major," the hulking Marine asked.

"No," she said.

"At least there's no extra weight," Flash said.

"How is everyone on ammo?" Mara asked, trading the round canister her automatic shotgun used for her lone replacement.

"About half," Ninja said.

"Ditto," Flash responded.

"Leave your empties," Mitch suggested. "Backpacks too. We carry weapons and water only."

"Roger that," Jingo said.

"Once we get a little closer, you should be able to reach Captain Marcs," Elaine told Mitch. "He's in charge of the SSO squads defending the colony."

"Alright, let's move out," Mitch said.

He still had three full ammo canisters, along with his pistol, and the mini-rocket launcher. His stomach was growling, but there was no time to eat. He took a long pull from his canteen, grateful for the water even if it had a medicinal tang to it.

They started running at what the squad of enhanced Marines thought of as a slow jog. It soon became clear that Major Swift was struggling just to keep up. The terrain was better than it had been. The swamp had given way to grassland, but it was uneven and rocky. Major Elaine Swift was wearing polished dress shoes, not combat boots. And despite the falling temperatures, she was soon sweating freely, her usually neat appearance was lost.

"Take this, bro," Jingo said, handing Flash his GAR and going down on one knee. "Climb on Major."

"Are you sure?" she asked.

"You probably weigh less than the backpack I usually carry," he said. "No sweat."

She stepped up onto his massive thigh and put her feet onto the thick gun belt he wore around his waist. His battle armor had a canvas strap at the back of his neck for pulling a wounded Marine out of harms way. She held onto that as he stood up. Mitch was seven feet, four inches tall. Jingo was a couple of inches taller and built like a power lifter. His back was so wide that Elaine had to stretch to reach his shoulders.

"You okay there?" Mitch asked her.

"Yes," Major Swift said.

"You get tired, one of us will help you," Mitch told Jingo.

"I can go thirty-five klicks with the major on board, no problem, LT."

"Then let's do it," Mitch said.

It felt good to run. The group formed pairs and ran at a steady pace, but much faster than before. Mitch was running beside Mara at the rear of their formation, with Hawk running beside Jingo, and Flash running beside Ninja at the front. They all felt a little lighter than they had running in the swamps. Mitch felt a spring in his step and was taking wide strides. Major Swift had no trouble hanging on. She didn't look comfortable, but she was secure. And Jingo didn't seem to even notice the additional weight.

"How long have you known the Major?" Mara asked Mitch.

"Four weeks, I think," he replied.

"Are the two of you..."

"What? An item? No," he said shaking his head.

"But she wants to be."

"I don't think so," Mitch told her.

"Come on, Lieutenant. Why would she risk her neck to come out here if she wasn't into you."

Mitch had to think about that for a moment. He respected

Major Swift. She had been his tutor on the *Wellington*, taking him through an abbreviated officer's training course."

"She's a scientist," Mitch said. "I think she sees me like a test subject."

"A test of what?" Mara asked, clearly not convinced.

"An officer maybe," Mitch said. "Most days we have a debrief together."

"Maybe that's her way of spending time with you."

"I just don't get that vibe from her," Mitch said.

"And you're good at reading people?"

That made Mitch give Mara a hard look. The light was fading. Mara's face was flushed, but not yet sweating. They were all filthy, but somehow Mara's tight braids were holding, and she looked all the more fierce.

Finally, he shrugged. "Maybe not."

"At least you know yourself," Mara said. "That makes you a better officer than most I've served with."

Mitch felt that having a love relationship with Major Swift would be inappropriate. Not that he really wanted one. She was attractive, but he saw her as a mentor, nothing more. His feelings for Mara were growing stronger, and there was chemistry there, but he felt like pursuing that relationship would be inappropriate as well. He was an officer, she was an enlisted Marine. He needed to maintain a certain distance from his squad, even though he felt like they were the only people in the galaxy who really understood what he had gone through with the LE Protocols. They alone knew how intoxicating his new abilities were. Navigating his way forward wouldn't be easy. He could control his feelings, but not those of others. Still, knowing that Major Swift might possibly have amorous intentions would help him as he moved forward with his new career.

"I see lights ahead," Hawk called out.

"A city on a hill," Ninja replied. "What a beautiful sight."

Major Swift turned her head and called out to Mitch. "Try your data cuff."

He would have used the satellite phone, but its battery had died. Instead, he brought up the messaging application and recorded himself as he ran.

"Captain Marcs, this is Lieutenant Murphy, Leo Squad, with Major Swift. We are approaching Alpha Colony, nine kilometers out, requesting instructions and aid. I repeat, Leo Squad is nine klicks from AC with Major Swift. We request instructions and aid. Over."

He hit the send button, but the data cuff was still out of range of the colony's wireless networks. They kept running, and it wasn't long before his data cuff vibrated with an incoming message. He held it up and tapped the messaging icon. A hologram of Captain Marcs' face appeared above his wrist.

"Well done, Leo Squad. Join Kilo squad at the power station on the north side of town. They'll have supplies and transport for the major."

The short message ended. The hologram disappeared. Mitch raised his voice. "Head for the power station."

They were near the end of their journey, and the squad sped up. It only took ten minutes to race the last seven kilometers to the power station.

"Look what the cat dragged in," Sergeant Stevens said.

"Leo Squad," Mitch said.

"We're Kilo," a short man with brown skin and gap between his two front teeth said. He had a single, silver bar on the collar of his fatigue shirt, and unlike the SSO Marines he commanded, he wasn't wearing a battle helmet. "I'm Lieutenant Sazar."

"I'm Murphy. We have Major Swift with us."

Sazar snapped to attention. "Welcome, Major."

"At ease, Lieutenant," Elaine said, as Jingo dropped to a knee and helped her down. She shook her hands and stretched her back, before patting Jingo on the shoulder. "Thank you for the ride, Corporal."

"Any time Major," he said.

"Captain Marcs said to send the major through, but we're here to help," Mitch told Sazar, who gave him a dirty look.

"You want food," he said. "Joker, Zorro, that's you."

"Yes sir, Lieutenant," a tall SSO Marine said. "Chow is this way."

Mitch led his people through the double doors of the power building. It was a big complex laid out like a circuit board, with various power banks, and battery systems that supplied power to the colony. Just inside the doors was a folding table with metal trays. One was nearly empty, the other had thick burritos wrapped in aluminum foil.

"I made these myself," said a Marine with a livid scar on his face that made his mouth pucker to one side. "They're mostly seasoned rice, with some grilled chicken, onions, corn, black beans, peppers, and cheese."

"Outstanding," Flash said. "We're starved."

"We've got powder for your canteens too," the tall Marine said.

Jingo picked up two burritos and immediately started eating. Mitch was starving too, but he let his squad get all they wanted first. Mara dumped the filter pond water from her canteen and rinsed it with fresh water from a drinking fountain, before refilling it and dumping in some of the electrolyte/BCAA powder in and shaking it up. Mitch followed her lead, refilling his canteen and drinking half of it down almost immediately.

"You guys had a long hike?" the Marine called Joker asked.

"Our wheels ran out of juice about forty klicks outside town," Ninja said.

"Y'all look like you was hip deep in the mud bogs before that," the taller Marine said.

"We were," Jingo told him, after swallowing a massive bite of food. "Training exercise."

"See anything while you was out there?" Joker asked.

"Lymies," Ninja said.

"Spider aliens," Flash added. "We hit 'em from behind, but they took off flying on us."

"So, the rumors are true," the tall man said. "How do they fly?"

"Like spiders," Jingo said. "They spin ribbon that catches the wind and carries 'em up."

"You have spotters?" Mitch asked.

"Gabe's our shooter. Sampson is his spotter. They're both on watch with night vision overlaid with thermal," Joker said. "Those bugs come this way, we'll know it."

"Outstanding," Jingo said.

Mitch got himself a burrito and was busy devouring it when Lieutenant Sazar came into the building with Major Swift right behind him. He was taller than she was, with a thick build and tight-fitting fatigues that showed off his muscles, but he still seemed very small in comparison to the SSO Marines he commanded.

"Our orders are to spot and slow down the enemy," he said to Mitch.

"We can help with that," Mitch said.

"You'll be under my command," Sazar said.

It was a challenge. Mitch didn't know what the man expected to happen, but he had no intention of breaking the chain of command. First Lieutenant Sazar was clearly the senior officer, at least without Major Swift stepping in.

"Yes sir," Mitch said. "Tell us what you want, and we'll get right on it."

"The enemy is coming, but there's time to prepare," Swift said. "I recommend you let Leo Squad arm up and come back to help you, Lieutenant."

He looked annoyed that she had put him a position to follow her orders, rather than give his own. But he nodded in acceptance of the order.

"You'll want non-conventional weapons too," she continued.

"Standard ammo isn't going to stop the Lymies if they've got hardened exo-skeletons in place."

"We could get flame throwers and mini-rocket launchers," Mitch suggested.

"Plasma rounds for the shotguns," Sazar said. "We'll stop the bugs one way or another. My squad is forming up on the rooftop. I want you to rally down here, just inside the building. I'll coordinate the attack once the Lymies get here."

"Roger that," Mitch said. "Leo Squad, on me. Let's get geared up for a fight."

"Boo-ya!" Flash said.

"Time to get some!" Jingo added.

They were still eating as they wound their way through the building, between the big power banks that hummed in the stillness and made their skin tingle. Major Swift stayed with them and jogged through the colony streets toward the base. Just inside the enclosed military area was an armory. As his squad mates got weapons and armor, Major Elaine Swift said goodbye.

"This is where I leave you," she said.

"We wouldn't be here without you, Major," Mitch said. "Do you want an escort to the evacuation site?"

"No, I'll be fine from here. Make us proud, Lieutenant Murphy. Show the galaxy what an SSO officer can do."

"I won't let you down," he said.

She hesitated for a moment, as if she was going to say more. But then she turned and hurried away. Mitch didn't have time to speculate. When he turned around Mara was handing him a fully functional battle helmet. He pulled the training helmet off and put the new one on. It immediately synced with his data cuff, the HUD came on illuminating the inner face shield. He selected squad commander and the unit connected with the battle armor of each member of his team.

"We're online," Mitch said. "Weapons?"

Jingo handed him a tactical shotgun and four twelve-round magazines of short-range plasma cartridges.

"We're ready," Flash said, holding up a flame thrower. He had a fuel tank strapped across his back.

"We've got mini-rocket crates too," Ninja said.

"We can carry two of them back," Mara said. "Flash take point. Let's get back into position."

Flash, Jingo, and Ninja all had flame throwers. Hawk brought up the rear, having refilled the empty magazine she had for the long range rail gun she carried. Mitch had a tactical shotgun, while Mara still had her automatic shotgun, albeit with three big round drums of plasma cartridges.

They hustled back through the colony and into the power station. Mitch connected his battle helmet's wireless system to Lieutenant Sazar's command chain and activated the platoon comlink.

"We're back, Lieutenant. We have enough laser-guided mini-rockets for our squad and yours."

"Very well, I'll send someone for them," Sazar said. "I'm holding your squad in reserve, since you haven't completed your officer training yet."

The words were a little hard to hear. Mitch knew he was just a rookie, but he wasn't helpless. It wasn't like his squad was brand new, and he could see the looks of irritation on their faces, but none spoke out. They were too disciplined for that.

"Yes sir."

"At least we can still eat," Jingo said, taking another burrito from the tray of food.

"Somebody wake me up when the shooting starts," Ninja said.

Mitch stepped through the open double doors. Beyond was a wide, concrete area where a fleet of electric vehicles were parked in neat rows. There was a wooden bench just outside the building to the right of the double doors. Mitch sat down, with Mara and Hawk. Estelle took the optical scope from her long rifle and held it up. The sky was clear from what Mitch could see, but they knew the enemy was coming. His data cuff had a weather app, which showed the temperature and wind direction. At the equator, it rarely got below freezing, but the temperatures were dropping from the low teens Celsius into the single digits. The wind continued blowing down from north to south.

"This wind should carry them straight toward us," Mitch said.

"Depending on how high, and how spread out they are," Mara said.

"I've got nothing," Hawk said, as she scanned the skies.

Mitch took a long drink from his nearly empty canteen and sighed. He was tired. Not exhausted, but he knew he needed time to regain his full strength. Sleep would help, but there was no time for that.

"Can I refill that for you, LT?" Flash asked from the doorway.

"Thank you," Mitch said, handing over his canteen.

"How many times have you been ordered to do that when you didn't spit in the canteen?" Jingo asked his friend as he munched on another burrito.

"I would never," Flash said, and both men broke into laughter.

"Get your people off the platoon channel," Sazar's voice crackled in Mitch's ear. He looked over at Jingo and Flash, who clearly hadn't heard the order.

"Yes sir," Mitch said, switching to his squad only channel. "You chuckle heads are on open coms."

They both whirled around, looking first at Mitch, then glancing up.

"Sorry, LT," Flash said.

"Our apologies, Lieutenant. That wasn't our intent."

"No worries," Mitch told him.

Mara bumped his shoulder with her. "It's been a long time since we had a commanding officer we could respect."

"I doubt that's true," Mitch said.

"Most are like Sazar. They have a chip on their shoulder when they get assigned to an SSO squad. They want to be special forces, but working with us rubs most of them the wrong way."

"It's called jealousy," Hawk pointed out, never looking away from her scope as she scanned the sky.

Stars were out but hidden by clouds that glowed pale silver.

"It's not that we blame them. They can't keep up. But few officers have the same endurance that a basic recruit has out of boot camp," Mara said. "Still, they struggle and feel a need to flaunt their authority at every opportunity. Just keep that in mind, Lieutenant. Sazar is not your peer, even if you think he is."

Mitch didn't reply, but he did make certain that Mara's comlink wasn't on the open channel. They sat there for nearly half an hour before the enemy appeared. Mitch could feel his exhaustion draining away into a general tiredness, which he was able to ignore when the time for action came.

"Contact," a voice that Mitch didn't recognize said. "Enemy units dead ahead."

"I see them," another voice echoed.

Hawk raised her free hand and pointed but didn't say anything. Mitch followed her lead and saw something dark against the silvery clouds.

"Captain Marcs, this is Lieutenant Sazar, we have enemy contacts inbound, over."

"Roger that, Sazar," Captain Marcs said. "Bravo, Delta, Indigo, respond when you see them."

There were several clicks of acknowledgement to the order. Mitch was slightly surprised he hadn't been included, but he was under Sazar's command and stayed quiet.

"Jingo, what's the range on the mini-rockets?" Mara asked.

"Four klicks maybe," he responded. "Let me check."

"You think the rockets will penetrate their armor?" Mitch asked.

"Maybe, maybe not," Mara said. "But I think it should severe their web support."

"Let 'em fall," Ninja said. "See if that kills 'em."

"Good thinking," Mitch said.

"Affirmative, four klicks," Jingo said from around the corner where the rocket crates were stowed in the power building.

"I want everyone with launchers," Mitch said quickly. "Make sure you've got reloads too."

The small, short-barreled launchers were simple weapons. Each one had dual pistol grips and took a wide magazine that loaded between them. The magazine was as long as a man's hand from the palm to fingertips. Inside was six rockets with solid fuel. They had extendable fins around the gas chamber at the bottom. It was filled with just enough flammable gas to propel the rocket out of the launcher and ignite the rocket fuel. The nose cone of the rocket was a low yield concussion warhead that would detonate on impact. Above the barrel was a laser that would guide the rocket to the target. All Mitch and his squad needed to do was to keep the laser on the body of the spidery aliens and the missile would hit it.

"Permission to engage," Lieutenant Sazar asked over the command channel.

"Granted. Give 'em hell, Kilo Squad."

"Fire at will!"

Mitch heard the hollow sounding pops as five mini-rockets were launched. The hollow pop from the rocket leaving the barrel of the launcher was followed by a savage hiss as the missile's fuel kicked in and sent the missile tearing through the sky. Mitch and his squad watched from the ground as the missile trails streaked through the sky.

"They're evading," Hawk pointed out.

Mitch could only see a few of the aliens, although there were dozens of dark spots against the clouds. All but one of the missiles missed their targets, lost power, and fell. It was, in many ways, a mistake that saved their lives. While the rest of his squad was looking up to see if the missiles hit, and Kilo Squad on the rooftop continued firing more laser guided mini-rockets, Mitch looked down to see the explosions from the rockets that missed. Their concussion warheads were still active. There were three distant booms, but that's not what caught Mitch's eye.

"Contact!" he shouted. "There's a ground force coming right at us!"

CHAPTER 26

THEY FIRED THEIR ROCKETS INSTINCTIVELY, probably because that's what they had in their hands. The little missiles popped out of the launchers like roman candles, almost instantly igniting the solid fuel boosters that sent them racing across the open ground at the edge of town. There was no need to aim. A swarm of well over a hundred Lymies were racing straight at the power building. Six mini-rockets exploded at the edge of the wide, paved, work yard. Mitch felt a surge of strength as the savage display of destructive power, but that feeling was dashed as more of the spidery aliens leaped through the still expanding flames.

"Jumpers!" Flash shouted.

The mini rocket launchers were fired again and again. The heat from the billowing explosions reached the Lion squad, who were forced back inside the building. Jingo, Flash, and Ninja took up their flame throwers, as Marauder, Hawk, and Mitch got behind them. Fountains of flames erupted. For a split second, while the aliens were screeching in pain, Mitch thought they were like dragons, but the sound of the aliens landing on the sides of the metal building shook him from the fantasy. Looking up, he saw the pointed ends of their feet punching through the metal siding. The power building was hot from the electrical currents passing through and didn't have insulation like most other structures on New Terra. Beside him, Mara raised her shotgun and fired. The plasma cartridge hit the metal and exploded, sending the super-hot gel onto the metal with a splat. In seconds, it burned through and left a jagged hole in the wall.

"These plasma rounds are useless," she said.

Mitch knew what was coming. The two SSO squads were formidable, but they were vastly outnumbered.

"Lieutenant, pull back," Mitch said, using the command channel.

"Who is this?" a frenzied voice snarled. "Stay off this line, Murphy!"

"Forget him," Mara urged Mitch.

It seemed outrageous that anyone would be so foolish, but Mitch knew pride had been the downfall of many people.

"Fall back," Mitch ordered. "Jingo, help me with the doors."

"Roger that, LT," the big man responded.

Flash and Ninja kept firing their flame throwers. The heat was intense, and it kept the Lymies away from the doors, but the weapons were sputtering as they ran low on the fuel in their tanks.

"Flash, Ninja, fall back," Mitch ordered.

They threw themselves backward through the building's doorway. Mitch was on one side, Jingo on the other. They swung the double doors closed and threw the locks which bolted into the top of the door jam, and down into the concrete flooring. They barely got the doors locked before a Lymie crashed into them on the other side. The doors were heavy metal, but the locks were metal bars. There wasn't much support on the inside of the entryway. The doors flexed in for a moment. Mitch knew they wouldn't hold the enemy back for long.

"What now?" Flash asked, dropping the spent flame thrower to the floor.

"We move," Mitch said.

He led the charge back through the building. They dodged the power banks and went around the stacks of industrial batteries, jumping over bundles of cables and ducking under metal conduits before reaching the exit on the far side of the building. All the while they could hear the shouting, shooting, and screams up on the roof. Some were human, some were alien. The Lymies had a unique way of moving, their pointed feet pounding on the metal roof.

Mitch pushed open the door and waved his people through. They didn't hesitate. Mitch was about to follow them through when a body hit the ground. For a moment Mitch froze in horror. Lieutenant Sazar lay face up, his eyes open wide in death.

"Up there!" Mara shouted. "Give them cover fire!"

Mitch dashed out of the building. It was dark outside, but on the rooftop and the far side of the power building, fires burned. The darkness was lit with yellow flames. Mitch looked up and saw four Marines on the edge of the building. It was twelve meters tall. The Marines up on the rooftop were blazing away with their Garrison Assault Rifles and seemed to be having some success with them. The Lymies were leaping to other structures and avoiding the deadly Marines.

"We have to help them," Mitch said, looking around.

"Here," Hawk said, standing next to an emergency fire node. There was thick, canvas hose, not the garden variety type, but the strong kind of hose used by firefighters. It was neatly coiled on a round spindle. Hawk was busy pulling it off.

"Jingo," Mitch said. "Can you throw that thing up to the rooftop?"

"On it," the big man said.

"Cover fire!" Mara shouted.

They were in a courtyard of sorts. The big power building was directly in front of them. To their left was the administration building, and to the right, where Hawk was uncoiling the fire hose, was the maintenance building. Neither were as large or as tall as the power building. Mitch fired his shotgun at a Lymie that leaped onto the roof of the admin building. The plasma cartridge hit the spider alien's body. He saw the blue plasma splatter as the cartridge exploded against flesh. The gel responded to the oxygen in the air. The chemical reaction was instant, the gel heating to nearly five hundred degrees celsius. Smoke billowed from the Lymie. It wailed in pain, a high pitched, keening noise. The plasma burned into the flesh, and caused the alien to limp, but it didn't stop the creature. It turned and lurched toward Mitch.

He fired again. The Lymie was on the edge of the roof, preparing to jump. Mitch didn't know if it could clear the thirty meters to where he stood, but he didn't like the idea of finding out either. His shot took the Lymie in its head segment, and once more the plasma did what it was designed to do. The alien didn't scream, but its burning head drooped, and it tumbled off the roof and landed with a crunch on the concrete below. It rolled onto its back, the four long, articulated legs curling in death.

Nearby, Jingo lifted the end of the fire hose. It had a brass nozzle, which he spun around and around, before flinging the hose up onto the roof of the power building.

"Kilo Squad, get that hose and tie it off," Mitch ordered over the command channel.

"We're kinda busy here," someone snapped.

But one of the Marines grabbed the hose and bent to tie it off. Mitch pointed to Jingo, but he and Hawk were already turning the spindle to tighten the line. The big man waited until the Marine on the rooftop straightened up, then he pulled the hose tight, bracing the spindle with his big body.

"Slide down, Kilo team," Mitch said. "That's an order."

The same Marine who had tied off the hose was the first one down. He grabbed the hose and jumped off the building. Jingo grunted at the sudden strain, but held the hose taut. The Marine from Kilo Squad slid halfway down then dropped. He landed lightly on his feet, his knees flexing on impact.

"That's one," Mara declared as she swapped out the plasma ammunition for a barrel of shotgun slugs.

Mitch still had his MAX on the harness. He dropped the tactical shotgun on the ground with half a mag of plasma cartridges still waiting to be fired and went to work with the .50 caliber machine gun. It blazed to life, sending fountains of hot lead toward a group of Lymies congregating on the corner of the power building's roof. Not every bullet penetrated the thick hide that covered their bodies. But some did, and those that didn't, knocked the aliens down with the kinetic energy transfer. The big machine guns bullets ripped through their spindly legs. The GARs were having even more success with their hardened tipped bullets. They punched inside the aliens and exploded, sending jagged shrapnel tearing through their vital organs.

Like a flock of birds, or a school of fish, the alien swarm shifted directions and dropped off the buildings to avoid the deadly fire of the SSO teams, just as a second member of Kilo Squad slid down the makeshift zip line.

"That's two," Mara said.

"They're running," Flash said. "We got 'em scared."

"They're just changing tactics," Mitch said. "Taking cover until they can get closer."

"What should we do?" Ninja asked.

His squad had stopped shooting and were scanning for any signs of the aliens.

"That's a good question," Mitch said, toggling his comlink to the command channel. "Captain Marcs, this is Lieutenant Murphy, Leo Squad. We got hit hard sir. Lieutenant Sazar is dead. Looks like Kilo is down to just four Marines, but we turned the aliens. They're avoiding our fire."

"Copy that, Lieutenant. What's working best to kill those bastards?"

"The GARs are making the most impact," Mitch said. "Not everything else penetrates."

"Copy that, we'll pass along the word. I want you to take command of Kilo Squad, Murphy. You draw back, through the colony. Harass the enemy wherever you find them. Make your way to the airfield for exfil. Is that clear, Lieutenant?"

"Yes sir. We will pull back, through the colony, harass the enemy, and rally at the airfield for exfiltration, sir!"

"Very good, Murphy. Watch your six. You've got half an hour. Don't be late. Marcs out."

By that point all four Kilo Squad's surviving members were on the ground. Joker and Zorro were there, along with Cheetah and Rocky. They moved close to Leo Squad.

"Kilo, you're with us now," Mitch told them.

"What happened to Ace?" Ninja asked the four survivors.

Joker explained. "Got hit by a Lymie. The bug jumped right on top of him."

"He killed it," Zorro said, "but it knocked him backward through a skylight."

"He was impaled on something," Cheetah said, shaking his head. "Might have lived through it, but it was some kind of live wire."

"Don't matter how he died," Rocky said, "only how he lived."

"Well said," Mara agreed.

"We're pulling back," Mitch said. "Our orders are to move through town."

"Looking for anyone who didn't get out?" Jingo asked.

Mitch shook his head. "There's no time. In half an hour the last transports will dust off. If we ain't on them..."

"What about the bugs?" Rocky asked.

"We kill them," Mitch said. "You see one, you take it down."

"Copy that, Lieutenant," the big man from Kilo Squad said.

Mitch didn't have to ask about special talents. Every SSO

member took on a nickname that explained what they were best at. It was obvious that Cheetah was a speedster, Rocky was a strongman. Zorro probably preferred blades, much like Ninja on Mitch's squad.

"Flash, Cheetah, take point," Mitch said. "We move fast, and we stay quiet when we can. I don't want to draw the Lymies down on our location. And stay away from narrow alleyways."

"Copy that, LT," Flash said.

"The rest of us will follow, but don't bunch up," Mitch ordered. "And stay away from tight places. We don't want to give these bugs the advantage."

"You want me to bring up the rear?" Rocky asked.

"I've got that," Mitch said.

"Pretty dangerous at the back, sir. You should let us take the heat."

"He can handle himself," Mara said. "Besides, our weapons are best at holding the bugs off."

"We'll keep them off our six," Mitch said. "You send them to hell, or wherever they go when they're dead."

"Yes, sir," Rocky said.

It was an obvious change for him. He was used to having to protect his commanding officer. That wasn't really much different from most Marine platoons. Leaders shouldn't put themselves into harms way too often if they can avoid it, but there was a feeling of brotherhood among the two SSO squads. They were depending on each other for survival, and it seemed that everyone was willing to pull their own weight.

"Let's move!" Mitch ordered.

The group spread out, following Flash and Cheetah away from the cluster of buildings where Mitch had fought his first real battle. Adrenaline, combined with the speed at which everything was happening, kept Mitch from dwelling on the fear he felt. He hadn't even noticed the power going out across the colony, which made the town dark and ominous. Somehow, it felt wrong to be moving away from the light of the fires behind them, and into the gloom of city.

"Switching to low light amplification," Mitch said.

It was an unnecessary order, but announcing it was how he was taught. In the shock of the attack, his training over the past two weeks, first on the *Wellington* and then with Leo Squad on Alpha Base, was kicking in hard.

"The colony is deserted," Flash reported. "Streets look clear."

"How far is the rally point?" Joker asked.

Mitch had to check the navigation app. His data cuff ran the information and projected it onto the Heads Up Display of his battle helmet's face screen.

"Eighteen kilometers," Mitch said.

"We better pick up the pace," Mara suggested.

"Stay in the middle of the road," Mitch urged his people.

"They can jump clear across it," Ninja said. "I'm not sure—"

"Contact!" Rocky shouted, his GAR blazing a three-round burst that tore through a flimsy safety railing around the top of a building. One of the Lymies dropped to the ground, curling up in death, but two more leaped away in opposite directions.

"Where'd it go?" Mara asked.

Mitch had tracked the alien that had jumped in their direction, but it fell into the shadows between the buildings.

"Stay alert," he warned.

"You want some of this!" Rocky bellowed. "Come and get it."

"Keep moving," Jingo told the big man.

"I ain't running," Rocky insisted.

"Move, Corporal! That's an order," Mitch said as he approached the big man.

Rocky didn't turn away or take a step. He was only an inch taller than Mitch, but thicker through the chest, shoulders, and neck. Mitch didn't back down either.

"We are on a mission, Rocky. Don't slow us down."

"Come on, bro," Jingo said. "There's plenty more to kill along the way."

Rocky made a sound that was part chuckle, and perhaps a choked off sob. He was a big, strong man, a warrior who could face any danger, but maybe seeing his friend get killed had wounded him in a way no alien or enemy could.

"Move!" Mitch ordered.

Rocky nodded, then turned and started up the street. It wasn't until then that Mitch noticed how close Jingo was. The big man was ready to step in if the situation required it. He gave Mitch a simple chin raise. It was a gesture of respect, no less than a salute at full attention would have been.

Suddenly, Mara's automatic shotgun chugged out a series of slugs. Mitch turned in time to see a Lymie in midair. It had leaped from the shadows straight toward Mitch and Rocky, but Mara had seen it. Her barrage of heavy slugs knocked it off course. It flew past Mitch, hit the sidewalk, and bounced through a plate glass window.

"Thanks," he said.

Mara nodded, as Rocky and Jingo both followed up with bursts from their Garrison Rifles. The harden points on their bullets punched through the walls and deep into the store. When there was no movement inside, Mitch pulled his attention back to the street.

"Move, move, move!" he barked.

Their flight through the town continued. Mitch kept his head on a swivel. The Marines in front of him turned around every so often, checking behind them as well as to either side. Mitch and Mara did the same.

"Contact," he said as they stopped on a cross street.

A cluster of Lymies were lingering over something. Mitch couldn't tell what it was at first. He and Mara raised their weapons at the same time. His MAX churned out fifteen rounds a second. Hers only fired five every second, but their combined attack was deadly. Four of the

Lymies went down, their legs hit and broken by the gunfire, or knocked over by the kinetic force of the impacting rounds. Two more jumped away, and a third screeched, before rushing toward them.

Mitch's tracers stitched across the alien's head. It dropped to the ground, rolling over, and curling up.

"This is taking too long," Mara said. "We need to move faster."

"We go faster and we risk running right into the aliens," Mitch argued.

"But at this rate, we won't make it. We need to run," Mara said. "The faster we get through this part of town, the better."

"Alright, Lions, Kilos, let's move," Mitch ordered. "Double time it."

"Running and gunning!" Cheetah said.

"It don't get no better, baby!" Flash cried out.

Mitch could run pretty fast but felt wrong to dash ahead knowing that at any moment a monster could attack. Perhaps it was inevitable that they would be ambushed. Maybe going slow would have only allowed the enemy to encircle them. Instead, the Lymies dropped from the dark sky right on top of the squad.

Ninja was hit first. A Lymie cut its ribbon when it was only a few meters over the group. It dropped nearly on top of Ninja and kicked him with one long, spindly leg. Ninja wasn't as tall as Flash, or as thickly muscled as Jingo. But he was still a formidable man. Stealth was his specialty. He could move through just about any terrain without being seen or heard, which was astounding for a man who stood seven feet tall and weighted two hundred and seventy-five pounds. Still, the alien's kick knocked him off his feet and sent him tumbling across the street.

Guns blazed, but there were nearly a dozen of the spidery aliens. Mitch fired a heavy volley, his tracers blazing into the dark sky. Some of the aliens dropped when they were shot and killed, others fell directly on their targets. Jingo was knocked to the ground, a Lymie landing right on top of him. It stabbed down with its barbed stinger. Somehow, Jingo caught the curved stinger in his hands and stopped it before it could stab into his chest.

Zorro wasn't so lucky. A Lymie landed on his back, pinning him to the ground. Its stinger rammed down and penetrated a gap in his armor at his lower back. It punctured his spine and injected some type of toxin. The man screamed. Hawk fired a round from her long range rail gun. At close range the rifle was so powerful, it made the alien's head explode. But the damage to Zorro was done. The alien dropped sideways, it's stinger retracting, its legs curling, but Zorro didn't move.

"Man down!" Hawk called out.

"I got him," Joker shouted.

But as he bent over his friend another Lymie dropped to the ground. Hawk was wracking in a new round, and even though Joker tried to dive out of the way of the Lymie's stinger, he didn't get far enough. The spidery alien raised a leg and stabbed down with the pointed foot. It stabbed through Joker's leg before Hawk could fire her LRRG. When she did, the Lymie was knocked backward, and nearly ripped Joker's leg from his body.

"Medic!" she screamed, running to help her comrade from Kilo Squad.

Mitch heard her, but had troubles of his own. A Lymie hit the street right in front of him. Mara raised her weapon, but the alien dropped to a prone position and swept her legs out from under her. Mitch had to jump back to avoid the same fate. He stumbled and fell on his side, the MAX pinned down beneath him. He was scrambling back up, moving faster than he would have thought possible, but not fast enough. The alien was on its feet in a flash. Mitch saw its stinger protrude, a drop of venom glistening on it as the alien started to jump on him. But just before it got off the ground, Jingo grabbed one rear leg, and Rocky got the other. The alien jumped but couldn't get away from the two big men.

"Wishbone!" Jingo shouted.

"Hell yeah!" Rocky replied.

They pulled in opposite directions. There was a loud crack and the leg Jingo was holding snapped. Rocky heaved and the leg he was holding actually tore out of the alien's body segment. It screamed, but Mara shot it in the face. Three heavy slugs made the head crack open and sent bloody brain matter flying into the air.

"Lieutenant!" Jingo shouted.

"Go!" Mitch replied. "Go!"

Mara was standing, but she couldn't put her weight down on her left foot. Mitch ran to her side.

"Damn thing cracked my ankle," she said.

"I got you," Mitch told her.

She threw her free arm over his shoulder and Mitch swiveled the MAX to his opposite side. He then wrapped his free hand around her waist, clutching her gun belt to lend his support.

"Thanks, Lieutenant," she said.

He was halfway carrying her as they ran around the bodies of the Lymies in the street. Ninja was shaken up, but okay. Joker wasn't as lucky. Hawk had gotten a tourniquet tied off on his upper thigh, but blood was still pouring out of the wound. Rocky picked the slightly smaller man up like he was a child. Joker was unconscious. Rocky hung him over one broad shoulder and started running.

Jingo knelt over Zorro and then looked back at Mitch.

"Is he dead?" Mitch asked.

"No, sir! But he's in bad shape."

"Can you—"

"Absolutely," Jingo replied. He rolled Zorro onto his back, pulled him up onto his broad shoulder, and started running.

The good news was they were almost out of town. The airfield and launch pad for orbital shuttles was only seven kilometers out of town, and a road ran straight out to it. But it was dark, and they could see shadows moving to either side of the road. They had only run a thousand meters when Flash and Cheetah started shooting at something in the road.

"Flash, what have you got," Mitch asked.

"Bad guy down," Flash said. "But you gotta see this, LT. It ain't right, man."

It was only a few seconds before Mitch caught up with the others. Their low light amplification took the color out of the world but allowed them to see in the dark. It wasn't like seeing in broad daylight, but clear enough for Mitch to know what he was seeing.

"Oh, hell no," Rocky said.

"They're eating them," Ninja said, referring to the Lymies eating one of the colonists.

The worst part was that the man, a balding, slightly overweight man in his forties, lay on the ground with his eyes wide open and shifting around from person to person.

"He's alive," Mitch said, although he couldn't see how. The Lymies had torn off huge chunks of flesh from his thighs and across his stomach. The man's intestines were bulging out of the wound. "Sir! Can you hear me?"

"Can't move," the dying man said, his voice barely a whisper.

"He's in shock," Mara said.

"I think it's the venom," Rocky said. "It must be some kind of paralyzing agent. I can't feel my hands. They're completely numb."

"Move out," Mitch said. "We can't save him."

The others took off, but Mitch hesitated. He drew his Desert Eagle and held it in front of the man.

"Please," the man said, tears streaming from the corners of his eyes. "End it."

Mitch pointed the gun at the man's forehead and fired. Mara looked away, and Mitch felt his own eyes stinging with tears as he holstered the Desert Eagle and started walking.

"I'm slowing you down," she said.

"No, you're fine," Mitch said.

"You could leave me," she said. "No one would blame you."

"That's crazy," Mitch said.

"You know I didn't like you at first," she confessed. "You were too calm, too willing to take criticism."

"I had a lot to learn," he said. "Still do."

"And you were humble. You look like us, but you act like you're not."

"What's that mean?" Mitch asked.

"We're different, Lieutenant. Special. We can do things normal people can't. How do you stay humble when you're physically superior to everyone around you?"

"I don't know," Mitch said. "I guess a decade of being walked on leaves a mark."

"But you're a good man," she said. "I could see that too. I didn't know how doing this would affect you. It can ruin a good person, you know?"

"You're good Mara," Mitch said. "Our squad is full of good people."

She leaned into him. "I'm glad it was you, sir. I'm glad you're our CO. Thanks for getting me out of here."

"We're not out of the woods yet," Mitch said.

They were close enough that they could see the air strip. There was a shuttle setting down on the landing pad, it's engines roaring. In their helmets over the command channel of the comlink they heard the order by Captain Marcs.

"This is us, SSO squads. Mount up or get left behind."

"We're almost there, sir," Mitch said. "Leo and Kilo Squads, with wounded."

"Move it, Murphy. This ship won't wait. The damn bugs are everywhere."

It was true. They had infiltrated the tall airfield building. The other SSO Marines were getting on board the shuttle via a metal staircase they had rolled into position. Mitch could hear screams from the airport building. There were still people inside, some fighting, others being eaten alive. The chatter from the Lymies was audible too, along with glass breaking and metal groaning as it was bent and broken.

"Let's go Lions, no time to waste," Mitch ordered.

He practically carried Mara, holding her up so that her good foot only touched the ground every so often. They had to run around the building, which was long, with a low roof and big windows. Perhaps going through the building would have been faster. Plenty of the windows were shattered, but Mitch could see dark shapes moving inside. They were too big to be people, and he shuttered at the thought of what was happening. Alpha Colony was lost, at least for the time being. Perhaps a battalion of Marines could land and clear it out again. He knew his squad alone had killed nearly a hundred of the Lymies. And a fight in broad daylight would be much easier to carry out.

"Move it!" an airman shouted to them as they raced around to the side of the airport where the ships landed and took off.

The shuttle was the only aircraft in sight. It was a standard military transport, not the posh civilian type of aircraft. But it had thick armor and a powerful engine. The rear hatch was folded down, making a ramp. Mitch followed his squad, and the survivors of Kilo Squad, across the tarmac. But they weren't the only people there. At least a dozen civilians were rushing toward the ship. Mitch, even burdened with Mara, outpaced them easily.

"It's about damn, time!" Captain Frank Marcs growled as they rushed up the ramp into the rear of the ship.

"Sorry for the delay sir," Mitch said, helping Mara into a jump seat.

She immediately strapped in.

"You're lucky, Murphy. This is the last vessel going out tonight," Captain Marcs said, moving to the rear control.

Mitch could hear the civilians screaming for them to wait as the shuttle's engines began to spool up.

"Sir," Mitch said, "what about the civilians?"

"No room," the captain said.

Mitch saw a man with a little girl in his arms. She had blood on her face from a cut in her scalp and looked terrified. Her father was screaming for them to wait.

"Sir!" Mitch said.

"There's no room, Lieutenant," Marcs snarled. "Grab a seat or get off the deck. Makes no difference to me. He pressed the intercom button, "Pilot, we are clear for lift off."

"Copy that," the pilot said calmly.

The rear hatch slowly began to close. Mitch was still standing on it. He saw a Lymie leap out of the airport and land on top of a woman struggling with a heavy suitcase. The running lights on the shuttle came on, illuminating the carnage. The man with the little girl was so close. Mitch could see the desperation on the man's face.

"Take her! Please! Save her!" the father yelled.

Mitch looked at Mara. She had pulled her helmet off and was pale from the pain of her broken ankle.

"Sorry Sergeant," Mitch said. "Look after the lions for me."

"Lieu—"

Mitch didn't wait. He jumped out of the ship, grabbed the father and his wounded daughter, and flung them over the end of the ramp. Then he slung his Max around and started shooting.

CHAPTER 27

THE MACHINE GUN'S tracer rounds stitched across the airport before hitting the Lymie who had leaped upon the woman. People were screaming, the shuttle's repulser's kicked on, and the transport lifted off. Mitch didn't even look over his shoulder. It didn't matter that he wasn't on the ship. He certainly wished he was on board, but why would he run and hide when he was more than a physical match for the Lymies.

His theory was soon tested. The ship's lights and roaring engines brought the aliens to the airfield. Mitch fired off a series of barrages that emptied the ammo box that was strapped to his over-sized hip. He pulled the next one around, ripped off the top that was made of thin strips of aluminum to keep the elements out. He fed the .50 caliber bullets into the breech of his MAX as a group of aliens formed up and started toward him.

The humans who had been left behind moved toward Mitch too, only they were trying to get behind him. Two things became immediately clear to him. The first was that the civilians would be no help in the fight to come. And the second was that he couldn't stay out in the open. He was too exposed, and the Lymies could come at him from all sides, including above.

He fired an angry barrage at the group of aliens. Many of his bullets ricocheted off their thickening hides, but a few found weak spots. Of the group of eight, only two survived, and both had injuries to their long, delicate legs.

"We have to get out of here," Mitch shouted to the group of civilians behind him.

There were more than a dozen people. They all looked shocked, terrified, and desperate. He wanted to help them. He glanced over his shoulder. There were two huge aircraft hangers behind him, and a smaller maintenance building. It was made from prefabricated materials, but constructed to house heavy machinery, replacement parts, and the tools to work on said machines. It had a metal frame, and big overhead doors at either end.

"There!" he shouted pointing at the maintenance building. "Get to that structure. You've got to move if you want to live."

Beyond the airport was the colony. Over the years, it had grown bigger and bigger. Alpha Colony was the first, and the biggest. Most of the other colonies used Alpha's airfield and massive fuel tanks to ferry people and goods from outer space to the planet. There was no need to build another space port a hundred kilometers down the line. The plan had been to encircle New Terra's equator with colonies, and eventually to build three more space ports so that no one was more than half a day's hover car journey to one. But the expansion had been halted by the various aliens who had begun arriving in the system shortly after the humans.

The airfield was the last bastion of civilization on the south side of Alpha Colony. Beyond the aircraft hangers was nothing but wilderness. To the north, grassy plains stretched from the city to the swamps. To the south, a forest grew between the city and the swamps. The forest was full of big trees with Spanish moss that hung from the branches, and a variety of wildlife that lived in the canopy. Mitch wasn't interested in the forest, but he was thankful that the Lymies didn't seem interested in it either. There was plenty of unoccupied land that any number of alien species could clear, cultivate, or construct colonies of their own on. The Lymies didn't seem to have an interest in doing that. They wanted the human colonies, or maybe they just didn't want humanity on the planet at all.

But as Mitch looked back toward the airport, he was reminded of what he had seen earlier that evening with his SSO squad. There were Lymies pulling the bodies of fallen humans toward the airport building.

"What are they doing?" someone behind him asked.

"Eating them," another person said. "They eat people."

"We're all going to die," a third declared.

"No," Mitch said. "Get to that maintenance building. Move! Secure the door on the far side. I'm coming."

He turned back to the aliens and drew out the mini-rocket launcher he kept in a special holster at the small of his back. It had six rockets inside. He took aim at one of the aliens and fired. The missile popped out of the weapon, then jumped forward so fast as its booster fuel lit that it was impossible to follow. But Mitch didn't try to follow the rockets. He kept the laser on the aliens. The first blew up close to the airport building. The rocket didn't kill the Lymie immediately, but flipped it backwards and set it on fire. The creature writhed in agony, throwing itself onto the pavement in a futile attempt to put out the flames. When it died, it rolled onto its back, the legs curling in, as the carcass burned. Something about the alien was combustible. Mitch didn't know if it was something in their blood, or just their thick, outer skin, but the light from the fire glittered in hundreds of black eyes inside the airport building. Mitch had already moved on to target the next alien. The second died just like the first.

"There's so many," a young man with muddy boots, and well-worn overalls said. He had a jacket on with a name tag sewn onto the front that said *Kirby*.

"We killed a lot of them, kid," Mitch said. "Let's move."

They were backing away from the airport building, watching for more of the aliens, when a pair of them dropped to the ground on either side of Mitch. They were too close to shoot with the rocket launcher, not without getting himself killed. Instead, he dropped the rocket launcher and drew his combat knife. It was a thick bladed kukari that was straight from the handle, then angled forward with a swell to the belly, before ending in a deadly point. The blade was as long as a grown man's forearm, from elbow to fingertips. Mitch intended to cut through the closest alien's leg, but while the knife bit deep, it didn't sever clean through the alien's delicate leg. Instead, it wedged in the hard, bony matter. The alien lashed out with the wounded leg, knocking Mitch backward. He stumbled and nearly fell but managed to keep his balance. The wounded alien with Mitch's kukari still in its leg, was hobbling away. The other was bending to puncture the kid named Kirby with its long stinger. The Lymies were tall, their spindly legs holding the body up a full two meters off the ground. The kid was in his late teens, but not very tall. He could have walked under the alien without stooping. But the alien could contort its body and was thrusting the stinger toward him.

"No!" Mitch shouted, pulling his MAX around on the harness to bring it to bear on the alien.

He was fast, but the Lymie was faster. The stinger hit the kid in his right shoulder, hooking under his collar bone. At first, Kirby screamed, but he soon went limp, even as Mitch shot the alien's pumpkin sized head pod. The body was well armored with thick skin, but its head was more vulnerable. The skin split in several places from the .50 caliber bullets fired at close range. A few even punched through the thick skull and turned its brain to jelly.

The Lymie died and did what they all did in death. It dropped to the ground, rolling over in the process. Kirby was thrown down, the stinger retracting in death. Mitch bent down over the kid. His shoulder was a bloody mess, and he wasn't moving, but his eyes darted around feverishly.

"Don't worry, kid," Mitch said. "I got you."

He flipped Kirby over his left shoulder, a move that made him think of the Lion Squad, and then Mara. Her memory was like a fresh wound. He didn't want to think about her. He had left her to stay and fight, to save the father and little girl. She would be furious, and maybe his team would be too. Captain Marcs probably thought he was crazy. The CMC had invested a lot of money to put him through the LE program, not to mention the signing bonus they had given him. But he couldn't just run away. There was fighting to do, and he was built to do just that. He was bigger, stronger, faster, and more agile than he had ever imagined. Running away was the wrong move.

But as he trotted toward the maintenance building, with Kirby flung over his shoulder, he couldn't help but wonder if the Lymie would have stung him, had the kid not been there. Mitch didn't know, and he didn't want to think about it. When he reached the maintenance building, he turned the kid over to some of the other survivors.

"Close the doors," Mitch said. "They roll up and down, so use a big wrench or something to jam the rollers shut. If more survivors come, let them in through the man door."

"What about you?" a woman asked.

"I didn't get off that shuttle to run and hide," Mitch said.

"Good luck," someone called out, just before the overhead door rattled shut. Mitch surveyed the launch pads and landing strips between himself and the airport building. He didn't see anyone. His battle helmet was using the light from the burning aliens he had shot to increase his vision. Mitch looked up, but didn't see any movement overhead. But he remembered the eyes. There had been so many of them inside the building. Mitch knew the aliens all had eight eyes. They were black, the size of plums, and lined up in a row across their insectile faces above the bony mandibles. He was going back to kill them all.

Perhaps it was a battle frenzy, or maybe his latent aggression was starting to take hold, but he wanted to fight. He would have wrestled with the aliens bare handed if that was what he had to do, but it wasn't. He still had a little over two hundred rounds in the MAX, and he knew where there were more weapons to be found. It was time to take the fight to the enemy. He was through running, through being hunted. What came next was carnage.

CHAPTER 28

MAJOR ELAINE SWIFT hurried into the command center of the *S.F. Marathon*. She had just arrived and insisted on being in the information center.

"Last shuttle is lifting off," a naval officer commented.

"There are still a lot of civilians down there," Michael Hughes, the ship's commanding officer, said.

"They'll have to look after themselves," Admiral Darcy Wilcox said. "We've got alien ships in the system."

"Hostile?" General Mercer asked.

"Unknown," Admiral Wilcox stated. "We've never seen them before."

Major Swift knew that most of the invasive aliens spent time studying the planet before landing any type of spacecraft. The Graylings had been around the longest, and even entered the atmosphere, but to her knowledge, had never landed any type of craft or set foot on New Terra. Unknown ships meant more players in the contest for the swampy world, and more species for her to study, but the colony was already in shambles. It seemed that humanity who was first in the system was being forced out.

She looked around the command center. The *Marathon* was a massive ship, with over a thousand naval crewmen, a full squadron of fighters, and space for an entire battalion of Marines. The nonessential spaces were already overflowing with both Marines and civilians. The command center was a busy place as the ship's senior officers oversaw the evacuation process. General Mercer and his second in command, Lieutenant Colonel Jerome Banks, were both there, but General Polk was absent. Standing against the wall just inside the doorway, she listened to the radio traffic and the orders going out from Admiral Darcy Wilcox, who was in charge of the *Marathon* and the battleships *Zama* & *Hastings*.

"No response to our hails," the communication officer said.

"Have the *Hastings* and the *Zama* form up behind us," Wilcox said. "We'll maintain orbit for now. Is the runner ready?"

"Aye, Admiral. Captain Dorski is ready to launch," another naval officer said.

"He has downloads of the complete tactical assessment from this system?"

"Affirmative, and will continue to receive updates until they pass through the portal to the Sol System."

"Let's just hope we aren't showing the bad guys the quickest way to our neighborhood," the admiral said. "Launch the runner. I want it moving to the wormhole at top speed."

"Roger that, launching the runner," one officer said.

"*Sprinter One* is away," a second officer announced.

Admiral Darcy Wilcox stood near the large holographic display of the system. Major Swift could see all the planets, and nearly a dozen ships. They were all labeled with little words and corresponding numbers. The Grayling ships were easy to identify. They flew small, saucer shaped vessels. The others belonged to various races that Major Swift had spent her entire career studying. The largest being the Grumbler ship. It was built like a giant cigar. No one knew how many of the forty story tall aliens were inside, but it was large enough for several dozens of them. It was as big as most human space stations and labeled Lima One. There were several Brascus raiding ships. They were long and slender and bristled with laser cannons. Despite their obvious capacity for battle, they stayed in a cluster well away from the New Terra orbit. The human ships held that territory for now, although they couldn't keep the aliens from making landfall. The Brascus ships were labeled Bravo one through six.

There were Kistor and Prog ships too. The latter being filled with water was by far the most interesting to Major Swift, but her focus at the moment was on the two new ships, labeled November One and Mike One. They looked different, more sophisticated somehow. Most interstellar ships were very economical and built for function over form. The two new ships both had an almost artistic flare but were completely different from one another. November One was small, and looked almost like a sleek, aerodynamic castle. It was on a direct course to the planet. Mike One was larger. It was shaped in a long curve, thick in the center, and tapering on the ends. It reminded Elaine of a crescent moon, only it was laying on its side.

"Tell me what we know about the new ships?" Admiral Wilcox ordered.

"Not much," Commander Hughes said. "We've got very little from long range scans. What I can say is that neither one has any sort of mechanical propulsion that we can identify."

"They're running cold?" the admiral asked.

"Yes, ma'am," Hughes responded.

"Admiral, I'm getting a report from the last shuttle," the communications officer announced. "One of the SSO Marines stayed behind."

"Wounded?"

"No, Admiral, he gave up his seat for a father and daughter at the last moment."

"Can you raise this Marine on coms?" Darcy Wilcox asked.

"Yes, Admiral, standby."

Mercer looked at Banks, then turned to stare at Major Swift. Their eyes locked as they waited to hear who had stayed behind. No one could be certain, but from the looks of things on New Terra, the planet was lost to humanity. Anyone who stayed behind wouldn't survive long.

"I've got Lieutenant Murphy, Admiral," the communication officer announced.

Mercer turned his attention back to the pilot and Elaine Swift felt the back of her throat sting. She was not an emotional person, but knowing that Mitch had given up his place on the last shuttle off-world was both heroic and tragic to her.

"Lieutenant, this is the *Marathon*," the communications officer said. "What's your status? Over."

"I'm still outside the airport," Mitch said, his voice tinged with just a touch of static. "Fourteen civilians are barricaded in the maintenance building. I'm moving to clear the main structure now."

Admiral Wilcox looked at General Mercer. "One of yours?"

"Yes, Admiral. An experiment."

"Is he capable?"

"His ratings are off the charts, which is why we made him an officer," General Mercer replied. "But he's only been down there a week. He hasn't been tested."

"Leo Squad was left on the north side of Alpha Colony," Major Swift spoke up. "They were in heavy fighting and had to make their way through the colony as the Lymies invaded."

"What about his squad?" Admiral Wilcox asked one of her officers.

"Leo Squad all made it to the shuttle," the officer replied. "One injury reported. They also had four members of Kilo Squad with them, two of which are in critical condition."

"What do you expect this Marine to be capable of?" Admiral Wilcox asked General Mercer.

"Just about anything we need," General Mercer said. "He's not invincible, but he's one of the most enhanced Marines to go through the procedures."

The admiral signaled the communications officer with a wave of her hand. "Lieutenant Murphy, this is Admiral Darcy Wilcox, Space Force commander in charge of the system. You are now our eyes and ears on the ground. That means no heroics, Lieutenant. We can't afford to lose you. What's your assessment of the colony?"

"It's completely overrun," Mitch replied. "The Lymies are collecting the bodies of our dead or captured. From what I've seen, they're feeding on us, Admiral."

General Mercer stepped closer to Admiral Wilcox and pointed at Major Swift. "Our xeno-biological expert, Major Elaine Swift."

"Is that normal, Major?" the admiral asked. "Do the Lymies eat humans?"

"We don't have much information on their species," Elaine replied. "And what we have, I believe, is just from their recon teams. There's never been a report of the Lymies attacking humans and consuming them for food, but they do appear to be carnivores. I wouldn't be surprised if that's the case."

"Lieutenant Murphy," Admiral Wilcox spoke up. "Can you tell if the aliens are doing anything else?"

"Anything besides killing everyone?" Mitch asked.

"Correct. Do they seem to be utilizing our structures, setting up some kind of headquarters, collecting any of our assets, that sort of thing."

"Negative," Mitch said. "They're in the airport and don't show any signs at this stage of conserving the building. They're ripping it apart looking for people hidden inside."

The admiral turned to General Mercer. "Are there survivors in the airport?"

"Probably," he said casually, as if he were talking about the weather and not human lives. "The airport was our rally position. We moved people out of there as fast as we could, but we had to prioritize Marines over civilians."

"Lieutenant Murphy, what is your plan?" Admiral Wilcox asked.

"To get inside the airport and kill every last alien in there," Mitch replied with an edge to his voice.

"That's too dangerous," the admiral said.

Major Swift felt a chill when she heard Mitch chuckle in reply.

"Dangerous for them, Admiral. Are there any other Marine forces on the planet right now?"

It was General Mercer who spoke up in reply. "No, Lieutenant. To our knowledge, you are the only Marine left alive on New Terra."

"That means you're an invaluable asset, Lieutenant," Admiral Wilcox said. "We need regular reports of what is happening down there. Do you understand that, Murphy?"

"Affirmative," Mitch replied. "But there are civilians down here too. They need food, water, medical attention, and security. If you can't supply that, then I'll have to do whatever it takes to get it for them."

"Lieutenant, you've been given a direct order to stand down," General Mercer said.

"All due respect, General, but I've been standing down my whole life. I'm not doing that anymore."

Major Swift was impressed, but she couldn't let it show. She was a Marine, and the first rule of being a Marine was following orders. Maybe not so much in the Research and Development Division, but for the grunts in the blood and mud, it was gospel. Mitch Murphy was truly on his own, and she didn't have any illusion about ever seeing him alive again.

CHAPTER 29

MITCH DIDN'T WAIT for confirmation, or permission. The voices in his helmet were safe in orbit. He was boots on the ground, and as far as he knew, the only thing stopping the Lymies from having the run of the place. Maybe it was foolishness, but he felt a burning sense of fury inside him. It was almost at the boiling point, driving away any fatigue and fear as he walked back toward the airport main building.

It looked like a scene out of hell. There were dead people lying on the pavement, shattered glass was everywhere, and several dead Lymies were on fire, illuminating the scene in a lurid, yellow light. As he got closer to the building, his connection to the information network, and communications with the *Marathon* in orbit, cut out, despite the fact that there was a transmitter on top of the airport's control tower that should have boosted the signal to full strength. He selected the video record function on his battle helmet. It wouldn't be perfect, and if he was killed, maybe no one would ever get the data, but he was seeing things both inside the building and out that the CMC needed to know.

Walking over to the nearest burning alien, Mitch took his time going around the dead Lymie. There was a pool of dark fluid beneath the body, and a jagged gash along one side where his mini-rocket had hit. Up close, it became obvious that it was the creature's thick outer skin that was burning. Like many insects, they appeared to be molting. Unlike insects on earth, which discard the dry, fragile outer skin, the Lymies outer skin hardened, forming a kind of armor. Mitch made sure that he recorded the fact that the old skin armor was flammable. He poked the body with a boot, then moved on. There was more to see.

At the edge of the building, he could look into the gloomy interior. Several of the metal I-beams were bent, the waiting area was practically destroyed, as were the coffee and travel kiosks that had once sold passengers all sorts of goods as they waited to board whatever transport they had booked. Worst of all were several bundles that hung from the ceiling. The Marines called the Lymies bugs, and they were very spider like in appearance. It seemed, they also held to the practice of wrapping their victims in silky bundles for later consumption.

Mitch stepped through a shattered window frame. The glass crunched under his boot. The firelight showed dozens of glossy, black eyes watching his every move. Mitch had no illusions about the danger that the Lymies represented. They were killing machines, but he was too. He flicked off the safety on his MAX and raised the barrel slightly. For just a second, he glanced upward, making sure there were no aliens moving around on the ceiling above him, then he opened fire.

The .50 caliber machine gun was a wrecking crew. The big bullets pulverized whatever they hit in the airport, including several aliens. The others jumped away from the blaze of the machine gun fire, squealing in protest. Mitch fired short bursts wherever he saw movement. The big weapon wasn't like a tactical or sniper rifle. He held it low, clamped against his side with the elbow of his right arm while that same hand worked the trigger. His left hand guided the weapon, and held it as steady as possible, all the while letting most of the machine gun's considerable weight be held by the harness around his back and shoulders. The tracer rounds made aiming easier, and he fired mostly on instinct, rather than trying to take careful aim. There was no time for that.

The Lymies had thick skin. Many took direct shots to their wide body segment without getting hurt. The high caliber rounds knocked them down, broke their fragile legs, and sometimes penetrated, but it certainly took more than one shot to bring them down. Their heads were the size of carving pumpkins, and much more vulnerable. Several Lymies flipped over and curled their legs in death, others scurried away, searching for safety. A few even jumped out of the airport and either raced away into the darkness or climbed the building.

Mitch checked his ammunition supply. He was running low on the current ammo box and had only one more remaining. He needed to be more judicious with his shooting and would need to resupply very soon. The base had plenty of weapons and ammunition. But getting to it would require a hike back into the city proper. Mitch wanted to wait until dawn to make that dangerous journey. He moved slowly through the airport, keeping his MAX ready to fire. The Lymies in the building appeared to be afraid of him. That was a change, at least in Mitch's experience. The Lymies they had fought on their way through the city had been savage and unafraid.

It was gloomy in the airport. A few of the aliens still burned outside, but that didn't cast much light into the building. His low light amplification setting helped too, but there were still pockets of deep darkness. Mitch was being careful, but nearly stumbled over a human body on the floor. He glanced down, knowing that it was risky to lower his gaze. The Lymies could jump and move quickly. And he guessed there were more of the spidery aliens hiding in the shadows. Still, something drew his attention downward. He knelt down and looked at the person on the floor. It was a man in some type of uniform, a gate attendant perhaps. He was half wrapped in silky threads. They pinned his arms to his body and his legs together. Some even crisscrossed over his face.

"You're alive," Mitch said in surprise as the man looked up at him.

He didn't respond, didn't even struggle against his bonds. Mitch reached down and felt his pulse just to be sure. The man's heartbeat was strong.

"Can you hear me?" Mitch asked.

Again, no response, just the terrified stare. Mitch shifted his focus to the man's body. There was a bloody gash just below his hip, in the meaty part of his thigh. The man had been stung. Mitch didn't know what the venom was, or what it did exactly, but many creatures on earth had a paralytic venom that didn't kill.

"I'll be back," Mitch said in a low voice.

He got up and moved toward where the bundles were hanging. He would need to get some type of ladder to cut them down. A ladder and a knife. His own had been taken away by a wounded Lymie. Pushing on, he came to a counter next to a conveyor belt for luggage. He looked behind it and was nearly pounced on by an alien hidden on the far side. It leaped, Mitch dropped to his knees and let the creatures sail over his head. His knee pads saved him from the glass shards that crackled as he turned, bringing his rifle up and around to track the Lymie. The spider alien didn't turn back to finish Mitch off. It was scrambling up one of the metal I-beams. He fired a burst. The bullets knocked the spider down. It dropped, rolled, sprang back onto its feet just as Mitch fired again. The second cluster of shots did more damage, taking out two of the alien's legs. It flopped, squealing in pain. Mitch made a fast turn all the way around, expecting more of the aliens to attack. But there was no movement in the airport other than the wounded Lymie. Two legs were broken on the same side, making it impossible for the creature to stand or walk. It was forced to drag its heavy body and broken legs. Mitch finished it with a quick burst of machine gun fire to the alien's head.

The search of the airport lasted several hours. Mitch was slow, and careful. He would have loved a straight up slug fest. His enhanced muscles wanted to be exerted, and the fury inside him was simmering, but the aliens were cautious. He had to search each one out before he could kill it. Those on the outer walls and rooftop could be heard moving around occasionally, but didn't seem in any hurry to attack him. Perhaps they would if he left the building, but Mitch stayed inside.

There were six people hiding in what had once been an office of some sort. It was a fully contained room near the back of the building. They locked the door and braced the metal desk against it. Every other room had been unlocked so Mitch knocked on the door just an hour before sunrise.

"Anyone in there?" he asked. "This is Lieutenant Murphy, CMC."

"Yes!" an anxious voice replied. "We're here. Is it safe out there?"

"Not yet," Mitch admitted. "How many of you are there?"

"Six of us," the voice said. "I'm Carter."

"Carter, stay put. I'll come back to you when the sun is up and it's safe to come out."

"Yeah, okay."

Mitch found the luggage area, a large open space with rows of conveyor belts. There were no windows in that section of the building and he decided not to risk searching it. In the morning, things would be easier to accomplish.

Just as the sun was starting to rise, a group of Lymies came skittering into the airport through one of the shattered windows. Mitch immediately opened fire and used the last of the ammunition in his second of three ammo boxes. The Lymies went down hard, most with shattered legs. One jumped back through the open window and raced away. Mitch would have preferred to shoot it down, but that wasn't an option with his MAX out of ammunition. He quickly removed the empty ammunition container from his gun belt and put the last one on. Then, he fed the ammo from the box into the MAX and pulled the charging lever to load the first round into the breach of the machine gun.

Finishing off the wounded didn't assuage his rage. But when the sun rose, he turned his attention to the humans. The six survivors in the tiny office were relieved to be alive but discouraged by the fact that he was the only Marine left to defend them.

"I thought the CMC was supposed to protect us," an older woman with graying hair and a stained white blouse said. "I can't believe they all left."

"When are they coming back?" Carter asked. He was a short man with bright red hair and a cut on the back of his hand.

"I don't know," Mitch said. "Communication with the ships in orbit is difficult."

"Shouldn't be," a thin man with a white mustache said. He had stooped shoulders and big hands. "There's a transmitter on the control tower."

"Power's down Bobby," Carter pointed out.

"The tower has backups," the mustached man said. "There's a solar power array up on the roof too. It should get enough juice to keep the transmitter operating. The computers are a different matter, but radio transmission can't go down. Not unless the aliens destroyed it."

"You know about that stuff?" Mitch asked the man with the white mustache.

"I'm a first gen colonist. My parents came through the portal in eighty-seven. I've been on the maintenance crew for thirty years. Took over a decade ago, that used to be my office," he said, pointing at the tiny room the six people had been hidden in.

"You can help me," Mitch said. "First, we need to get everyone safely out of here. Bobby, do you have a knife?"

"Several," he said.

"Here?" Mitch asked.

The man pulled a finger-length lock blade folding knife from his pocket. He handed it to Mitch, who immediately went to the man he had nearly stumbled over. Mitch opened the knife and cut through the silk bands wrapped around his body. The man was still breathing, but obviously in a lot of pain. He couldn't move or talk, but he was moaning, which was an improvement over the night before.

"Good knife," Mitch said, handing it back to Bobby. "You keep it sharp."

"It ain't much good dull," the man with the white mustache said. "You think those people could be alive?"

He was pointing at the bundles hanging from the ceiling. There were over a dozen of them.

"The Lymies were eating some of their victims," Mitch admitted.

"Oh, God," the gray-haired woman declared.

"It's okay, Grace," Bobby told her. He put a sturdy arm around her trembling shoulders. "We're going to make it."

She put her hands over her face and cried. Mitch didn't stop her. His own emotions were still tuned to a fever pitch. He wanted to do more than just survive, he wanted to take the fight to the enemy.

"We need to cut them down and find out for certain," Mitch said. "Is there a ladder tall enough?"

"No," Bobby said. "But there's a scissor lift in the maintenance building. Carter and I can do that."

A shuffling noise was heard. Grace stifled a scream. One of the other survivors was a young woman in a dark blue skirt, her brown hair pulled back into a ponytail. She had make-up smears down both cheeks.

"What's that?" she asked.

"This is Adele," Bobby said.

"Lymies," Mitch admitted. "There are several on the roof."

"Oh, God," Grace said again.

"Are we going to die?" A man with a loosened necktie and stubble on his dark chin and cheeks asked.

"What's your name?" Mitch asked.

"Eugene Rice," he said.

"Eugene, I'm going to do everything I can to protect you. But we can't just hide out somewhere. There are other survivors in the maintenance building. For now, that's home base. We'll secure that building and keep working until there are no more aliens in the city."

"That's a pretty lofty goal for one dude," Carter said.

"I'm not just a regular dude," Mitch said.

"You're one of the super soldiers?" Grace asked.

Mitch was nearly seven and a half feet tall, muscular, and well-proportioned. It was obvious he was not a normal man.

"That's right, Grace," Mitch said. "And I'm going to kill the aliens on the rooftop."

"There's access from the luggage area," Bobby said.

"Show me," Mitch said. "The rest of you stay here and keep watch for more Lymies."

"There's more?" Adele asked.

"In the city," Mitch said. "I can't say how many more, but yes, there are more of them. Maybe a lot more. And the other colonies were attacked too."

"We need to make contact with them," Bobby said.

"If they have the resources they'll contact the ships in orbit," Mitch said. "But the Lymies jammed our signals. If I can clear the roof, I should be able to keep in contact with Admiral Wilcox and the fleet in orbit."

"Then they can come and get us," Grace said.

Mitch didn't want to say that he had doubts about getting

rescued. Space Force didn't like the idea of risking multibillion-dollar ships just to save a few people. But if he could make the colony safe enough, there was always hope.

"We'll be back soon," Mitch promised.

Bobby led the way to the luggage area. It was still dark inside, but there were several transparent roof panels. As the sun rose, the gloom in the luggage area receded. Mitch took point once they were inside the large room. They searched between the conveyor belts and around the loading docks. There was no sign of any of the aliens. A metal staircase led up to the roof access.

"Is there a door up top?" Mitch asked.

"Yes," Bobby said. "It locks automatically when it closes."

"I won't have time to fool with that," Mitch said. "I'll go through, you stay put on the stairs until I call for you to open it again. If you don't hear from me in five minutes, just leave."

"I could help," Bobby said.

"You get the other survivors to the maintenance shed," Mitch told him. "Contact the Space Force. That's how you help."

"Got it," the older man said.

Mitch went up the stairs three at a time. Bobby hurried to keep up and was breathing heavy when they reached the top.

"You good?"

"Yeah, I'm fine," the older man said.

Mitch checked the safety on his MAX, then shoved the door open. There were five Lymies on the roof. He stepped forward to allow the door to close and opened fire. The aliens all reacted instantly. Two scurried down the sides of the building. One was hit and killed, another was knocked off the rooftop by a round from the MAX. The fifth jumped to attack Mitch. He had to dive out of its way. He hit the gravel and tar rooftop and rolled back to his knees. The Lymie reared, intending to impale him with one pointed leg. Mitch fired first. His MAX roared, and the bullets tore through the Lymie's leg. Instead of stabbing him to death, it fell to the side. The alien screeched as it stumbled back.

Mitch's first instinct was to shoot the alien, but a second thought reminded him he wasn't alone on the rooftop. He turned in time to see the two aliens that had scurried down opposite sides of the airport building were back. One rushed at him and the other leaped into the air, spinning out a ribbon of silk that slowed its fall toward the ground on the city side of the airport building.

The .50 caliber machine gun roared again and stopped the charging alien in its tracks. The Lymie had charged at him headfirst and was completely exposed to the full force of the large caliber rounds that came churning out of the machine gun. The first few bullets knocked the alien senseless, and those after that split the spidery skull in half. The final rounds churned the alien's brain to mush. It dropped, face-first, and slid forward a couple of meters on the rough roofing materials. Mitch spun back around and found the wounded alien limping away. They could be savage in their attacks, but they didn't throw their lives away without reason. Mitch fired again. His shots tore the back legs off the creature and it toppled from the roof.

Mitch scanned the roof, but it was empty. Then, he looked around the airport grounds. The control tower was at the far end of a runway. There were several hover carts parked near the big hangers. Mitch couldn't see any aliens on the runway side of the airport property. The city side was a different matter. The survivor from Mitch's attack was on the ground and running across the open space toward the city proper. Mitch could see the bodies of the aliens that had attacked his squad on the road leading to the airfield. He could have killed the last Lymie, but Mitch was acutely aware of how his ammunition was dwindling. He needed to get to the base and get as much ammunition for his weapons as possible, but there was one more task that was even more important.

He toggled on the long-range communication application. "*Marathon*, this is Lieutenant Murphy in Alpha Colony, do you read me? Over."

"Five by five, Lieutenant," a familiar voice said. "You are one crazy SOB, you know it, Murphy?"

"Yes sir, Captain Marcs. I am fully aware."

"Glad to know you're alive, Marine. What's your status?"

"The airport building is clear of Lymies," Mitch said. "At least the ones that are still drawing breath. Sir, I've had my helmet recording everything since I last spoke to the Admiral. I'd like to transmit it if that's possible."

"Major Swift is right here, she'll be thrilled to get it," Captain Marcs said. "The Admiral isn't too happy with you right now, though. General Mercer is trying to calm her down. Some good news will go a long way toward that goal."

"I've got civilians here willing to be her eyes and ears, Captain," Mitch said. "There are nearly twenty survivors at the airfield alone. And sir, I think maybe more are being detained by the Lymies."

"They're taking prisoners?" Captain Marcs asked.

"More like they're saving some people to eat later, sir," Mitch said. "My squad saw some eating the colonists on our way through the town. And I think that maybe the venom in their stingers is some kind of paralytic."

"We've got a solid upload on your data stream, Lieutenant. For now, let that finish. Then we'll plan your next move. If you're going to take the fight to the enemy, we'll do all we can to help from up here."

"That's the best news I've heard in a while, sir," Mitch said.

"Make us all proud, Murphy. Let me get this data to the admiral. I'll be in touch. Marcs out."

Mitch stepped to the door and knocked.

"It's me, Bobby. The roof is clear."

The door opened and the man with the white mustache grinned. "Did I hear you talking to someone?"

"You were right about the transmitter," Mitch said. "With the Lymies gone, I was able to make contact with the *Marathon*."

"And they're coming to get us?"

"They will," Mitch said, feeling guilty about lying, but not knowing what else he could tell the man at that moment. "But first, we've got work to do."

"We?"

"Yeah," Mitch said. "We get everyone to safety, then I want you in the control tower."

"What if the aliens come back?"

"Then we'll kill them," Mitch said. "Every last one of them."

CHAPTER 30

THE CMC MAY HAVE GIVEN up on the survivors, but Mitch was impressed with those he had ordered into the maintenance building. They had not only barricaded the big roll-up doors, but they stockpiled food from a vending machine, and water too.

"A hundred and eighteen bottles of water," a man named Bart explained. "It's still flowing from the tap too. We filled some of the barrels to have for washing up. And we're refilling our individual bottles too. We won't break into that stockpile until we have to."

"What about Kirby," Mitch asked.

"He's alive," the older man said. "We stopped the bleeding. Patricia is a nurse. But we don't have anything other than a first aid kit. Nothing for his pain. He was moaning some this morning. I don't think he slept much."

"Is he able to move?"

Bart shook his head.

"I've got the radios," Adele said. There was rack of handheld walkie-talkies for the maintenance personnel and baggage handlers.

"How many?" Mitch asked.

"Twelve. There's no electricity here, but they're all fully

charged," she said. "If we use just one or two at a time, we can make them last a few days."

"Good idea," Mitch said.

"So, what's the plan?" Carter asked.

"Right now, we have two objectives," Mitch explained to the crowd of survivors in the maintenance building. "First, we're going to rescue the captives the Lymies captured and left hanging in the airport. If there's a chance those people are still alive, we have to help them. Bobby is getting the lift ready, and we'll be bringing those folks back here."

"We need more medical supplies," the woman named Patricia asked. She was a middle-aged woman who was favoring one leg. "What we've got isn't sufficient for the one patient we've got."

"It's on the priority list, just behind weapons and food," Mitch said. "Once we get the captives from the airport building, we're going to secure the control tower. It will give us eyes on the surrounding terrain, as well as a vital link to the Space Force ships in orbit."

"We're ready here," Bobby called out.

"One radio, Adele. Channel thirty-three."

The young woman had cleaned the make-up from her face and tied her hair back into a ponytail. Her cheeks were red where she had scrubbed them, and her eyes will a little puffy from crying, but she looked better than before. She held out a handheld radio to Mitch, but he shook his head and tapped the side of his helmet.

"I've got coms," he said. "We just need to be able to communicate with you all here."

She nodded and turned the switch that powered on the walkie-talkie. Another knob set the device to the right frequency. Carter and Bart helped open the overhead door nearest the airport building. Then Bobby used the scissor lift's controls to move the small machine out. It was a very plain looking utility vehicle, with four small wheels. The lift was rectangular in shape, with the top section being a passenger platform with safety rails and power controls. Beneath that was the hydraulic lift that could extend the platform up to ten meters. It moved slowly and they had over two hundred meters of open ground to cover.

"Should we leave this door ready to open?" Bart asked.

"No," Mitch said. "We only need the scissor lift to get the bodies down."

"We can leave it in the airport," Bobby agreed.

"Lock it back up," Mitch said.

"Will do," Bart said.

As Bobby drove the cart across the open runways and around the elevated landing pads, Mitch watched for any signs of the enemy. There was no doubt in his mind that the enemy knew he was there. Of course, that was assuming the spidery aliens thought and reasoned like humans did. From a strategic standpoint, there wasn't a lot of benefit in crossing the open ground between the city and the airfield. Whatever the aliens wanted, it was surely in the town. But Mitch wouldn't assume anything. There were more of them than he could keep up with, and while he sometimes felt invincible, he knew that it would only take one mistake to end his life. And maybe not just his alone, since there were nearly twenty people all counting on him to keep them safe.

Bobby and Carter went to work as soon as they reached the airport. The first hanging victim was cut free, and the cocoon of silky material cut apart. The person inside was dead.

"We're too late," Bobby said, bringing the body back down.

"They're probably all dead," Carter said.

"You think she suffocated in there?" Mitch asked.

"Can't say for sure," Bobby said. "But there's a lot of blood."

"Let's check the next one," Mitch said.

The second cocoon was a little bigger. Inside was a man, still alive, but just barely. He wasn't conscious. The third, fourth, and fifth cocoons all held dead people. Two had clearly died of their injuries. The third was an older woman with no visible puncture wounds from the Lymie stinger.

"I think maybe she was already dead," Bobby said. "Heart attack maybe."

"Do we keep going?" Carter asked.

"We have to be sure," Mitch said.

The sixth victim was alive, and even able to talk. It was a younger woman in a chef's jacket. The name tag on her chest said Penny. Bobby and Carter carried her down and moved her to a clear space on the floor where Mitch had swept away the shattered glass from the windows.

"Tell me how you're feeling," Mitch asked.

"Hurts..." she said, her face pinched from the pain. "All over."

"She's got a wound on her leg," Carter said. "It looks like it clotted though."

"Bobby, are there medical supplies here in the airport?"

"First aid kits," he said. "Maybe a portable defibrillator."

"Get us a first aid kit," Mitch said. "I want to wrap that wound. Penny, is that your name."

She gave a curt nod.

"Can you tell me what happened to you?" Mitch asked.

"One of the aliens got me coming out of the kitchen," she said softly. "I came to when it was wrapping me up. I couldn't move."

"Can you move now?"

"My fingers move a little. I can flex my toes."

"That's good. How's your breathing?"

"My chest is heavy," she said. "I thought it was the cocoon, but it still feels tight. It's hard to get a full breath."

"And the pain?"

"Like my whole body is on fire," she said.

Mitch was recording the interview while Bobby and Carter cut down the next victim. He immediately uploaded the footage to the *Marathon*. It was Major Elaine Swift who answered his hail.

"We're here, Lieutenant," she said. "The report you sent is matching up with what some of the victims up here are reporting.

They need fluids, Mitch. Get her drinking something as soon as possible. Dehydration seems to be the biggest danger."

"Roger that," Mitch said.

Of the two dozen victims only four were alive. Bobby got a luggage cart, the kind the baggage handlers used to haul suitcases from the shuttles to the airport. It was electric powered, and down to thirty percent power, but big enough to lay all the survivors on. Carter drove it back across the airfield to the maintenance building. Then, he had orders to return and clean out the small kitchen of any useful supplies, while Bobby and Mitch secured the flight control tower.

It was mid-day by the time they searched the entire structure. It was a cylinder-shaped structure with four levels. The first was where the generators were stored. Some were big, built in models that had battery reserves that were powering the transmitter. There were several smaller models that could be moved.

"We'll transfer those to the maintenance building," Bobby said. "Round up some solar panels to keep 'em juiced up."

"Let's check upstairs," Mitch said.

The second level was a few offices for the flight control supervisors. The third level was a lounge with comfortable furniture and a kitchen area. The fourth floor was the control room. The airport's radar, guidance computers, and communications systems were all still powered up. There were floor to ceiling windows, tinted to keep the sun out. Mitch had a view that stretched for fifteen kilometers in almost every direction. There were binoculars too. Mitch focused his attention on the town.

"See anything?" Bobby asked.

"Movement," Mitch said. "But that's it. I can't make out any details."

"People?"

"No," Mitch said. "Has to be the Lymies. They're too big to be people."

"Wonderful," Bobby replied.

"Hey, at least they're not coming this way. See if you can raise Adele in the maintenance building."

Mitch established communication with the *Marathon* and gave a full report on the situation at the Alpha Colony airfield.

"We need to know what the aliens are doing in the city," Admiral Wilcox said.

"That's my next objective," Mitch said. "I'm running low on ammunition and I need to get weapons to the people out here, unless you're sending help down."

"Negative, Lieutenant," the admiral declared. "You're on your own until we know what the approaching vessels intend."

"A single platoon could hold this area," Mitch said. "Drop a couple of SSO squads from high altitude. They can secure the landing pads and ensure a safe troop landing."

"It's already been decided to hold off any offensive measures at this stage," General Mercer said. "We've lost all the colonies. There's no sense in throwing away the lives of our Marines if there's nothing to gain."

Mitch was glad that he alone could hear the senior officers on the *Marathon*. Bobby was in the same room, but Mitch was communicating with the Space Force ship on a private channel. The audio was delivered via a tiny speaker in one side of his helmet. He could feel his anger rising again. Initially, it had been directed at the aliens who over ran the colonies, but more and more, his rage was being stoked by the decisions of the senior leadership.

"There are survivors down here," Mitch said, working hard to keep his voice calm. "When do you plan to come and rescue them? We have several that need medical attention."

"It's in the works," General Mercer said. "What we need from you is solid intel. We need you to recon the city, Lieutenant. Find out where the enemy is going. The entire system is in flux right now. We've got a lot of movement up here."

"You're going back to Alpha Base for supplies?" Captain Marcs asked.

"Yes sir," Mitch replied.

"That's a dangerous mission, Lieutenant," Admiral Darcy Wilcox said.

"What's your plan?" Marcs asked.

"Get in, get what I need, and get out again," Mitch said.

"You need to recon the area first," Captain Marcs said. "Take your time. Study what the Lymies are doing. Use that intel to make a solid plan for getting to the base."

"We don't know what the Lymies are capable of," Major Swift added. "We believe they have excellent vision and some type of auditory ability. Odds are they're watching for any sort of counter offensive."

"You won't be helping anyone by throwing your life away," General Mercer said. "All we're asking you to do is get some intel on the enemy and report in before you try to reach the base."

"I can do that," Mitch said.

It was irritating. Part of him wanted to ask why he should do anything for the fleet if they wouldn't even commit to rescuing the hostages at the airfield. If they really cared about keeping him safe, they would send a shuttle back down to get him. But Mitch knew he couldn't leave. There were more people in need of rescue in Alpha Colony, and probably every other city and farm on the planet. Leaving was the wrong thing to do, especially for Mitch who had the strength and abilities to defeat the Lymies and save lives.

"Very good, Lieutenant. We'll be awaiting your report," the admiral said. "*Marathon* out."

Mitch didn't like her. At that moment he didn't like any of them. They hadn't even shared how his squad was doing. His idea of the right thing to do was completely different from the senior leadership. They saw resources and investments, essentially giving everything on the planet a numeric value. To them, the transport ships, and Marines, were more valuable than the civilians on the ground. Mitch couldn't help but wonder if things would be different if the survivors on New Terra were the admiral's loved ones, or if General Mercer's reputation was dependent on regaining the lost colonies.

It was all just speculation, and he turned his mind to the task at hand. He could be angry at the brass later if he lived long enough. There was an internal struggle going on inside him. He felt an urge to throw off restraint and attack the Lymies head on. At times, he felt so strong, so fast, and so full of energy that he didn't believe anything could stop him. On the other hand, he only had one ammo pack left for the .50 caliber machine gun. If he wasn't judicious with his approach to the city, he might run out before reaching the base. Mitch didn't want to die. He didn't know if the Lymie venom would affect him any differently with his enhanced circulatory system and metabolism. It might not paralyze him at all, but he couldn't count on that. It had made Jingo's hands go numb. Still, taking his time, and reporting back to his superiors seemed like a waste of time.

"Adele and Carter are joining me here," Bobby said. "We'll keep an eye on things until you get back. Just make sure you come back, Lieutenant."

"That's the plan, Bobby. If you see Lymies coming, get back to the maintenance building."

"And if they come for us there?"

"An exit strategy wouldn't be out of place," Mitch said. "They can go anywhere, and they're faster than we are on foot."

"If we can get that old transport running, we could all get away on it," Bobby said. "Assuming there aren't a lot of other survivors."

"If there are, we'll cross that bridge when we come to it," Mitch said.

The two men shook hands. Mitch didn't remember the last time he had slept or eaten a decent meal. But there would be plenty of MREs at the base, he just had to get there in one piece.

CHAPTER 31

SKAR HAD SECURED THE TOWN. His swarm had nearly two hundred humans in food sacks spread around the colony. The other human settlements had fallen too. All that remained were the farms and estates in between the colonies. The would be overrun in time, and the queens could begin a proper invasion of the planet. It was no small feat to have secured the planet. There were other races spread across the new world, Kistors, and Brascus Raiders, perhaps one of the massive aliens that trudged around in the wild places. But they would be eradicated. If they were smart, they would flee. Skar had claimed the new world for his people. It was Lymie territory, and they wouldn't give it up once their spawn was entrenched.

"You forget the resistance at the human flight center," Skar's second in command said.

"It is of little consequence," Skar replied as the pair scrambled up the side of what had once been a church. It wasn't the tallest building, but it had a tall steeple that the aliens could easily climb. From there, they could see the entire city, and even the surrounding land.

"We have lost half our swarm," Reks pointed out.

"The losses are acceptable."

"If the humans had stayed and fought us, the outcome might have been different."

"But they did not," Skar said. "As our scouts predicted."

"Is it not wise to prepare for a counterattack?"

"Unlike the humans, we are embedded in the city they built. To exterminate us would require more time and effort than they are willing to commit. They value the life of every person in their swarm. It is a weakness we have exploited. They will not risk losing so many of their warriors to regain the colonies."

For a while, the two spidery aliens were silent. Their pointy feet easily penetrated the polymer material the steeple was molded from. Skar marveled at the human machines. They had no ability to secrete the materials necessary to thrive, but they could build mechanisms to do it for them. The Lymies had tiny, retractable barbs near the pointed ends of their spindly legs that could hold them fast on vertical platforms, or even completely upside down.

"This world is too cold," Reks said, as a chilly wind blew past them near the summit of the steeple.

"It will satisfy," Skar said. "There is much to feast on here."

"What about the cold season?"

"Our spawn will be safe underground," Skar said. "Let the Workers decide what is best. We will not be here that long."

"I expected more from the humans," Reks said. "They have many weapons."

"Theirs is not an efficient species. Each of them is worker, each is warrior, each looks to mate, and have offspring. They are not adept at any one thing. They rely too heavily on their weapons."

"What if they drop their bombs from the sky?"

"Why would they destroy all they have built?"

"Revenge," Reks said.

"It is a destructive emotion," Skar pointed out. "Our scouts believe they will withdraw."

"And if they are wrong? It has happened before."

"I will not waste time contemplating what is outside my control," Skar said. "We will assemble the gifted. They will send word to the cluster. The food is gathered. Soon, the queens will spawn. That is all that matters."

"And the enemy at our gate?"

"Assemble those not already tasked," Skar ordered, turning his eight-eyed gaze to the south. The alien could see the airfield and its auxiliary buildings. There was no movement that he could detect, but many brothers had died there. Skar would ensure that there was no threat to the cluster before it made planetfall. "We will clear the last of the human resistance. Nothing can stop us now."

†††

From space several species of intelligent life were watching. The Porgs and the Brascus had reserves waiting to make landfall. The Graylings moved in and out of orbit, their small, saucer shaped ships seemed to defy the laws of physics. There was the trio of human battleships in orbit, and two more at the far end of the system. They were all watching and waiting to see what would transpire on the planet.

Only one ship made steady progress toward New Terra. It wasn't moving terribly fast, nor did it seem to be in the process of slowing down. Not far behind it was another ship. The crescent shape was unique among the vessels in the system. From the obser-vation platform, a trio of Nagani watched everything, not with their eyes, but with other, more potent senses.

"We should intercede," the being known as Qwii suggested.

"Everything in due time," the senior being, known as Arq replied. "The outcome is certain."

"We must test the humans," the third being said. It was known as Juj and was the shortest of the three.

The Nagani were bipedal creatures with wide heads and

curved, white horns. They were covered with short white hair and wore long strips of lightweight fabric over their shoulders. They had powerful arms, but their hands were more like split hooves, which they used somewhat like pincers. Each had a long tail with a shock of longer hair at the end. Their tails hung straight down almost to the floor.

"It may be their time," Arq said. "There is one among them that is of interest."

"It is too dangerous," Qwii said. "The humans are war mongers. Just look at their vessels. They know nothing of peace."

"Peace is the exception in this galaxy, not the rule," Arq said.

"This is their first foray outside their solar system," Juj pointed out. "They do not appear to be up to the challenge."

"What they do next will tell us much about them," Arq said.

"And the Fray?" Qwii asked.

"It knows we are here," Juj said.

"And doesn't care," Arq said. "Not every race is capable of living with the power and knowledge."

"We three can stop it," Qwii insisted, "before it can damage the planet."

"It is not our world to save," Arq said. "Let us observe, as is our mandate. When the Scion raises up a human worthy of the power and knowledge, we much be ready to supply it."

"I just hate to see such waste," Qwii said.

"It is not a waste if it leads to an expansion of the order," Arq reminded him.

"You are wise, Star Saver, but I do not hold out hope for the humans," Juj said. "Better if they remain in their own system."

"Was there's not visited by the Scion, just as ours was?" Arq said. "We do not judge, we do not decide. It is our place to listen and obey."

"Even when the outcome is almost certainly dire?" Juj asked.

"Especially then," Arq said.

CHAPTER 32

MITCH WAS WATCHING the city from a thousand meters out. Alpha Colony was essentially a series of concentric circles, with the residential buildings in the very center, surrounded by the shopping and entertainment rings. Beyond that, the rings were a mix of professional, government, and industrial sections. Alpha Base was three rings deep on the eastern side of the city, less than a kilometer from the outer most ring.

Mitch had walked slowly toward the city. He was able to maintain radio contact with the flight control tower most of the way, although the resolution dropped off the closer he got to the city. It had been a risk traveling in broad daylight. But Mitch had no idea how well the Lymies could see in the dark. The aliens had attacked in the night, which suggested to his logical mind that they could probably see as well in the dark as in the daylight — maybe even better.

Humans used radar to keep tabs on anything approaching their installations, and sonar worked in underwater environments. Mitch had no idea if the Lymies had similar tools, or if they even needed them. Major Swift believed they could communicate telepathically.

It wasn't a very large leap from there to believe that they had a mental radar that would alert them to danger.

Daylight was the best for Mitch to see by. The power was down and his low light amplification was good on the battle helmet he wore, but it was a poor imitation of good daylight. Mitch settled behind a cluster of rocks and watched the city for nearly an hour. Occasionally, he saw a Lymie moving between the buildings, but never more than one at a time. They didn't seem to be on patrol, or moving in regular patterns like sentries. He knew he needed to get closer to find out more.

Between his position and the base was a large manufacturing plant. It was surrounded by a tall fence that had been torn down in the invasion. Not all of it, but the support posts were bent in several places, or the metal fence links were severed, leaving gaping breaches in the containment barrier. Mitch fully intended to use the facility to hide his approach. There were two buildings in the complex. One was a big factory type building, with exhaust vents extending from the roof. The other was a massive warehouse, and the property around both was stacked with the various materials being manufactured, from galvanized drainpipes, to 3D printed, interlocking blocks used for building a wide range of structures. The blocks were hollow and could be stacked together to form walls and roofs, before being filled with insulating foam that made the buildings extremely strong and energy efficient.

Mitch wasn't interested in the goods being created by the manufacturing facility, he wanted to use them to hide his approach. From the plant to the base was just one city block. Mitch was certain he could reach the base as long as he could get through the manufacturing facility safely.

His orders had been to recon the aliens and report back before attempting to get to the base. Unfortunately, he could see what the Lymies were doing without getting much closer. Added to that issue was the limited amount of daylight he had left. He knew Captain Marcs and General Mercer will have pushed him to wait on the raid until the next day, but Mitch had no idea what the enemy might do that afternoon and all through the night. If they attacked the survivors, his single machine gun and mini-rocket launcher wouldn't be enough to guarantee the safety of the survivors. And if he was going into the city to scope out the enemy, he might as well get what he needed to defend himself and the refugees before leaving again.

The outer fence was intact on the outer side of the city. Mitch had to go to the side, between the manufacturing property and a large recycling center. The fence there wasn't down completely, but it was sagging enough that he could get over it without trouble. When he moved, he felt strong and fast. In his old life, just walking around the block would have winded him. Years of sitting behind a desk ten hours a day had taken a heavy toll. But since the LE Protocols, he seemed to grow stronger every day. He dashed across an open space and slid down behind a pallet of building block material. His MAX was loaded with the belt-fed rounds and ready to fire. All he had to do was point and shoot. Holding the weapon steady was the hard part. But as he peeked out from behind the stack of building materials, he couldn't see the enemy. He got to his feet and dashed to a stack of neat, round, pipes that would one day be turned into a culvert, to allow water to drain through. The stack was tall enough that Mitch could stay upright without being seen from the street.

He turned his attention to the warehouse. It was dark and quiet, but he could see in through the big loading docks. The interior of the building was lined with more goods waiting to be shipped to their destination. Each of the colonies specialized in certain things. Most were built around harvesting resources from the planet, whether that was foods, minerals, gases, or fossil fuels which were still used on Titan and Europa to help thicken the atmosphere on those lunar bodies.

Alpha Colony had more manufacturing equipment than the other colonies. Raw materials could be brought in via the nearby airfield. It was then made into useful products that were shipped to the other colonies ready to sell or use. Mitch saw no movement inside the building, but he decided to get a closer look. It wasn't necessary to go inside, or even very close to see in the warehouse. When he did, the materials looked undisturbed, the walkways between the tall stacks were empty. But hanging from the ceiling, suspended by ribbons of silky material, were over twenty Lymies. They didn't congregate together. If they had, there would have been room for over a hundred of the large-bodied aliens. Instead, they were spread out all across the warehouse's roof, their web lines attached to the metal girders that held up the ceiling.

Mitch made a short recording for the bigwigs in the *Marathon* and then turned his attention back to the city. He moved as close as he dared to a gaping hole in the fence. There was no sign of Lymies. He knew they were there, maybe in every building, maybe sleeping, but as soon as he fired a bullet, they would know he was there. His big .50 caliber machine gun didn't have a silencer. Mitch didn't think they made anything like that for such a high-powered weapon. That meant he needed to move silent and unseen.

Mitch couldn't help but think of Ninja. He wished his friend was with him. Mitch could nearly keep pace running with Flash, and he enjoyed lifting heavy weights with Jingo, as well as shooting with Hawk, but he sometimes felt clumsy and awkward next to Ninja. The man seemed able to glide over any type of terrain, always surefooted, and almost graceful when he moved. He reminded Mitch of the big cats his squad was named for. A stalker, silent and deadly.

Doing his best imitation of the stealthy Marine, Mitch left the manufacturing plant and went across the wide road to a brick building that had been filled with various government offices. Mitch didn't want to go inside. It would be crowded with small rooms and office furniture. The Lymies could have a hundred of their kind hidden inside. Mitch went around the building, stopping every few steps to look in every direction for the enemy, even up.

At the far side of the government office building, he saw the complex of buildings that made up the base. They too were surrounded by a fence, but it was made of stacked blocks and hid most of the military installation from casual view. Mitch was just about to run across the street toward the base when a Lymie went skittering from one building to another less than a hundred paces from where Mitch was hiding. He ducked back, pressing himself against the building and looking up. Still no sign that he had been spotted. The enemy wasn't rushing to stop him, and if he could just get inside the base, he would have all the weapons he needed to take the fight to the enemy.

He waited for a full minute, then looked down the street. The alien was gone. Alpha Colony seemed like a ghost town. He knew it wasn't deserted, just quiet. The enemy was there, and if he woke them, getting out of the city would be an uphill battle he wasn't anxious to fight. Taking a deep breath, he dashed out from his hiding place beside the government offices building and ran across the street. He rotated his MAX around his body as he ran, so that when he stepped up onto the curb by the wall that surrounded Alpha Base, it was on his back. With one jump he nearly hurtled the two-meter tall barrier. It was flat on top, and wide enough to get easy purchase. His hands went down flat on top of the wall and he brought his feet up and over the obstacle, just as he had been trained to do. He came down on the far side, flexing his knees, and bringing his MAX around, ready to fire at the enemy. But there was no enemy to fire at. The wide courtyard was clear. Mitch had come down between two utility buildings. One was a garage, the other held equipment for the groundskeepers. Mitch moved to the end of the garage. There was a wide-open space between the utility buildings and the barracks, offices, and logistical buildings. Mitch had seen the regular platoons marching back and forth in the open space. At the far end of the compound were the smaller SSO barracks, each with their own designations. His had been Leo Squad, and so naturally they were the lions. But his squad was safe on board the *Marathon*. Mitch missed their camaraderie and confidence, but he was also glad that he wasn't risking their lives to carry out the mission he had given himself. Perhaps if he hadn't seen the man and his frightened daughter begging to be let on board the last shuttle, he would be with Leo Squad. They would be working out, maybe participating in training simulations. But that seemed like hollow, meaningless work to Mitch at that moment. He had been given incredible physical gifts for a reason, and he was anxious to put them to use.

He looked into the garage and found what he was hoping for. An armored personnel carrier was parked inside. It was a long-range ground transport, although it used repulser lifts and could traverse any sort of terrain imaginable. He checked the dark recesses of the garage. There was no sign of aliens in the utility building. It wasn't large, and it reeked of repulser coolant. The walls were lined with tools and boxes of spare auto parts. Mitch climbed into the personnel carrier and pressed the power button on the dash. The console lit up in front of him, and the repulsers came online.

Having never driven or operated a personnel carrier, Mitch didn't know much about it. But he did know they could operate in near complete silence on stealth mode. He checked the power supply. It was at ninety-eight percent, with a warning that the charging device was still attached. Mitch flipped through the digital display until he found the various operating modes. Stealth was clearly listed, and when he tapped the touch display, it shifted into quiet operating settings.

Mitch stepped out of the driver's compartment and walked quickly to the back of the transport. It was big enough to fit a full platoon in the rear compartment. Mitch looked inside, found it completely empty, the jump seats folded onto the sidewalls, with straps hanging from the ceiling for a person to hold onto while standing. On the far side was the power line. He unfastened the safety clamps. The power to the base was off, and he put the charging cable back into the docking station.

After coming back to the driver's compartment, he pulled off the MAX. It had been his trusted weapon during the battle with the Lymies and he had no intentions of getting rid of it, but he needed a smaller, more versatile weapon for the time being. With the big .50 caliber in the passenger seat, Mitch got into the armored personnel carrier and shut the door. The vehicle would be easy to see, but it was quiet, and he didn't think the aliens could get to him inside it.

He eased the big transport out of the garage then backed it up to the armory just inside the gate that barred entry to the base. Mitch still hadn't seen any Lymies on the property, but he knew his luck couldn't last forever. He left the vehicle powered up and got out. At the rear, he opened the passenger compartment, then turned to the armory. The doors were constructed of heavy metal, with an electric biometric locking device. Fortunately for Mitch, the lock automatically disengaged in the event of a power failure. He slowly opened one of the doors. There was no light inside the armory, but he didn't need light to see the big alien hanging from the center of the room. Just inside the door was a rack of combat knives. They were all different, from Bowie knives to old fashioned daggers, and even slightly curved Japanese Tantos. Mitch grabbed the biggest knife on the rack, a straight edge Sax knife with a clipped point. At the same time the Lymie hanging from the ceiling uncurled its long legs and dropped lightly to the floor. Mitch could have drawn his .45 and shot the creature. At close range, it was highly likely that he could have killed the alien by shooting its head pod. He could even have aimed for the bulbous black eyes, there were eight of them staring at him. But he didn't want to draw any more attention than was absolutely necessary. So, the knife would have to do.

He stepped inside the armory, closed the door, and went to work.

CHAPTER 33

"WHAT DO YOU MEAN, NOTHING?" Major Elaine Swift asked.

"Exactly what I said. We do nothing," General Mercer said. "The good Admiral is in charge now."

"You want to just leave Murphy down there?" Swift asked.

They were in the Ward Room. It was slightly bigger than the one on the *Wellington* but not by much. They were drinking hot coffee and discussing the situation on the surface of New Terra. Not much had changed in the system. It felt like a stand-off of sorts.

"It's not what I want," General Mercer said. "We certainly have the personnel to take Alpha Colony back, but what then? We'd be fighting a war on two fronts with an enemy we don't understand."

"So why not just rescue Murphy and the civilians?"

General Mercer spread his hands on the table. The look on his face was almost devious.

"What we have here is a perfect opportunity to see what an SSO Marine can do. Think of it like a case study."

"He's one of our own, General," Captain Frank Marcs said. "It doesn't seem right."

"Of course it doesn't," Mercer said. "But this is what being a leader is all about. We make the tough choices. We do the hard work that others can't or won't do."

Elaine thought it was easy for the general to say that when it wasn't his life in danger. Elaine would freely admit she had grown too attached to Lieutenant Mitch Murphy. He was a dynamic man, so incredibly talented, and yet humble. She felt like the potential for him was incredibly high, and yet he was being used as a test subject to do the dirty, dangerous work on the ground, while the senior officers were safe in orbit.

"Look, no one is arguing that having Murphy on the ground isn't valuable. We need intel, and he can get it for us," General Mercer said. "Let's keep in mind that he volunteered to stay. No one forced him, or even asked him to do that."

"If only we could get comms and a visual feed," Lieutenant Colonel Jerome Banks said. "If something happens to him, we'll never know it. He could trip and break his leg, get stuck somewhere and die of dehydration and we'd never know it."

"I don't see that happening," Captain Marcs said. "Murphy is extremely capable."

"He's also extremely green," Mercer said. "You read his file. The guy never got into a fight in his life. He was a total loser in the business world."

"The protocol changes people," Major Swift said. "It can bring out the best in people."

"Or the worst," General Mercer said.

The door to the Ward Room swished open. There was a whole other command staff on the *Marathon* but General Polk had not been seen since retreating to space. The members of his staff tried to avoid Mercer's people. Major Swift was not surprised to see Lieutenant Johnny Tosh come in. He took a seat behind the general, who turned to face him.

"Well?"

"I'd say best case scenario," Tosh replied. "Leo Squad won't stop singing his praises. They want to know when they're going back to get him."

"And Kilo Squad?" Mercer asked.

"They're in bad shape, but those that can talk say that Lieutenant Murphy is the real deal. They're saying he took charge, got them out of the city, and saved their wounded squad mates."

"Now we know," Major Swift said.

"He's not a coward, that's good," the general said, turning around.

"He led his team, and the remnants of another through the city to reach the airport," Captain Marcs said. "I'd say he's pretty resourceful. There were no comms. He was out of contact once the bugs arrived."

"Strategically, he's making good use of the resources at the airport too," Colonel Banks said. "The maintenance building is the only reinforced structure in the complex. The hangers are too big to properly defend."

"Getting those giant doors open and closed without power would be exhausting," Captain Marcs added.

"The control tower isn't as secure, but it gives them the best vantage point to watch over the airfield. Plus, securing communications with us is a vital priority."

"Which tells us he's smart," General Mercer said. "He soaked up what you taught him, Major."

"His mental acumen is high," she said, "just like everything else about him. He's not just another Marine. That's why I'm fighting so hard to get him back. We've only scratched the surface of what can be learned about the LE program with Lieutenant Murphy. Marines like him are the future of the Corps."

"So why, after hundreds of subjects, has he been the only one with such high marks?" General Mercer asked.

"Goes back to the subjects," Colonel Banks said. "Our recruiting tactics aren't appealing to the right people."

"We got lucky with Murphy," Captain Lindsey Priss said. "His failures in his personal and professional life made him open to the recruitment, whereas most people are settled into a career track that they're unwilling to leave."

"If he hadn't been overlooked by the shot callers at his job he probably would never have left," Banks said.

"It's the conundrum of the program," Major Swift said. "Young people just starting out in life don't think they need it. The best candidates are often too entrenched in their plans by the time they begin to notice their deficits."

"We'll write up a report," General Mercer said. "See if we can entice the Commandant to sweeten the pot and go after prime candidates. Murphy will be the proof that we can do even better than we already have with the SSO division."

"If he survives," Captain Marcs pointed out.

"He doesn't need to survive," the general said. "He only needs to do a few things while he's on his own down there. Some things no regular Marine would be able to pull off. He does that and we can write our own ticket."

The general smiled, as did Colonel Banks, but Elaine Swift wasn't happy. She was pleased to see that Captain Marcs didn't seem to be either.

"What's going to happen to the colonies if we don't go back," Captain Marcs asked. "We're just giving them up?"

"This system is getting awfully crowded," the general said. "My guess is the admiral pulls the pin on the colonies."

"We just run away?" Colonel Banks asked.

"In the cost/benefit analysis, New Terra just isn't worth the cost it would take to keep it," General Mercer said. "And the risk of having the Sol System exposed is too great. My guess is we'll bomb the territories. No sense in giving the enemy our resources. They'll pull back through the portal and mine the worm hole to ensure no one follows us."

"And Lieutenant Murphy?" Swift asked.

"He'll die a hero," General Mercer said without an ounce of compassion. "But his sacrifice will usher us into the next stage of physiological advancement. He should be checking in soon. Let's get back to the CIC and give the admiral the support she needs."

Elaine Swift didn't get up when everyone else did. She felt a sinking feeling in the pit of her stomach. Maybe other candidates could do what Mitch Murphy had accomplished in the LE program. But there were no guarantees. She felt like leaving him to die was the most wasteful thing they could do.

CHAPTER 34

THE LYMIE DIDN'T HESITATE, but Mitch expected as much. The armory wasn't a vast space. Most of it was filled with scissor shelving that folded against the side walls and were loaded with weapons, explosives, ammunition, and armor. The spidery alien was right in the center of what little open space there was. Mitch didn't have room to dodge the alien, which drew up one leg to strike at him. But Mitch was ready for it. The spider was fast, but Mitch had the Sax knife held up to the side. When the Lymie stabbed it's pointed leg at Mitch, he swatted it away with the Sax. The knife was forged for the SSO squad, with a handle that fit in Mitch's hand. The blade was three fingers wide. It had a tapered edge that was designed for chopping and was honed as sharp as a razor. The knife hit the alien's leg just before the pointed tip of that leg made contact with Mitch's chest armor. The blade passed clean through, severing the bottom of the alien's leg in one smooth pass. Mitch hardly even felt any resistance. The point tip hit Mitch's armor, but no longer had the force of the alien's strength or weight behind it and bounced off him without doing any damage.

The Lymie pulled back, shrieking in pain, but Mitch didn't

wait to see what it might throw at him next. It was holding up the wounded leg, propped on the other three. He stepped forward, the alien's pincer mouth opening wide with a menacing hiss. Mitch lashed out with the Sax and again severed the alien's leg. It was the uninjured front leg. Mitch chopped it in two at the halfway point, just below where it bent back toward its big, hairy body. The alien screeched again, but the wail was cut off as it fell face first onto the concrete floor with a crunch.

The alien had only one thing left that it could do, and Mitch jumped to the side just before the Lymie's powerful back legs thrust the body forward. He crashed into a rack of Kellton Infantry Light rifles, or KILs as the regular Marines called them. The alien hit the front wall, then curled around, trying to get onto its side where it could bring its stinger to bear. Mitch didn't wait for that happen. He slashed at the alien's thick body segment. To his surprise, the incredibly sharp Sax knife just bounced off the Lymie's thick hide.

He shuffled backward, away from the writhing alien, which suddenly managed to lunge toward him, still pushing itself on the floor. If the pincers had been close enough, they might have clamped onto Mitch's leg, or maybe snapped clean through. But it wasn't on target, and Mitch dodged backward, once more crashing into a shelf. Boxes of ammunition clattered to the floor as Mitch stabbed down with the angled point of the big knife. There were eight perfect targets on the alien's hairy head pod. He stabbed the knife through one of the eyes and straight down into whatever type of brain it had. The Lymie shuddered, its intact legs tapping wildly for a moment, then it somehow managed to roll over, it's back legs curling over its body which seemed to deflate.

Mitch found himself breathing hard. It was more from the stress than the physical exertion. But he didn't have time to relish his kill. Black blood was spreading across the floor. Mitch turned toward a stack of crates filled with KILs. It was the standard weapon for rifle platoons and would be useful for the survivors at the airfield. Each crate weighed well over a hundred pounds and was normally carried by two Marines. Mitch lifted one by himself without even straining. He carried it to the armory door, pushed it open, and looked outside. It wouldn't have surprised him to see Lymies rushing toward the armory from every direction, but the base still seemed deserted. He set the crate of rifles in the back of the armored transport, shoved it forward and went back for more.

The SSO weapons were on one of the scissor shelves. Mitch had to pull them apart, then step back to reach a Garrison Assault Rifle. He slung it across his back, then hung another around his neck on the simple carry straps that came standard with the weapon. It was built bigger than a normal rifle, with longer grips and a much wider trigger guard. There wasn't time to load ammunition, but fortunately, there was a crate full of forty-round magazines with the standard hollow point bullets, filled with the gel explosive and jacketed in depleted uranium. He rammed one home in the GAR, then stuck two more into the empty loops on his armor before carrying the crate of ammunition to the personnel transport.

For the next ten minutes, he loaded weapons, everything from .50 caliber machine guns with remote controls, to automated rocket launchers. He loaded entire crates of ammunition too, and then big, reinforced boxes of explosives. There were laser motion detectors, weight sensitive mines, shotguns with a variety of shells, and shoulder held rocket launchers. His final loads were crates of body armor and battle helmets. With more than enough weapons and ammunition to outfit the survivors at the airfield, Mitch started for the driver's compartment. That's when he saw the aliens massing on the wall he had vaulted over. The sun was starting to go down. He guessed there was maybe half an hour of daylight left. It was time to get out of the city, but he couldn't ignore the aliens. The armory was close to the gate, which was nothing but a wooden beam on a rotating hinge. He could have easily lifted it up, but he didn't want to turn his back on the aliens along the wall.

One glance in the street looked clear, but he didn't have the luxury of really scoping things out. Turning back to the wall, he lifted the GAR on his chest. His MAX had a much higher rate of fire, and the belt-fed ammo would give him access to many more rounds than the Garrison rifle, but he remembered how the Sax knife had bounced harmless off the Lymie's thick hide in the armory. The aliens seemed to be getting tougher and tougher to kill. Mitch hoped the ultra-hard depleted uranium tipped bullets from the GAR would be more effective.

The GAR had a metal stock with a rubber pad. He pressed it against his shoulder, his eye easily finding the aliens on the wall in the square aiming reticle. The sounds of the first three rounds from the Garrison rifle were loud in his ears. The report boomed off the buildings and echoed across the city as the first alien dropped backward off the wall in a spray of dark blood.

The others leaped forward. Some merely jumped to the ground, but others tried to close the distance between Mitch and the wall in one leap. His enhanced muscles and reflexes helped him target and fire on the creatures. Six were down within seconds, the others scattering wide, trying to avoid the deadly rifle fire. But Mitch was just one man. More Lymies were appearing every second, jumping over the fence, bursting through the windows of the tall admin and officer's quarters building. Mitch would have liked to have gone into the logistics building to gather clothing, survival supplies, and MREs. He knew that if they were left on New Terra for long, they would need all sorts of things, from shoes to medical supplies. But there was no time. Somehow, other Lymies had known where he was. The time for sneaking around was over.

He dove into the armored transport and slammed the door just a split second before a Lymie smashed into it. The aliens pointed feet didn't penetrate through the armor, but he heard the bony legs pinging against the hardened steel, followed by the grinding scrape of the creature's stinger. The door had narrow slats of reinforced plexiglass to give the driver the ability to see out the armored door.

Mitch glanced over, saw the Lymie's writhing underbelly, and the pointed stinger dripping venom as it gouged a groove in the metal.

The vehicle had simple controls, a steering wheel, acceleration and brake pedals, and an altitude lever. The battery was still at ninety-five percent. He stomped on the accelerator and cranked the wheel over. The troop carrier was five meters long, the tail end swung around from the sudden burst of power to the repulser drive thrusters. Several of the Lymies were caught off guard. Mitch heard the crunch of their hardened bodies as the transport slammed into them. The entire vehicle rocked from the impacts too, and some of the aliens wailed in pain. Others were jumping onto the transport as it rammed into the wooden barrier blocking the exit from Alpha base.

Mitch could see the enemy converging on his location. There were dozens, some on the streets, others on the buildings. They came scurrying and leaping toward the transport. Mitch slewed back and forth, driving closer to the buildings to knock the aliens off the sides of the troop carrier. There were plenty of narrow allies, but not a lot of connecting streets between the rings. It was designed for people to walk or use public transports rather than driving their own vehicles. Mitch found a road and turned onto it. There were still Lymies on the roof of the carrier. There were no bridges or tunnels he could drive under to get them off, that would have to wait. He raced toward the road that led to the airfield. When he reached it, he turned out of the city and pressed the accelerator to the floor. While the troop carrier raced ahead at top speed, he swapped out the magazines on his GARs so that both of the rifles were fully loaded. Then, he stomped the brake pedal. The repulsers reversed their thrust, and the vehicle lurched to a stop. Several of the Lymies went flying off the roof.

Mitch stomped the accelerator again, charging straight toward the aliens. Just before he reached the spidery creatures, who were shocked by being flung off the transport, and just getting back onto their spindly legs, Mitch hit the brakes and turned the wheel hard.

The transport spun around, smashing into the aliens, and flinging more off the roof.

As soon as the vehicle was fully stopped, Mitch jumped out of the driver's compartment. He had a rifle in each hand. They were meant to be held with two, but he was a big man and very strong. He brought the rifles and fired quick bursts at the three aliens still on the transport. The uranium tipped bullets punched a few centimeters into the hard skin of the aliens. From what Mitch had seen, it was like they were covered in thick, rubber sections. The hardened skin was difficult to penetrate, but the explosive rounds, while not tremendously powerful, pushed the hot lead deeper into the aliens, while the kinetic energy from the bullet impacts knocked them from the roof of the vehicle.

He ran around to the far side. There were eight aliens, some with broken legs, others shocked by the crash, but a couple that tried to attack him. He gunned them down. Their head pods were more vulnerable to the GAR bullets. Mitch felt a grim satisfaction seeing them blow apart when he shot them. A few of the aliens tried to run, but Mitch was in full battle rage. He wasn't going to let them escape. The guns roared, the bullets flew, and the aliens died. It was chaotic and fast. Mitch used up his ammunition and the rest was in the back of the transport, which was a jumble of crates. One look back toward the city showed him there was no time to go searching for more bullets. At least forty Lymies were running from the city onto the open plain. And more were rising into the air on their long, streaming ribbons of silk. Fortunately, the wind was blowing more west than south. Mitch hurried back to the driver's compartment and raced to the airport. He drove around the main building and stopped by the maintenance structure. The big over-head doors were still closed and barricaded from the inside, but several people ran out of the man door.

"Take this inside," Mitch ordered, pulling open the rear doors of the transport. Get what you can and get back inside. The aliens are coming."

Some of the survivors jumped to obey, while others cowered back in fear. He heard people starting to cry. One woman grabbed his arm as Mitch was opening a crate with two .50 caliber machine guns on tripods inside. They were designed for SSO Marines, who like Mitch were taller and stronger than the average human, with bigger hands. The machine guns on tripods had two handed parallel grips, with thumb triggers. Mitch set one up on either side of the transport.

"Can we help?" Bart said.

"Get someone on these .50 cals," Mitch ordered. "They shoot anything they see in the air."

Mitch found the crate of GAR ammo. He ripped it open with his bare hands, and started reloading the two rifles which were still hanging by their straps, one from each shoulder.

"What are you going to do?" Bart asked.

"Hold them off," Mitch said. "If I go down, you get back inside and lock everything. There's no sense in your people getting killed. Just wait for the CMC rescue."

"Are they coming back?" Bart asked.

"Sooner or later," Mitch said. "They have to."

He knew it wasn't true. If his experience in business had taught him anything, it was that loyalty was a costly virtue that most people weren't willing to pay for. And the Space Force didn't owe the colonists anything. They had put out the word to evacuate, and those that didn't make it were probably going to be written off as casualties. He didn't see it that way, but he knew some people did.

The Lymies had slowed as he reached the airport. They weren't stupid. Mitch wasn't trying to draw them back to the airfield, but if there was going to be an ambush, they weren't willing to rush right into it. That gave him just enough time to sprint into the airport main building. Mitch was fast, perhaps he couldn't beat Flash in a footrace, but he could keep up. It took him less than a minute to sprint to the airport building, make his way to the baggage area, and up the metal staircase. He burst through the metal door, not caring that it would lock behind him. The Lymies were less than a hundred meters from the building Mitch was on. He brought one of the GARs to his right shoulder and took aim.

The Lymies reacted as one might expect once the shooting started. The bullets from the first three round bursts hit one of the aliens a split second before the report of the shots reached the group. They saw one of their own get knocked backward. Despite the thickening hide that protected them, the alien rolled onto its back and died. That sent some backpedaling, and others running away, but the majority, more than thirty of the spidery aliens, charged toward the airport.

Mitch fired over and over again until his rifle locked in the empty position. He popped out the first magazine, dropped it on the gravel covered rooftop, and slid a fresh one into the weapon. He had just yanked back the charging lever when the survivors by the maintenance building started shooting the .50 caliber machine guns. They made a distinctive rattling sound as the bullets were fired. Mitch glanced to the side and saw tracer rounds flying up toward a group of Lymies floating from their long, silky ribbons. Some began dropping to avoid the gun fire, others continued on, the wind blowing them wide of the airport complex.

Below him, several of the Lymies had reached the main building. They weren't directly below him, but he knew they were coming. Half a dozen jumped through shattered windows into the safety of the ruined airport. A couple tried to climb up the side of the building. They were fast, their spindly legs almost a blur of motion, but Mitch was fast too. He shot one, then the other, almost on instinct. There was no thought to his actions, no careful aim being taken. He just pointed the weapon at the aliens and fired, then moved to the next.

The battle slowed down after that. Almost half of the attacking horde was killed, and most of the rest had pulled back to what they thought was a safe distance. But there were at least ten in the building beneath Mitch's feet. He stepped back from the edge of the structure that faced the colony town. Moving as quietly as he could, Mitch walked to the other side of the building. Bart and another man named Riley were pointing toward the airport main building. Mitch didn't need them to tell him some of the aliens were climbing the far side of the structure hoping to take him from behind. He leaned out over the side of the building and fired. Three more aliens fell. They weren't all dead, but they were all injured. Broken legs made the spidery creatures clumsy and slow. They preferred not to fight if their legs were shattered from a burst of gunfire.

Mitch swapped out another depleted magazine, pulled the pin on one of the concussion grenades he had picked up from the armory, and tossed it inside the airport. It was a risky tactic. The entire building might collapse, or the roof where he stood might be compromised. Mitch was gambling that the steel girders that supported the building could withstand the concussion grenade, which was designed to injure and kill without being completely destructive. A second later, a deafening boom sent smoke and debris flying out of the airport. The rooftop seemed steady enough, so Mitch pulled the pin on another, and after running several meters along the roof, tossed it down and into the structure through the shattered windows. Then, he went to the other side and tossed another grenade down.

In the distance, he could see dozens more of the insectile aliens. They were gathering around a big specimen who was facing the rooftop. Mitch pulled his mini-rocket launcher and took aim at the big Lymie. He pulled the trigger, and watched the rocket shoot out of the weapon's barrel, then streak across the open ground. To his surprise, one of the Lymies in the group leaped up straight into the approaching rocket.

Mitch chuckled. He fired two more rockets, then holstered the mini launcher. He had the feeling that something was behind him. When he turned around, he found a pair of Lymies coming over the far side of the building. Their bodies were singed and smoke wafted from them. They were moving slow, but steady. Mitch raised his GAR and fired. One went tumbling backward off the roof, the other fled. Mitch glanced back out at the open plain. Three Lymies were burning as the twilight began to darken. The aliens were marching back to the city. He estimated the number of survivors to be well below a hundred, but that didn't mean there weren't hundreds more still in the colony. They had nested in the buildings and probably had more colonists wrapped up in their silky webs just waiting to be eaten.

Mitch went to where the last two Lymies had come onto the roof. One lay dead on the ground, the other was nowhere in sight. Mitch looked at where Bart was manning one of the .50 caliber machine guns. He pointed to his eyes, then made a spidery gesture with his fingers moving like the Lymie legs. Bart held up three fingers and pointed at the building.

Three more, Mitch thought, walking toward the door to the stairs. He wondered if the aliens from the colony would attack again. He would have to keep watch, or make sure someone did while he got a few hours of sleep. He was beginning to feel the exertion of the fight. His eyes felt sandy, and his mouth was extremely dry. The rumbling in his stomach was constant. Since having the LE procedure, he always seemed to be hungry. And he was a little clumsy, his boots dragging on the gravel rooftop. It wasn't until he reached the door to the roof that he remembered that it locked automatically. He pointed at the handle and fired the GAR. The bullets punched through the thin metal, shattered the lock, and destroyed the handle. He pulled the door open and descended down into the darkness.

CHAPTER 35

MITCH HAD no idea that as he walked down the metal stairs from the airport roof, that a ship was entering New Terra's atmosphere. It wasn't visible from Alpha Colony, or any of the human cities. The ship was made of dark material that seemed to soak up the sunlight. It came down through the clouds with no visible exhaust or engine rumble. But it slowed in midair, drifting for a while until it came to a clearing to land in.

On the ground, the ship looked like a castle from a fantasy novel. It had two tall spires that twisted like soft serve ice cream, and a domed roof between them. A few moments after the ship landed, a hatch opened in front like a draw bridge over a moat. The ship wasn't in the swamp. It had found a small clearing that was elevated enough to be dry. A being came out that was different than anything the humans had seen and recorded. From orbit, the *Marathon* was scanning the ship, but finding no heat signature that would indicate engines.

"Can we get visuals?" Admiral Darcy Wilcox asked.

She was exhausted. Since the order had gone out to evacuate

the colonies, she hadn't left the Command and Control Center of the spaceship. She was monitoring everything.

"Launching surveillance drones now, Admiral," one of the ship's officers said.

General Mercer was there, along with his staff. The general was allowed to approach the holographic projection of the system, but the rest of his people were left by a communications console reserved for the CMC. He watched as the admiral ran a hand across her tired face.

The System had gotten busy, and despite that fact, Admiral Wilcox had left the *Hastings* in geo-synchronous orbit over Alpha Colony. They were still waiting to hear a report from Lieutenant Murphy, and General Mercer was beginning to doubt that one would ever come. It was much more likely that Mitch Murphy had gotten himself killed. It was one of the dangers of the SSO program, especially for new Marines seeing their first taste of battle. Many of them just felt so good, so strong and full of energy, that they took mortal risks without hesitation. It was a recipe for disaster, but General Mercer was well practiced in turning bad situations into positive outcomes. With the right spin, Murphy would be a hero. The SSO program would take center stage with the Colonial Marine Corps, and of course, General Mercer would ride that wave into the highest rank possible, and then into a political career. He might even become President of the Expansion Coalition, of which was composed of most of the larger countries on Earth, as well as the colonies on Mars, Titan, and Europa. He felt it was his destiny to be a great leader, not just another politician, but a man of historic achievement.

"Admiral, we just got word from Sol," the communications officer said.

"And?" Darcy Wilcox snapped, her fatigue getting the best of her self control.

"The Coalition Leadership Collective agree with your assessment, Admiral. Permission is granted to use the Non-Reactive Kinetic Torpedoes to destroy the colonies."

"Very well," Admiral Wilcox said. "Have *Hastings* and *Zama* spool up their torpedoes and calculate firing solutions. We can't risk dawdling once we've begun the attack. I want surveillance drones ready as soon as the warheads make impact. They should be able to get full scans once the Lymies are destroyed."

"Aye, Admiral," the communications officer said, sending the message along to the other two ships in orbit.

"Navigation, plot our course back to the wormhole," Admiral Wilcox continued giving orders. "Have communications drones ready for launch. I want to keep tabs on the planet as long as possible. We'll drop one every ten thousand kilometers until we're well out of New Terra's orbital plane."

"Should we inform the people left behind?" General Mercer asked. He knew the answer, but he also knew that every order given on a Space Force vessel was recorded and logged for after action analysis. General Mercer wanted it on the record that the order not to inform the refugees still on New Terra had come directly from Admiral Wilcox. Not that Mercer disagreed with her, but should public sentiment fail to see it their way, he would have proof that he tried to save those wretches left behind.

"Negative," Wilcox said. "We can't risk the enemy intercepting the transmission and learning of our plan."

Mercer nodded sagely, but his back was to Captain Marcs and Major Swift. He didn't see the horror on their faces. Nor the look that passed between them. Major Swift stepped out of the CIC and began typing up an emergency message. She sent it to Captain Marcs, who was seated at the communications console. Sent as a priority message, it would display on his helmet's HUD even though it was just a text message which normally wouldn't be noticed until a person had the leisure time to check the mail app on their computer tablet. Since Major Swift had typed up the message, all Captain Marcs had to do was forward it on, adding the priority designation. There was no need to record himself, or be seen typing anything, and wouldn't rouse suspicion. But both Frank Marcs and Elaine Swift would sleep better knowing they at least tried to warn Mitch Murphy of what was coming.

The hologram in the center of the Command and Control Center of the warship changed suddenly. The Terra system disappeared, and in its place, was an aerial feed from a surveillance drone. It showed a rocky hill where the castle-shaped ship had landed. More importantly, it showed the being who had left the ship.

"Is that human?" Admiral Darcy Wilcox asked.

"Certainly looks like one," General Mercer said.

"Can we get a better angle?" the admiral said. It wasn't really a question so much as a suggested order to the drone operator nearby.

"He's moving fast," the drone pilot said.

"I don't see any sort of transport," General Mercer said.

The person on the ground was racing across the terrain, no longer walking, the biped's body seemed still, yet somehow it was moving faster than the drone could fly.

"Fascinating," Major Swift said as she rejoined the rest of General Mercer's staff.

"Do we have any records of something like this?" Admiral Wilcox asked in a loud voice.

When no one spoke up, Major Swift answered. "No, Admiral, this is all new."

"Obviously intelligent," the admiral said. "Are we picking up anything from the scans?"

"Negative," a naval officer replied. "No chemical reactions. No heat signatures. No exhaust, or fusion reactor off gassing."

"Their power reactor must be well insulated," General Mercer said.

"A ship that size should have some sort of electronic signature," the officer continued. "I'm not even getting EM waves. On the scopes, it looks like a rock."

"Can you get a hit on the composition?" Admiral Wilcox said.

"It isn't metal," the man said. "Whatever it is, the ship is natural."

"Like it was grown?" General Mercer asked.

"No sir, more like it was carved."

"We're losing the pilot," the drone operator said. "Whatever it is shouldn't be able to move that fast without mechanical help."

"Not every intelligent race in the galaxy would build things the way that we do," Major Swift said. "Technology is one of the things that makes humanity unique."

"We've seen enough. Are the warheads ready?" Admiral Wilcox asked.

"Aye, Admiral," the weapons officer said. "*Hastings* and *Zama* are ready to launch tungsten kinetic rods to destroy the colonies. Awaiting your order, Admiral."

"Very well. The order is given. Launch the communication satellite. Have the signal buoys ready once we break orbit."

General Mercer felt his heart rate speed up. The hologram changed to a view of the two battleships launching the hundred-meter long rods. They would circle the planet, picking up speed with minimal guidance, then dip into the atmosphere to rush at hypervelocity speed before impacting the colonies with enough kinetic energy released to match a hundred kiloton nuclear bomb, but without the destructive, radioactive fallout. Each of the colonies would be swept away, along with the aliens who had taken them over. General Mercer thought of Lieutenant Murphy for a moment, and the survivors he was fighting to save. Their lives would be lost, but not wasted. Not if General Mercer had his way.

CHAPTER 36

THERE WAS no movement in the baggage room. It was the one part of the airport building that had sustained the least amount of damage. He reached the bottom of the stairs thankful for the low light amplification of his helmet's view screen. The sun was almost down, and the windowless baggage area was too dark to see much.

Mitch went through the doorway into the main concourse. There were areas where the grenades had gone off leaving the debris blown clear. There were also several Lymie bodies, all on their backs, their legs curled. But Mitch felt immediately that something wasn't right. Two of the nearest aliens were larger than the others. They didn't seem deflated in death the way most of the kind did. Mitch, with a full magazine, fired a burst at the nearest alien's head. The result was a gory explosion of skin, bone, blood, and brain tissue. The other Lymie nearby rolled quickly to its feet and lashed out with one leg. It was too far away to reach Mitch, but it kicked what had once been a chair. The metal legs were simple metal rods that made into a square that the plastic molded seat was attached too. Only the legs were crumpled, the seat back cracked.

Still, it flew towards Mitch, who had to jump out of the way to avoid it. When he did, he tripped.

Luck is a part of any endeavor. No one can predict every move and every outcome. Mitch knew the trio of Lymies in the airport were dangerous, and that they might even be setting a trap for him. But in his caution, he had failed to look up. As Mitch fell, the third spidery alien was dropping toward him from above, it's stinger out ready to impale him. It just so happened that in falling, Mitch turned, landing on his back. He saw death descending on him and fired his GAR without a single conscious thought. The bullets didn't penetrate deep, but they were on the alien's belly. They hit and exploded, wounding the Lymie and knocking it off course. Mitch saw it all in a black and white slow motion. The alien screeched, and tumbled to his left, saving him from the death the spidery creatures had planned for him.

Mitch was up fast, rolling to one knee, his rifle held ready. The unwounded Lymie was charging at him. It moved fast, bouncing back and forth in a skittering rush. Mitch was reminded of being a child and trying to kill a spider. It would never stop moving, and when he hit it with his shoe, it somehow survived the blow and kept running from him. But the Lymie, for all its speed and dexterity, couldn't avoid Mitch's gun fire. He fired several bursts as he swung his rifle toward the alien. Several of the bullets bounced off the Lymie's thick skin, but one hit its left foreleg. The bullet snapped the bony leg and caused the alien to stumble. It lifted its head in pain, and Mitch took the opportunity to target the vulnerable part of its anatomy.

Two were dead, one was wounded and trying to escape, when the message from Captain Marcs flashed onto the HUD of Mitch's battle helmet. It was a text message displayed in red letters at the bottom of his vision. Mitch ignored it at first, thinking it was some type of low power warning, or some other system information. There was still a lot about the complex armor he wore that he had yet to learn. He knew that it kept a check on his vitals, and he was feeling himself wear down. Maybe the warning was just a way of keeping him from pushing too hard. He had heard stories about Marines newly out of the LE program that felt invincible, only to wear themselves down to the point of exhaustion before they knew it. Mitch was too busy shooting the last alien. It was facing away from him, and Mitch targeted the legs. It took two bursts from the Garrison rifle to hit one of the alien's spindly legs, but it shattered beneath the Lymie as it attempted to crawl out of one of the broken windows. Mitch followed it. The spidery alien was dripping blood from its wounded belly and dragging its broken leg. He could tell by the way it moved that it was nearly out of strength. It certainly wouldn't make it back across the plain to the colony, and he decided to let it go. It would be dead soon enough and was no longer a threat to him.

The cluster of Lymies in the distance, however, were a completely different matter. He could see them, just a dark smudge on the horizon. They were moving, probably advancing toward the airport. It crossed Mitch's mind to get some explosives set. They could mine the airport building and when the aliens reached it, blow the entire thing up. He would have to see how much time he had to set up the ambush. But before he did that, his eyes glanced down at the priority message in red letters: *Orbital bombardment ordered. Get the survivors out of the city ASAP. The Fleet is being recalled. You are on your own. Good luck, Marine.*

Good luck? Mitch thought. His mouth was suddenly terribly dry, and his entire body sagged. The fleet was running, but not before they sent bombs to destroy the colonies. It had never occurred to him that they might destroy everything the colonists had worked for. His fury at the cowardice of his own leaders made him throw back his head and scream.

But there was no time for indulging in his personal feelings. The bombs could drop at any second. He turned and ran, leaping through a shattered window frame and sprinting toward the maintenance building while toggling his comlink to transmit.

"Bobby, do you read me?" Mitch asked.

"Yeah, you're coming in crystal clear now, Lieutenant. Why are you running?"

"We have to get out of the city," Mitch said. "The Space Force is going to bomb it from orbit. Get everyone out of the tower."

"There's more of the aliens," he said. "A lot more. They're coming this way. I can't see much now that it's getting dark, but they're out there."

"I know," Mitch said. "We don't have much time. Get out of there!"

Mitch slid to a stop by the armored personnel carrier. Bart looked at him from behind the tripod mounted machine gun.

"Some of them got away," the man admitted. "They drifted off to the west."

"It doesn't matter," Mitch snapped. "Get everyone on board the carrier as fast as possible."

"Why? Are there more aliens coming?"

"Yes, but that's not why," Mitch said. "The fleet is going to bomb the city."

"No," Bart said. It wasn't a denial of the news, but an order, as if they could hear him from orbit and would obey his commands. "No, they won't do that."

"I just got word," Mitch said. "We have to get everyone out of here."

Riley wasn't as stricken by the news. He was young, only twenty or twenty-one years old. Maybe, like many young people, he had become smitten with one of the other fugitives. Hope springs eternal, and for the young who have yet to be broken by the hardships of life, they feel that the future, however bleak in a general sense, is still full of opportunities that they believe will be in their favor. He ran into the maintenance building and began calling the others out.

"This doesn't make any sense," Bart said.

"Standard military protocol," Mitch said, although he had only read about such things a couple of weeks ago. "You don't leave valuable material resources behind for your enemy when you're forced to retreat. You scuttle the ships. You blow up your own artillery and disable anything you aren't using."

"It's not right," Bart said. "This is my home. I've lived here my entire life."

"I'm sorry," Mitch said. "But they don't care about that."

"They'll destroy it all just to kill the Lymies?"

Mitch nodded, his mouth so dry, his tongue was beginning to feel too big for his mouth. The survivors were starting to come out of the maintenance building. They carried the KIL rifles and bottles of water. Riley had an extra and handed it to Mitch. He pulled off his helmet and took a long drink. The water tasted sweet in his mouth, and it ran like a cool, refreshing river down his parched throat. He instantly felt the effects of the hydration as his body absorbed the liquid, but he forced himself to slow down and sip from the bottle, which was already half empty by the time he got control of himself.

"It's dark," Mitch said. "Can you see anything out here?"

"Some," Riley said. "We could get the armor you brought. There are helmets like yours."

"No time," Mitch said. "Get everyone loaded up."

It took longer than expected. Many of the survivors were injured. Those that weren't were tasked with carrying out those who couldn't walk. People were arguing about what to take and what to leave behind, but soon, they heard glass crunching and objects inside the airport being tossed around.

"We're out of time," Mitch said, putting his battle helmet back on and turning toward the airport.

"They sent scouts ahead of the main group," Bobby called, and he, Carter, and Adele came jogging to the personnel transport from the control tower.

"We're leaving," Mitch said.

"Going where?" Bart asked.

"This vehicle will get higher than the trees," Mitch said. "Head for the forest. Look for a clearing to land in, then stay inside. It's armored, and the best protection you've got."

"Aren't you coming?" Riley asked.

"No," Mitch told him. "I'll hold off the Lymies while you get clear, then I'll make a run for it."

"When are the bombs dropping?" Bobby asked.

"I don't know, but I was told to get clear of the city as soon as possible. Get these people to safety, Bobby. I'll find you when I can."

"Alright, Lieutenant. But don't get yourself killed."

He could see the aliens. They hadn't moved past the airport building yet, but with his helmet's low light vision he could see them just inside watching as the survivors loaded up in the transport. Bobby took the controls. It was a simple vehicle, made to be easy enough that a raw recruit could drive it. They lifted off the ground, and at the same moment, as if seeing the vehicle move was their signal to attack, the Lymies jumped from the gloomy interior of the airport building and charged toward the maintenance building. Mitch had moved over to one of the .50 caliber, belt-fed machine guns. He opened fire on the scouts as the armored transport moved off between the maintenance building and hanger. The tracers from the machine gun showed Mitch where the bullets were going. They weren't designed to penetrate armor, but they packed a punch, and Mitch was learning how to fight the aliens. He aimed low. The bullets either hit the legs of the spidery aliens or hit the concrete and ricocheted up into their more vulnerable parts. It wasn't enough to kill them, but Mitch didn't need to kill them. The wounded aliens sought to survive. A broken leg, or other wound, would take them out of the fight.

As the transport rose upward, moving past the airport buildings and toward the forest to the south, nearly a hundred Lymies took to the air. Mitch saw only dark shapes and long ribbons of spidery webbing that carried them aloft. He raised the weapon upward and began shooting. Some of the Lymies dropped and died, others began a controlled descent to stop him.

Mitch ran the first of the two big machine guns dry. The barrel was smoking as the air turned colder. He ran to the other machine gun and continued shooting. He probably wasn't hitting the aliens. The issue was that the bullets didn't penetrate and kill them. And being in the air, they weren't knocked into anything by the kinetic energy release. As long as they didn't lose their ribbons, or get shot in the face, they survived the attack. The Lymies were spreading wide too, preparing to flank him. It was only a matter of time before he was surrounded and overwhelmed by sheer numbers.

Mitch turned and ran. But his path between the maintenance building and the hanger was blocked. The Lymies were coming down all around him. They had given him a healthy distance, not descending right on top of him, but that would change soon enough. He had nowhere to go. And the bomb was coming. He didn't hear it or get any sort of message from the ships in orbit. Maybe it was just fear, but he felt the impending doom. There was only one place to go, one course of action. Mitch dashed into the maintenance building and locked the metal door. It was dark inside, but with his helmet, he saw where the survivors had been spending their time. There were pallets of corrugated cardboard on the ground, and an older transport where the refugees had been sleeping on the padded seats. More importantly to Mitch at that moment was a vehicle lift positioned over a pit in the concrete floor. There was a big, wheeled vehicle on the lift, the kind used for pushing shuttles and transports around the airfield. It was almost a meter off the ground, and the pit below it was dark like a tomb. Mitch snatched up a fresh bottle of water that had been left behind and dove into the pit, just as the bomb from orbit went off.

CHAPTER 37

"ADMIRAL, THERE'S AN ISSUE," the weapons officer announced.

"Spit it out, Lieutenant," she growled.

"Something is pushing the bombs off target," he said. "It's not possible."

"What does that mean?" Admiral Darcy Wilcox said.

"The trajectory has changed," the weapons officer said. "Impact is in twenty-eight seconds, but they're off target."

Major Elaine Swift was watching the video feed being uploaded by high altitude surveillance drones. It was dark over the side of the planet where the colony towns were located. And there was a strange sort of interference as well, a kind of signal fog that they couldn't explain other than to say that it came from the Lymies who were in control of all the colonies.

Captain Frank Marcs had come across the estimated numbers that the Space Force shuttles had brought up to the *Marathon*. It was only a fraction of the total civilian population. Where the others had gone, or why they hadn't been rescued was a mystery. Some would certainly have stayed behind. Major Swift understood that many of the colonists had been born and raised on New Terra. They had survived numerous threats and attacks from various alien groups. The Brascus were a constant threat, raiding for technology, food, and taking slaves. The towering aliens known commonly as Grumblers sometimes wandered close to the colonies or destroyed farms. They weren't always hostile, usually it was just their extreme size and clumsiness that resulted in catastrophic destruction. But it wasn't the aliens that would be doing the damage or killing so many colonists. The orbital bombardment would wipe out any sign that humanity had ever been on New Terra.

"Where are they going?" the admiral demanded in a shrill voice. She was operating on caffeine and sheer willpower.

"They're going to impact in the spaces between the colonies," the weapons officer said. "I don't know how the Lymies are doing it."

"Maybe they aren't," General Mercer said. "That newcomer is on a direct course for Alpha Colony."

"One person can't alter those bombs," another officer said in a patronizing tone. "They weigh in excess of fifty tons."

"They shouldn't be able to move like that either," General Mercer said, pointing to one view screen that showed the alien flying like a superhero over the terrain. "But it is. Who are we to say what it can or cannot do."

"Time to impact?" Admiral Wilcox asked.

"Five seconds," the weapons officer said. "Four, three, two, one..."

The video feed went white from the sudden brightness of the bombs. The CIC was a circular room. The walls were all display panels. Most of them showed live feeds from high altitude drones. The signal fog was replaced by massive clouds of dirt and debris kicked up by the impact of the kinetic bombs. The colonies were themselves swamped as thousands of tons of dirt, rocks, and vegetation was kicked up into the air and carried by the blast wave in all directions.

"That's it," the weapons officer said. "No direct hits, Admiral."

"We could launch another volley," the *Marathon's* commanding officer suggested.

"Admiral, November One is on a direct course to intercept the *Hastings*, the navigation officer said. "May I bring up the plot again?"

"Show me," Admiral Wilcox said.

The hologram in the center of the room changed back to the view of the Terra system. It seemed the crescent-shaped ship was in orbit and moving toward the two battleships that had just launched the kinetic gravity bombs.

"Get them moving out of orbit," Admiral Wilcox ordered. "They've done all they can do. Lieutenant Rogers, can we fire at the colonies?"

"Negative Admiral," the weapons officer replied. "We're out of position."

"Admiral," another officer spoke up. "Look at the other ships. Everyone is leaving."

On the plot they could see the other ships, each one marked with a military designation. They had been there for weeks, some moving in and out of orbit, others hovering close by. Some were in clusters, others in tight formation, and a few were alone, but they were all leaving as if they had gotten an urgent message and knew something the humans didn't.

"Get us out of orbit," the admiral demanded. "If we're contending with forces that can alter the trajectory of our weapons, we are well out of our depth. Set course for the worm hole and get the buoys ready to eject."

"Aye, setting course for the anomaly," the navigation officer replied.

"Climbing out of New Terra orbit now, Admiral," the pilot said.

"Full power," the admiral ordered. "Have all defensive measures ready."

It was, Major Swift knew, a standard protocol for leaving a hostile system. The *Marathon* would drop sensor buoys that would boost the signals from the surveillance drones, which had already been set on autopilot. They would continue circling in high orbit until their power failed in three- or four-days time.

"Goodbye, Lieutenant Murphy," Major Swift whispered.

"Think he survived it?" Captain Marcs asked.

"If anyone could," she replied. "But I don't envy him."

"If he survives," Marcs said. "He'll have a shot of getting off that world when the CMC sends recons teams back to the surface."

"You think they will?" Major Swift said. "In our lifetimes?"

"From the looks of things," Captain Marcs said. "I would say yes."

"Good," she said. "No one deserves to be left behind with no hope."

CHAPTER 38

"HOW LONG SHALL we allow the dust clouds to linger?" Qwii asked.

"For now, they serve a purpose," Arq replied. "The humans are using their technology to watch what we do."

"We can bring those down too?" Juj said.

"Better not to reveal ourselves too much," Arq said. "Bring the ship down to the surface. Set us down just outside their primary settlement."

Juj nodded, and the crescent-shaped ship dipped down into the planet's atmosphere. If the crew on the human battleships were watching them closely, they would be surprised at the ease in which the crescent-shaped ship moved. Most shuttles used a planet's gravity to its advantage, but the alien ship seemed to defy gravity. It didn't need to sail into the wind, or to battle the friction of the atmosphere. It drifted down in an almost lazy fashion, moving directly toward it's intended landing spot.

"The Fray has reached the city," Qwii said. "He has turned his attention to us."

"If you need assistance..." Arq said.

"Unnecessary," Qwii said. "He is probing, that is all."

Arq closed his eyes and turned his powerful attention to the city they were descending to. It was damaged, both by the fighting from the Lymies, and from the bombs. Arq had no great concern for the damage to the colony. He would have spared it all, but that was not his intent. Below him, he could feel the bright spark of life that had drawn the trio of powerful aliens to New Terra in the first place. It still lingered, as did some of the Lymies. Arq had altered the course of the bombs, dropping them close enough to wipe out most of the spidery aliens. Normally, he did not interfere with matters on such a small scale. The Lymies would continue to invade and overwhelm planets across the galaxy. It was their nature, and short of driving them to extinction, they would continue their hostile ways.

But the blast had broken the power of the aliens. A few might still have fight left in them, but not many. The hordes in the other settlements had weathered the bombing much more efficiently. They were protected by the human structures that were engineered for such purposes. Arq wasn't surprised that so many of the Lymies were drawn out into the open at the primary settlement. Nor was it a mystery why. They were there for the human that the trio from Nagani sought.

"We can land close by," Qwii said. "On the very ground the humans used for that purpose."

"Excellent," Arq said.

"The Fray is waiting just outside the city," Juj explained.

"He will attack," Qwii said. "They always do."

"Then we shall deal with it," Arq said. "As we always do."

"It is so," Juj said.

The three aliens fell silent as their ship settled onto the airfield. The dust cloud was over them, while closer to the surface, the air was surprisingly clear. The shockwave from the bomb had toppled the control tower and ripped the roof from most of the structures, including the maintenance building. The Lymies had been sent sprawling as if they were hit by an invisible hand. When the trio of aliens came out of their crescent-shaped ship, only a handful of Lymies were moving toward the building where the human was hidden.

"They want to kill him," Juj said.

"Dissuade them of the notion," Arq ordered.

Qwii extended one arm, the gauzy fabric draped over his shoulder fluttering in the wind. The Lymies intended to take advantage of the building's missing roof. It had no windows, and breaking through the big, metal doors would take more time than simply climbing over the walls. But as they started up the side of the structure, they suddenly flew up into the air. The spidery aliens writhed, the legs waving madly. Qwii moved his arm away and the aliens flew back toward the crumbling city.

"He is here," Juj said. "His defenses are strong."

"Spread out," Arq said. "Prepare for battle."

It was dark outside, but a soft glow from the debris cloud above them made the airfield visible. Not that the Nagani needed much light to see by, their eyes were excellent in the darkness. Juj reached his hoof hands into a sheath at the small of his back. It was covered from view by the robes he wore. His arms came out with triangular blades over his hooves. They looked like an Indian Katar, only the blades were matte black and seemed almost like shadows in the darkness.

Qwii had two weapons made of short, curved blades that were mounted on short handles. They hung like tools from a belt on his robe and were similar to the Japanese Kama. He held them firmly in the cleft between his hooves and began to move them in an intricate pattern as he loosened the muscles in his shoulders and back. The blades on the sickle-shaped weapons were matte black, the same as Juj's.

Arq had a short, slender sword, slightly curved. It was tucked into his robes, but he didn't draw it out. Instead, he hung back, letting his associates move ahead. Across the expanse of the airfield, their opponent moved with confidence. It was a tall being, thin, and walking upright on two legs, although they bent backward at the knee, and gave the Fray a bouncy gait. The approaching alien had a staff nearly as tall as he was, with two small, straight blades mounted to either end. The Fray began twirling the staff around its body and over its head, as it approached. It was an impressive display, but Arq had seen many such fighting styles. The alien was no doubt deadly with his weapon. He had a long head, rounded on the lower front portion, and narrow as it rose up and back over his shoulders. The eyes were large and mounted to either side of the head, which the alien turned from side to side as it approached. Arq could see gill-like openings on the side of its long neck.

"You do not have to die this day, brother," Arq called out. "Throw down your weapon, and we can take you home. You will not be the first."

"Your mountain fortress is no home," the alien shouted in reply. "It is a viper's pit. I no longer hold to your creed, old Gani. My eyes have been opened, and I will not be seduced by your evil ways."

"We didn't come here to debate philosophy," Juj warned. "If you attack us, we will have no mercy."

"Nor will I," the alien said, as he came bouncing toward the trio.

Arq felt a wave of sadness, but he drew his sword just the same.

CHAPTER 39

MITCH WASN'T UNCONSCIOUS, but the blast had rattled him. The ground had shook and the sound of the metal roof being ripped off by the shock wave of the blast was deafening. But when things settled down, Mitch crawled out of the recessed work pit. He pulled off his helmet and drank an entire bottle of water. His body soaked the liquid up like a dry sponge.

When a shadow passed over the maintenance building, Mitch feared that the Lymies were floating over to drop on top of him. But instead of the spidery aliens, Mitch saw the crescent-shaped ship. It was big but descending gracefully. There was no sound of engines, thrusters, or repulser lifts. The ship was silent, and nearly as large as the airport main building. Mitch watched it drift by overhead, then turned his attention to his top priority... survival.

He had no idea what the bomb blast had done to the Lymies. Mitch was no expert on kinetic gravity bombs, but he was surprised that the maintenance building was still standing. Hurrying toward the back of the building, he unlocked the rear man door and opened it. Some of the trees had been knocked down by the shock-wave of the bomb, but the forest was only a few kilometers away. If he could get there, he would have cover and the chance to escape the Lymies. But getting across the expanse wouldn't be easy. He checked the load in his GAR. He had a full magazine in both of the tactical assault rifles that hung from straps around his shoulders, but only a few more in the loops of his armor.

Most of the weapons and armor he had risked his life for had survived the bombing. They were stacked near the far side of the maintenance building, still in their crates. If they could avoid the Lymies, Mitch decided it would be worth returning for. He even considered getting more of the uranium-tipped bullets for the Garrison rifles, but before he could make up his mind, he heard the familiar tapping of Lymies climbing up the building. Mitch thought he knew what was coming. He could stay where he was, take cover, and try to fend off the aliens, or he could dash out the back door. Maybe, he considered, if they saw him running away, they would just let him go. It was a long shot, but anything was possible. And Mitch could run very fast. His muscles were trembling from the long days of fighting without rest, and the idea of fleeing for his life was distasteful. But he had to consider the survivors. Somewhere in the forest was a transport full of people who were counting on him.

He was caught in a moment of indecision. Since becoming a Marine second lieutenant, he had worked to be decisive and make smart decisions, but the combination of fear and fatigue had left his mind sluggish. And before he could decide what to do, the Lymies began to squeal in fear. The chatter of their pointed, spindly legs against the sides of the building ceased, and Mitch saw them floating upward. The aliens could harness the wind by utilizing their long strands of silky webbing, but something else was carrying them upward. They seemed in a panic and then were whisked out of sight by a strange force. That got Mitch moving, he ran out the back door, then around the side of the building, staying between the two structures for cover.

At first, he didn't notice the aliens. He was looking upward, just catching sight of the Lymies as they were carried back toward the city. Then he heard the whisper of blades leaving their sheaths. It was an unmistakable sound. Mitch looked around the edge of the big hangar and saw the three Nagani aliens in their loose robes. He thought maybe it was a trick of his low light amplification that made them appear to be covered in white fur. Their curving horns seemed bright, while their blades were so dark, they were hard to see.

From the opposite side of the airfield, near the control tower which Mitch realized had fallen over during the blast, came a single alien. He was tall and slender, with leathery-looking skin. His only clothing was a wide belt, with what appeared to be a stiff panel of embroidered cloth that rose up from the belt-like armor. There were strips of some kind of thick material hanging from the belt too, almost like a skirt, but the strips weren't connected, leaving the alien's long legs free to move. And they moved in a way that was almost shocking to Mitch. The knee, and ankle joints were backwards, at least compared to human anatomy. Not that the alien looked human, he had two arms and two legs, but that's where the comparison ended. It had skin like an elephant, a long, serpentine neck that looked aquatic, and a strange head that looked both equine and reptilian. Mitch heard it speak to the trio in white, but he couldn't understand what was said. But the body language of the lone alien warrior was undeniable. Especially as he bounded toward his adversaries.

Mitch didn't move. He was shocked by what had happened, and what he saw. At times, he even thought maybe it was all a dream. Perhaps he had died in the bombing and he was seeing angels and demons doing battle. The gray-skinned loner was fast. He lashed out with his spear staff at the being with triangle blades. The alien in white blocked the spear attack, and Mitch heard the strange clash of the weapons. It didn't sound like steel, more like two rocks hitting together.

The lone alien bounced away from the first opponent and toward the second, stabbing out with the butt of his spear which also had a dark blade mounted to the staff. The alien in white blocked the spear thrust with one curved, sickle-shaped weapon, and countered with the other. The lone attacker swayed backward in a fashion that made Mitch wonder what the alien's backbone was like. When he straightened up, he spun around, slashing the spear blade at his opponent's feet. The alien with white fur jumped and then hovered in midair. Mitch couldn't believe what he was seeing. The sickle-shaped blade swung down at the tall alien's pointed head. To avoid the blow, the being with the spear dove to the ground. The alien with the triangular blades jumped into a flip, avoiding the sweep of his opponent's spear, and scoring a shallow cut across the alien's shoulder. The leathery skin parted, and dark blood spilled out.

The alien grunted, rolling backward and springing up, only to find the floating alien had followed. The spear came up in a two-handed block, but the floating alien's downward chop with the mysterious curved blades was too much for the staff. It splintered between the lone aggressor's hands. At that point, the aliens with white fur and flowing robes took a step back. The one in the air landed gracefully on his feet. Mitch was not an expert on ancient weapons or even hand-to-hand combat. He had been a Marine in training for a little over three weeks, but it seemed obvious to him that the trio in white were giving the lone alien a chance to retreat. Unfortunately, the alien with the splintered spear either didn't realize what was happening or didn't care. He rushed forward when he could have fallen back to safety. With the two ends of the spear, the alien thrust one at each of his adversaries, who once more fell back, moving in opposite directions. In that instant, the third of the aliens with white fur rushed forward. The lone fighter was standing exposed, both arms extended out from his body, when the horned alien with white fur stabbed him with a thin-bladed, slightly curved sword. The weapon punctured straight through the stiff garb the lone alien wore, into his stomach, and straight through the body. It stuck out the other side, dripping blood. The spear-wielding fighter dropped both pieces of his ruined weapon and sagged backward. The aliens on either side of him stepped forward and caught the lone fighter by the arms. They lowered him gently to the ground. There were some words spoken by the three aliens as they stood over the fighter and eased him into death.

Then they turned and stared straight at Mitch.

CHAPTER 40

"DON'T BE AFRAID," the alien with the sword said. "We mean you no harm."

"Who are you?" Mitch said, mystified by everything he had seen. It also wasn't lost on him that the alien was speaking to him in his own language.

"We have many names, but we are from the Order of Scion. I am Arq, this is Qwii, and Juj."

Mitch stepped out of the shadows and lowered his gun. He would have dropped it on the ground, but it was still hanging from the strap on his shoulder.

"I'm Lieutenant Mitch Murphy, at least I was."

"Your military is leaving the system," Arq said. "And the Lymies here will no longer trouble you, although they still hold the other cities."

"You know about all that?" Mitch asked.

"We've been watching for a while," Arq explained. "It is time your race discovered the power and knowledge."

"The what?" Mitch asked.

"There is so much to explain," Arq said. "And it's best if we show you. We want you to come with us, Mitch Murphy. We are extending you the offer to join the Order of Scion. But I must tell you that it is not an invitation to a life of peace and tranquility. You would be the first of your race to join us. And being the first is never easy."

"I really don't understand what you're talking about," Mitch said. "What is this order?"

"We are the True Navigators," Qwii said. "Some call us light benders."

"The Order of Scion seeks to restore the Creator's order to the universe, Mitch Murphy," Arq explained. "To restore the races to knowledge of his love and purpose."

"And to stand against the Fray who would use the power and the knowledge for selfish gain," Juj said, looking back at the dead alien.

"You're saying that you're wizards or priests or something?" Mitch said.

"Yes," Arq said. "Something of both those things. We are defenders of the Way. Come with us and learn more about it."

"I can't just leave," Mitch said, looking around.

He was still wearing his armor, including the battle helmet which allowed him to see in the dark. There wasn't much left of the airport, just the shell of a few buildings, none with roofs. Bodies were scattered across the runway and landing pads. The stench of decay was beginning to reach him in the night wind. He had no place to stay, and nowhere to go, except to the survivors somewhere in the forest.

"There are people here who are depending on me," Mitch added.

"They will survive," Arq said. "The threat from the Lymies has passed. You did all you could for them, but it is time that you think of your race. They are ready for someone to lead them into the future. The Son has chosen you, and we will help you. Come with us, and learn the way of the Order, before your people are lost or enslaved. There are more formidable enemies than the few you have encountered here."

Mitch was surprised by how much he wanted to go with the aliens. He knew almost nothing about them. They talked in riddles about things he had never heard of. The only thing he knew for certain was that they killed the alien with the spear. Perhaps he was an evil being. He had certainly initiated the fight and refused to retreat when given the chance, but they were killers. Of course, so was he. And he found himself madly curious about what the Power and Knowledge was.

"Alright," Mitch said, surprising himself a little with the answer. "I'll go with you."

"Very good," Arq said. "This is but the first step into a universe that is bigger and more mysterious than you ever imagined."

They turned. Mitch was shocked when Arq held out his sword. Without a word the blood and gore that was clinging to the black blade floated up and away. When the weapon was clean, he slipped it back into the sheath hidden inside his flowing robes.

"Did he do that on purpose?" Mitch asked the alien called Qwii.

"Indeed, he did. You shall learn to do it too."

"That and much more," Juj replied.

They walked to the crescent-shaped ship. A wide hatch was open. Lights came on as they approached. The three aliens didn't stop, but Mitch did. He took off his helmet and sat it on the ground. Then, he laid down the two Garrison Assault Rifles he had been carrying and laid them on either side of his helmet. He didn't think he needed them where he was going, and if anyone came looking for him, maybe they would realize that he wasn't taken against his will or murdered when they saw his helmet and weapons. Standing up, he looked around one last time. It wasn't Earth or even the Sol

System. It was a planet that had been abandoned by its own people, yet Mitch still felt a connection to the place. He had lived there. He had fought to defend it. It was part of him in some small way. He promised himself that if he was able, he would come back one day.

Then, he followed the aliens onto their ship.

CHAPTER 41

"IT'S hard to say for certain," the naval officer was explaining. "With so much dust in the atmosphere, we had to use thermal imaging."

"And you're saying that blob is Lieutenant Murphy?" Admiral Darcy Wilcox asked.

General Mercer leaned closer to the screen, his heart thundering in his chest. He couldn't believe what he was seeing.

"Yes, Admiral, the Marines in full armor have a certain thermal exposure. I'm certain that's him."

"And who are they?" she asked, pointing to the other four blobs moving toward where Mitch Murphy was hiding.

"Aliens," the officer said. He was a radar control specialist. The images were coming to them from the drones in high altitude above Alpha Colony. "Three from the crescent ship. The other I can't say for sure."

"He's the flyer," General Mercer said. "Has to be."

They watched in awe as the blobs came together.

"What are they doing?" the admiral asked.

"Fighting," General Mercer said. He had seen enough combat

engagements in a variety of formats to recognize what was going on. "See there," he continued. "They killed the flyer."

For the next few minutes, they watched in silence.

"Is he going with them?" the admiral asked.

"He might not have a choice," the radarman said.

"We can't just let them capture a Marine Corps officer," Darcy Wilcox said, even though everyone knew she wouldn't actually do anything about it.

"It's all in how you look at things, Admiral," Mercer said. "I'm choosing to see that we have a Marine on that alien ship. Murphy's made contact. I imagine that sooner or later we'll get a full report from him."

General Mercer didn't care about Mitch, and he didn't care about the aliens. All he really cared about was what the video feed would do for his career.

"It's taking off," the radarman said. "At least I think it is. There's no heat signature on that vessel."

Once again, the group fell silent. They saw the crescent-shaped ship float up through the cloud of debris. It moved too slowly and yet somehow it kept rising until it passed the drone.

"Do we have eyes on that ship?" Admiral Wilcox asked.

"It should be on the plot, Admiral," the systems engineer replied.

"Long-range scanners engaged," Commander Micheal Hughes said. "Activating the ship's reconnaissance cameras too."

"Unbelievable," the pilot of the *Marathon* said.

"What is?" Admiral Wilcox asked.

"A ship shouldn't be able to do that," the pilot said. "It's like it isn't operating by the laws of physics."

"A truly advanced civilization," General Mercer said, holding back his chuckle of excitement.

"It's leaving orbit," the radarman said. "Still no sign of thrusters or heat bloom from engines of any kind."

They all fell silent as the ship accelerated. It went from an almost languid pace to moving faster than they could keep up with. All any of them knew for sure was that the ship hadn't simply vanished. It raced away. They saw that before the speed grew so great, it couldn't be tracked by the human eye. But they had more than human eyes on the ship.

"Tell me we got that," the admiral said in a tremulous voice.

"Aye, Admiral. Video in all spectrums," the radarman said. "Scans and trajectory too."

This time Mercer couldn't hold back his giddiness. He chuckled with delight.

"We have to get this information back to the Sol System," Admiral Darcy Wilcox said.

And General Mercer knew that his superiors wouldn't believe it even after they saw the evidence for themselves. It was the greatest moment in the history of mankind's quest across the galaxy. And he would make sure that he rode the wave of command success as far as it would take him.

AUTHOR'S NOTE

Thanks for reading *Latent Prowess*. It was a dream come true to write this novel. If you follow me on social media you know that this is my 100th published novel. It's also the beginning of a series I've wanted to write for a long time. The Order of Scion is my homage to the stories I grew up with. Grand mythologies like the trials of Hercules, and wonderful fantasies like the Tarzan novels, to the movies that I've loved all my life such as Star Wars. I wanted to write something that made sense on a cosmic level but was a real mix of science fiction and fantasy adventure. I hope to write many more books this this universe. As I write this note I'm over halfway finished with the second book in the Order of Scion series. It will be released in March 2024. You can keep reading for an unedited sample of *Gravity Masters* (Order of Scion book 2)

GRAVITY MASTERS CHAPTER 1

He could never say why he did it. Sometimes events happen in a person's life and they report feeling like spectators watching from the outside and seeing themselves do something they would never have imagined. That was no what Mitch Murphy, Second Lieutenant, Colonial Marine Corps, experienced. He was fully aware, and fully in control, but what motivated him to follow the three strange aliens was a complete and utter mystery. It wasn't until several minutes later, after watching the ship rise up through the dust clouds caused by the Space Force bombardment, and into space, that he contemplated his decision.

"You are tired," the alien called Arq said.

Mitch still didn't know how they knew his language, or how their strange mouths could even form the words. All three of the aliens looked like animals. They stood on two legs and had two arms, but all four limbs seemed identical to Mitch. They all had split hooves on the ends instead of hands. They were all covered in short, white fur. They had heads shaped somewhat like bulls, with thick, white horns that curled around the back of their skulls. Their appearance was shocking to his mind and simultaneously calming. Mitch thought of them, especially Arq, as wise old men, sages, or counselors of some type. Perhaps it was the clothing they wore, which consisted of long strips of loosely woven fabric that were wrapped around them, and hung loose from their shoulders and upper arms, forming what Mitch thought of as a robe.

"I'm fine," Mitch replied. He was exhausted, hungry, and tense, but he didn't want that to show. He was a guest on their very fine spaceship and the last thing he wanted to do was insult his hosts.

"Our vessel has many services available," Qwii said. "We have everything you will need to be very comfortable."

"He's eager," Juj said. "Who can blame him?"

"May we can satisfy your curiosity enough that you will feel comfortable resting," Arq said. "Food is being prepared for you. Soon you can bathe, then sleep. Our journey will last several Earth days."

"Where are we going?" Mitch asked.

He was standing in what felt like a throne room, even though there were no thrones. It was a large space with a transparent wall that was so clear it almost looked like there was no wall or glass there at all. He could see so much and it wasn't like looking at a display screen showing live video, or a hologram. It was more like he was standing outside the ship rather than inside.

Nothing about the alien vessel was anything like human starships, which were small and cramped spaces. Mitch was seven and a half feet tall, and in most spaces on the S.F. *Wellington*, he had been forced to duck a little to keep from banging his head. In many of the corridors, he had to turn his shoulders to avoid banging into the narrow walls. But the alien ship was open and airy. Mitch admitted he had only seen two parts. They had entered via a ramp that led into what looked like a garage or staging area. There had been several platform vessels parked inside. But it had a tall ceiling and plenty of light, even at night. The light came from glowing orbs that hung suspended in mid-air. Mitch couldn't see how they hung, or what they were exactly. There was no sight of a bulb or diode, just light.

From the garage, they passed into the throne room. As far as Mitch could tell it was a huge room with no purpose. He knew the very existence on a spaceship was a grand extravagance. Through the huge window, Mitch saw the trio of battleships. They were spread out in a line hundreds of kilometers apart, but from a distance, they appeared close together. They were stubby, ugly vessels in comparison to the alien, crescent-shaped starship. The battleships bristled with guns but didn't seem like much of a threat as the alien vessel began to accelerate out of orbit. Mitch was no aerospace engineer, but he had seen a few documentaries on space travel and found it odd that the alien didn't seem to be held back by the planet's gravity at all.

"We will start on Vodex," Arq said. "The Order of Scion has a spacious facility there that will meet our needs."

"And what are those?" Mitch asked.

"Eager," Juj said, with what Mitch learned later was considered a smile by the Nagani.

"A proper introduction to the Power & Knowledge," Arq said. "It is not our intention to hold anything back from you, but we must pace ourselves. Too much of a good thing, too quickly, can still be bad."

Mitch had a thousand questions, but at the top of his mind was the fight between the three members of the Order of Scion, and the other alien. Mitch had seen the aliens move in ways that didn't seem possible. Juj had even floated in mid-air for a time. It didn't seem real.

"How are you doing the things you do?" Mitch asked. "How did you fly?"

"We are Gravity Masters," Arq said. "It isn't magic. We don't fly. But we can manipulate the gravitational forces all around us."

"This entire ship is an example," Qwii said.

"Propulsion is one of the easiest ways to understand," Arq said.

"You are aware of how your human vessels move through space. We manipulate gravity to move our vessels."

"That's impossible," Mitch said.

"And yet, you are experiencing it now," Arq said, waving an arm toward the opening.

Mitch could see the ship racing through the system. Things were moving too fast for any spaceship. New Terra and the Space Force battleships were lost to sight behind the alien vessel. Ahead of them were the system gas giants. It was like watching a movie. He could see their movement, but he couldn't feel it. And so, his mind told him it wasn't real.

"Gravity is the sinew that holds the entire universe together," Arq said. "From the smallest hydrogen atom with its lone electron in constant motion, to the largest celestial bodies, they are all joined and fixed in space by gravity."

"Even your human scientists have known this for hundreds of years," Qwii said.

"It is the gift of the Creator, given through the Scion to the people of every system," Arq said. "We are committed to helping restore the universe to the glorious state it was created in before the fall corrupted everything."

Mitch suddenly felt weak. It was a novel sensation. His body was stronger than it had ever been. Despite being physically tired, he was still more capable than he had been on his best day before the LE Protocols had transformed him into a super soldier. But his mind was overwhelmed. The alien ship was still gaining speed. It raced by one gas giant in a flash, as if he were watching a simulated flight through the Terra system on fast speed.

"Maybe some rest would be good," he admitted.

"Yes," Arq said. "Rest, nourishment, refreshment, those should be your priority now."

"I will assist him," Juj said. "Come with me."

Mitch followed the alien. They went into a tower-like room with a wide, spiral staircase. They went up and into a room that looked almost familiar. There was a wide bed with ivory blankets and square pillows. Two pieces of furniture took up the space on one side of the bed, one appeared to be a simple, wooden side table. The other was soft with a wooden frame that was covered with loose cushions of various colors. Juj walked to a nook built into the wall. A shelf rotated down with a tray of food on it. The alien took the tray over to the side table and set it down.

On the other side of the bed was a doorway. Mitch could hear water flowing. It sounded like a stream. He was beginning to question his sanity. It was such a surreal experience that he thought it was a dream.

"Food," Juj said, pointing to the tray, then at the bed, "rest, and in that room is a place for washing. You will find simple garments there that you may wear. There will be time to clean and mend your clothing, but for now please avail yourself of anything you need.

"Thank you," Mitch said.

Juj gave a little bow, then left the room. The door closed behind him, and Mitch dropped onto the sofa. It was comfortable, even for his oversized body. The food was some kind of stew. A large bowl sat on the tray, with several small loaves of bread and small blocks of soft cheese neatly arranged around it. There was a smaller bowl of fruit and a large mug. Mitch settled the tray on his lap and tasted the stew. It was rich, with a touch of spicy heat. He could see stewed vegetables and some type of dark meat. There was no way to know what it was, or if it was natural or artificial. Most space vessels carried either vat-grown or protein imitation meat. Mitch didn't care though. After one bite his stomach demanded more, as much as he could get. The bread was soft and excellent at soaking up the stew gravy. The cheese was a cool contrast to the stew's spicy heat. And when he had eaten every last morsel from the bowl, he tasted the fruit in its own smaller container. It was fresh, perfectly ripe, and sweet. There were grapes, a plum, an apple, and even some blueberries. When he finished eating he returned the tray to the nook where the shelf rotated as it rose upward and out of sight.

"This place is a trip," Mitch said.

He pulled off his armor. It was rank, spattered with dirt and gore on the outside, and soiled with his sweat on the inside. He carried it into the bathroom, which was nearly as large as the bed chamber. He hadn't been wrong about the water either. It was a stream that started high on one wall and then flowed across a narrow channel that looked as if it were made of stones. The artificial stream wrapped around three walls before ending in a pool that looked deep enough to bathe in. Mitch bent down and touched the water. It was warm. There was a bar of soap on a bundle of towels. It made Mitch wonder how the aliens knew he would join them. Maybe he didn't have a choice? Maybe they had gone to New Terra to harvest humans? Sure, they seemed nice enough, but it could all be an act. Yet try as he might, he couldn't take the idea that Arq, Qwii, and Juj were a threat to him. He took a bath, scrubbing his entire body and letting the tension drain from his muscles in the warm water.

The clothes he found were simple. Linen pants that cinched at the top with a silky belt. A long, sleeveless tunic that slipped over his head and hung to his knees. The clothing was comfortable, and so was the bed. It was soft and warm. His oversized body sank into the soft mattress. The blankets were lightweight and wrapped around him. He didn't even have time to ponder his strange circumstances before sleep overtook him. No dreams disturbed his mind as he rested from his labors. It would not always be so peaceful for him.

Mitch wasn't built for peace, but for war, and it was sure to find him, even on an alien ship in a system on the far side of the galaxy.

GRAVITY MASTERS CHAPTER 2

Sergeant Mara James was perched on the edge of her bunk. She was one of the lucky SSO Marines. At only six and a half feet tall after the LE Protocols had altered her body, she could still fit on a standard bunk. Across the narrow bunk-room of the S.F. *Marathon*, her squad mates Flash and Jingo had to curl up on their sides and still, they barely fit on the Space Force bunks.

"That hurt?" Estelle "Hawk" Flemming asked as Mara flexed her foot. It was part of the physical therapy assigned to her by the ship's doctor after her broken ankle had been scanned.

"Not really," Mara said. "It was just a fracture."

"By the time they scanned it," Flash pointed out.

"It looked pretty bad on the ground," Jingo added.

"It's fine," Mara said. "I'll baby it a few days. They didn't even keep me in the med bay."

"No room for us," Ninja said.

He was standing up with his shirt off. He had a small, hand-held shaving mirror in one hand, and his other lightly probed the bruise on his chest.

"I'd say we were lucky," Flash announced. "Only one casualty. Kilo Squad is no more."

"You hear something about Joker?" Jingo asked.

Flash shook his head. The run through Alpha Colony had been difficult and frightening. They were Marines, trained to put away fear and run toward danger, but giant spiders in the dead of night were stressful. They had succeeded in reaching the airfield for exfil only after one member of Kilo Squad was killed in action, and another severely wounded. The six-man team had already lost two members before joining Leo Squad for the run through the city. What would happen to the remaining two members was up to someone with a much higher pay grade.

"We've all lost people," Mara said. "And we always move on. They'll be okay."

"Damn shame about the LT," Flash said. "It was nice to have an officer I didn't have to bend down to look in the eye."

"What was he thinking?" Ninja said.

"He was thinking about that little girl," Jingo said.

They had all seen Mitch Murphy jump from the shuttle as it began to lift off. And they saw the colonist with his little girl who was practically tossed inside the ship as the hatch began to close up.

"Wish he'd given us some notice," Hawk said.

"You would have gone with him?" Mara asked.

She had been thinking the same thing but didn't know how the other members of the squad felt. They were all fiercely loyal to one another, but Mitch Murphy had been their new lieutenant. He was the first, and to her knowledge, only officer to have gone through the LE Protocols. But he had barely been in charge of Leo Squad for a week. The field survival training exercise had been their first time together off Alpha Base. So maybe the others weren't as attached to Mitch as she had been. But it appeared her thoughts on that score weren't exactly on target.

"Hell yeah," Jingo said.

"For sure," Flash added.

Hawk only nodded. She was a naturally quiet person.

"I wouldn't have liked it," Ninja said. "But I'd rather be down there in the mud and blood with him than safe up here without him."

"They'll go back for him," Flash said. "Right?"

Mara shrugged. Never before had she cared what her commanding officers did when they weren't barking orders at her. She was the highest-ranking NCO on Leo Squad, but even she wasn't privy to what the brass would do if one of their own went missing.

Before she could answer someone in the room shouted, "Officer on deck!" There were four SSO squads crammed into the bunk room normally occupied by a single, regular platoon. Everyone was clustering together, and Mara hadn't seen the officer come in, but she jumped up onto her good foot and stiffened into attention like every other Marine.

"Sergeant James," a gruff voice called out.

"Sir, yes sir!" Mara replied.

"You're with me," the man at the hatch snapped. "Let's go."

"Dang, Mara's in trouble," Jingo said.

"Told you not to kiss the sailors, Sergeant," Ninja joined in.

She ignored them as she slipped her bad foot back into the support boot and tightened the velcro straps. Pain was starting to throb in her ankle, but she ignored it and hurried after the officer. She didn't recognize the man, but the Lieutenant bars on his collar were easy to see. That meant he could tell her to do just about anything, down to and including scrubbing toilets with a toothbrush.

The man led through a narrow corridor. The Marine section of the ship was like a labyrinth. Every hallway was little more than a maintenance corridor with conduits running along the walls near the ceiling, and access hatches for various engineering spaces along the way. The rooms were sandwiched between other essential parts of the ship. They came to a stairwell, which was little more than a glorified ladder. She climbed it easily, despite the boot on her bad foot. At the top, they turned quickly into a series of offices. Captain Frank Marcs was waiting inside one.

"Captain, I've got Sergeant James," the lieutenant said.

"Very well," Captain Marcs said as he set his computer tablet down and looked up at Mara James who stepped into the small office. "Have a seat, Sergeant."

"Yes, sir," she said. "Thank you, sir."

For a moment there was silence between them. Mara was starting to feel uncomfortable. It was impossible not to feel like she was in some sort of trouble, although, to her knowledge, she had done nothing wrong. Then Captain Marcs sighed and leaned onto his elbows, reclining slightly in his desk chair.

"What was Lieutenant Murphy's state of mind before we left New Terra?" he asked.

"State of mind, sir?" Mara repeated. "He was focused on completing the mission, I know that. It was his first taste of combat, and if I'm honest, sir, I think he liked it."

"Yeah, that's not surprising, is it, Sergeant. A lot of new SSO Marines want to see what they're made of."

"True, sir, but that doesn't really describe Lieutenant Murphy. He was more disciplined than that."

"You found him disciplined?"

"Extremely sir. Not fanatical, but very self-aware. He wasn't rattled, not on the training mission and not when the Lymies attacked. His orders were concise and on point. It didn't seem like his first command, sir."

"Would you describe him as happy in the Corps?"

Mara thought about that. She was close to Mitch. Over their week together, she had tested him both socially and more importantly, professionally. He listened and learned quickly. He could take everyone's input and then decisively make decisions that showed he had heard the collected wisdom of the group. Physically, he was their equal in nearly every way. Not as strong as Jingo, or as fast as Flash, but unlike the rest of them, he could do it all. He had the flexibility and stamina to keep up with Mara and Ninja when they sparred, and he could even give Hawk a run for her money on the sniper range.

"Extremely happy, sir. I got the impression it was a real step up from his old life."

"Did talk about that much?" Captain Marcs asked.

Mara shook her head. "None of us do, sir. We all had our reasons for volunteering, and the transformation is such a change that we just don't talk about what came before very often."

Captain Marcs sighed. "We have a problem, Sergeant. I'm going to ask for your opinions, and then I'm ordering you not to talk about this meeting to anyone. Is that clear?"

"Sir, yes sir," she replied.

"Good. I was there when Murphy jumped ship. Hell, I didn't even blame him. He wanted to fight and to be honest, I did too. But orders are orders, Sergeant. We all answer to someone, and the mission always comes first."

Mara nodded, not sure what to say. Jumping off the shuttle at the last minute was a heroic thing to do. Mara certainly respected it. And had it not been for her broken ankle she would have followed Mitch right off the transport. But in technical terms, it was a dereliction of his duty. They had been ordered to evacuate the planet, and staying behind could be considered Absence Without Leave.

"We've been in contact with Murphy," Captain Marcs continued. "He was doing everything we asked. Not always the way we asked, but..."

"Is he in some kind of trouble, sir?"

"More trouble than being left on a planet that was bombarded from orbit with kinetic warheads, Sergeant?"

"We bombed the colonies?"

"What do you do when you have an infestation? You have to

fumigate the place, or burn it down and start over. Orders to use the nuclear option came from the Sol system, Sergeant. One kinetic warhead from orbit should have been sufficient to kill everything in Alpha Colony."

"Is he…" she couldn't bring herself to say the last word.

Mara James wasn't an overly emotional person. And she didn't usually have trouble controlling herself, but she found her body trembling at the idea of Mitch Murphy being killed.

"Alive," Captain Marcs said. "Some strange things went down on New Terra. Most of it is classified, which is why I'm ordering you not to tell anyone what I'm about to tell you, Sergeant.

Mara nodded, her mouth suddenly dry. She was gripping the edges of her seat with both hands and leaned forward slightly. The pain in her ankle completely forgotten.

"Aliens, not Lymies, these were something different, something we haven't encountered yet, were on site when the bombs fell. And for some reason we can't explain, the warheads missed their targets."

"Missed?"

"They dropped between the colonies. We checked and rechecked the data. It wasn't an error on our part. The warheads themselves are dumb, nothing about them can go wrong, and the fact that they all behaved the same way, and at the same time, suggests something outside the bombs themselves."

"Strange," Mara said.

"In the extreme," Captain Marcs said. "We don't have good visuals of what took place on the ground. Our surveillance feeds were blocked by the debris kicked up by the bombs. But we have this on thermal imaging."

He spun his table around and lifted it so that Mara could see the picture. It was a paused frame from a video feed, all gray except for several blobs of bright color.

"Are you familiar with SSO Marine armor's thermal output?" Captain Marcs asked.

She was. Mara nodded.

"So then, you can see that Lieutenant Murphy is there with the aliens."

"Yes, sir," she said, her throat tight from the tension gripping her body.

He tapped an icon and the blobs began to move. Three of them led Mitch away until they disappeared.

"What happened to them?" Mara asked.

"This," Marcs replied as he turned the table around, tapped a few commands, then swiveled it back so she could see.

On the screen was another video feed, this time of an alien ship rising from the dust clouds. It was dark and shaped like a crescent moon on its side. It rose up until it disappeared from sight.

"They took him?" she asked in horror.

"Or he left with them willingly," Captain Marcs said. "That's what we're trying to determine."

"He wouldn't leave us, sir," she insisted. "The Lieutenant wouldn't just abandon everything we fought for."

"And yet, he abandoned ship despite being ordered to retreat," Captain Marcs said. "Technically, he follows orders, but he does things his way. It's possible he left with the aliens because they enticed him to."

Mara didn't need to say that after the fleet had bombed the planet, Mitch Murphy didn't have much left to feel loyalty to. His own people were abandoning New Terra and would have murdered him from orbit if things had gone their way.

"Anything is possible, Captain."

"Obviously," he replied. "And you're sure he wasn't suffering some form of depression?"

"None," she said confidently.

"Did he ever complain about orders? I was his commanding officer. Did he talk about me with you, Sergeant? He won't be in trouble and neither will you. I need the truth."

"Never sir. Like I said, I think he loved his job. He certainly

loved training with the squad. PT, range time, and sims all seemed
to jazz him up. Lieutenant Murphy was the first one up and the last
one to leave at night, sir. If you're trying to ask if he was a disgrun-
tled Marine, the answer is no."

"Very well, Sergeant. Thank you for the information. Your job
is to forget this meeting ever took place. That's an order."

Mara stood to attention. "Sir, yes, sir!" she said, snapping out a
tight salute.

"Dismissed, Sergeant."

"Thank you, sir."

Mara walked out of the little office and started a slow return to
the bunk room where she knew the rest of Leo Squad would be
waiting. Her mind was a whirlwind of competing thoughts. Mitch
was gone. Not dead, but not on New Terra anymore. She didn't
even know if Captain Marcs knew where he was. The ship on the
video had just disappeared. She guessed maybe it had broken orbit,
but she had never seen any ship fly like the one on the video. It
didn't even look real.

There were too many unanswered questions. And she knew they
were going to haunt her for the rest of her life.

GRAVITY MASTERS CHAPTER 3

Mitch didn't know how long he had slept. He could have checked the chrono on his data cuff, but it was in a pile of his stinky clothes in the bathroom, and he woke up feeling good. It had been enough sleep to rejuvenate him, which was all he could hope for.

He was only on his feet in the bed chamber a few moments when a soft chime sounded and a tray of food descended in the nook built into the wall. He walked over and eyed the small feast with appreciation. There was what looked to be a stack of five, very large pancakes, a bowl of scrambled eggs, and a saucer that had what appeared to be real bacon and sausage. There was also a bowl of fruit, a bowl of yogurt, and a bowl of granola. Along with the food, there was a glass of orange juice and a mug of coffee. Mitch had just picked up the tray when the door to his bedchamber swished open.

"Will you take food with us?" Arq asked.

"Sure," Mitch said.

The white-furred alien gave a slight bow, then turned and began walking through the ship. Mitch stayed behind him, observing his host. There was no reason to be wary, but Mitch thought it was best if he stayed cautious. The aliens obviously wanted something from him. Maybe it was okay, maybe not. He would have to wait and see, but when the ask came, he wanted a clear mind when he answered.

Arq led Mitch to a room with a round table in the center, and several decorative tapestries hanging from the walls. Mitch wasn't sure what they were about, but it seemed like more of the religious philosophy that his hosts espoused.

"Welcome. Did you rest well?" Qwii asked.

"Very well, thank you," Mitch replied, setting his tray down on the table. The aliens each had large silvery bowls that were filled with what appeared to be a green salad of some sort, along with smaller bowls of water.

"We thank the Creator for this repast," Arq said softly.

"Thank you," his two companions said in soft unison.

The aliens didn't use utensils or their hooves to eat with. They bent forward and ate straight from the bowl, and lapped up water to drink. It was a surreal experience, but hunger overrode Mitch's wonder at his companions. His pancakes were excellent and his big body was eager for food. For a while, they ate in comfortable silence, but once their hunger had been satisfied they slowed down and began to talk between bites.

"How far are we from our destination?" Mitch asked.

"Two Earth days," Juj said.

"Normally, we would travel faster, but we wanted to give you time to acclimate," Arq said. "You are the first human we have invited into the order."

"Can you tell me more about it?"

"The Order of Scion is an ancient association of individuals from a variety of species," Arq explained. "Each dedicated to the principles outlined by the Creator for the universe. It is hoped that as we carry on the restoration it will elevate and unite our people."

"There's so much of that I don't understand," Mitch said. "Who is the Creator?"

"The source of everything that is," Qwii said.

"The first of all living things," Juj said.

"And a mystery," Arq added. "Yet one that is recognized by every intelligent species in the galaxy."

"How's that?" Mitch asked.

"You tell us," Arq said. "What do humans believe about how they came to be?"

Mitch shrugged. "No one knows," he said. "For a long time it was believed that we evolved from simpler forms of life over millions of years."

The aliens chuckled but in a polite way. "How inventive," Arq said.

"But that is not the prevailing thought any longer?" Qwii asked.

"I'm no scientist," Mitch said. "But I was taught that the evidence no longer supported the theory."

"Back to square one," Juj said.

"Are there other prevalent theories?" Arq said.

"Sure, but no real proof of anything," Mitch said. "Most people believe we were seeded on the Earth, that's our home world, by an advanced race."

"No belief in the divine?" Arq asked.

"Well, yeah, sure, there are plenty of people who believe in God. Is that what your Creator is?"

"A divine being in the sense that it exists outside our reality," Arq said. "One who initiated the creation of the universe. We call him Creator. The beliefs of our order run deep, and there will be plenty of time for you to study them in detail. For now, it is enough to know that we believe the universe was created, and finely tuned for life, but that creation was marred. The wonderfully diverse races were separated by vast distances of empty space. Many of the systems were misaligned, resulting in worlds that are completely inhospitable to life. It is our work to help restore what the Creator made so very long ago."

"Restoration," Mitch said. "What do you mean by that?"

"Long ago the first of the order were taught the means to control the power given by the creator," Arq explained.

"Gravity manipulation," Mitch said.

"That is one description of it," Qwii said.

"There are forces in the universe at work all the time," Arq said. "Gravity is the weakest, yet the effects of it are the easiest to see. Planets in motion. Light, attraction, even time itself is acted on and affected by gravity."

"When we understand the Creator's intent in giving us access to the Power, what we call the Knowledge is essentially knowing how, when, and why to use it," Juj said.

"All this you will learn," Arq said.

"Why me?" Mitch asked.

"You are the first who is ready," Arq said. "We have been watching. Every intelligent species grows in knowledge and abilities. Humans have long been in a phase of rapid growth. Your technology is phenomenal. And you have discovered the expansion portal left in your star system. Once you passed through it, the Terra system was discovered. First by you, then by others who were watching."

"The Graylings," Mitch said.

"They are one, yes, but there are others," Arq explained. "Hence the struggle for control of that system."

"If the aliens fought us for New Terra, will they invade the Sol system too?" Mitch asked.

"Eventually," Juj said. "For now, your military resources are formidable enough to secure your home system, but that will change."

"Every race goes through periods of strength and weakness," Arq continued. "It appears as though your people are pulling back. Perhaps they focus their technological resources, or perhaps they fall into apathy in their own system, believing they will never be threatened."

"Not a comforting thought," Mitch said.

"Nor should it be," Juj said.

"It is the work of the Order of Scion to share the Power and Knowledge, first to our own people, and then to others, as we work to restore the universe."

"How exactly are you doing that?"

"Only the most advanced of our Order can do the work," Arq said. "It takes decades of practice."

"What does?"

"Outline the levels of mastery for him," Qwii said.

Arq nodded. "Those who learn to use the Power and the Knowledge grow in stages. Many train to become Scion Warriors. They use the Power and Knowledge to protect the innocent."

"Protect them from who?" Mitch asked, wondering who would be foolish enough to fight these strange, alien wizards.

"There are many enemies of the Way," Juj said.

"Anyone who uses violence to take what does not belong to them is outside the truth," Arq said. "Is it not the same on your Earth?"

Mitch nodded. Stealing, of any form, had always been illegal as far as Mitch knew. Violence, be it via an individual or a nation, was seen as barbaric.

"Warriors grow in strength," Arq continued, "becoming Navigators, or what you might think of as space benders."

"What?" Mitch asked.

"Those with enough mastery over the Power and Knowledge can bend space time, and open portals like the one from your Sol system, to the Terra system. A race with a True Navigator will have access to a wide array of worlds."

"Where they may grow in the truth," Qwii said. "Under the tutelage of a True Navigator."

"It is possible, although rare, for Navigators to grow into World Movers," Arq said. "These incredibly powerful members of the order can correct the orbit of planets, pushing them into what your scientists have coined the *Goldilocks zone*. Entire atmospheres can be pulled from gas giants to worlds and moons that allow life to thrive. Their control is both powerful and precise."

"Is that the highest level?" Mitch asked, realizing just how incredible the aliens were. To be able to move planets would give the human race unlimited space. Nearly every star system had planets, but the number of worlds that could support life of any kind was nearly zero. A habitable world, like New Terra, was one in a trillion. A world like Earth was more than anyone dared hope for. But if planets could be moved, their atmosphere manipulated, any system had the potential for a vibrant planet.

"There is one more," Arq said. "But in the history of our order, only a handful have ever reached it."

"The Star Savers," Qwii said, his voice hushed with awe.

"None in a century," Juj said.

"A Star Saver?" Mitch asked. "What does that mean?"

"Stars are delicately balanced, self-contained systems," Arq said. "The weight of the hydrogen drawn to the molten core eventually fails. The star grows weak, but exponentially bigger as the hydrogen expands into a red giant, before it all collapses back down, forming a unique gravity phenomenon your people call a black hole."

"And the most powerful members of the order can stop this?" Mitch asked.

"In some cases," Arq said. "The stress on a person is so great that few who attempt it survive."

"Wow," Mitch said, leaning back. "That's incredible."

"And it is yours," Arq said, "should you accept it. But the training is not easy. Many attempt the training and fail. Perhaps you will succeed."

"I think it is time for a demonstration," Qwii said.

"Excellent," Juj agreed.

"I believe your people say, there's no time like the present," Arq added.

Mitch nodded. The entire conversation felt surreal. He was on an alien ship, with furry creatures who claimed they controlled gravity. He missed his squad and wished he could share his adventure with them. Especially, Mara. He couldn't help but wonder how she was feeling. Mitch even missed Major Swift with her inquisitive mind. Of all the people he had met since volunteering for the LE Protocols, she would be the most fascinated by the Nagani.

"I'm game," Mitch said.

"Wonderful," Arq said.

They all three stood up and Mitch followed suit. They left their bowls and dishes behind. Mitch stayed with them but kept an eye out for whoever else might be on the ship. Someone was cleaning up and cooking his meals. Mitch decided that he wanted to talk to that person. If he wanted the real scoop on who his hosts truly were, the hired help would be the ones to know. All he had to do was find them.

ALSO BY TOBY NEIGHBORS

Gravity Flux

Modulus Echo

Zero Friction

Planet Fall

Charter

Jack & Roxie

My Lady Sorceress

The Man With No Hands

ARC Angel

Battle ARC

Broken Crucible

Hidden Kingdom

War INC

Carthage Prime

Cronus Team

Skandia Seven

Mercurial

Magnificus Prime

Incursio

Merlin Appears

Runners

Survivors

Infiltrators

Resistance

Conquest

Occupation

Extraction